image® comics presents

Wayward

Volume Six: Bound To Fate

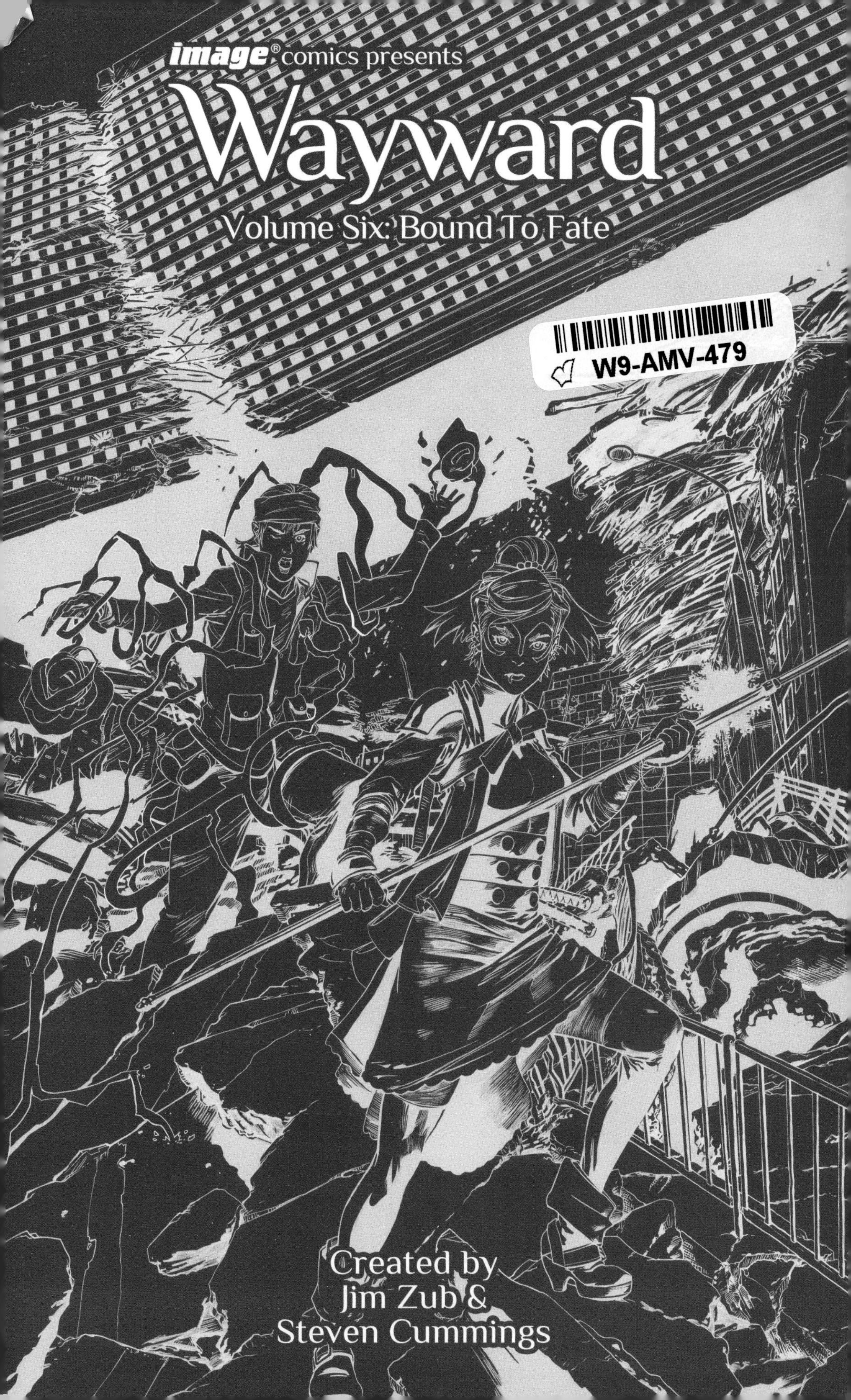

Created by
Jim Zub &
Steven Cummings

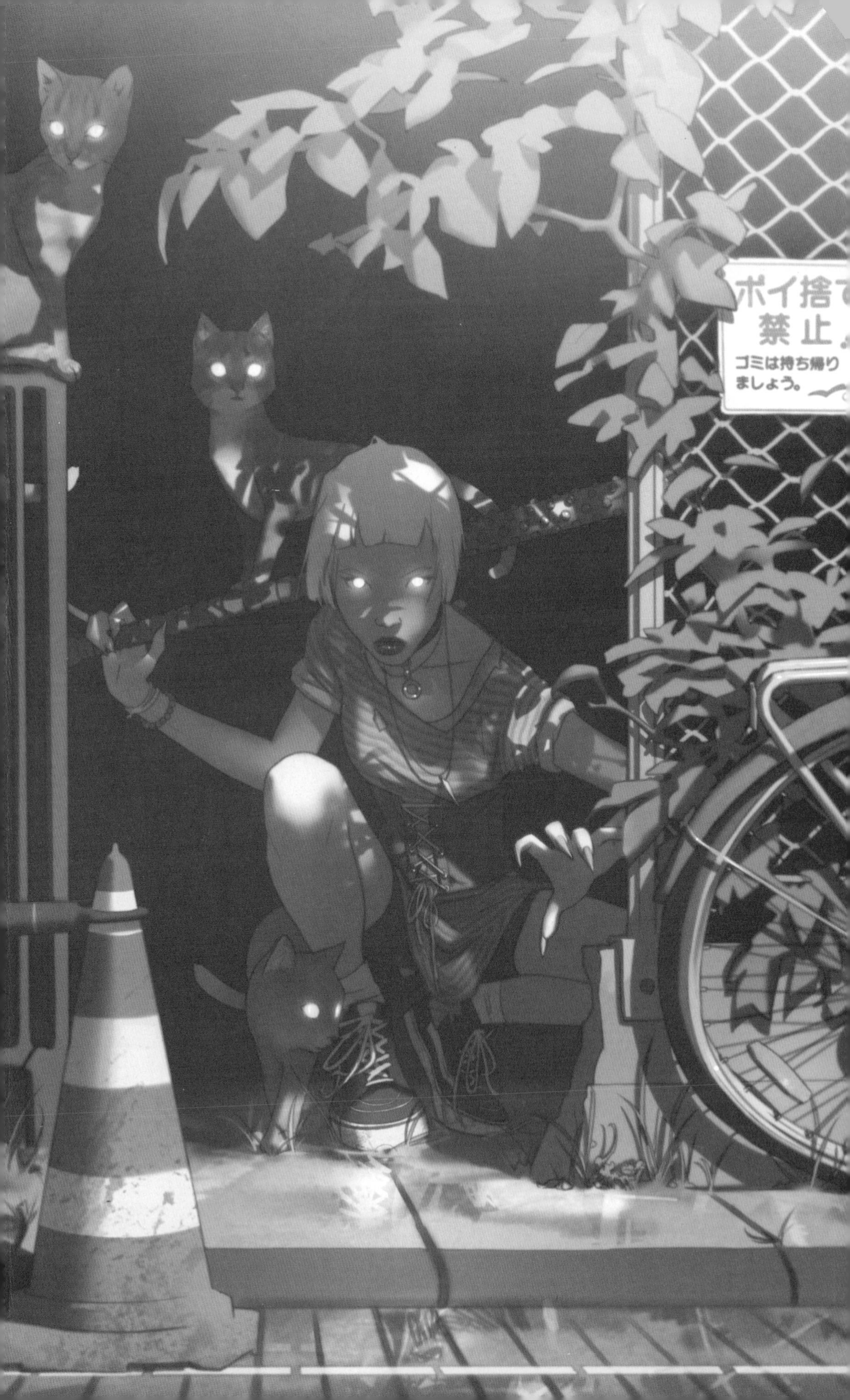
ポイ捨
禁止
ゴミは持ち帰り
ましょう。

Previously

A group of teenagers in Japan discover they have strange supernatural powers. **Emi Ohara** can alter the form of manmade objects and change her body to match them. **Nikaido** senses and controls emotions. **Inaba** is a ronin kitsune, a shape-shifting fox warrior. **Segawa** can manipulate networks and technology. At the center is **Rori Lane**, a half-Japanese, half-Irish girl called a 'Weaver', a powerful conduit for the strings of fate that define power and destiny.

Soon after these powers emerge, the teens are hunted by **Yokai**, mythical Japanese creatures and spirits. The Yokai sense these striplings are the next generation of the supernatural in Japan, but they're not willing to relinquish the control they've built over the centuries.

After destroying Tír na nÓg and unleashing its magical energy in Ireland, Rori has reunited with the rest of the group in Japan, but her return heralds a shift in the balance of power. The Yokai, led by **Nurarihyon** and the Japanese military forces he manipulates through a proxy, prepare to escalate their assault...

story
Jim Zub

line art
Steven Cummings

color art
Tamra Bonvillain

color assist
Brittany Peer

color flats
Ludwig Olimba

letters
Marshall Dillon

back matter
Zack Davisson

® **IMAGE COMICS, INC.**
Robert Kirkman—Chief Operating Officer
Erik Larsen—Chief Financial Officer
Todd McFarlane—President
Marc Silvestri—Chief Executive Officer
Jim Valentino—Vice President

Eric Stephenson—Publisher / Chief Creative Officer
Corey Hart—Director of Sales
Jeff Boison—Director of Publishing Planning
                        & Book Trade Sales
Chris Ross—Director of Digital Sales
Jeff Stang—Director of Specialty Sales
Kat Salazar—Director of PR & Marketing
Drew Gill—Art Director
Heather Doornink—Production Director
Nicole Lapalme—Controller
IMAGECOMICS.COM

special thanks
Chris Butcher
W. Scott Forbes
Melissa Gifford
Stacy King
Deanna Phelps
Briah Skelly

Chapter Twenty-Six

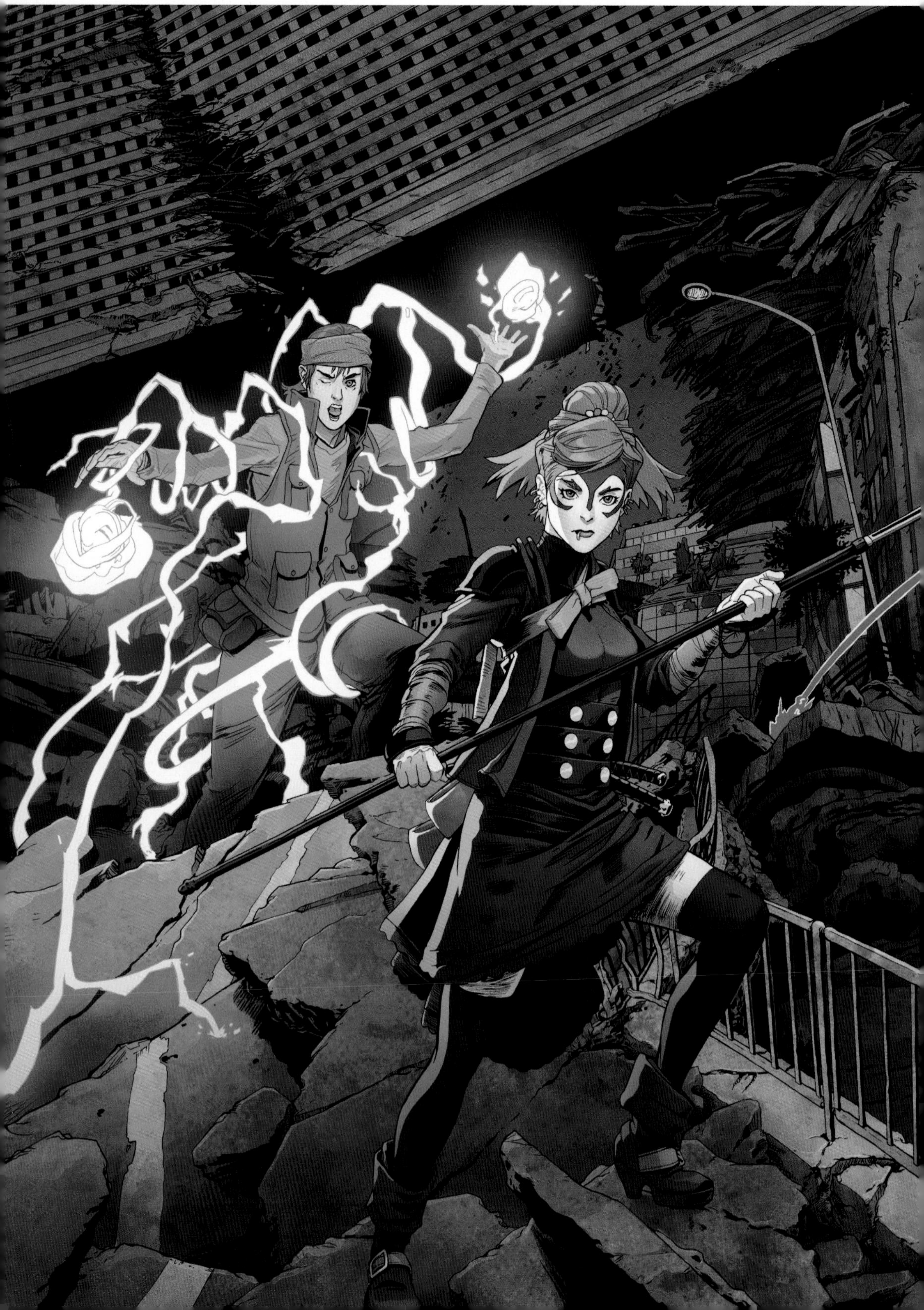

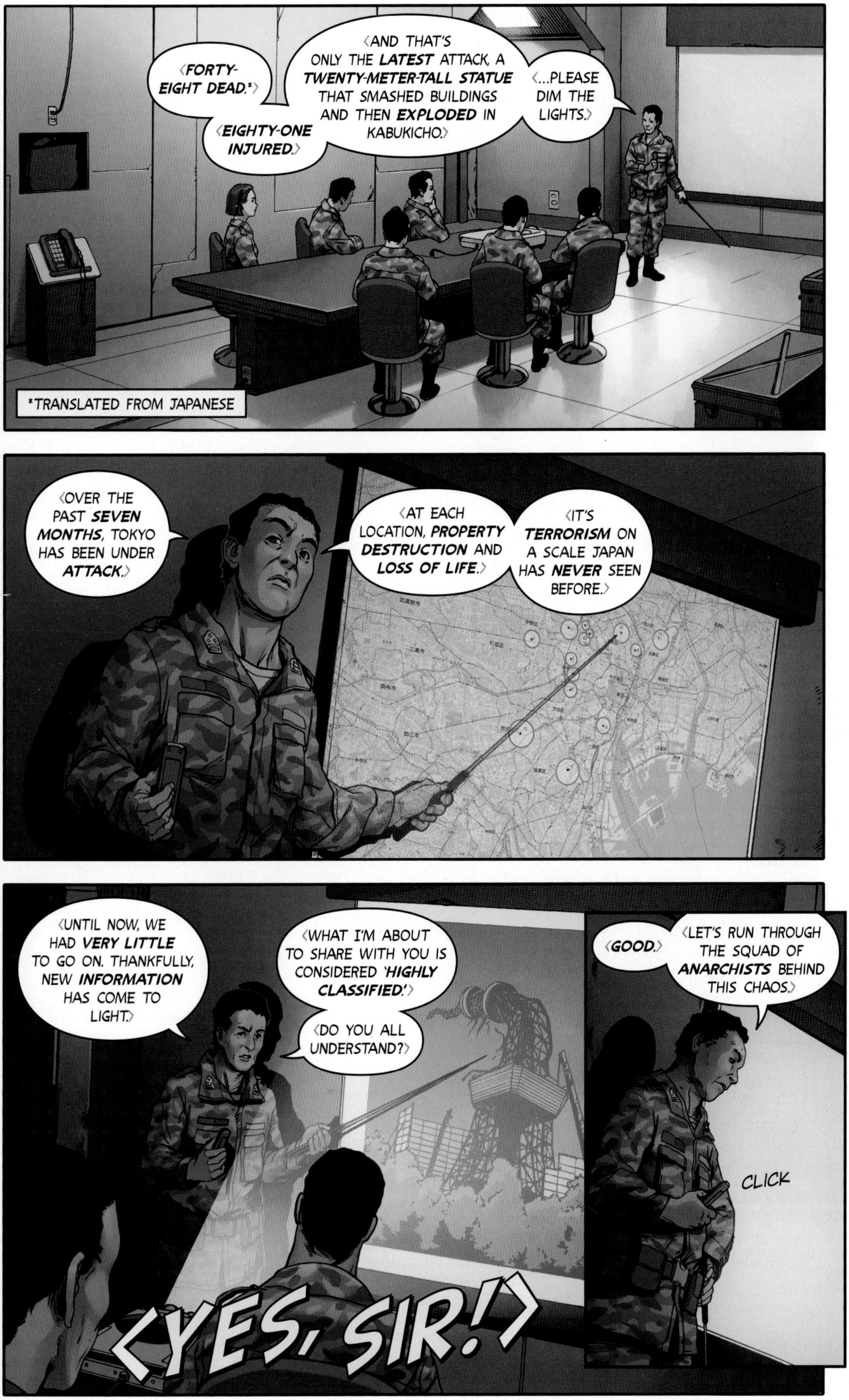
〈FORTY-EIGHT DEAD.*〉
〈EIGHTY-ONE INJURED.〉
〈AND THAT'S ONLY THE LATEST ATTACK, A TWENTY-METER-TALL STATUE THAT SMASHED BUILDINGS AND THEN EXPLODED IN KABUKICHO.〉
〈...PLEASE DIM THE LIGHTS.〉
*TRANSLATED FROM JAPANESE
〈OVER THE PAST SEVEN MONTHS, TOKYO HAS BEEN UNDER ATTACK.〉
〈AT EACH LOCATION, PROPERTY DESTRUCTION AND LOSS OF LIFE.〉
〈IT'S TERRORISM ON A SCALE JAPAN HAS NEVER SEEN BEFORE.〉
〈UNTIL NOW, WE HAD VERY LITTLE TO GO ON. THANKFULLY, NEW INFORMATION HAS COME TO LIGHT.〉
〈WHAT I'M ABOUT TO SHARE WITH YOU IS CONSIDERED 'HIGHLY CLASSIFIED.'〉
〈DO YOU ALL UNDERSTAND?〉
〈YES, SIR!〉
〈GOOD.〉
〈LET'S RUN THROUGH THE SQUAD OF ANARCHISTS BEHIND THIS CHAOS.〉
CLICK

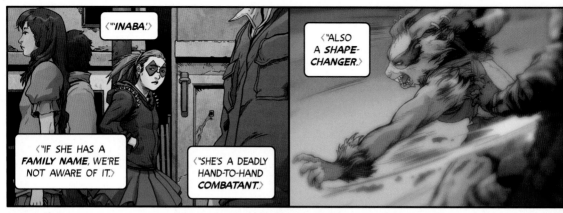

⟨"'INABA.'⟩

⟨"IF SHE HAS A **FAMILY NAME**, WE'RE NOT AWARE OF IT.⟩

⟨"SHE'S A DEADLY HAND-TO-HAND **COMBATANT**.⟩

⟨"ALSO A **SHAPE-CHANGER**.⟩

⟨"'AYANE.'⟩

⟨"SAME HERE. NO KNOWN FAMILY NAME.⟩

⟨"THIS ONE'S **ALSO** A SHAPE-CHANGER, BUT IT'S BEEN **WEEKS** SINCE SHE'S BEEN SPOTTED WITH THE OTHERS, SO SHE MAY BE **DEAD**.⟩

⟨"'SHIRAI TOMOHIRO.'⟩

⟨"HE'S A POWERFUL RECRUIT WITH VAST AMOUNTS OF **STRENGTH** AND **ENDURANCE**.⟩

⟨"HIS FAMILY HAS DISAVOWED ALL KNOWLEDGE OF HIS **TERRORIST ACTIVITIES** AND HAS BEEN LITTLE HELP IN TRACKING HIM DOWN.⟩

⟨"'SEGAWA TOURU.'⟩

⟨"A LAYABOUT **OTAKU** FOR THE PAST FIVE YEARS, RECENTLY HE'S NOW BEEN SIGHTED IN THIS **TERRORIST CELL**.⟩

⟨"HE CAN **TELEPATHICALLY COMMUNICATE** WITH **MACHINES** AND **NETWORKS**, WILLING THEM TO DO AS HE **COMMANDS**."⟩

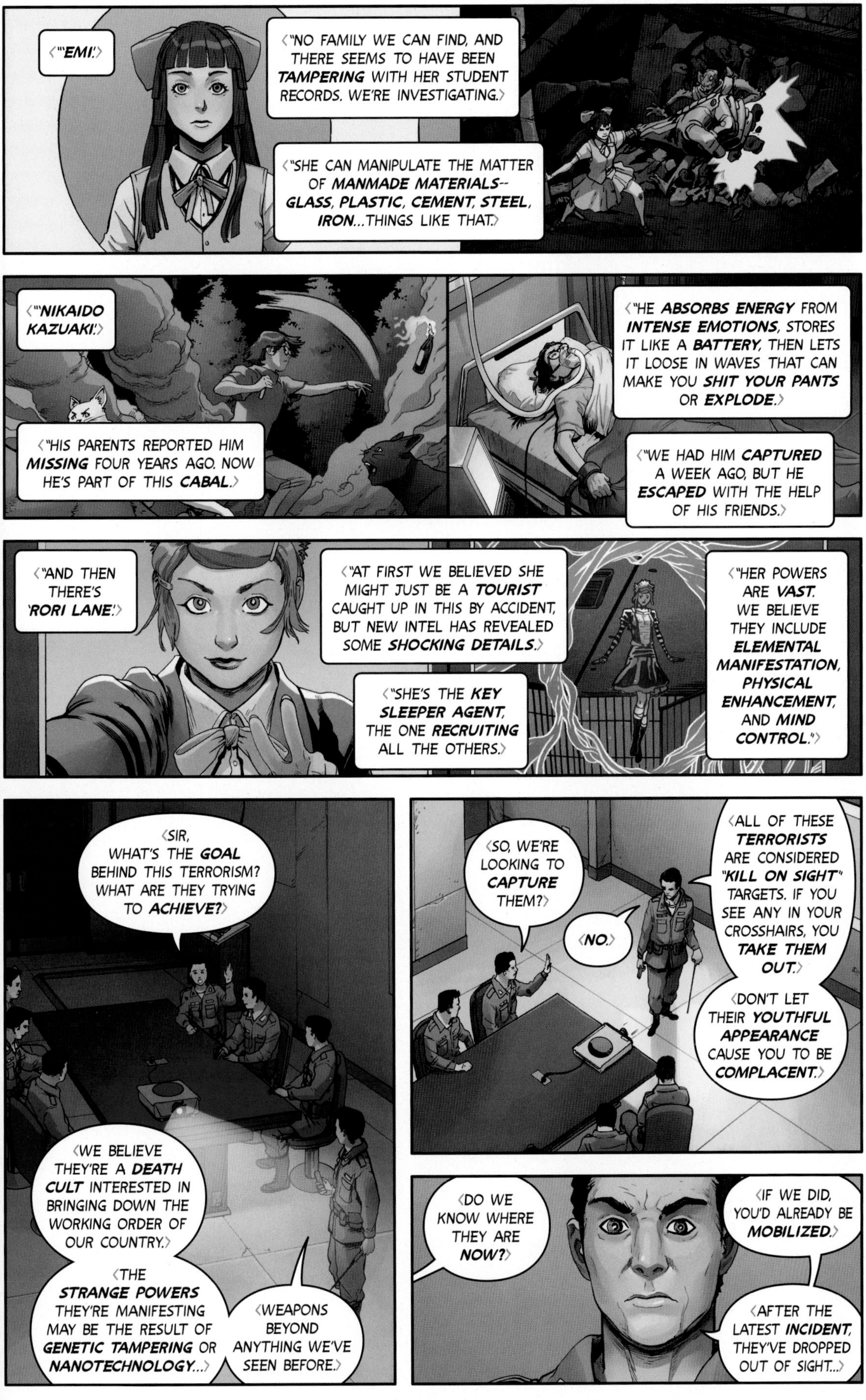
<"'EMI.'>
<"NO FAMILY WE CAN FIND, AND THERE SEEMS TO HAVE BEEN TAMPERING WITH HER STUDENT RECORDS. WE'RE INVESTIGATING.>
<"SHE CAN MANIPULATE THE MATTER OF MANMADE MATERIALS-- GLASS, PLASTIC, CEMENT, STEEL, IRON...THINGS LIKE THAT.>
<"'NIKAIDO KAZUAKI.'>
<"HIS PARENTS REPORTED HIM MISSING FOUR YEARS AGO. NOW HE'S PART OF THIS CABAL.>
<"HE ABSORBS ENERGY FROM INTENSE EMOTIONS, STORES IT LIKE A BATTERY, THEN LETS IT LOOSE IN WAVES THAT CAN MAKE YOU SHIT YOUR PANTS OR EXPLODE.>
<"WE HAD HIM CAPTURED A WEEK AGO, BUT HE ESCAPED WITH THE HELP OF HIS FRIENDS.>
<"AND THEN THERE'S 'RORI LANE.'>
<"AT FIRST WE BELIEVED SHE MIGHT JUST BE A TOURIST CAUGHT UP IN THIS BY ACCIDENT, BUT NEW INTEL HAS REVEALED SOME SHOCKING DETAILS.>
<"SHE'S THE KEY SLEEPER AGENT, THE ONE RECRUITING ALL THE OTHERS.>
<"HER POWERS ARE VAST. WE BELIEVE THEY INCLUDE ELEMENTAL MANIFESTATION, PHYSICAL ENHANCEMENT, AND MIND CONTROL.">
<SIR, WHAT'S THE GOAL BEHIND THIS TERRORISM? WHAT ARE THEY TRYING TO ACHIEVE?>
<WE BELIEVE THEY'RE A DEATH CULT INTERESTED IN BRINGING DOWN THE WORKING ORDER OF OUR COUNTRY.>
<THE STRANGE POWERS THEY'RE MANIFESTING MAY BE THE RESULT OF GENETIC TAMPERING OR NANOTECHNOLOGY...>
<WEAPONS BEYOND ANYTHING WE'VE SEEN BEFORE.>
<SO, WE'RE LOOKING TO CAPTURE THEM?>
<NO.>
<ALL OF THESE TERRORISTS ARE CONSIDERED "KILL ON SIGHT" TARGETS. IF YOU SEE ANY IN YOUR CROSSHAIRS, YOU TAKE THEM OUT.>
<DON'T LET THEIR YOUTHFUL APPEARANCE CAUSE YOU TO BE COMPLACENT.>
<DO WE KNOW WHERE THEY ARE NOW?>
<IF WE DID, YOU'D ALREADY BE MOBILIZED.>
<AFTER THE LATEST INCIDENT, THEY'VE DROPPED OUT OF SIGHT...>

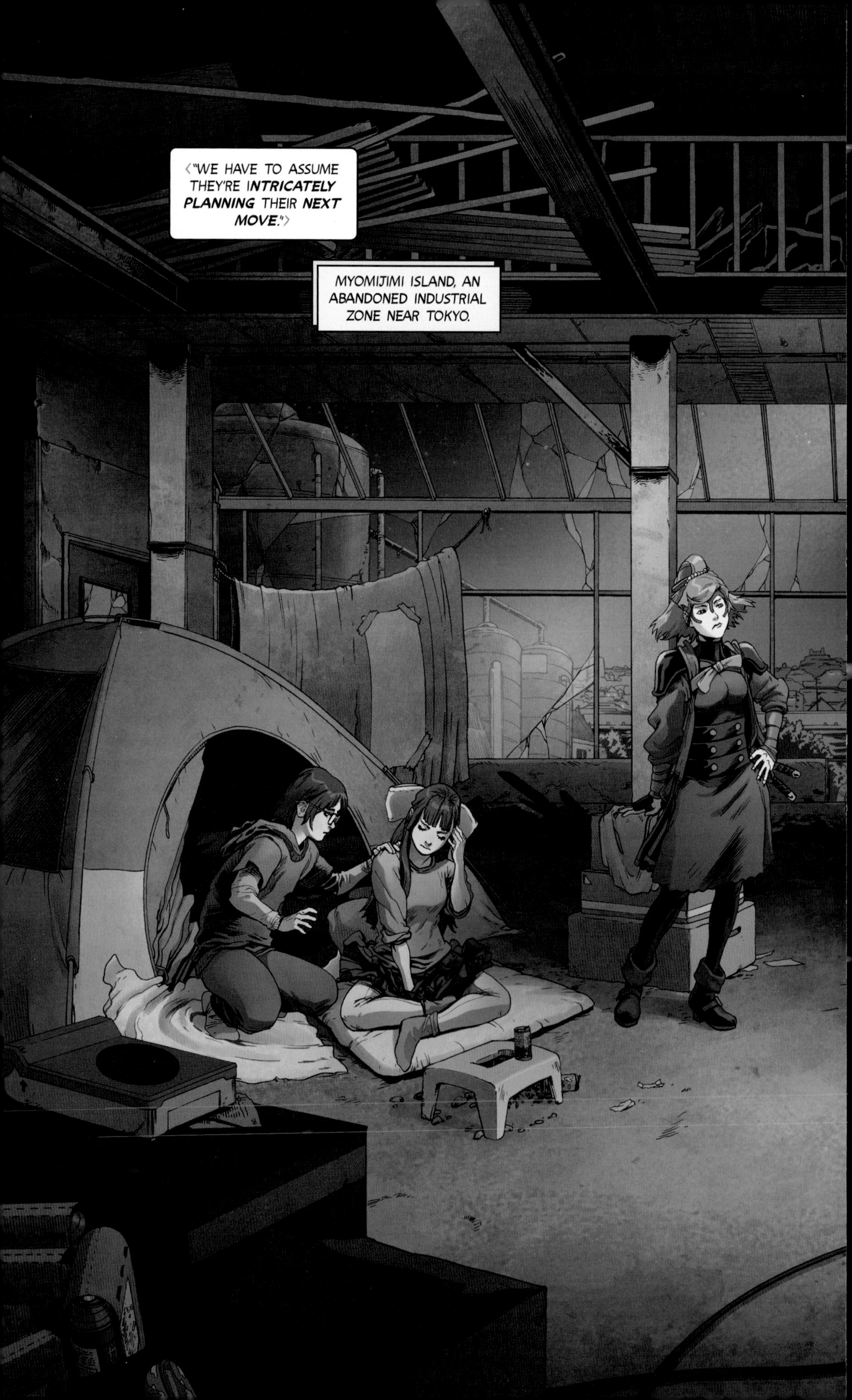
〈"WE HAVE TO ASSUME THEY'RE INTRICATELY PLANNING THEIR NEXT MOVE."〉
MYOMIJIMI ISLAND, AN ABANDONED INDUSTRIAL ZONE NEAR TOKYO.

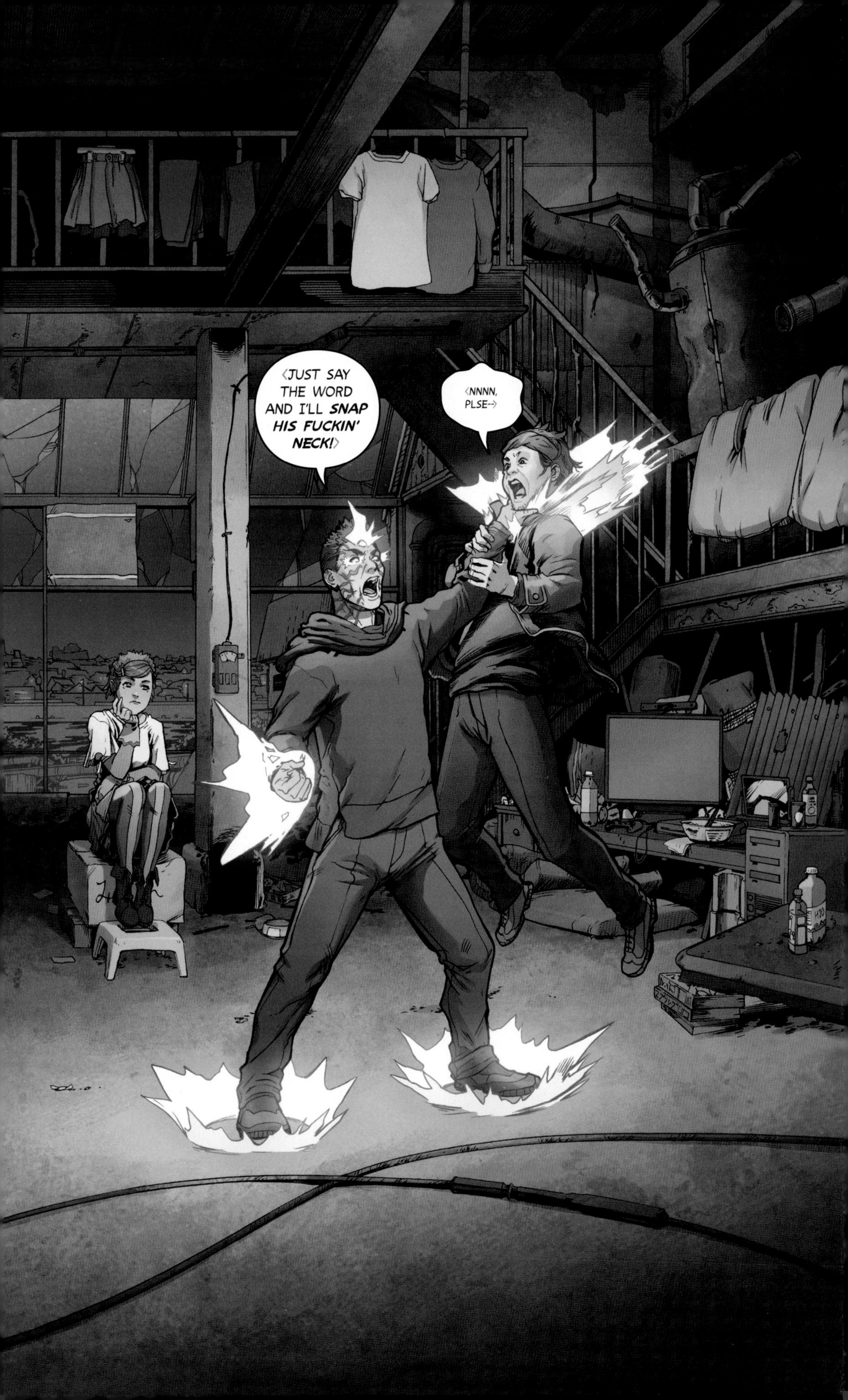

⟨JUST SAY THE WORD AND I'LL SNAP HIS FUCKIN' NECK!⟩
⟨NNNN, PLSE--⟩

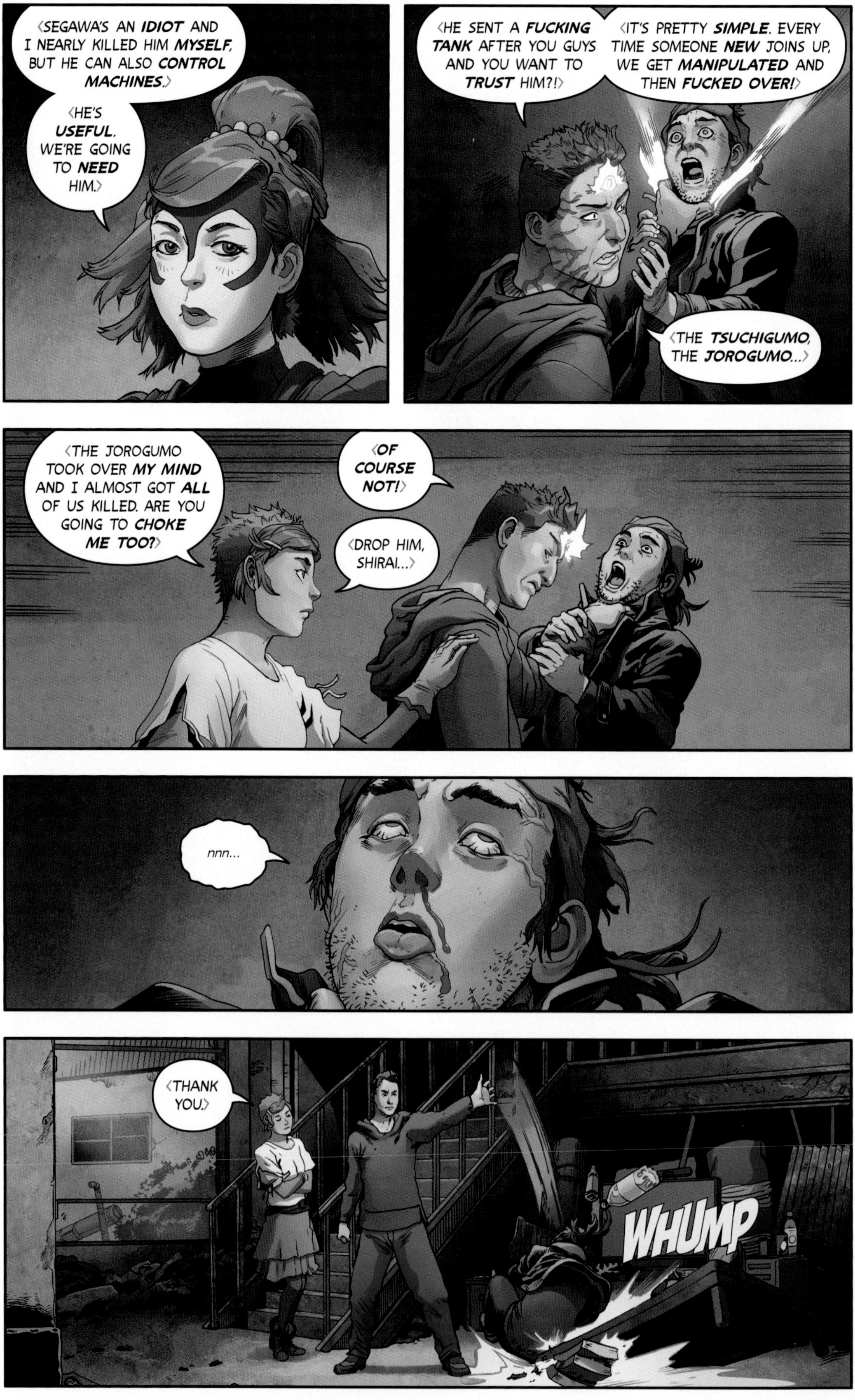

‹SEGAWA'S AN IDIOT AND I NEARLY KILLED HIM MYSELF, BUT HE CAN ALSO CONTROL MACHINES.›
‹HE'S USEFUL. WE'RE GOING TO NEED HIM.›
‹HE SENT A FUCKING TANK AFTER YOU GUYS AND YOU WANT TO TRUST HIM?!›
‹IT'S PRETTY SIMPLE. EVERY TIME SOMEONE NEW JOINS UP, WE GET MANIPULATED AND THEN FUCKED OVER!›
‹THE TSUCHIGUMO, THE JOROGUMO...›
‹THE JOROGUMO TOOK OVER MY MIND AND I ALMOST GOT ALL OF US KILLED. ARE YOU GOING TO CHOKE ME TOO?›
‹OF COURSE NOT!›
‹DROP HIM, SHIRAI...›
nnn...
‹THANK YOU.›
WHUMP

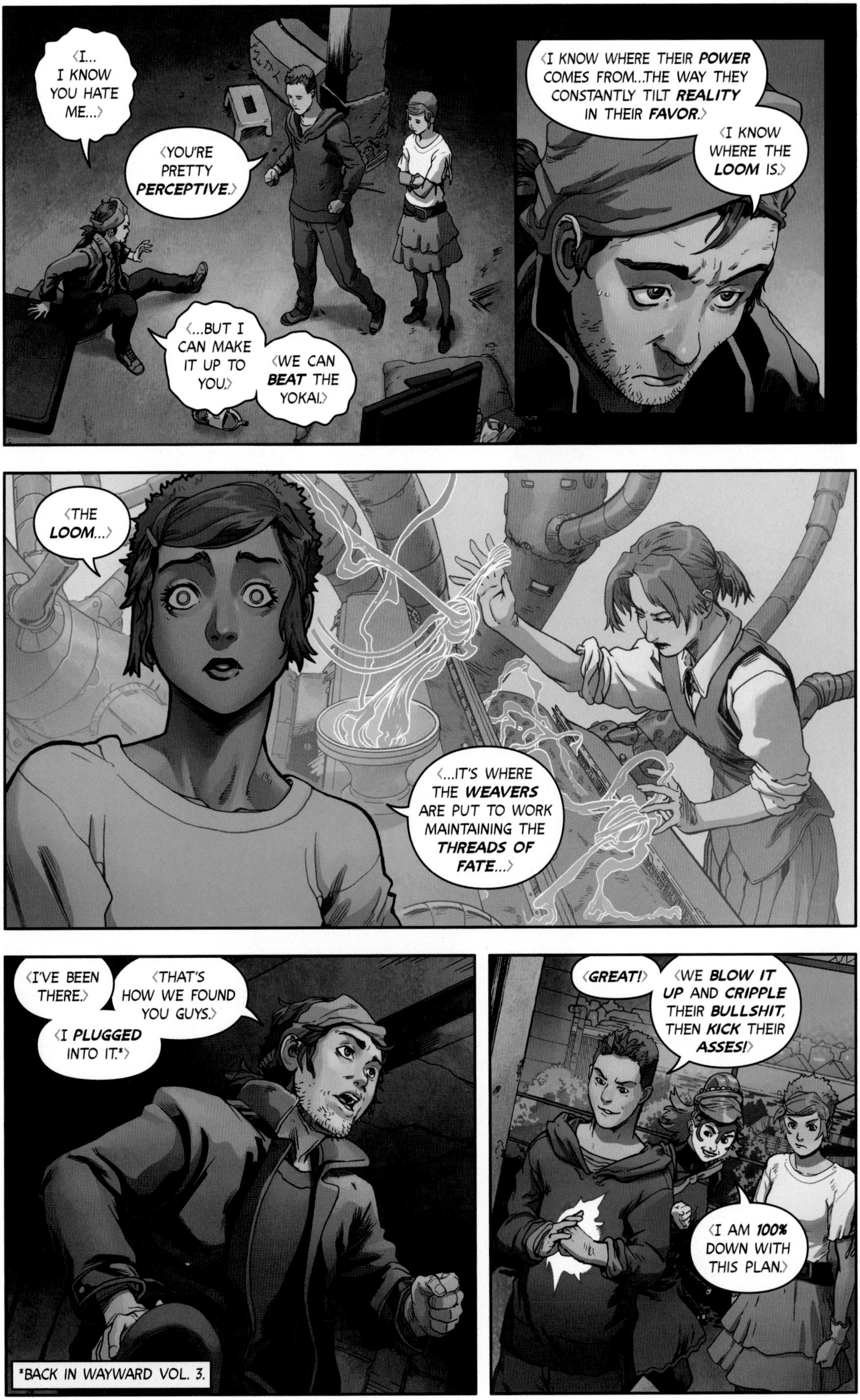
⟨I... I KNOW YOU HATE ME...⟩
⟨YOU'RE PRETTY **PERCEPTIVE**.⟩
⟨...BUT I CAN MAKE IT UP TO YOU.⟩
⟨WE CAN **BEAT** THE YOKAI.⟩
⟨I KNOW WHERE THEIR **POWER** COMES FROM...THE WAY THEY CONSTANTLY TILT **REALITY** IN THEIR **FAVOR**.⟩
⟨I KNOW WHERE THE **LOOM** IS.⟩
⟨THE **LOOM**...⟩
⟨...IT'S WHERE THE **WEAVERS** ARE PUT TO WORK MAINTAINING THE **THREADS OF FATE**...⟩
⟨I'VE BEEN THERE.⟩
⟨THAT'S HOW WE FOUND YOU GUYS.⟩
⟨I **PLUGGED** INTO IT.*⟩
*BACK IN WAYWARD VOL. 3.
⟨**GREAT!**⟩
⟨WE **BLOW IT UP** AND **CRIPPLE** THEIR **BULLSHIT**, THEN **KICK** THEIR **ASSES!**⟩
⟨I AM **100%** DOWN WITH THIS PLAN.⟩

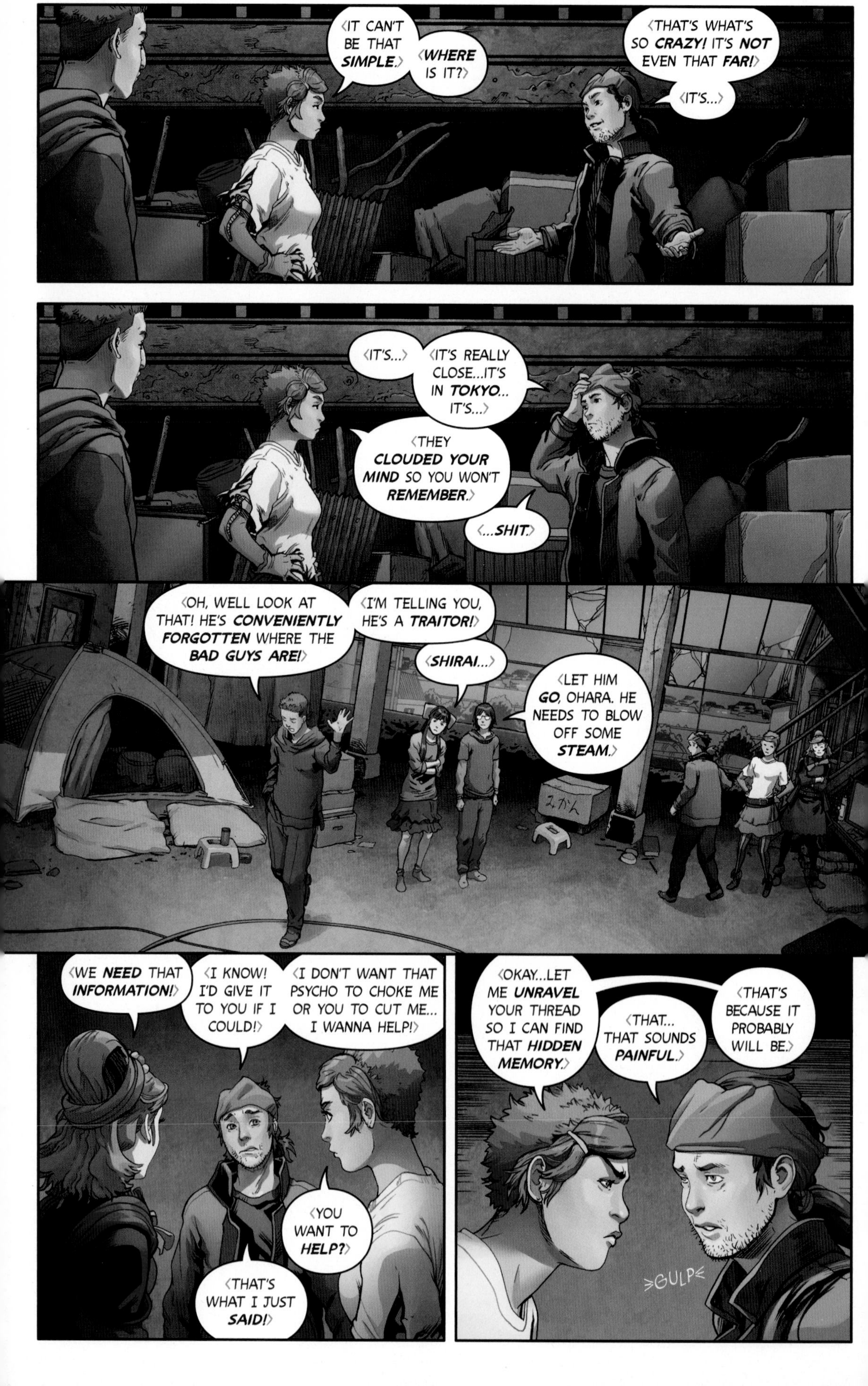

‹IT CAN'T BE THAT SIMPLE.›
‹WHERE IS IT?›
‹THAT'S WHAT'S SO CRAZY! IT'S NOT EVEN THAT FAR!›
‹IT'S...›
‹IT'S...›
‹IT'S REALLY CLOSE...IT'S IN TOKYO... IT'S...›
‹THEY CLOUDED YOUR MIND SO YOU WON'T REMEMBER.›
‹...SHIT.›
‹OH, WELL LOOK AT THAT! HE'S CONVENIENTLY FORGOTTEN WHERE THE BAD GUYS ARE!›
‹I'M TELLING YOU, HE'S A TRAITOR!›
‹SHIRAI...›
‹LET HIM GO, OHARA. HE NEEDS TO BLOW OFF SOME STEAM.›
みかん
‹WE NEED THAT INFORMATION!›
‹I KNOW! I'D GIVE IT TO YOU IF I COULD!›
‹I DON'T WANT THAT PSYCHO TO CHOKE ME OR YOU TO CUT ME... I WANNA HELP!›
‹YOU WANT TO HELP?›
‹THAT'S WHAT I JUST SAID!›
‹OKAY...LET ME UNRAVEL YOUR THREAD SO I CAN FIND THAT HIDDEN MEMORY.›
‹THAT... THAT SOUNDS PAINFUL.›
‹THAT'S BECAUSE IT PROBABLY WILL BE.›
GULP

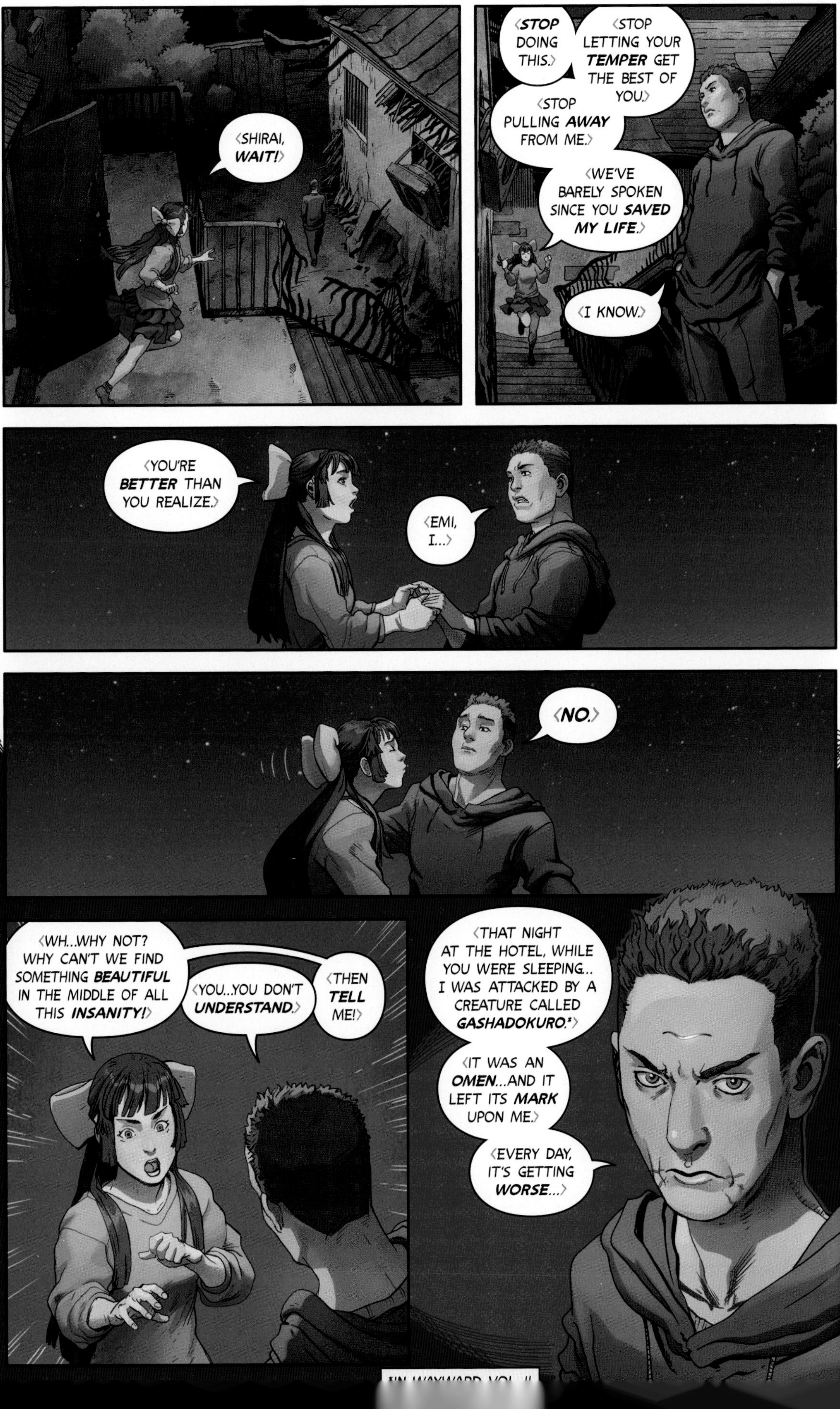
‹SHIRAI, WAIT!›
‹STOP DOING THIS.›
‹STOP LETTING YOUR TEMPER GET THE BEST OF YOU.›
‹STOP PULLING AWAY FROM ME.›
‹WE'VE BARELY SPOKEN SINCE YOU SAVED MY LIFE.›
‹I KNOW.›
‹YOU'RE BETTER THAN YOU REALIZE.›
‹EMI, I...›
‹NO.›
‹WH...WHY NOT? WHY CAN'T WE FIND SOMETHING BEAUTIFUL IN THE MIDDLE OF ALL THIS INSANITY!›
‹YOU...YOU DON'T UNDERSTAND.›
‹THEN TELL ME!›
‹THAT NIGHT AT THE HOTEL, WHILE YOU WERE SLEEPING... I WAS ATTACKED BY A CREATURE CALLED GASHADOKURO.*›
‹IT WAS AN OMEN...AND IT LEFT ITS MARK UPON ME.›
‹EVERY DAY, IT'S GETTING WORSE...›
*IN WAYWARD VOL. I

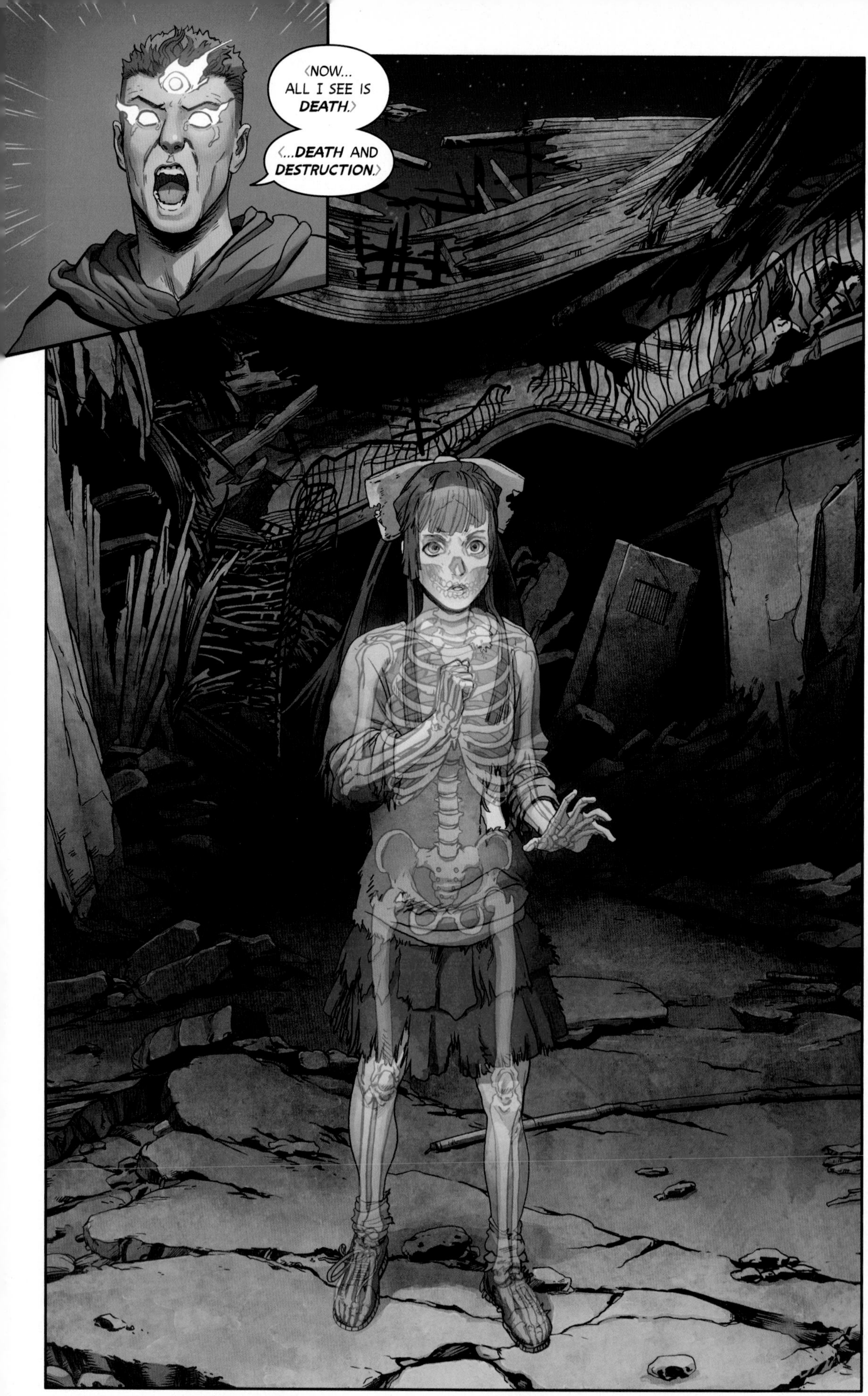

‹NOW... ALL I SEE IS DEATH.›
‹...DEATH AND DESTRUCTION.›

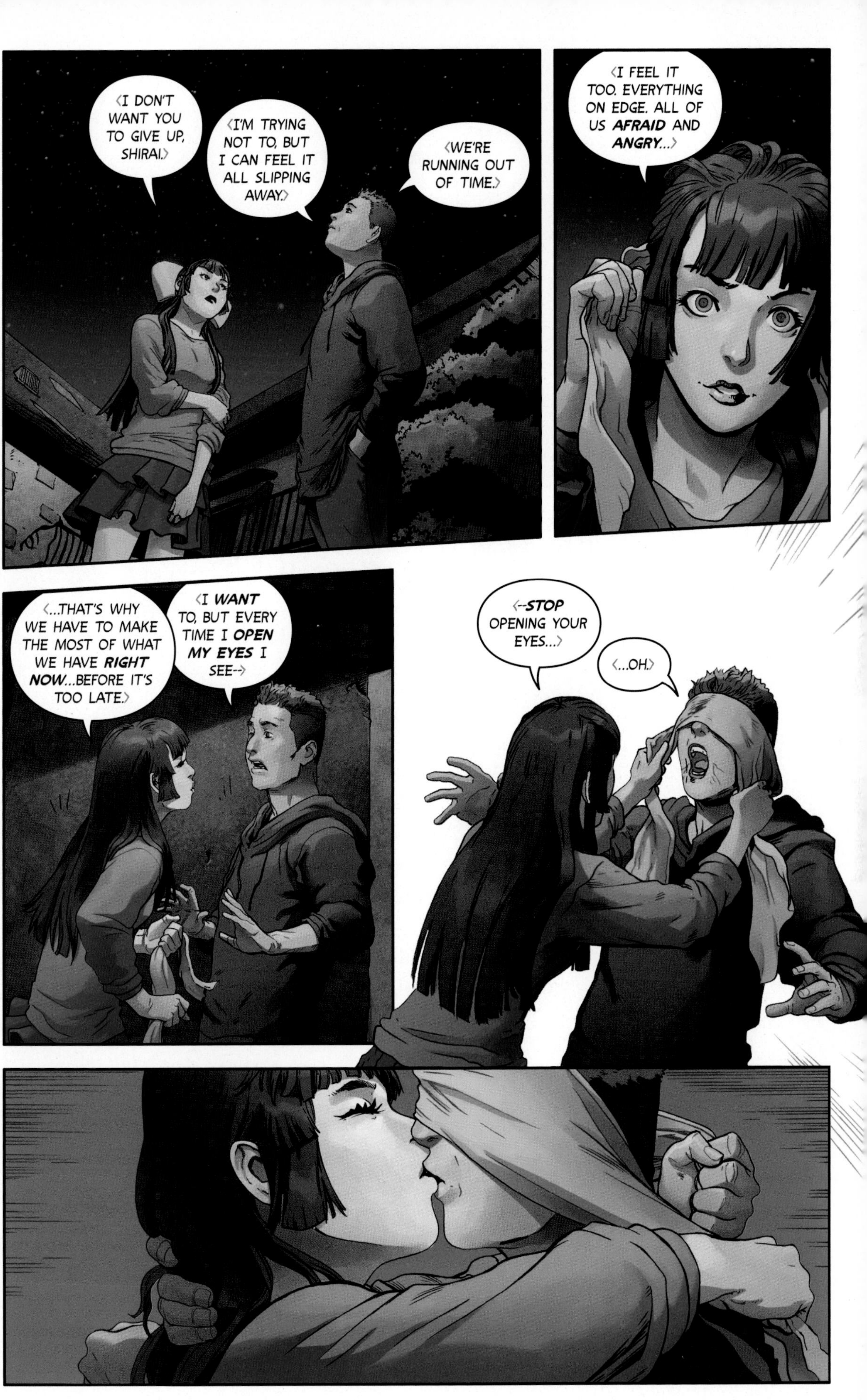

‹I DON'T WANT YOU TO GIVE UP, SHIRAI.›
‹I'M TRYING NOT TO, BUT I CAN FEEL IT ALL SLIPPING AWAY.›
‹WE'RE RUNNING OUT OF TIME.›
‹I FEEL IT TOO. EVERYTHING ON EDGE. ALL OF US **AFRAID** AND **ANGRY**...›
‹...THAT'S WHY WE HAVE TO MAKE THE MOST OF WHAT WE HAVE **RIGHT NOW**...BEFORE IT'S TOO LATE.›
‹I **WANT** TO, BUT EVERY TIME I **OPEN MY EYES** I SEE--›
‹--**STOP** OPENING YOUR EYES...›
‹...OH.›

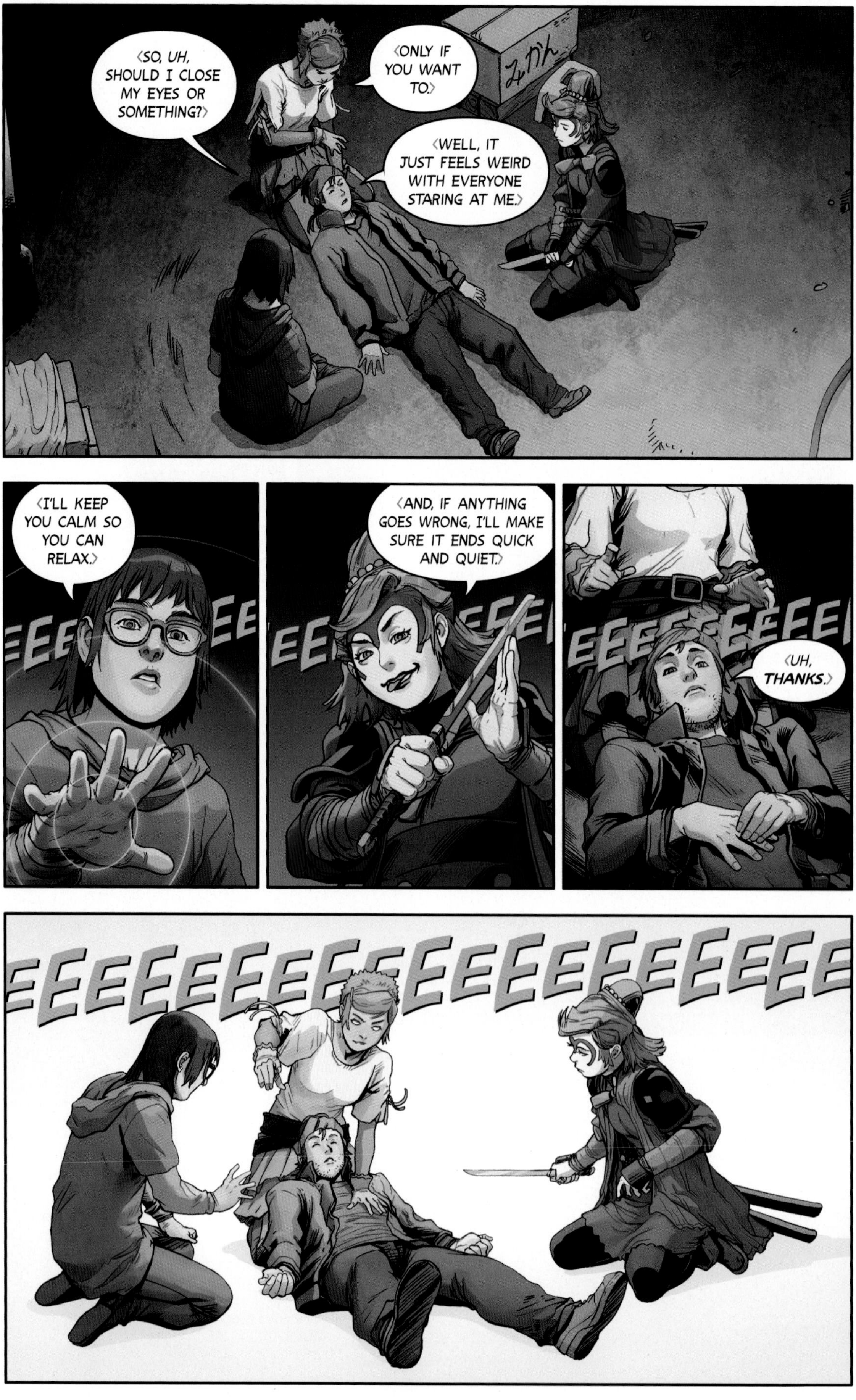
〈SO, UH, SHOULD I CLOSE MY EYES OR SOMETHING?〉
〈ONLY IF YOU WANT TO.〉
みかん
〈WELL, IT JUST FEELS WEIRD WITH EVERYONE STARING AT ME.〉
〈I'LL KEEP YOU CALM SO YOU CAN RELAX.〉
〈AND, IF ANYTHING GOES WRONG, I'LL MAKE SURE IT ENDS QUICK AND QUIET.〉
〈UH, THANKS.〉

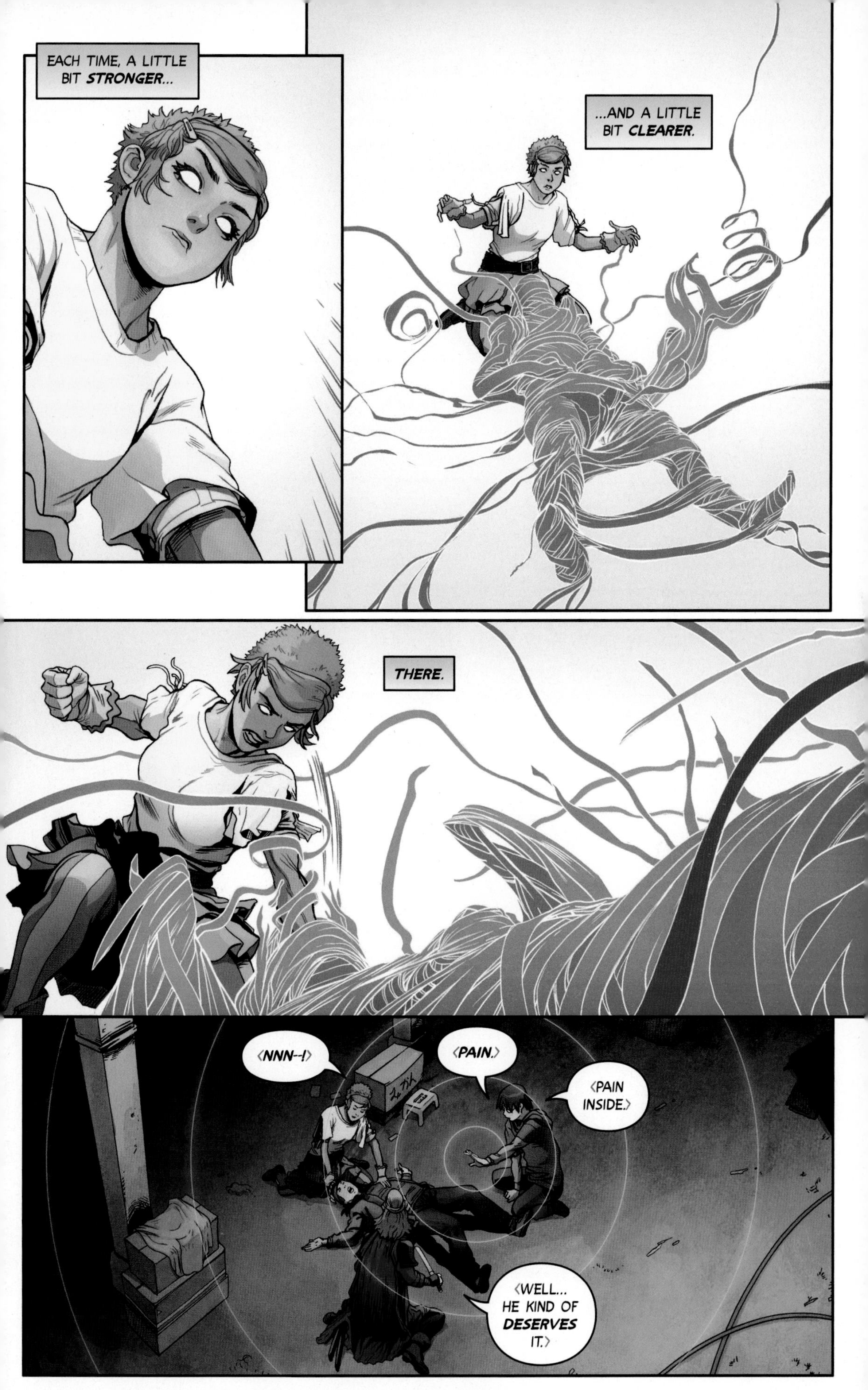
EACH TIME, A LITTLE BIT STRONGER...
...AND A LITTLE BIT CLEARER.
THERE.
‹NNN--!›
‹PAIN.›
‹PAIN INSIDE.›
‹WELL... HE KIND OF DESERVES IT.›

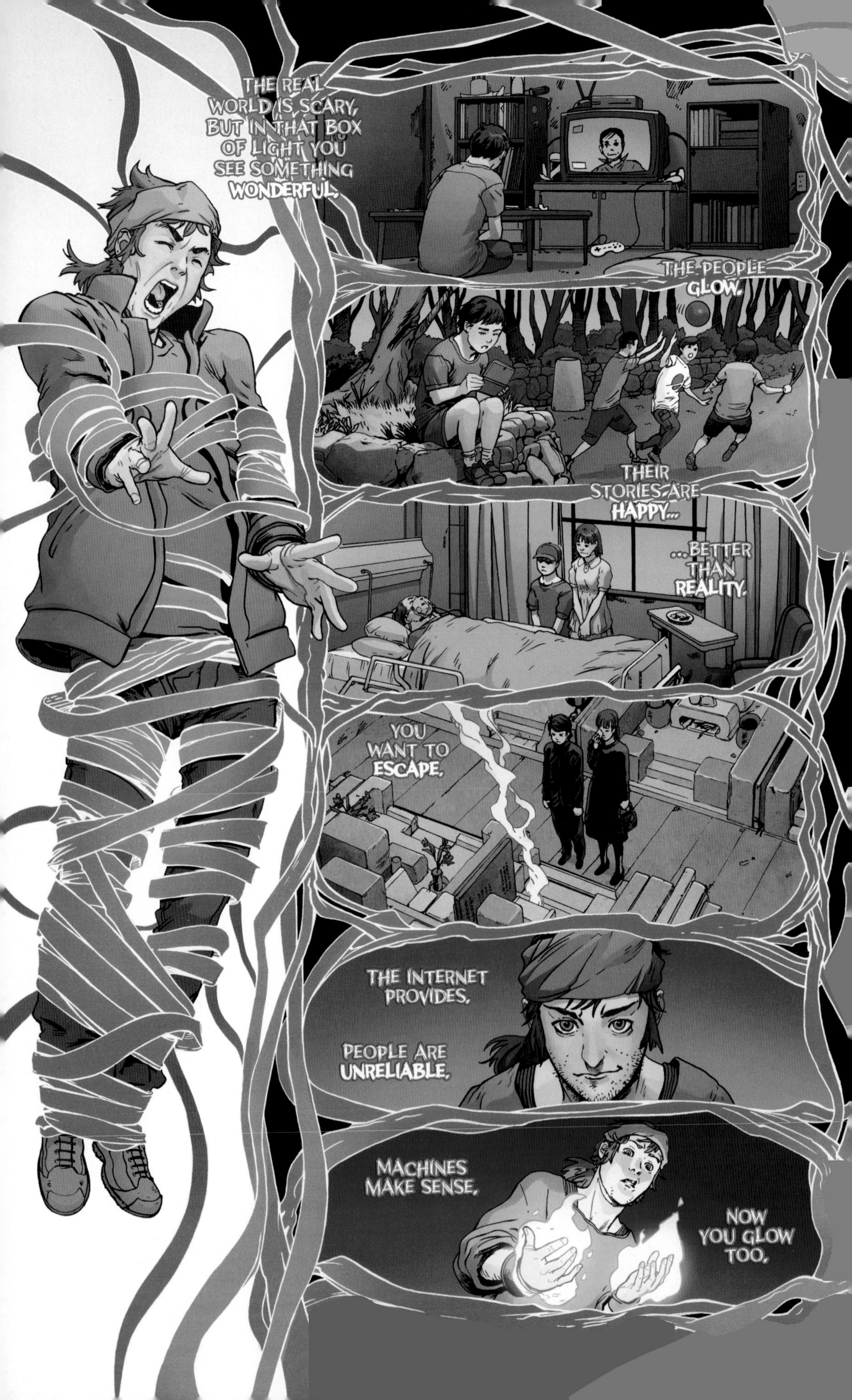
THE REAL WORLD IS SCARY, BUT IN THAT BOX OF LIGHT YOU SEE SOMETHING WONDERFUL.
THE PEOPLE GLOW.
THEIR STORIES ARE HAPPY...
...BETTER THAN REALITY.
YOU WANT TO ESCAPE.
THE INTERNET PROVIDES.
PEOPLE ARE UNRELIABLE.
MACHINES MAKE SENSE.
NOW YOU GLOW TOO.

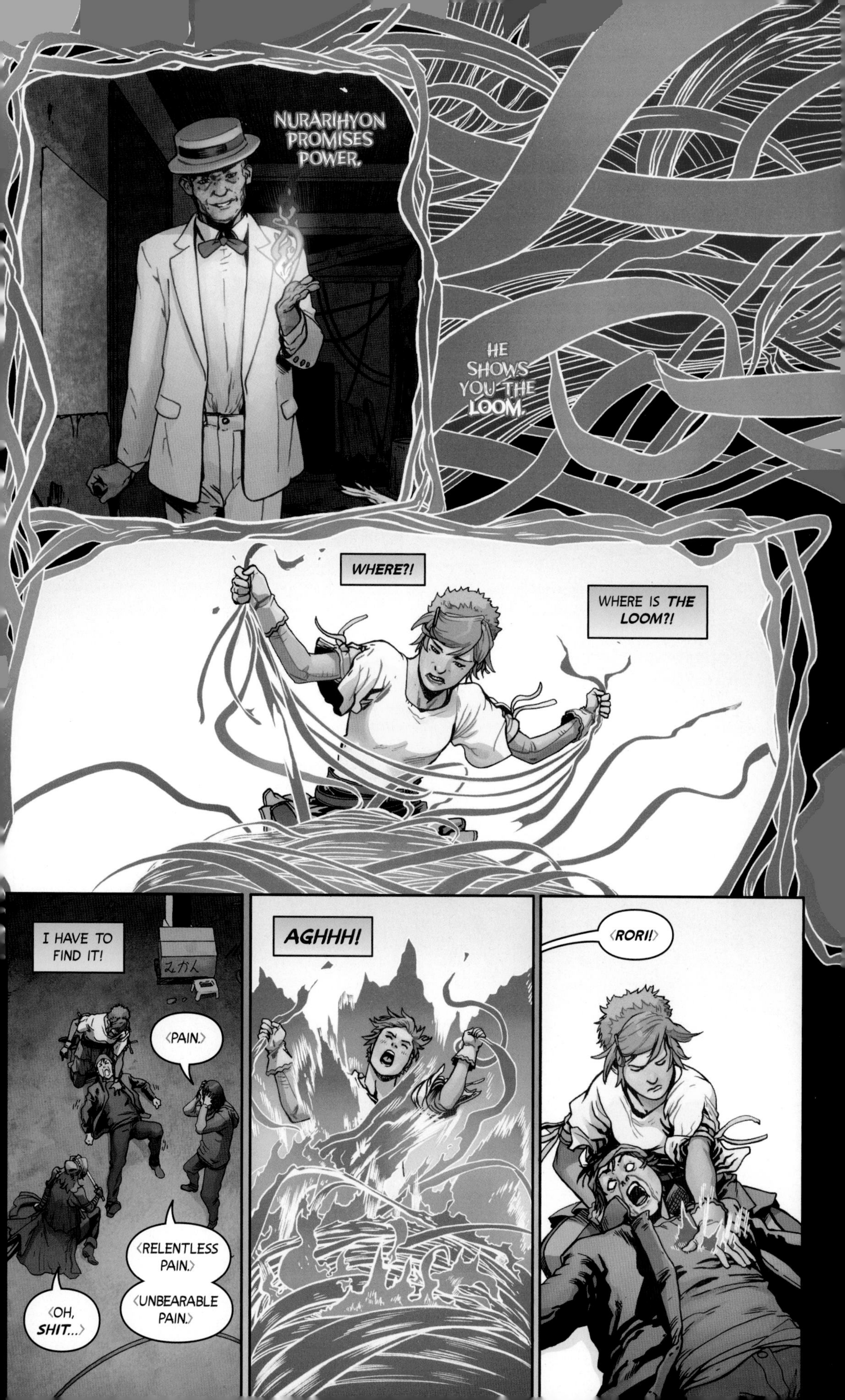
NURARIHYON PROMISES POWER,
HE SHOWS YOU THE LOOM.
WHERE?!
WHERE IS THE LOOM?!
I HAVE TO FIND IT!
‹PAIN.›
‹RELENTLESS PAIN.›
‹UNBEARABLE PAIN.›
‹OH, SHIT...›
みかん
AGHHH!
‹RORI!›

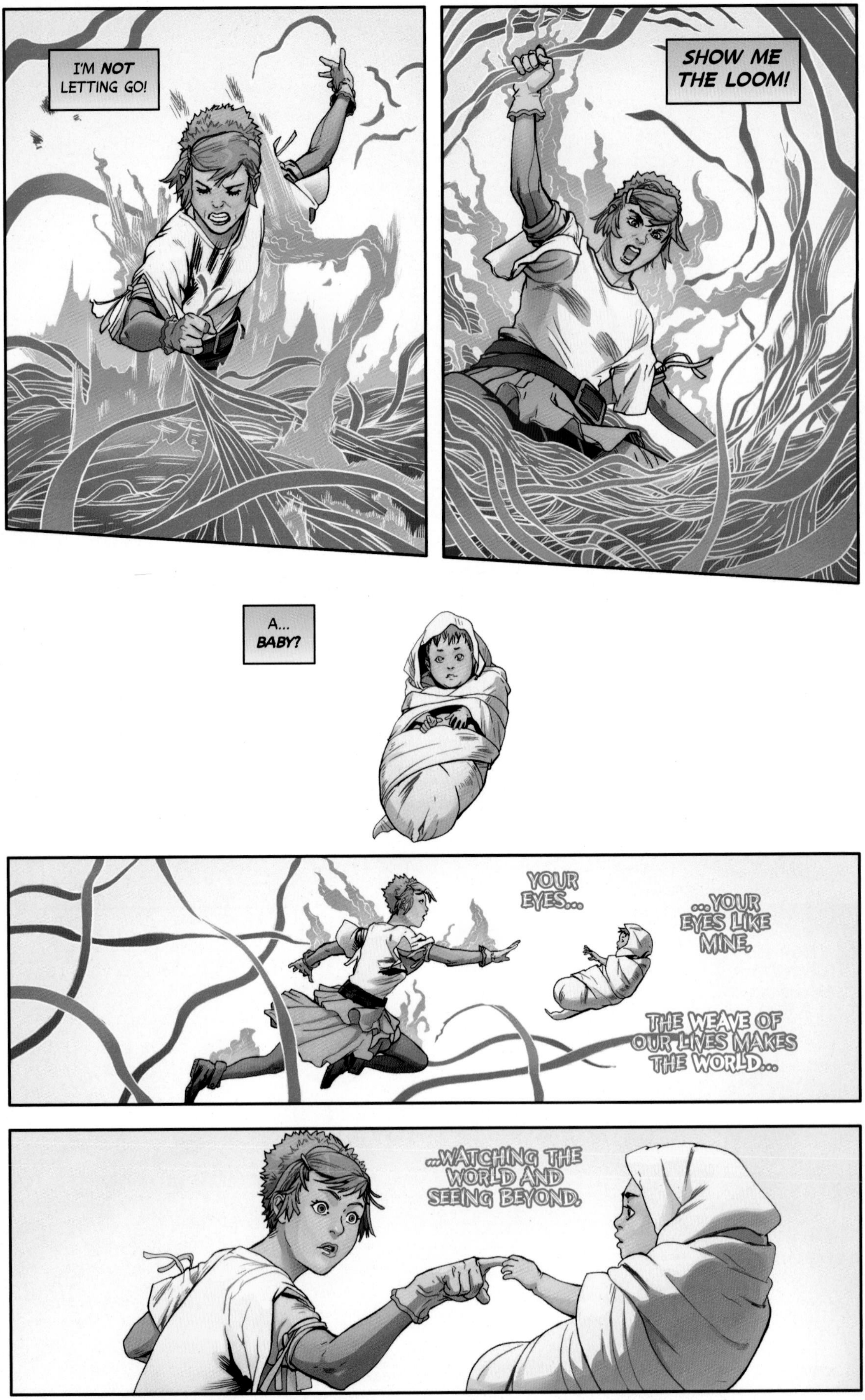
I'M NOT LETTING GO!
SHOW ME THE LOOM!
A... BABY?
YOUR EYES...
...YOUR EYES LIKE MINE.
THE WEAVE OF OUR LIVES MAKES THE WORLD...
...WATCHING THE WORLD AND SEEING BEYOND.

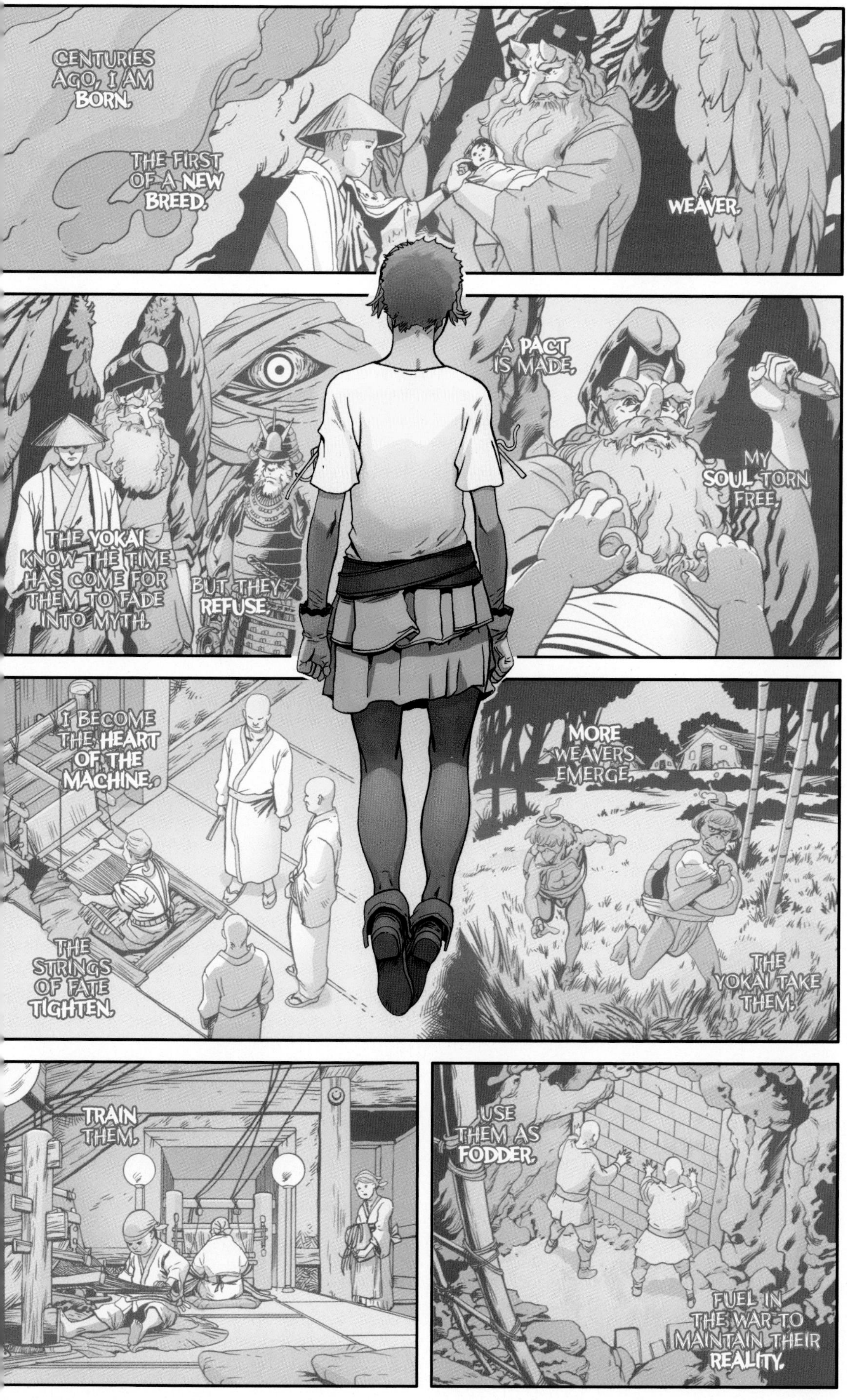

CENTURIES AGO, I AM BORN.
THE FIRST OF A NEW BREED.
A WEAVER.
A PACT IS MADE.
MY SOUL TORN FREE.
THE YOKAI KNOW THE TIME HAS COME FOR THEM TO FADE INTO MYTH.
BUT THEY REFUSE.
I BECOME THE HEART OF THE MACHINE.
THE STRINGS OF FATE TIGHTEN.
MORE WEAVERS EMERGE.
THE YOKAI TAKE THEM.
TRAIN THEM.
USE THEM AS FODDER.
FUEL IN THE WAR TO MAINTAIN THEIR REALITY.

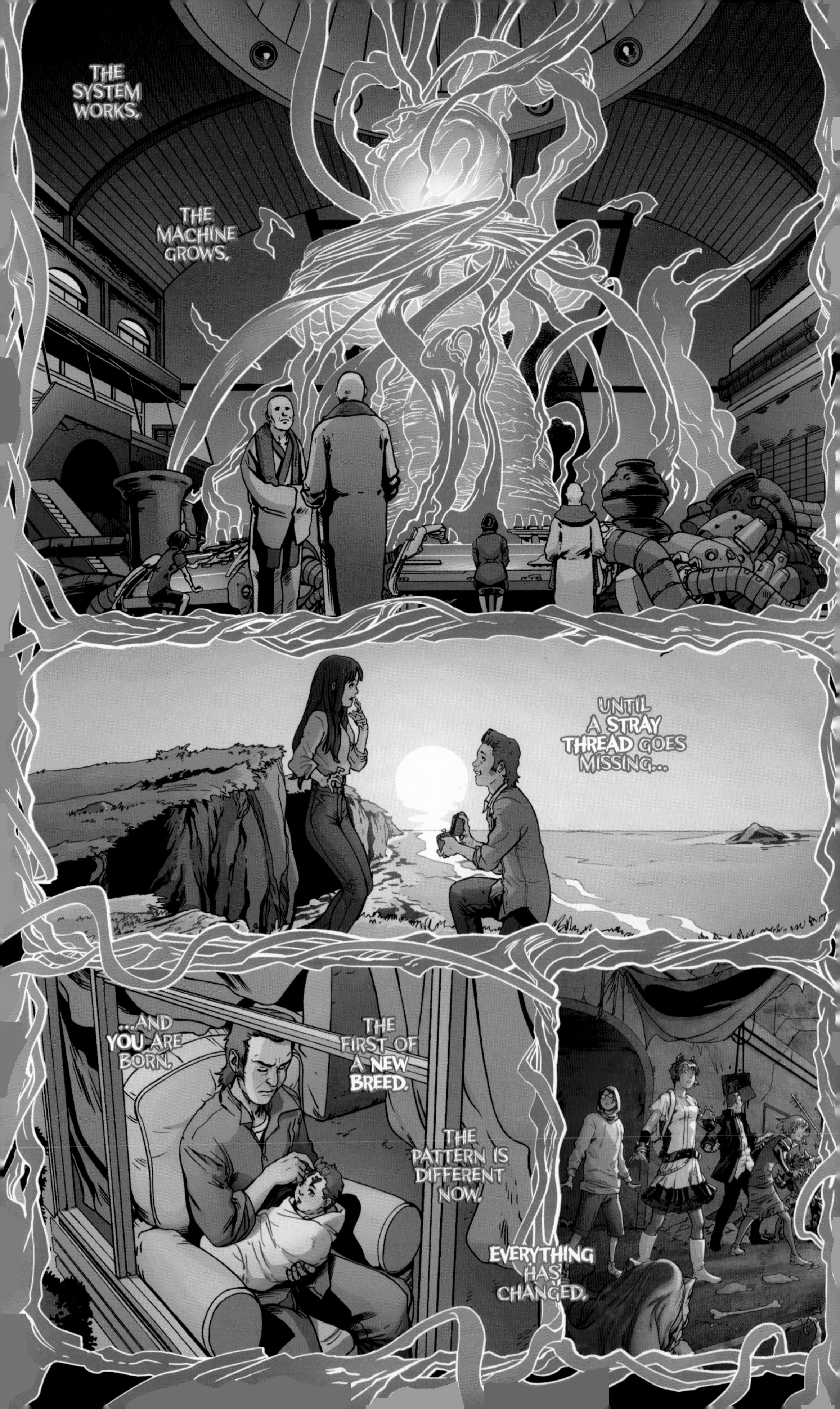
THE SYSTEM WORKS.
THE MACHINE GROWS.
UNTIL A STRAY THREAD GOES MISSING...
...AND YOU ARE BORN.
THE FIRST OF A NEW BREED.
THE PATTERN IS DIFFERENT NOW.
EVERYTHING HAS CHANGED.

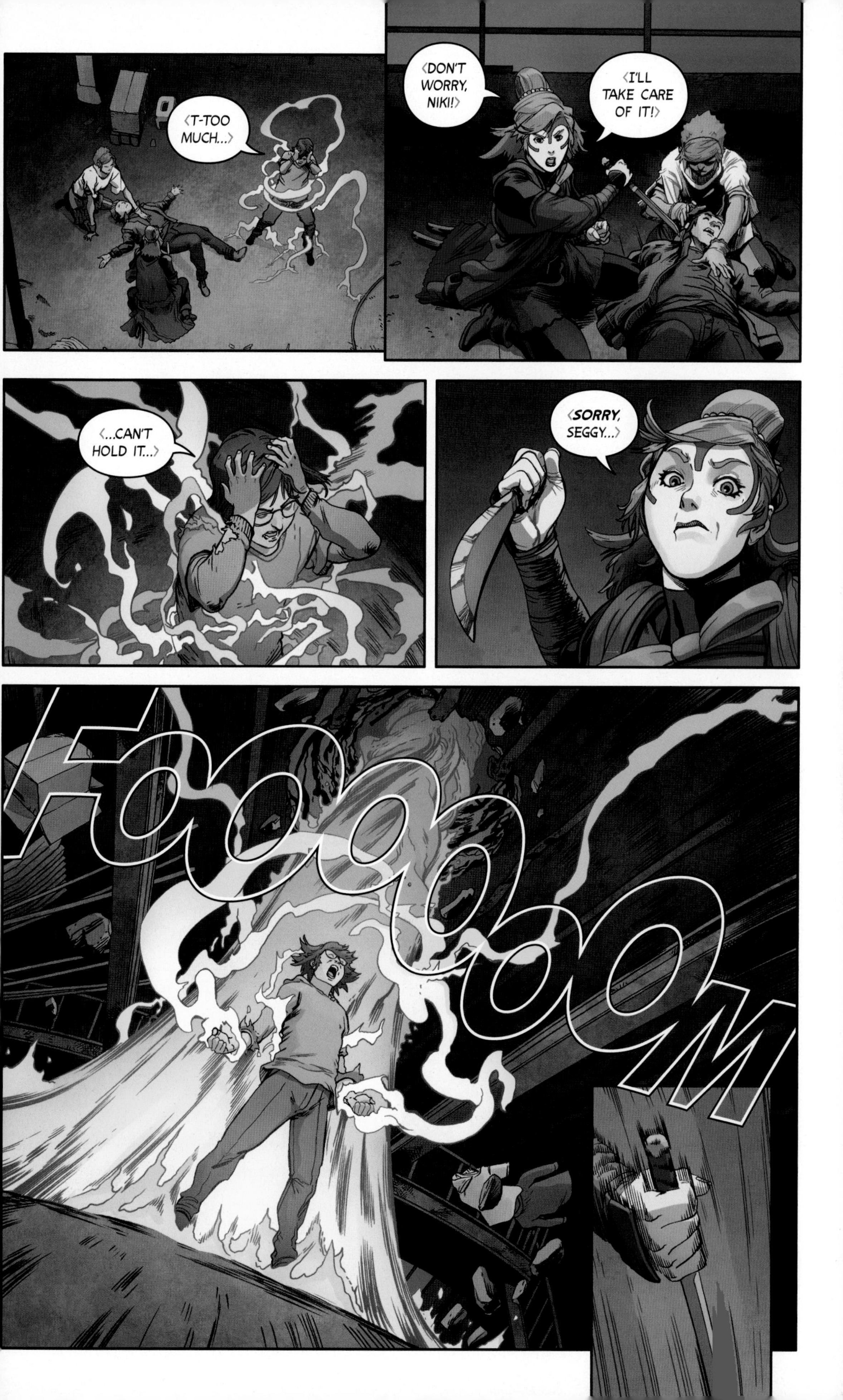

‹T-TOO MUCH...›
‹DON'T WORRY, NIKI!›
‹I'LL TAKE CARE OF IT!›
‹...CAN'T HOLD IT...›
‹SORRY, SEGGY...›
FOOOOOOOM

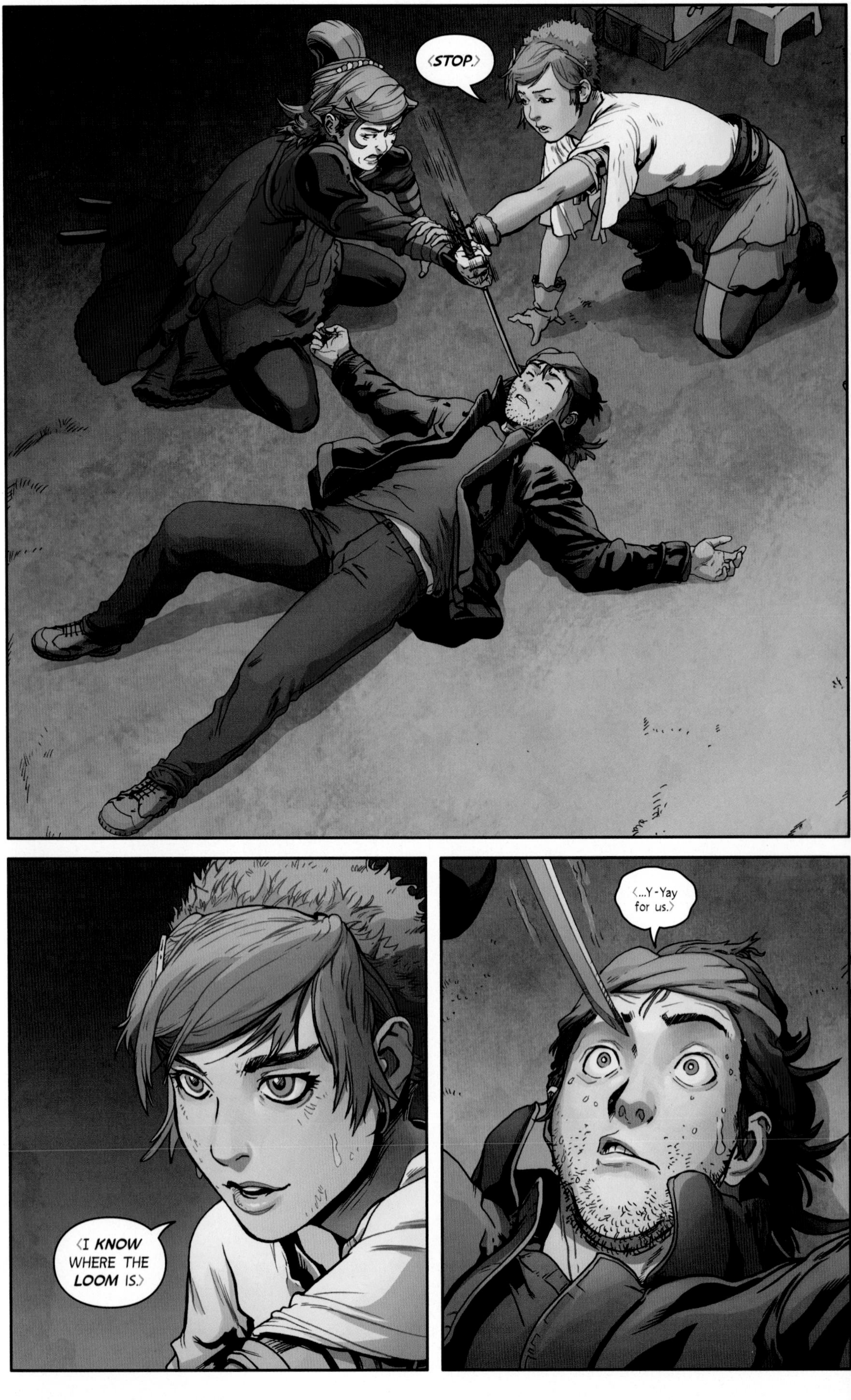
⟨STOP.⟩
⟨I KNOW WHERE THE LOOM IS.⟩
⟨...Y-Yay for us.⟩

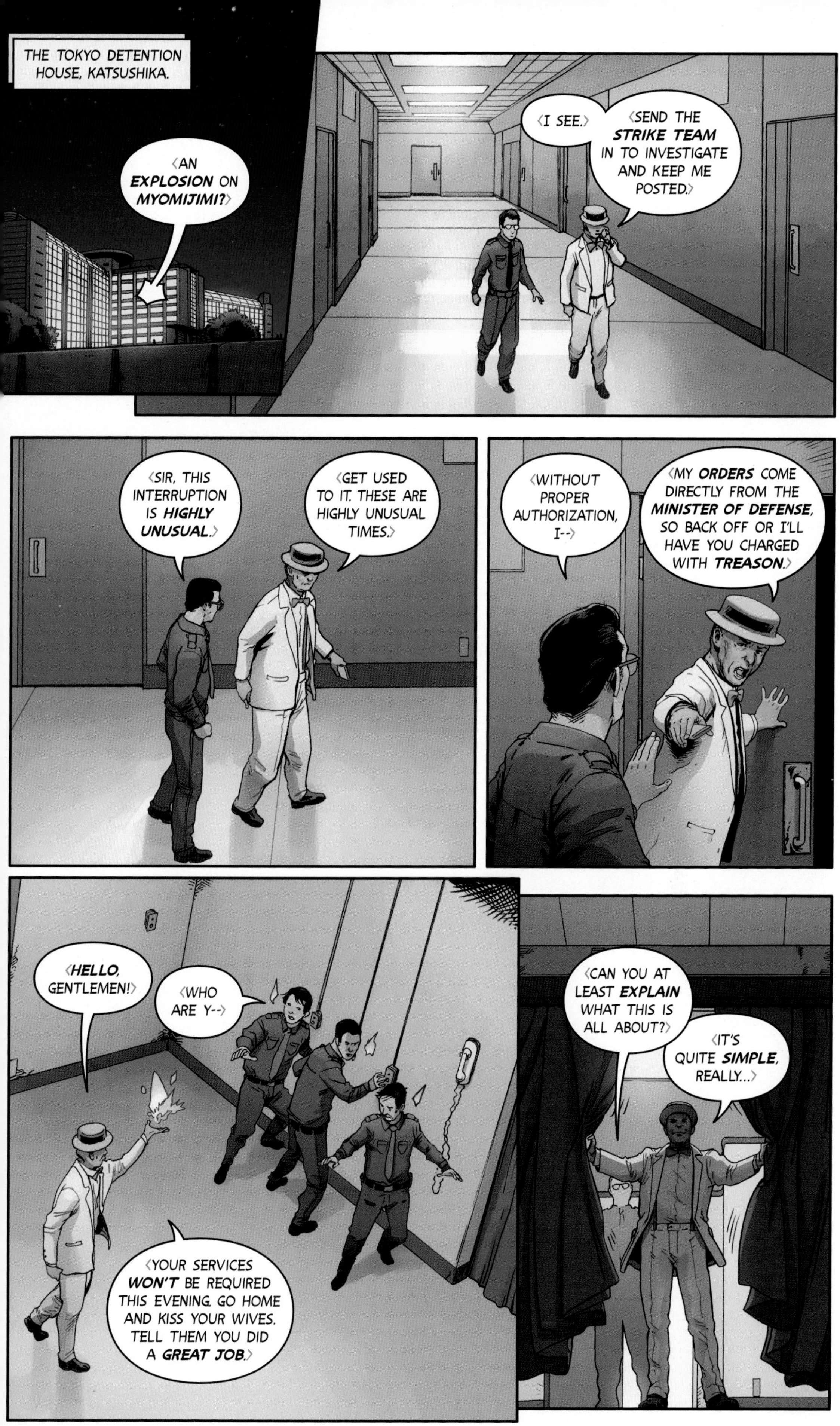
THE TOKYO DETENTION HOUSE, KATSUSHIKA.
⟨AN EXPLOSION ON MYOMIJIMI?⟩
⟨I SEE.⟩
⟨SEND THE STRIKE TEAM IN TO INVESTIGATE AND KEEP ME POSTED.⟩
⟨SIR, THIS INTERRUPTION IS HIGHLY UNUSUAL.⟩
⟨GET USED TO IT. THESE ARE HIGHLY UNUSUAL TIMES.⟩
⟨WITHOUT PROPER AUTHORIZATION, I--⟩
⟨MY ORDERS COME DIRECTLY FROM THE MINISTER OF DEFENSE, SO BACK OFF OR I'LL HAVE YOU CHARGED WITH TREASON.⟩
⟨HELLO, GENTLEMEN!⟩
⟨WHO ARE Y--⟩
⟨YOUR SERVICES WON'T BE REQUIRED THIS EVENING. GO HOME AND KISS YOUR WIVES. TELL THEM YOU DID A GREAT JOB.⟩
⟨CAN YOU AT LEAST EXPLAIN WHAT THIS IS ALL ABOUT?⟩
⟨IT'S QUITE SIMPLE, REALLY...⟩

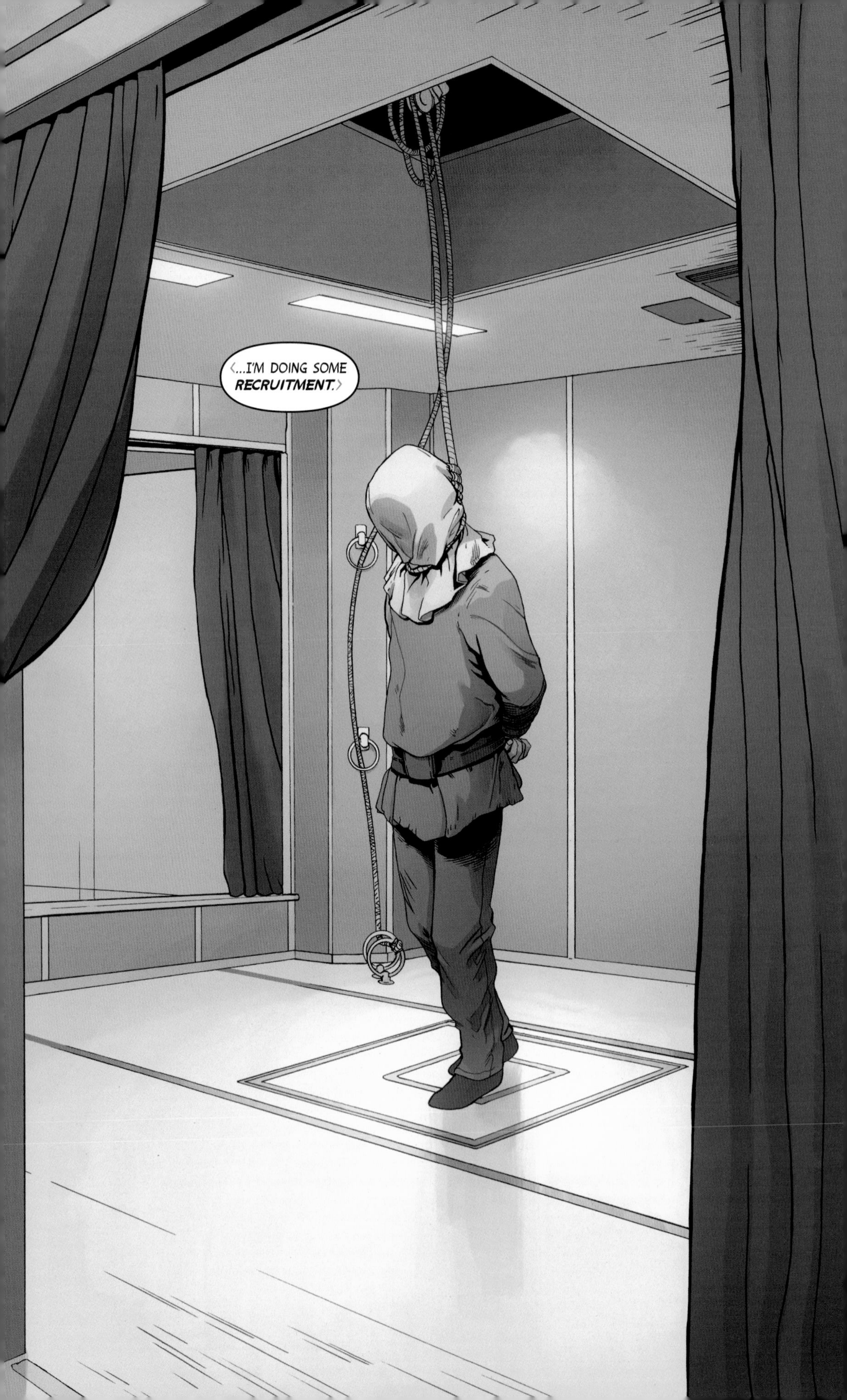
<...I'M DOING SOME RECRUITMENT.>

Chapter Twenty-Seven

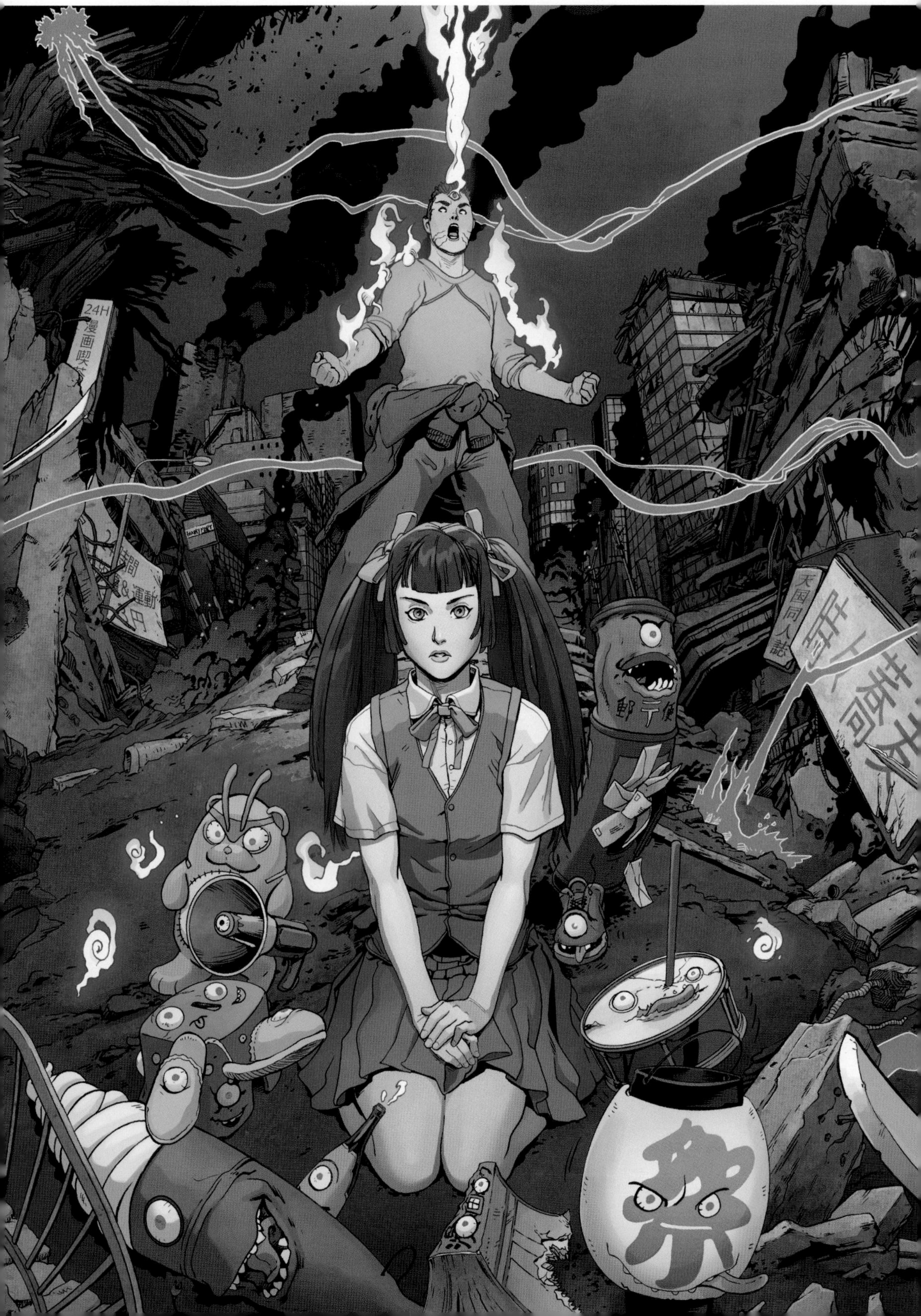
24H
漫画喫
天国同人誌
祭

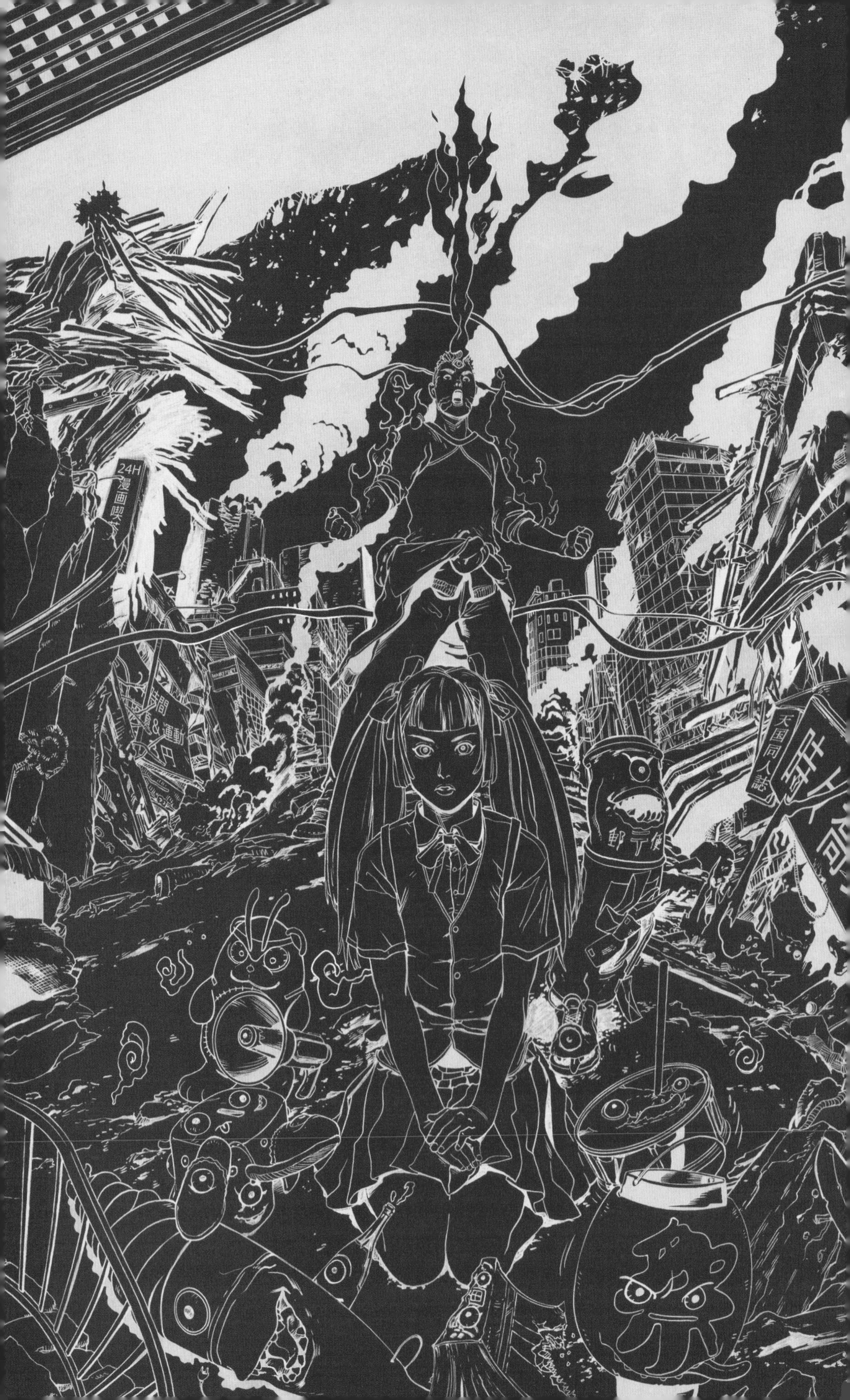
24H
漫画喫
天国同人誌

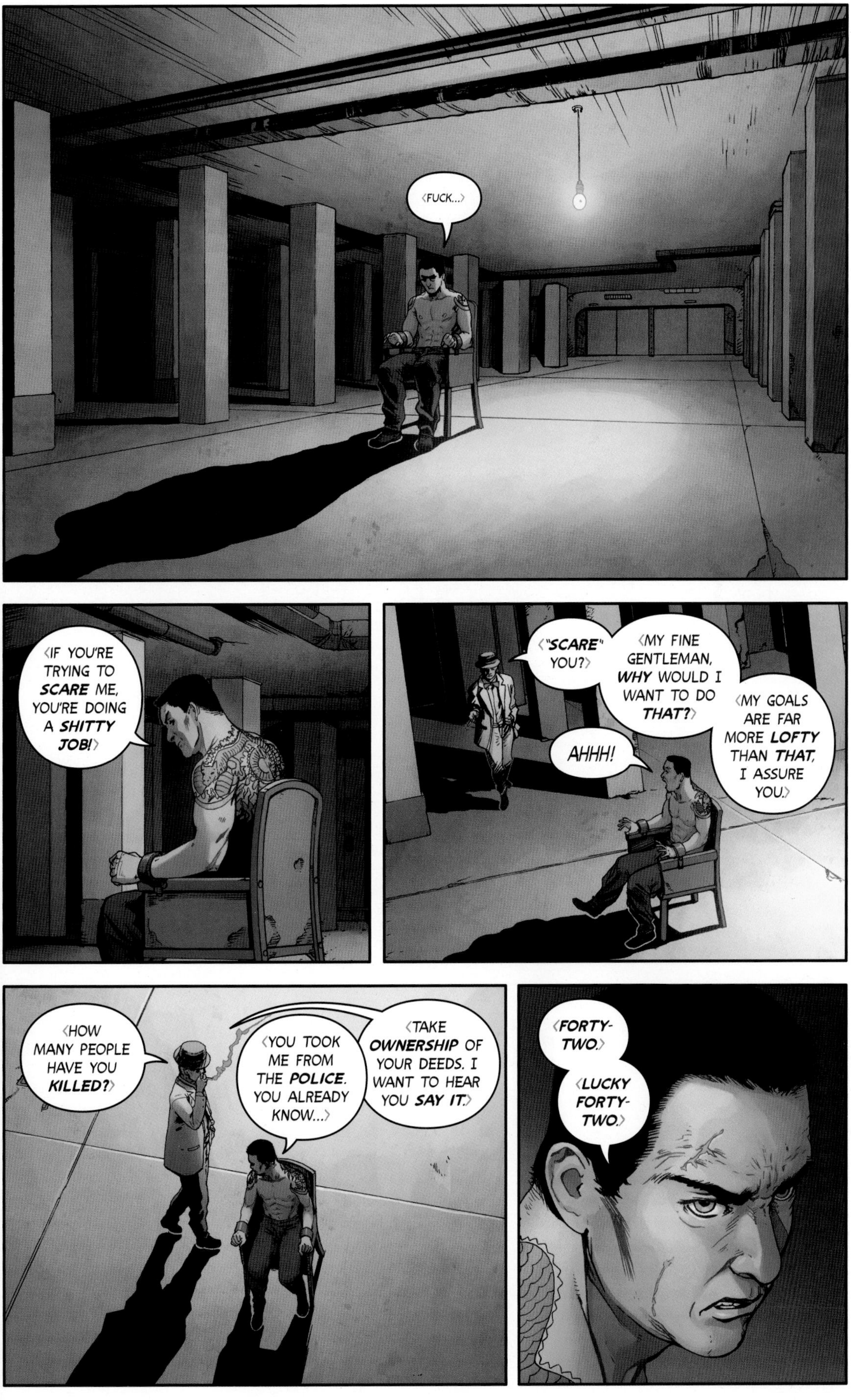
‹FUCK...›
‹IF YOU'RE TRYING TO SCARE ME, YOU'RE DOING A SHITTY JOB!›
‹"SCARE" YOU?›
‹MY FINE GENTLEMAN, WHY WOULD I WANT TO DO THAT?›
AHHH!
‹MY GOALS ARE FAR MORE LOFTY THAN THAT, I ASSURE YOU.›
‹HOW MANY PEOPLE HAVE YOU KILLED?›
‹YOU TOOK ME FROM THE POLICE. YOU ALREADY KNOW...›
‹TAKE OWNERSHIP OF YOUR DEEDS. I WANT TO HEAR YOU SAY IT.›
‹FORTY-TWO.›
‹LUCKY FORTY-TWO.›

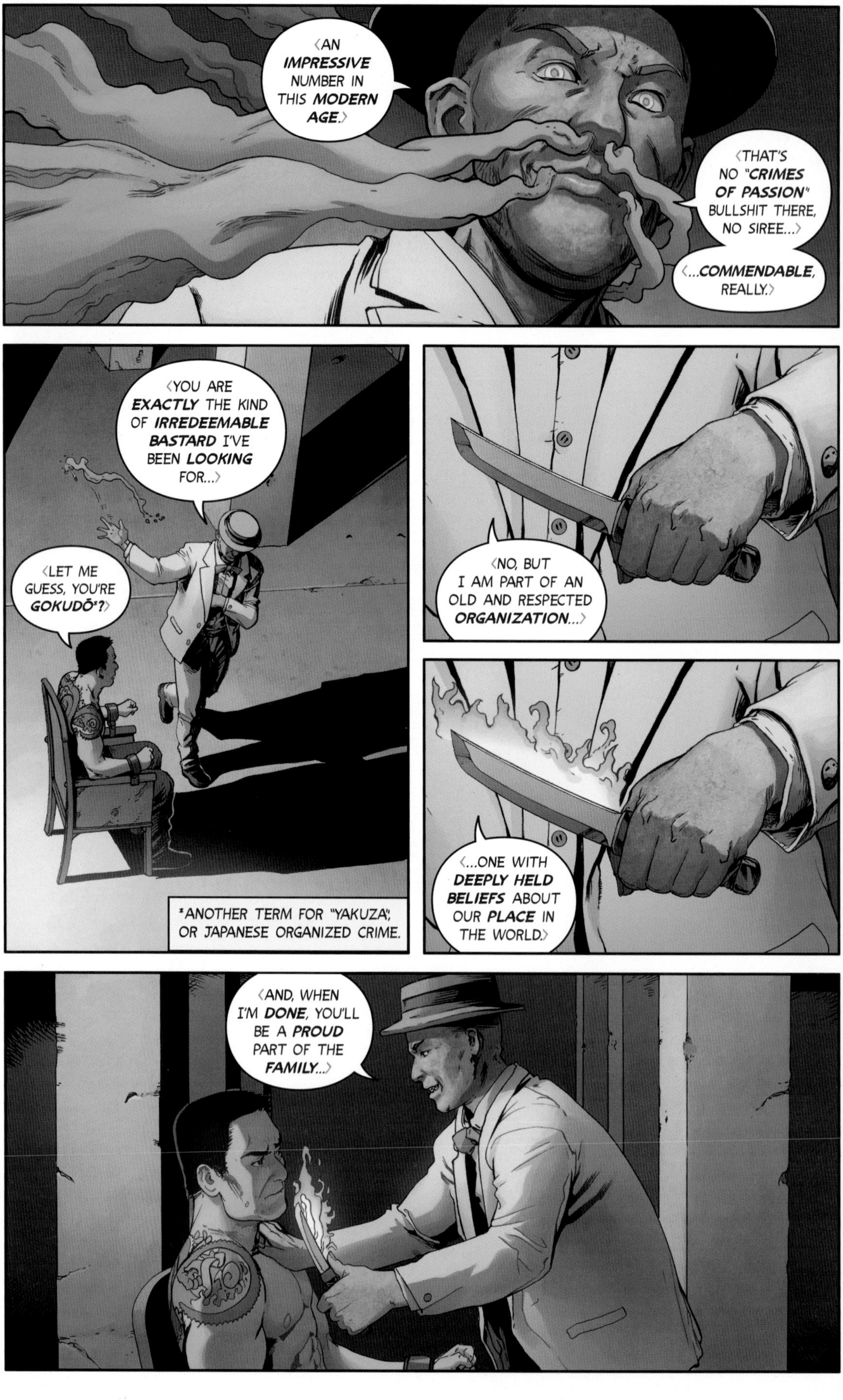

⟨AN IMPRESSIVE NUMBER IN THIS MODERN AGE.⟩
⟨THAT'S NO "CRIMES OF PASSION" BULLSHIT THERE, NO SIREE...⟩
⟨...COMMENDABLE, REALLY.⟩
⟨YOU ARE EXACTLY THE KIND OF IRREDEEMABLE BASTARD I'VE BEEN LOOKING FOR...⟩
⟨LET ME GUESS, YOU'RE GOKUDŌ*?⟩
*ANOTHER TERM FOR "YAKUZA", OR JAPANESE ORGANIZED CRIME.
⟨NO, BUT I AM PART OF AN OLD AND RESPECTED ORGANIZATION...⟩
⟨...ONE WITH DEEPLY HELD BELIEFS ABOUT OUR PLACE IN THE WORLD.⟩
⟨AND, WHEN I'M DONE, YOU'LL BE A PROUD PART OF THE FAMILY...⟩

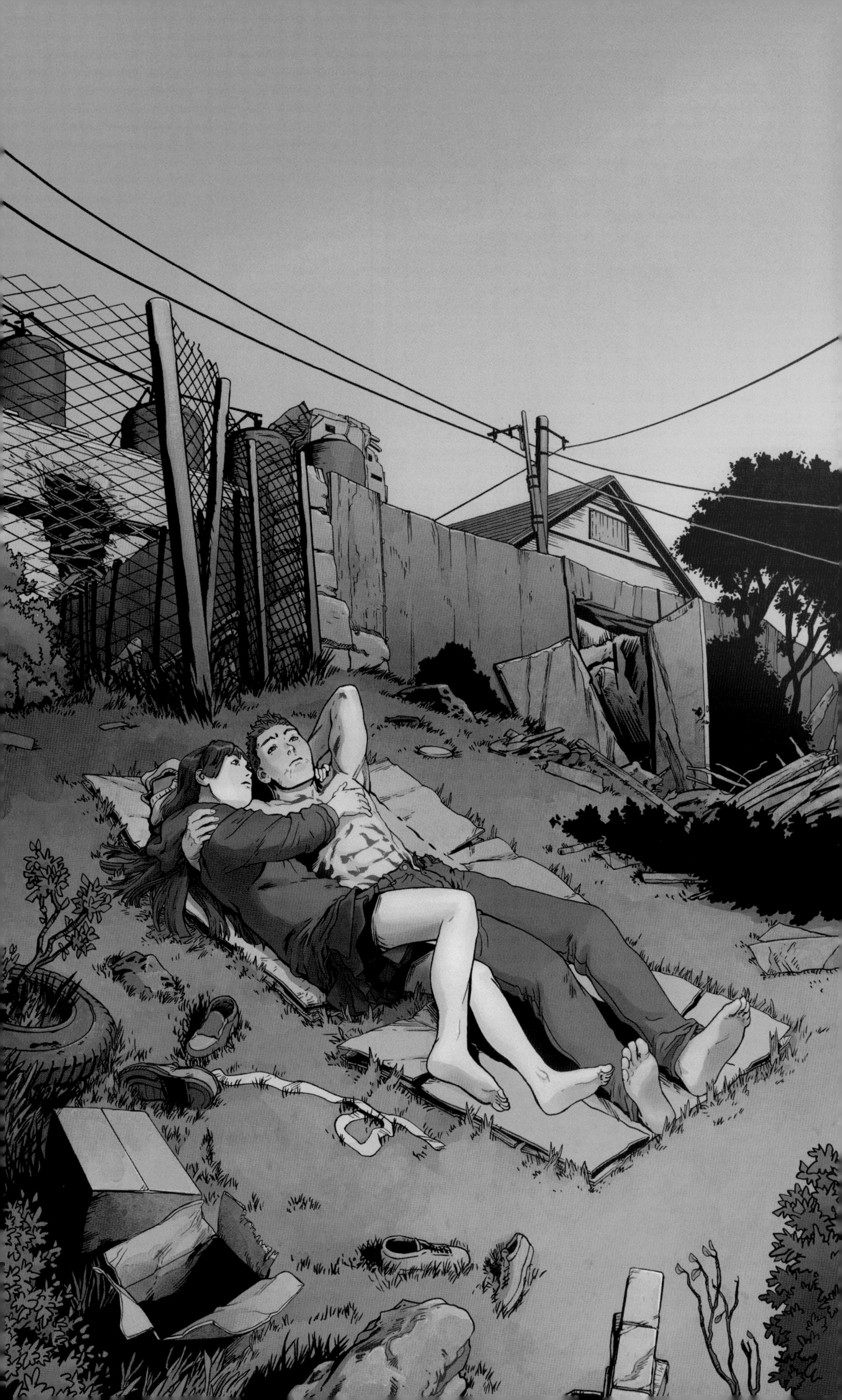

⟨I CAN'T BELIEVE WE FELL ASLEEP ON THE GRASS.⟩

⟨AFTER EVERYTHING WE'VE BEEN THROUGH, I'M AMAZED WE'RE NOT SLEEPING ALL THE TIME.⟩

⟨THE AIR'S COLD THIS MORNING, BUT YOU'RE SO WARM.⟩

⟨BLAME THE SPIRIT ENERGY RUNNING THROUGH MY VEINS.⟩

⟨I DON'T MIND. IT'S NICE.⟩

⟨ARE YOU STILL SEEING IT ALL... ALL WRONG?⟩

⟨YOU MEAN "DEAD"?⟩

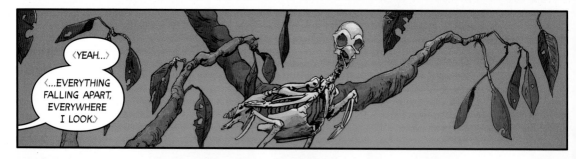

⟨YEAH...⟩

⟨...EVERYTHING FALLING APART, EVERYWHERE I LOOK.⟩

RUSTLE RUSTLE

⟨DID YOU HEAR THAT?⟩

⟨RODENTS?⟩

⟨NO.⟩

⟨IT'S SOMETHING ELSE...⟩

⟨...SOMETHING UNNATURAL.⟩

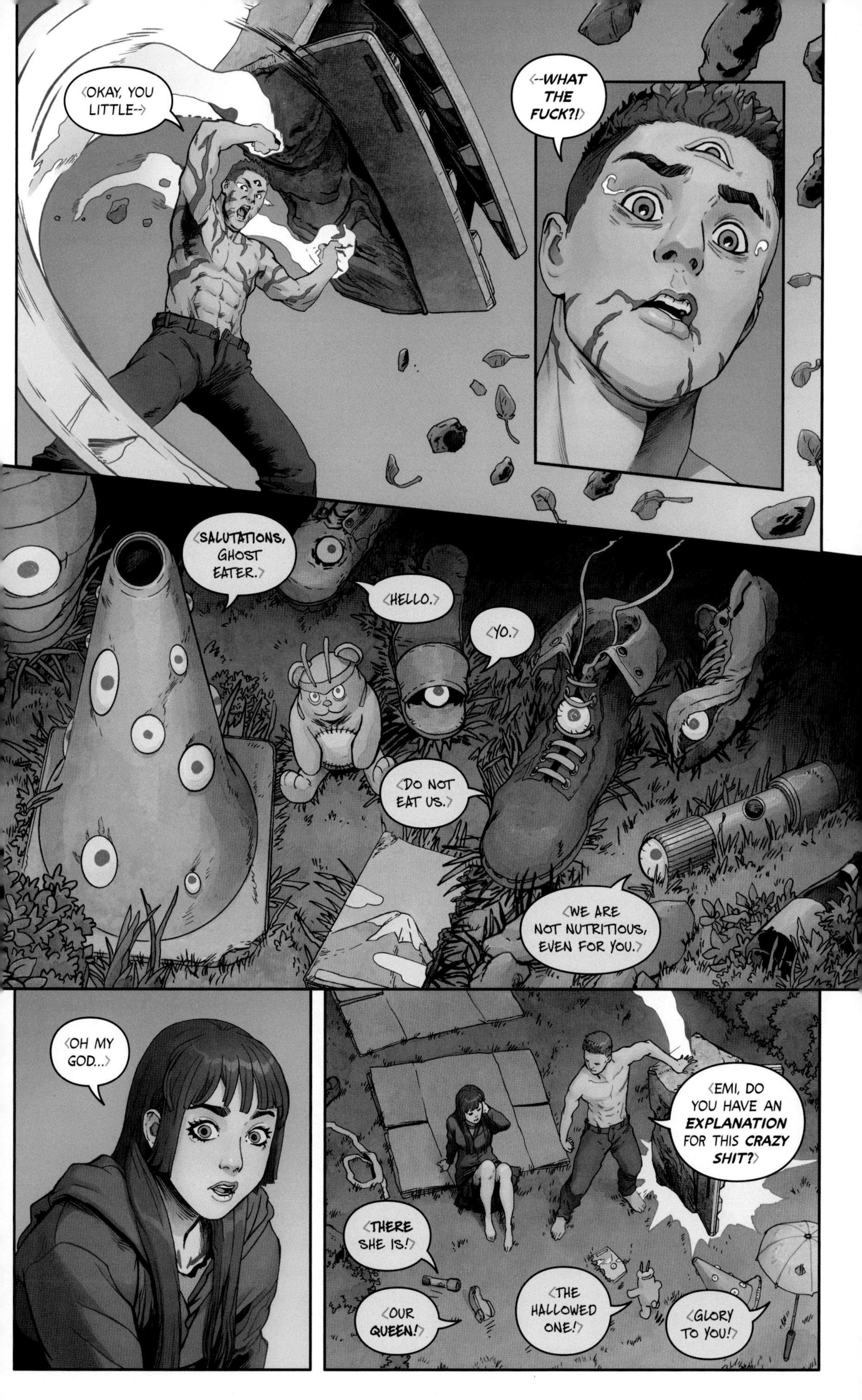
⟨OKAY, YOU LITTLE--⟩
⟨--WHAT THE FUCK?!⟩
⟨SALUTATIONS, GHOST EATER.⟩
⟨HELLO.⟩
⟨YO.⟩
⟨DO NOT EAT US.⟩
⟨WE ARE NOT NUTRITIOUS, EVEN FOR YOU.⟩
⟨OH MY GOD...⟩
⟨EMI, DO YOU HAVE AN **EXPLANATION** FOR THIS **CRAZY SHIT?**⟩
⟨THERE SHE IS!⟩
⟨OUR QUEEN!⟩
⟨THE HALLOWED ONE!⟩
⟨GLORY TO YOU!⟩

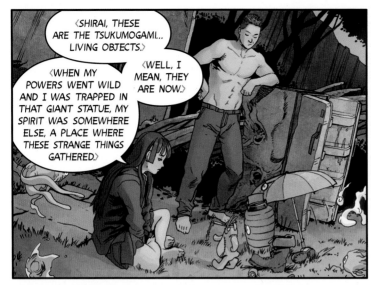

‹SHIRAI, THESE ARE THE TSUKUMOGAMI... LIVING OBJECTS.›

‹WHEN MY POWERS WENT WILD AND I WAS TRAPPED IN THAT GIANT STATUE, MY SPIRIT WAS SOMEWHERE ELSE, A PLACE WHERE THESE STRANGE THINGS GATHERED.›

‹WELL, I MEAN, THEY ARE NOW.›

‹OKAY, BUT NOW THEY'RE HERE.›

‹YES, THANKS TO OUR QUEEN, THE LIFE-BRINGER!›

‹I DID THIS?›

‹WHEN YOU ESCAPED OUR REALM, YOU PULLED US WITH YOU AND MANY OF US FOUND LIFE WITHIN OBJECTS NEARBY.›

‹OH MY...›

‹NOW THAT WE'RE ALIVE, CALLING US ALL BY THE SAME NAME IS A BIT CRASS.›

‹YOU MAY CALL ME "KUTSU".›

‹TOO OBVIOUS.›

‹OKAY... HOW ABOUT "SUNĪKĀ"?›

‹BETTER.›

‹I AM "KUMA-SAMA"!›

‹SIGH.›

<WHERE ARE YOU GOING?>

<I'M GONNA GO GET THE OTHERS AND LET 'EM KNOW WE HAVE A RIDICULOUS ARMY OF *TOYS* AND *CLOTHES* AND *SHIT...*>

<GREETINGS, FOOT-FRIEND!>

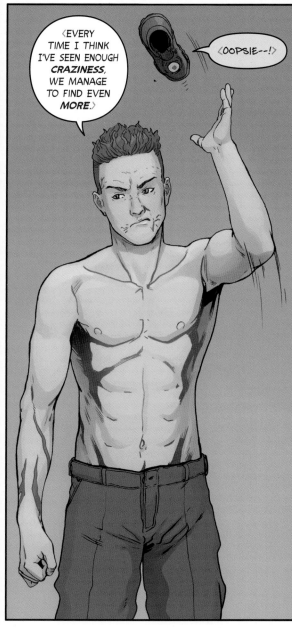

<EVERY TIME I THINK I'VE SEEN ENOUGH *CRAZINESS*, WE MANAGE TO FIND EVEN *MORE.*>

<OOPSIE--!>

<AT LEAST THEY'RE NOT TRYING TO HURT US. I'LL TAKE SHOES OVER SPIDERS ANY DAY.>

<THE QUEEN!>

<THE QUEEN!>

HEH.

<I CAN'T ARGUE WITH THAT...>

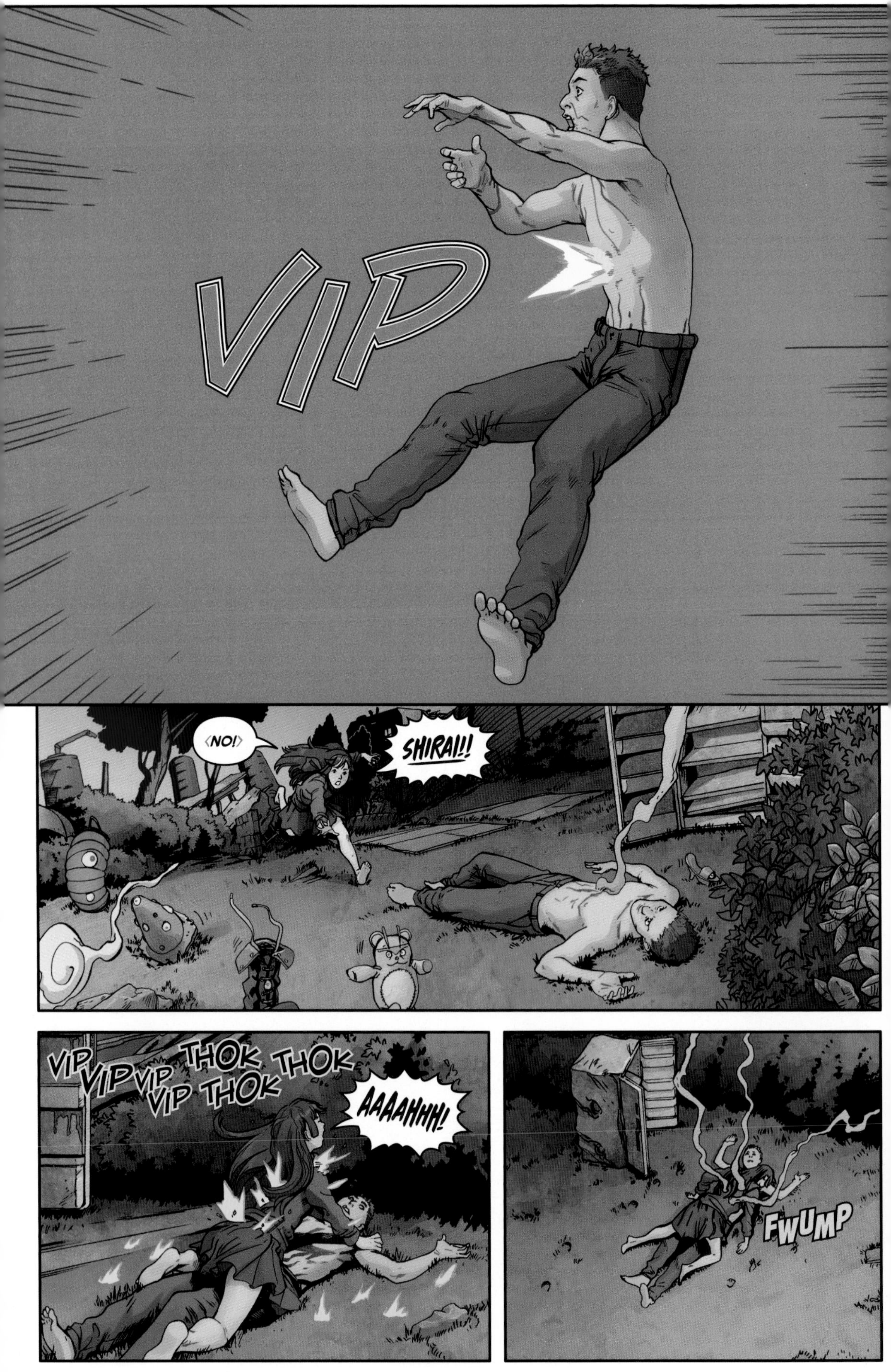
VIP
⟨NO!⟩
SHIRAI!!
VIP VIP VIP THOK THOK VIP THOK
AAAAHHH!
FWUMP

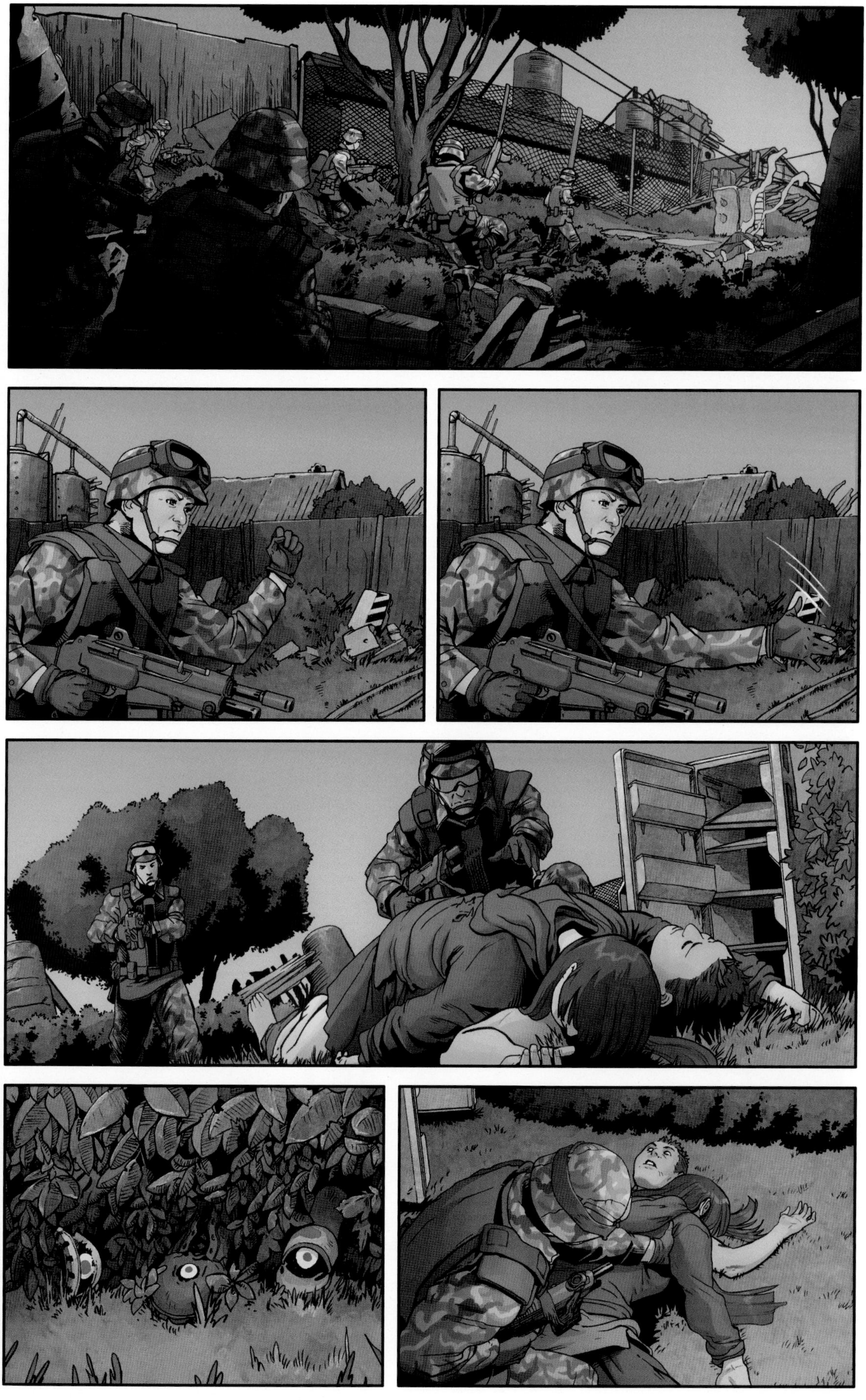

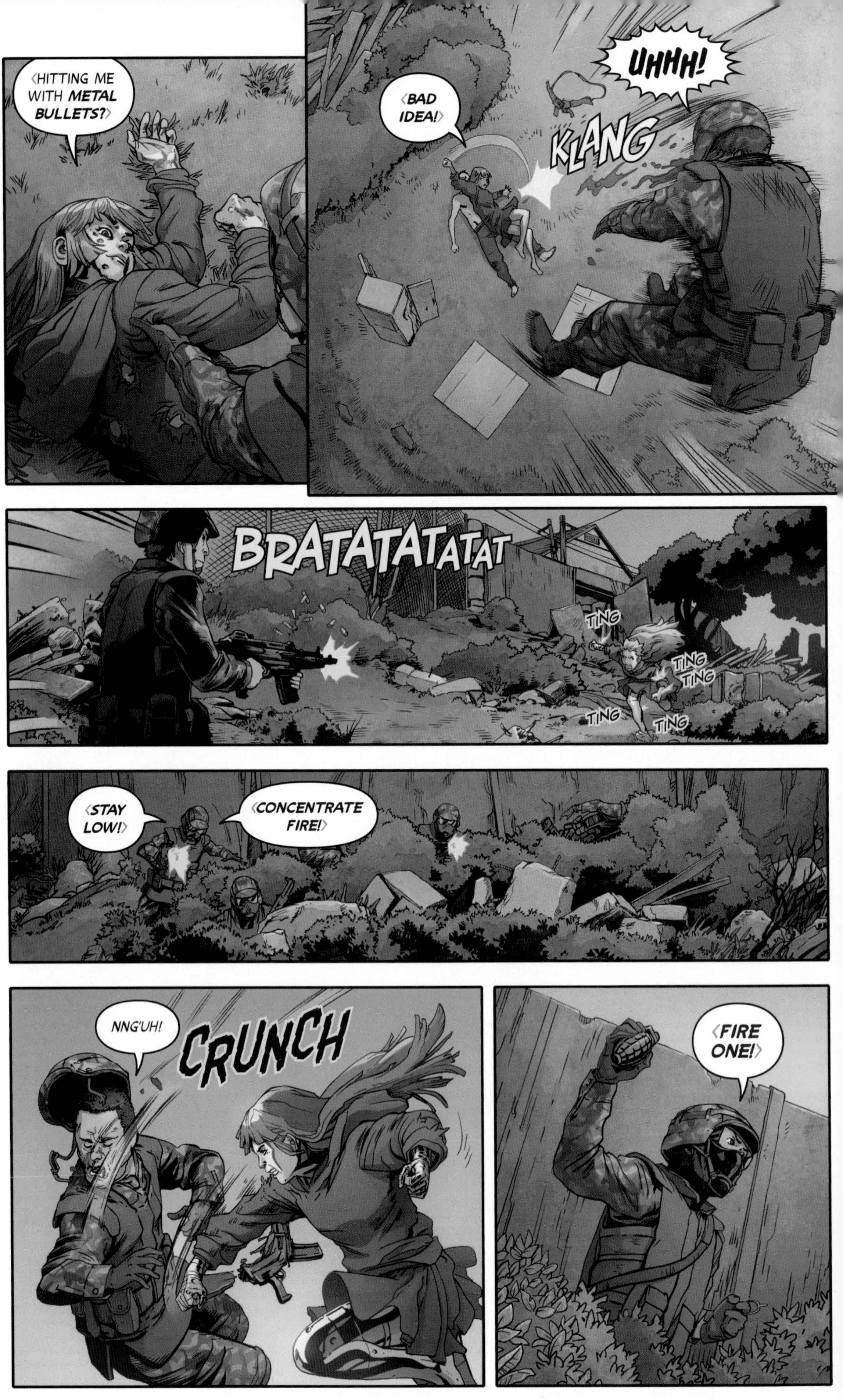
‹HITTING ME WITH METAL BULLETS?›
‹BAD IDEA!›
KLANG
UHHH!
BRATATATATAT
TING
TING
TING
TING
TING
‹STAY LOW!›
‹CONCENTRATE FIRE!›
NNG'UH!
CRUNCH
‹FIRE ONE!›

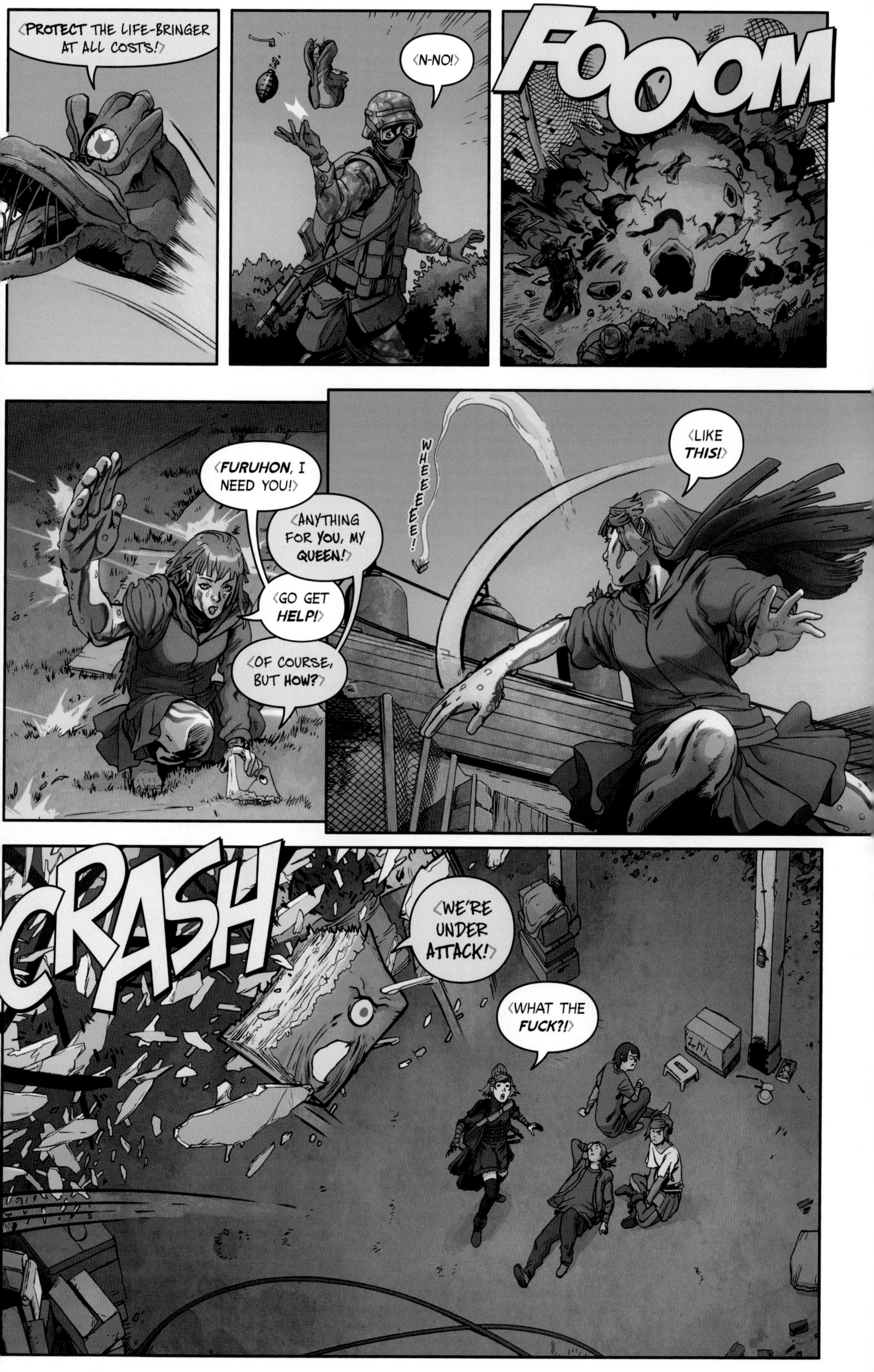
⟨PROTECT THE LIFE-BRINGER AT ALL COSTS!⟩
⟨N-NO!⟩
FOOOM
⟨FURUHON, I NEED YOU!⟩
⟨ANYTHING FOR YOU, MY QUEEN!⟩
⟨GO GET HELP!⟩
⟨OF COURSE, BUT HOW?⟩
WHEEEEEE!
⟨LIKE THIS!⟩
CRASH
⟨WE'RE UNDER ATTACK!⟩
⟨WHAT THE FUCK?!⟩

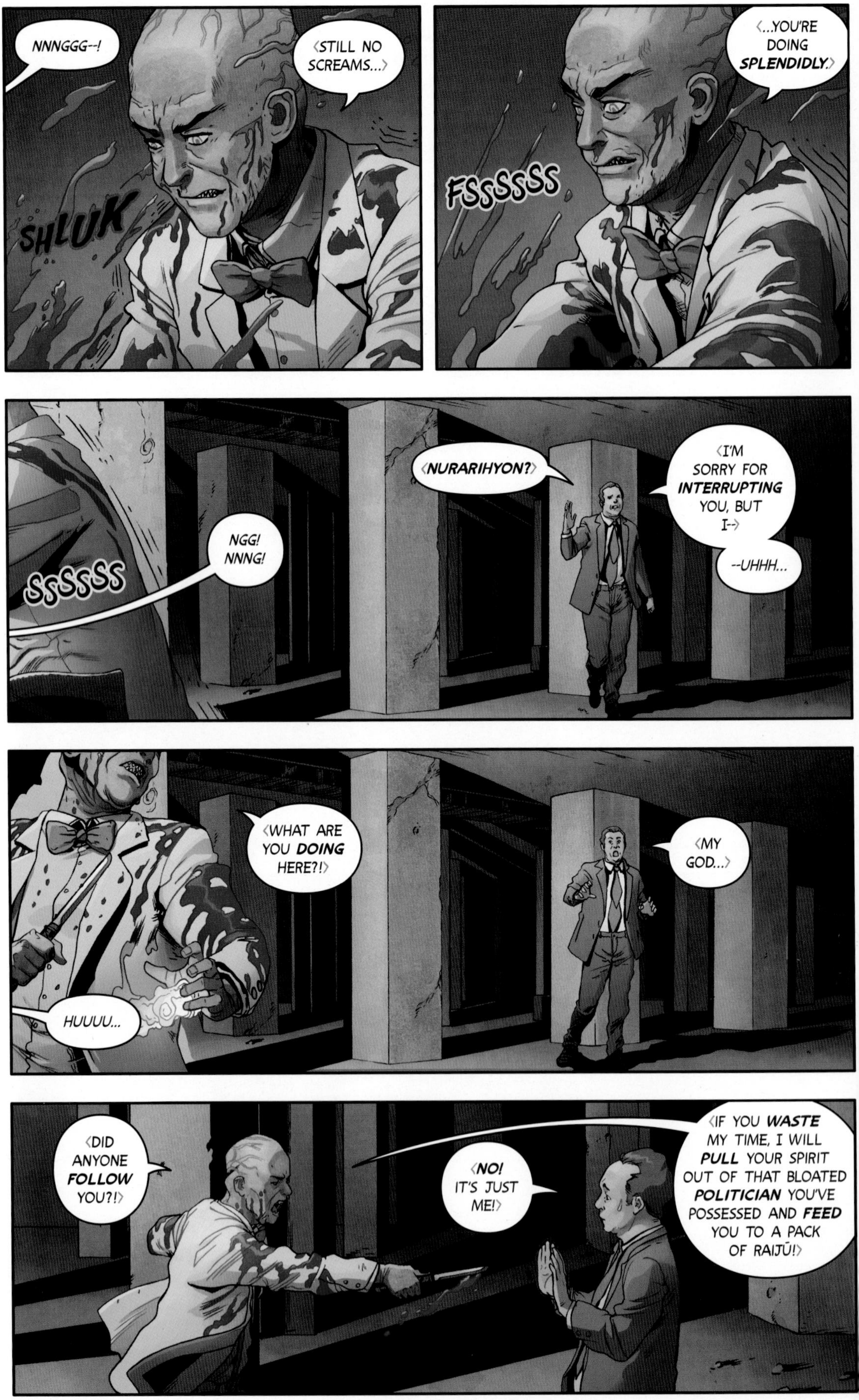
NNNGGG--!
SHLUK
‹STILL NO SCREAMS...›
FSSSSSS
‹...YOU'RE DOING **SPLENDIDLY.**›
SSSSSS
NGG! NNNG!
‹**NURARIHYON?**›
‹I'M SORRY FOR **INTERRUPTING** YOU, BUT I--›
--UHHH...
‹WHAT ARE YOU **DOING** HERE?!›
HUUUU...
‹MY GOD...›
‹DID ANYONE **FOLLOW** YOU?!›
‹**NO!** IT'S JUST ME!›
‹IF YOU **WASTE** MY TIME, I WILL **PULL** YOUR SPIRIT OUT OF THAT BLOATED **POLITICIAN** YOU'VE POSSESSED AND **FEED** YOU TO A PACK OF RAIJŪ!›

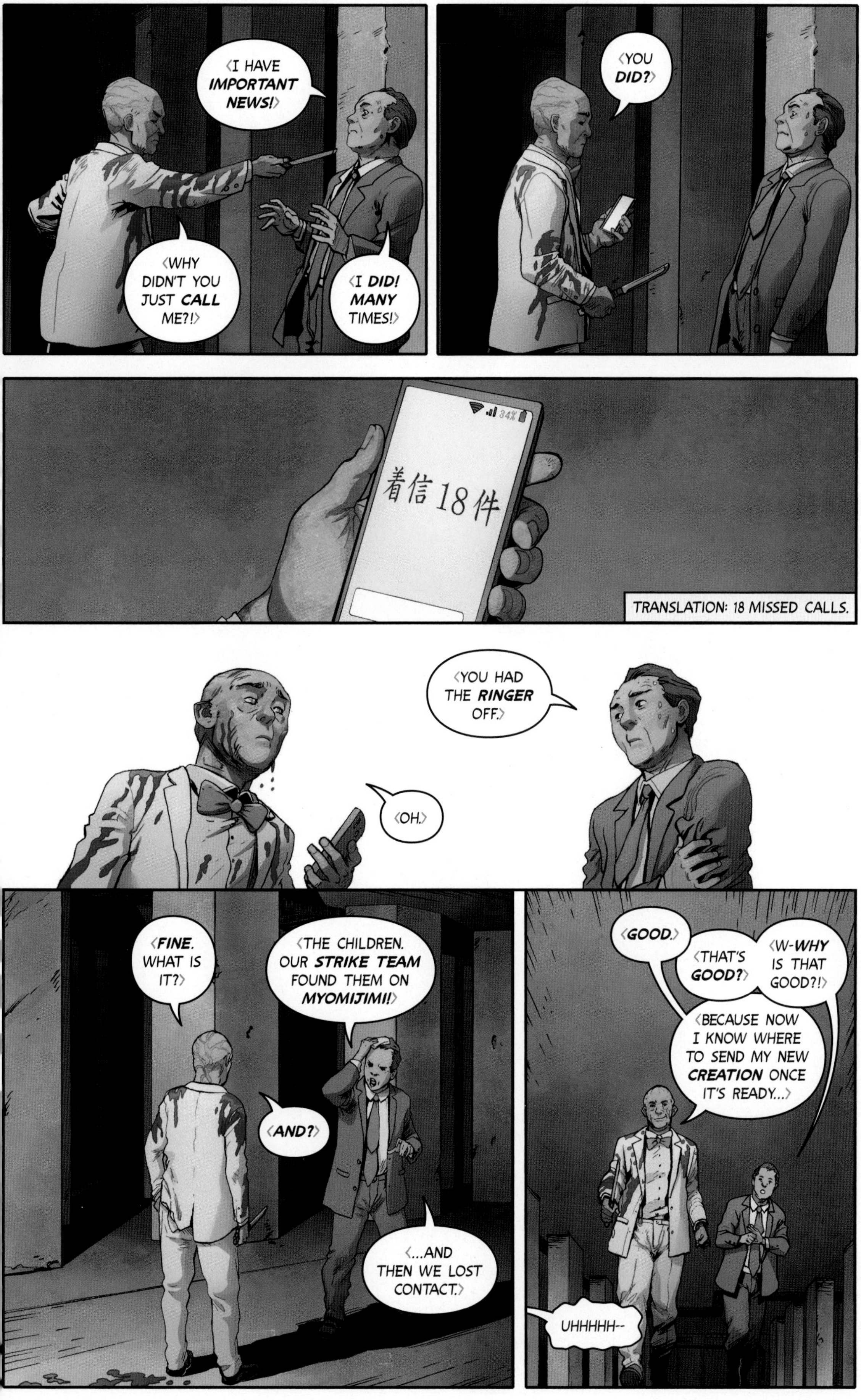
‹I HAVE IMPORTANT NEWS!›
‹WHY DIDN'T YOU JUST CALL ME?!›
‹I DID! MANY TIMES!›
‹YOU DID?›
着信18件
TRANSLATION: 18 MISSED CALLS.
‹YOU HAD THE RINGER OFF.›
‹OH.›
‹FINE. WHAT IS IT?›
‹THE CHILDREN. OUR STRIKE TEAM FOUND THEM ON MYOMIJIMI!›
‹AND?›
‹...AND THEN WE LOST CONTACT.›
‹GOOD.›
‹THAT'S GOOD?›
‹W-WHY IS THAT GOOD?!›
‹BECAUSE NOW I KNOW WHERE TO SEND MY NEW CREATION ONCE IT'S READY...›
UHHHHH--

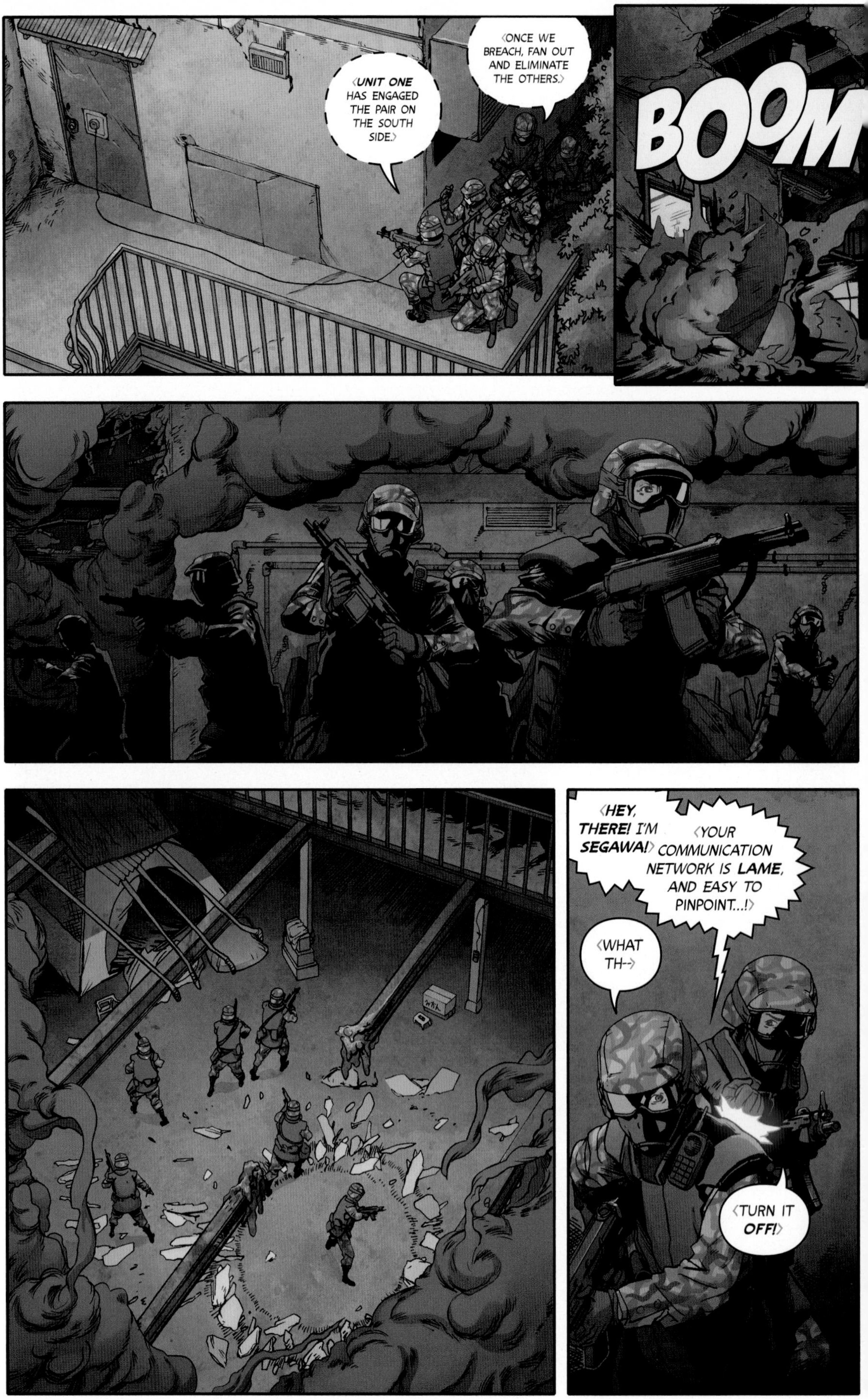

〈ONCE WE BREACH, FAN OUT AND ELIMINATE THE OTHERS.〉
〈UNIT ONE HAS ENGAGED THE PAIR ON THE SOUTH SIDE.〉
BOOM
〈HEY, THERE! I'M SEGAWA!〉
〈YOUR COMMUNICATION NETWORK IS LAME, AND EASY TO PINPOINT...!〉
〈WHAT TH-〉
〈TURN IT OFF!〉

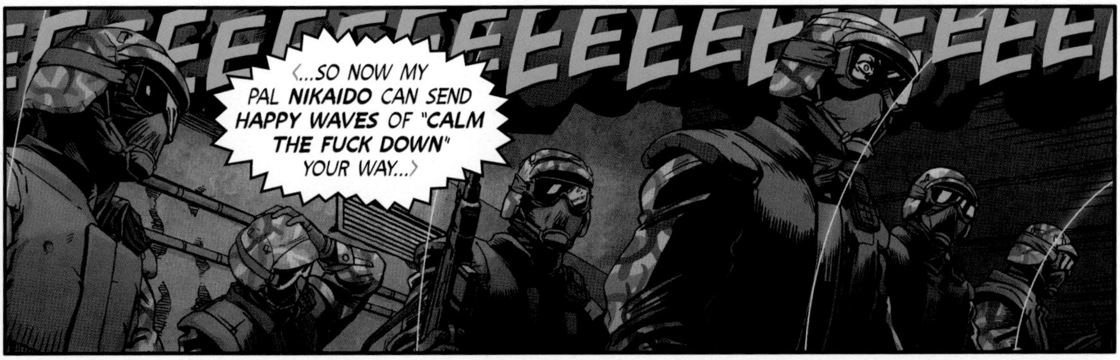
‹...SO NOW MY PAL **NIKAIDO** CAN SEND **HAPPY WAVES** OF "**CALM THE FUCK DOWN**" YOUR WAY...›

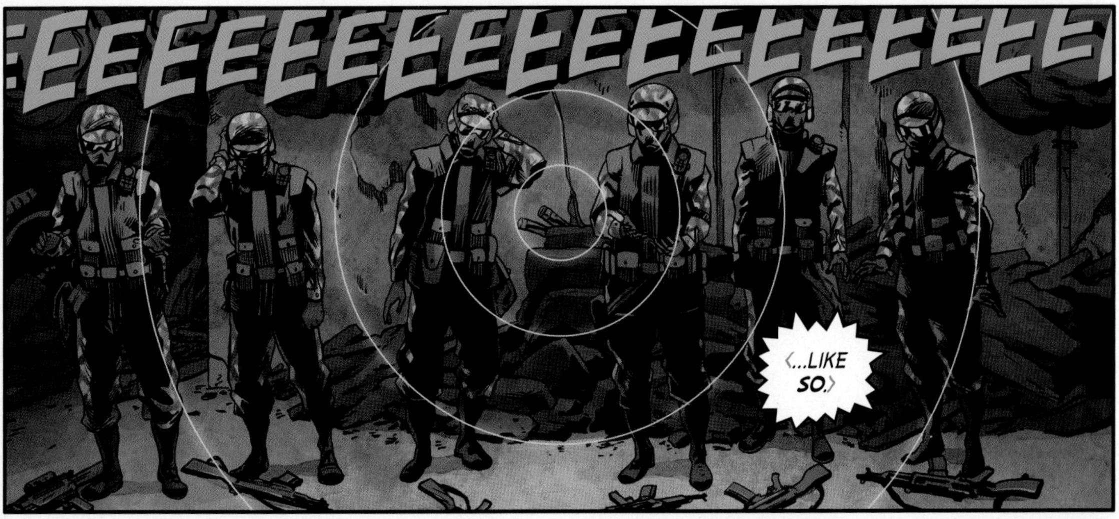
‹...LIKE **SO.**›

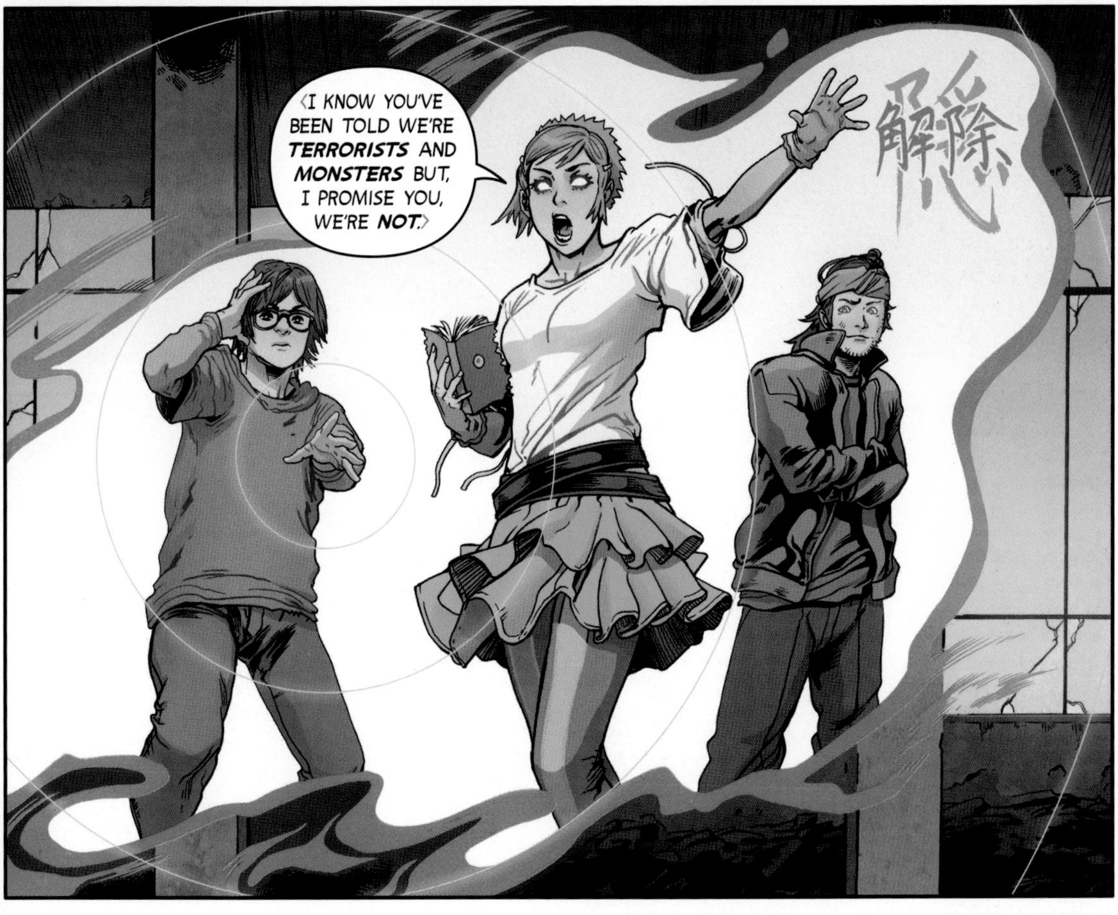
‹I KNOW YOU'VE BEEN TOLD WE'RE **TERRORISTS** AND **MONSTERS** BUT, I PROMISE YOU, WE'RE **NOT.**›
解除

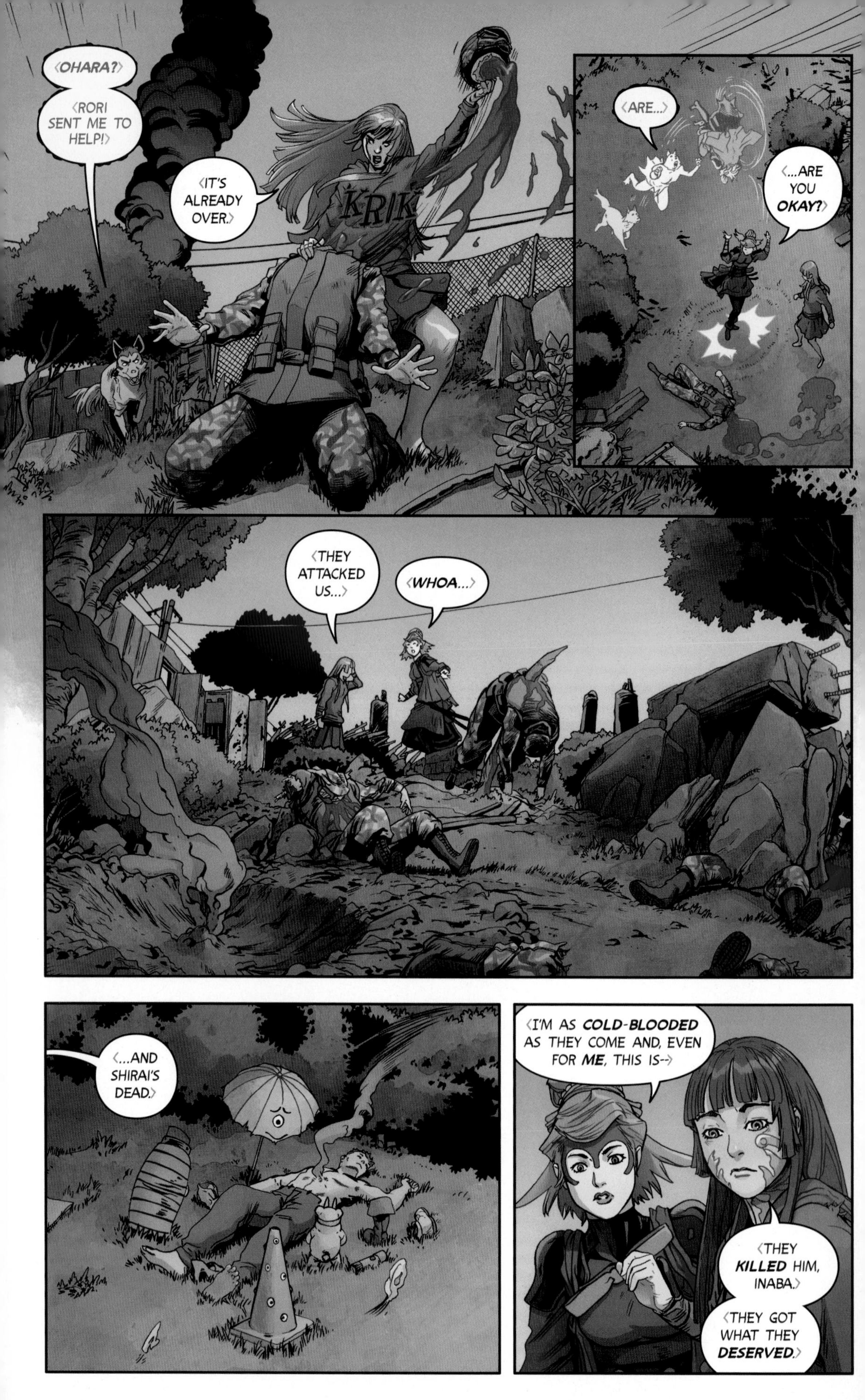

⟨OHARA?⟩
⟨RORI SENT ME TO HELP!⟩
⟨IT'S ALREADY OVER.⟩
KRIK
⟨ARE...⟩
⟨...ARE YOU OKAY?⟩
⟨THEY ATTACKED US...⟩
⟨WHOA...⟩
⟨...AND SHIRAI'S DEAD.⟩
⟨I'M AS COLD-BLOODED AS THEY COME AND, EVEN FOR ME, THIS IS--⟩
⟨THEY KILLED HIM, INABA.⟩
⟨THEY GOT WHAT THEY DESERVED.⟩

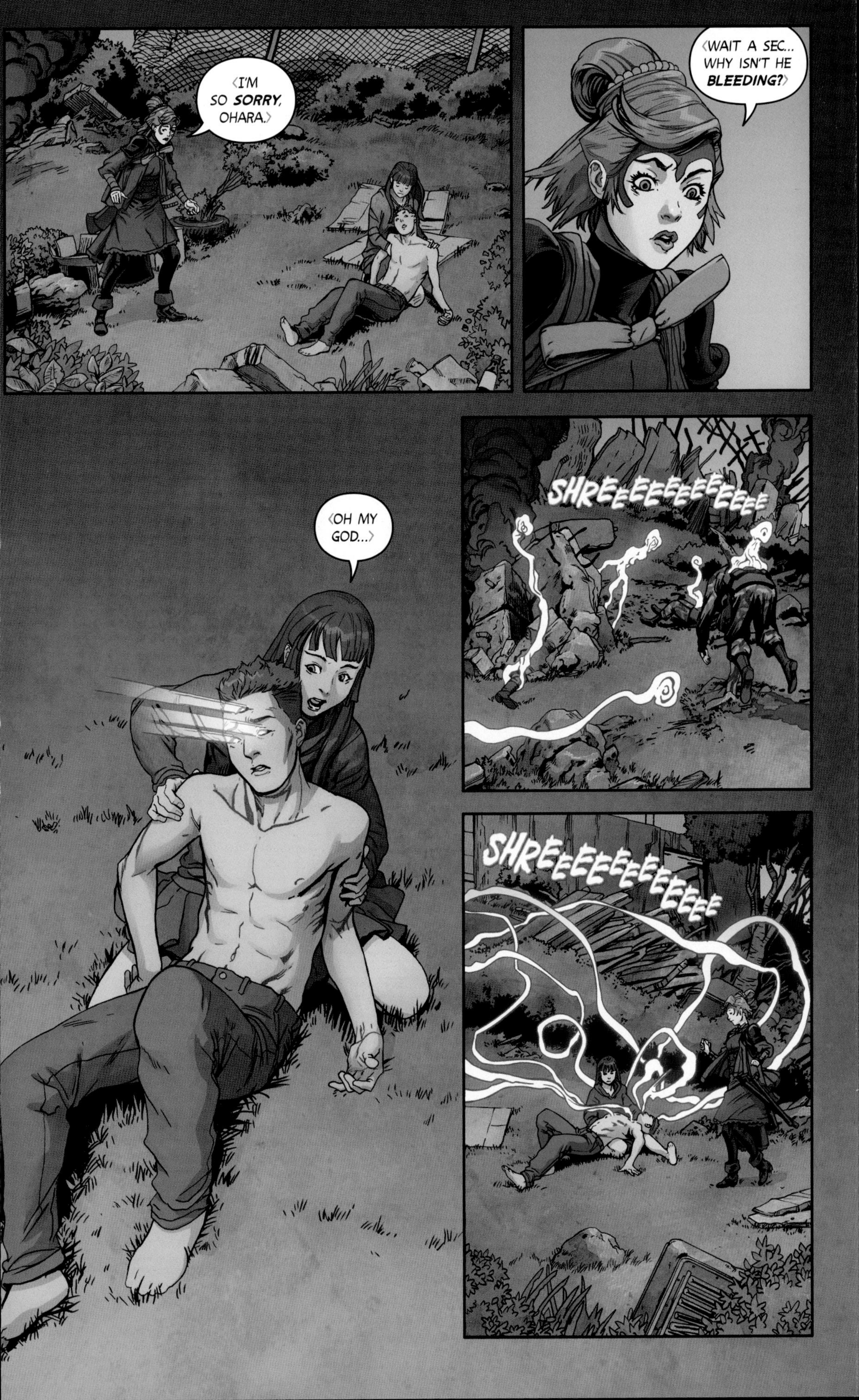

⟨I'M SO **SORRY**, OHARA.⟩
⟨WAIT A SEC... WHY ISN'T HE **BLEEDING?**⟩
⟨OH MY GOD...⟩
SHREEEEEEEEEEEE
SHREEEEEEEEEEEEEE

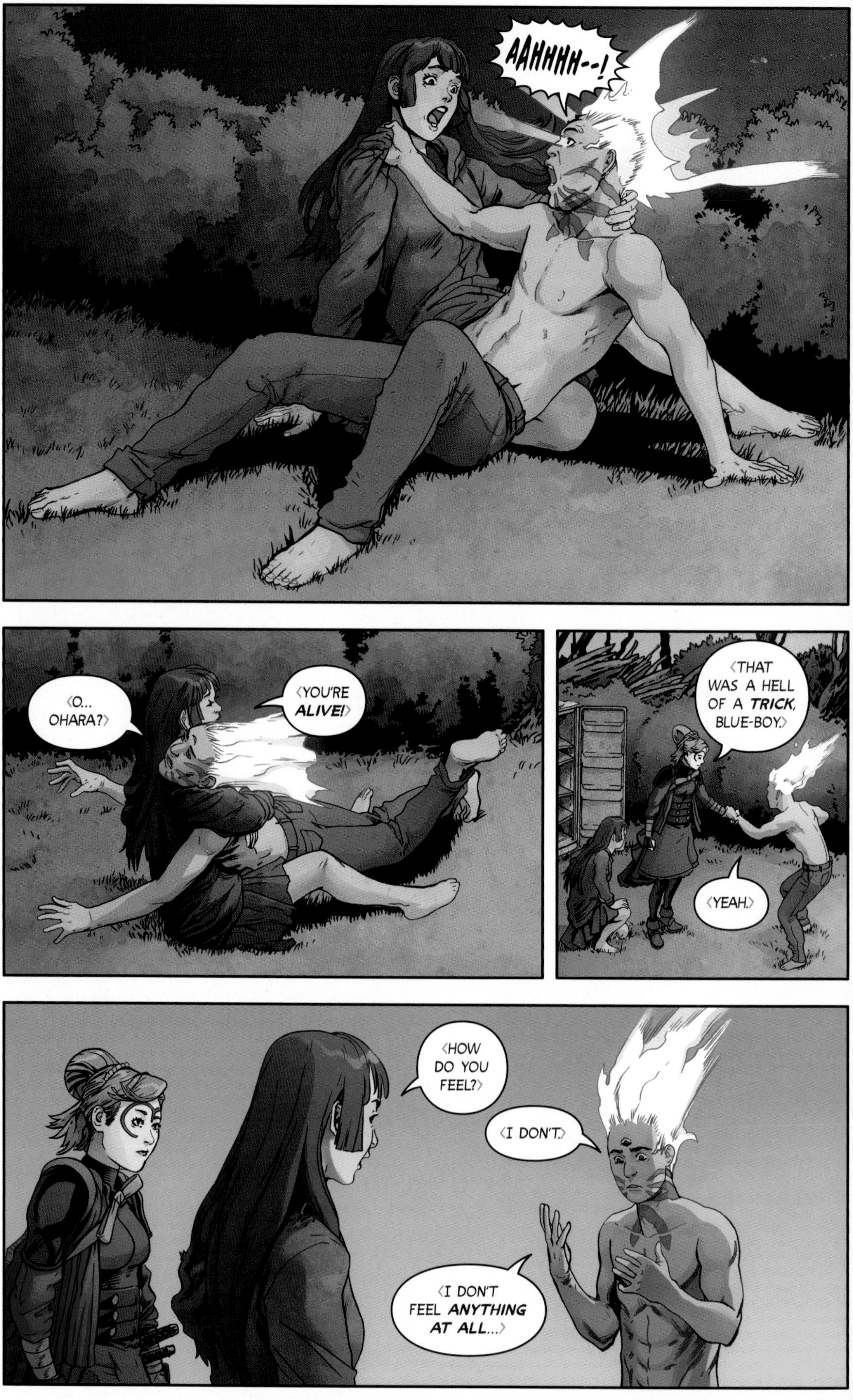
AAHHHH--!
⟨O... OHARA?⟩
⟨YOU'RE **ALIVE!**⟩
⟨THAT WAS A HELL OF A **TRICK**, BLUE-BOY.⟩
⟨YEAH.⟩
⟨HOW DO YOU FEEL?⟩
⟨I DON'T.⟩
⟨I DON'T FEEL **ANYTHING AT ALL**...⟩

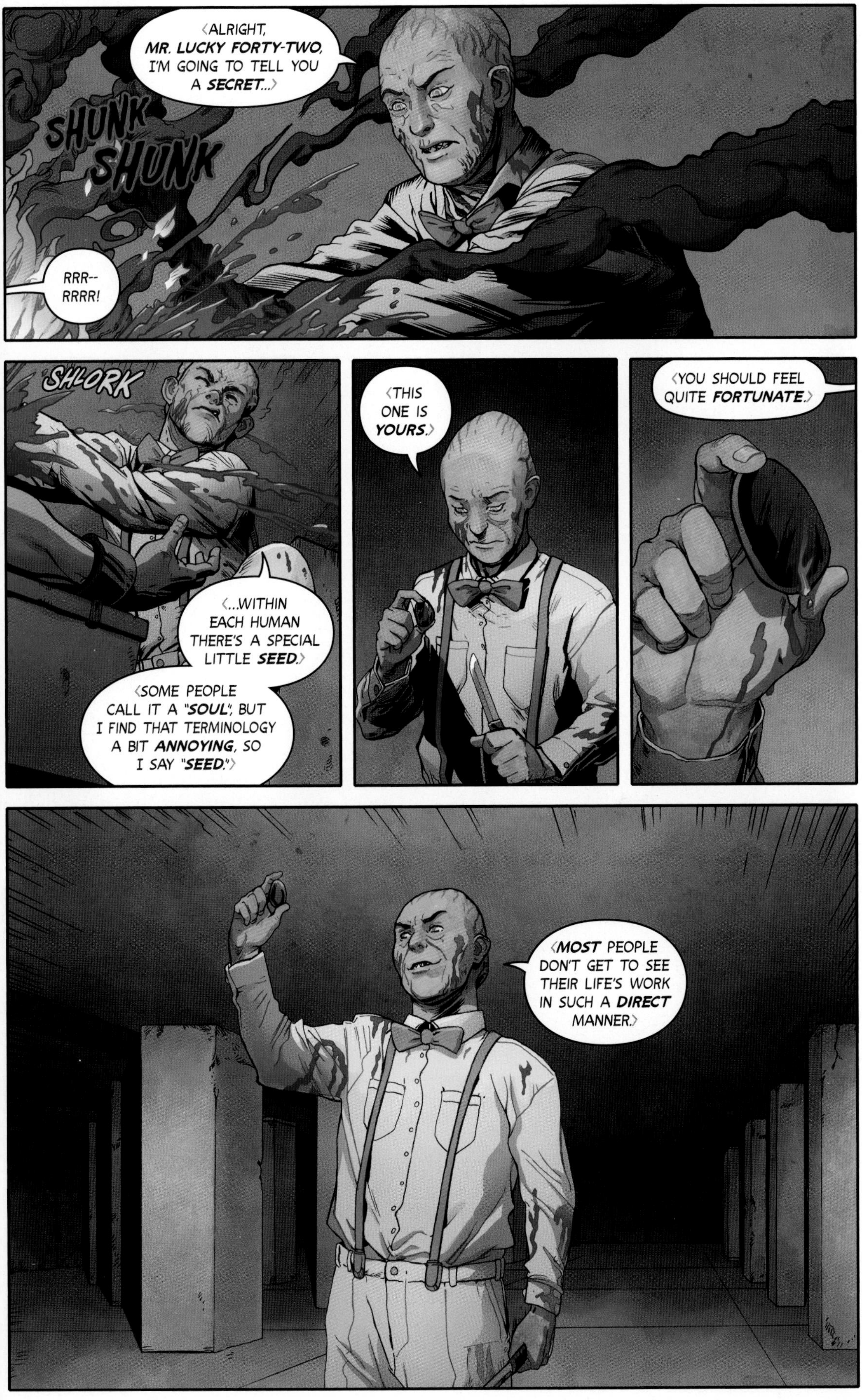

‹ALRIGHT, MR. LUCKY FORTY-TWO, I'M GOING TO TELL YOU A SECRET...›
SHUNK SHUNK
RRR-- RRRR!
SHLORK
‹...WITHIN EACH HUMAN THERE'S A SPECIAL LITTLE SEED.›
‹SOME PEOPLE CALL IT A "SOUL," BUT I FIND THAT TERMINOLOGY A BIT ANNOYING, SO I SAY "SEED."›
‹THIS ONE IS YOURS.›
‹YOU SHOULD FEEL QUITE FORTUNATE.›
‹MOST PEOPLE DON'T GET TO SEE THEIR LIFE'S WORK IN SUCH A DIRECT MANNER.›

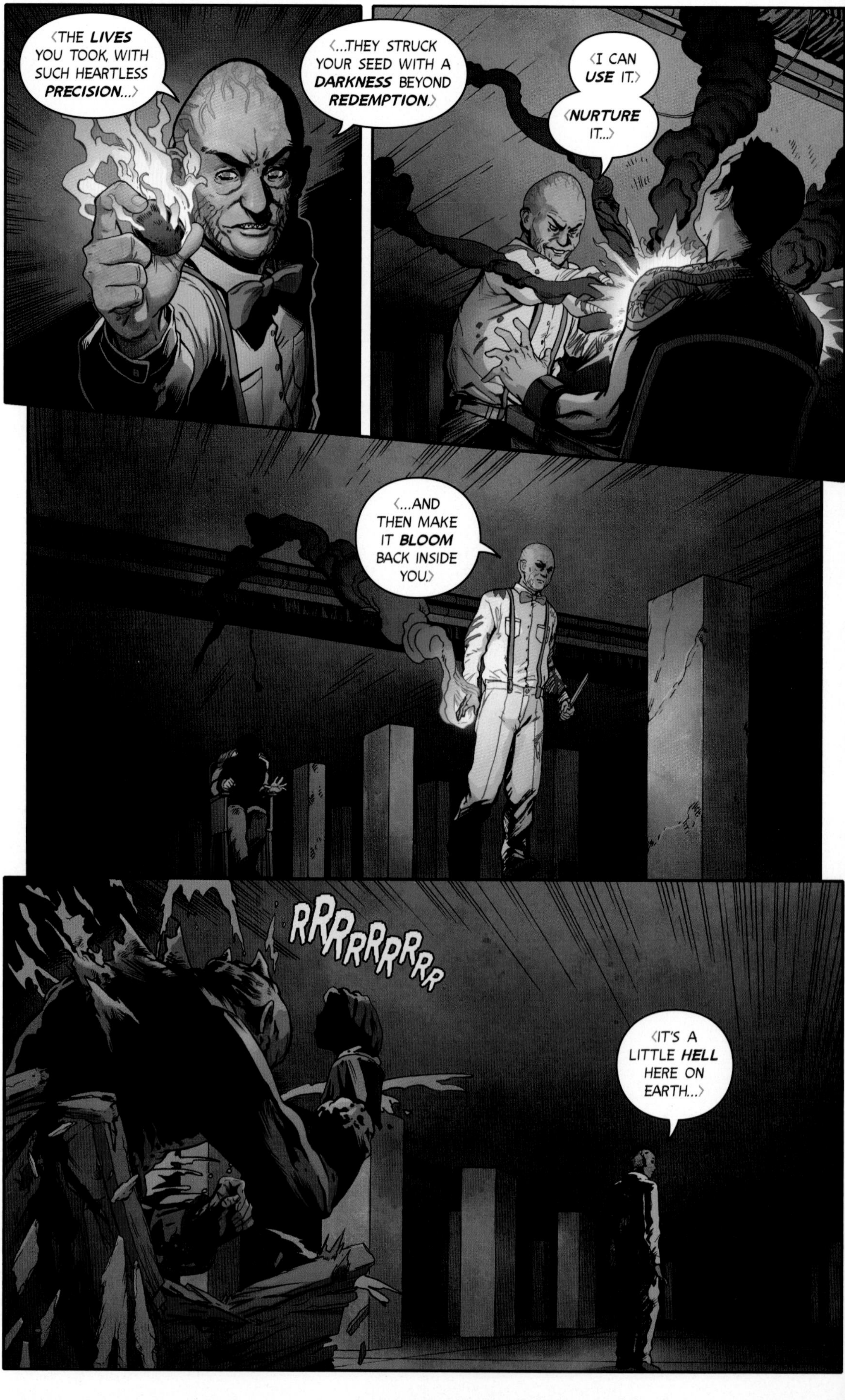

⟨THE LIVES YOU TOOK, WITH SUCH HEARTLESS PRECISION...⟩
⟨...THEY STRUCK YOUR SEED WITH A DARKNESS BEYOND REDEMPTION.⟩
⟨I CAN USE IT.⟩
⟨NURTURE IT...⟩
⟨...AND THEN MAKE IT BLOOM BACK INSIDE YOU.⟩
RRRRRRRRR
⟨IT'S A LITTLE HELL HERE ON EARTH...⟩

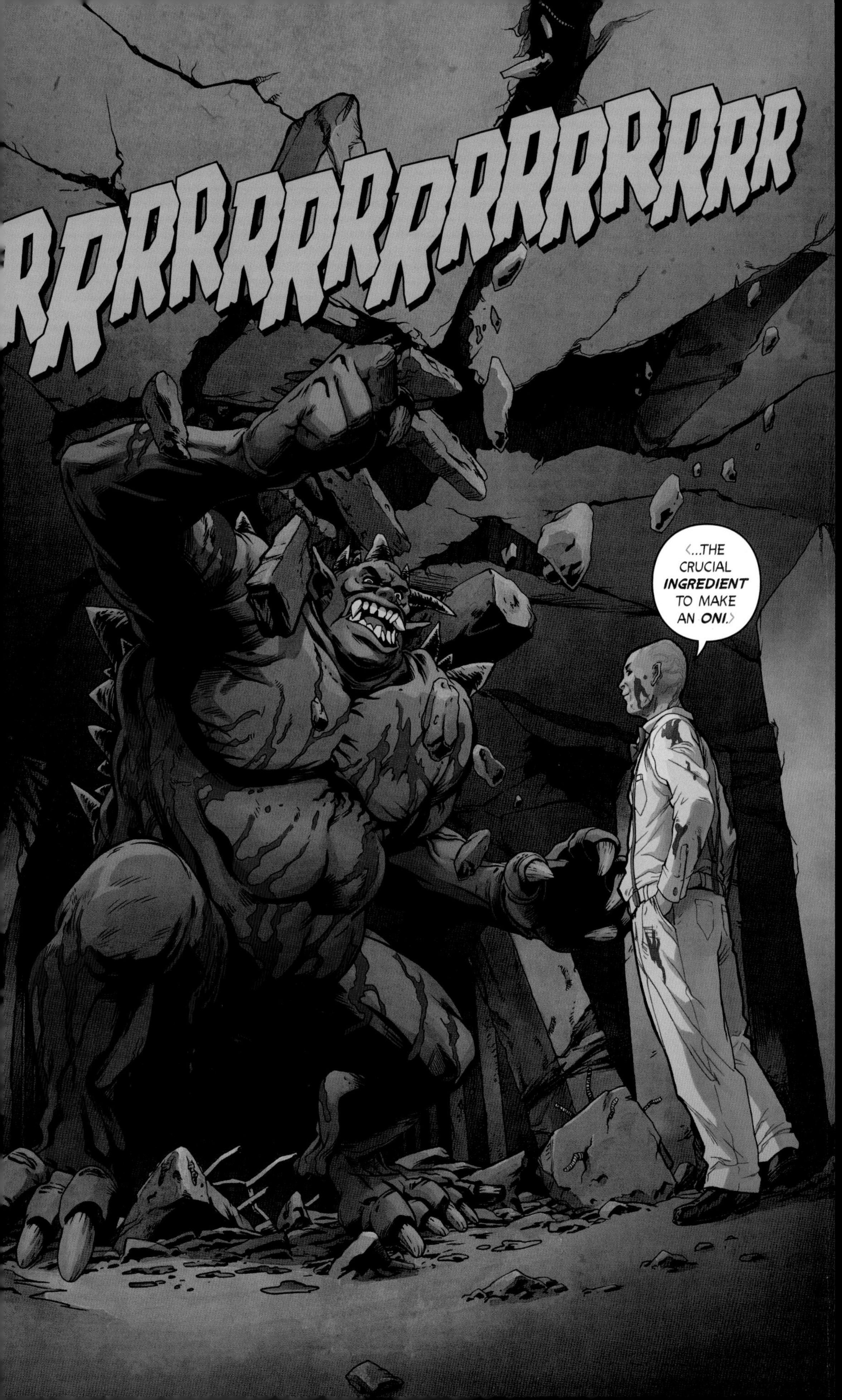

RRRRRRRRRRRRRRRRRR
〈...THE CRUCIAL INGREDIENT TO MAKE AN ONI.〉

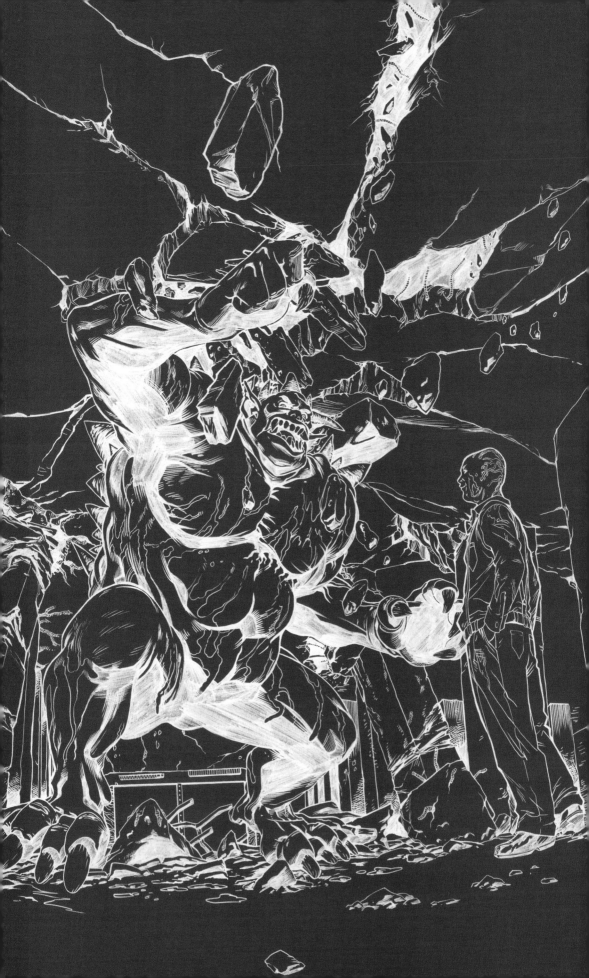

Chapter Twenty-Eight

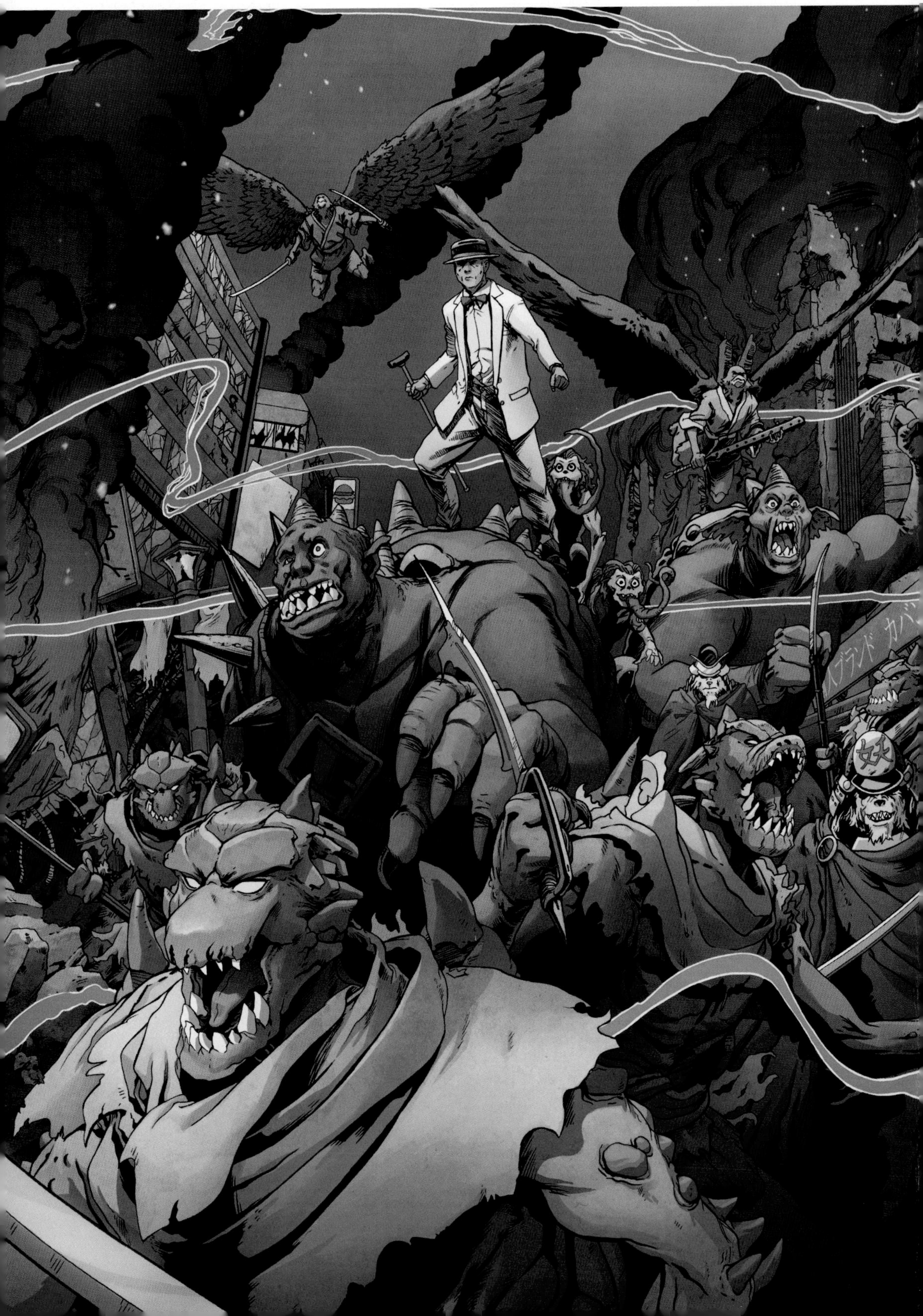
ブランド カバ
妖

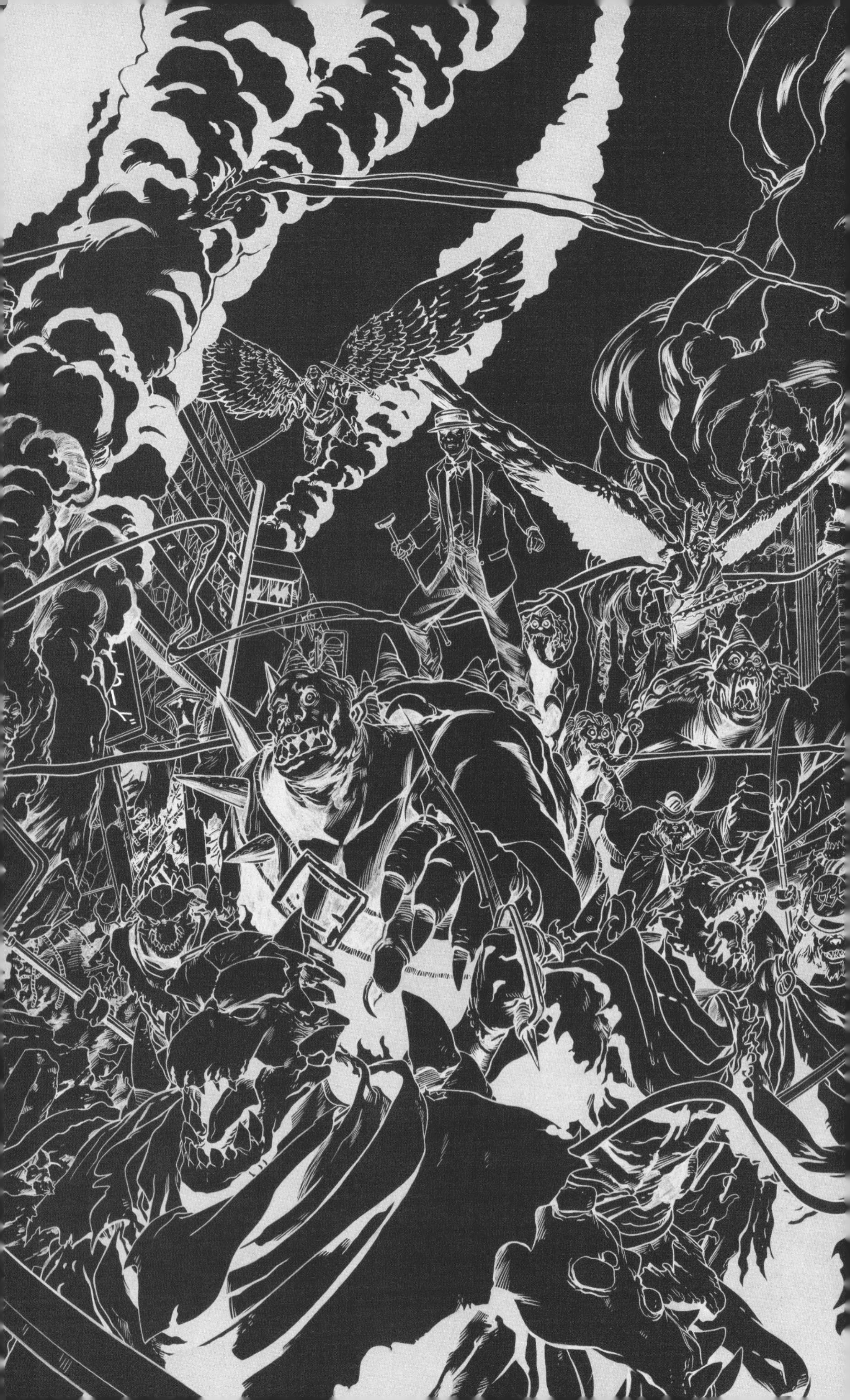

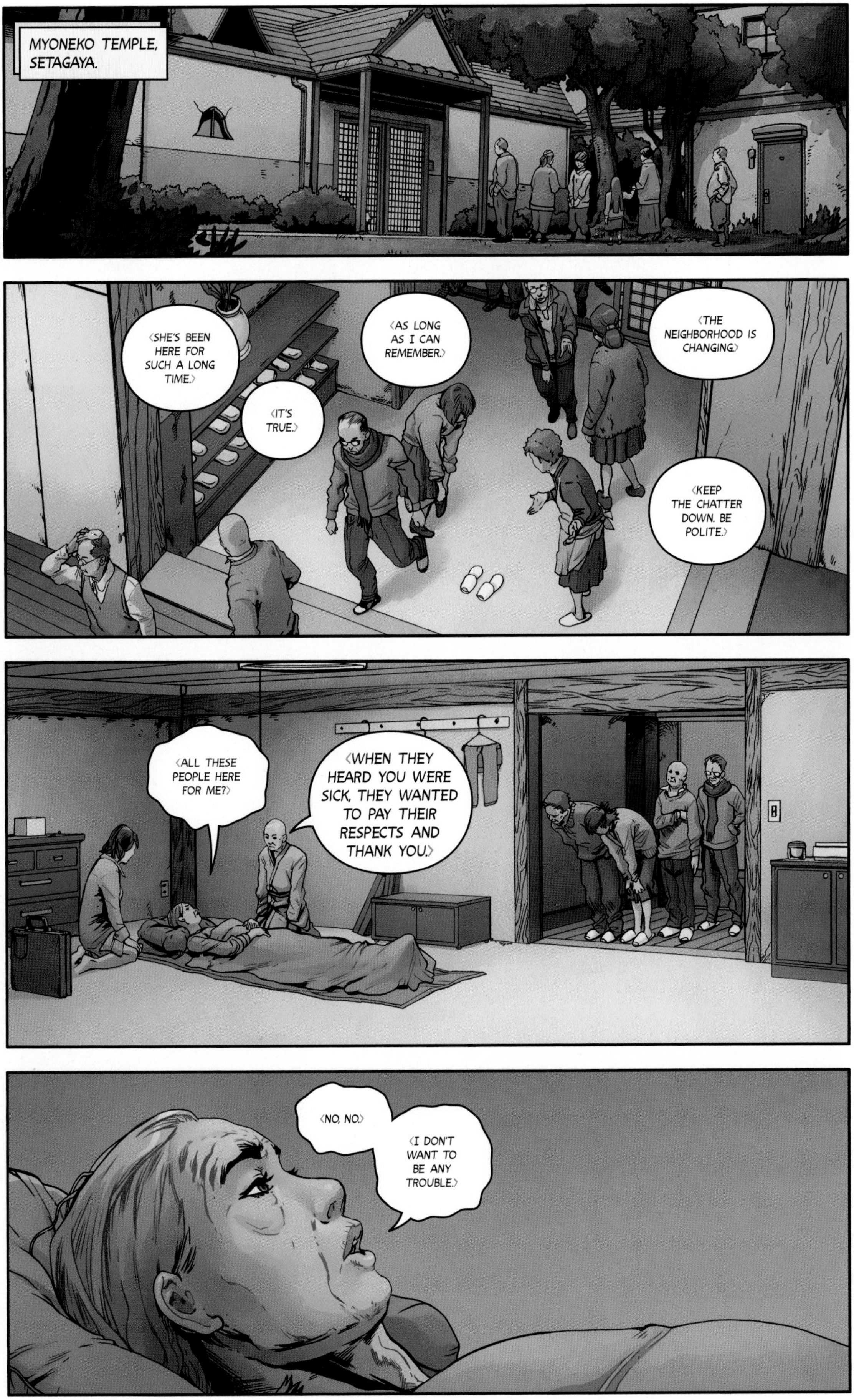
MYONEKO TEMPLE, SETAGAYA.
<SHE'S BEEN HERE FOR SUCH A LONG TIME.>
<IT'S TRUE.>
<AS LONG AS I CAN REMEMBER.>
<THE NEIGHBORHOOD IS CHANGING.>
<KEEP THE CHATTER DOWN. BE POLITE.>
<ALL THESE PEOPLE HERE FOR ME?>
<WHEN THEY HEARD YOU WERE SICK, THEY WANTED TO PAY THEIR RESPECTS AND THANK YOU.>
<NO, NO.>
<I DON'T WANT TO BE ANY TROUBLE.>

⟨THANK YOU FOR CARING FOR THE SHRINE.⟩

⟨THERE'S NO NEED FOR THANKS. IT'S BEEN MY PLEASURE.⟩

⟨WHERE ARE YOUR CATS TODAY, AUNTIE AYANE?⟩

⟨THEY WENT AWAY A FEW WEEKS AGO.⟩

⟨BUT WHY?⟩

⟨MAYBE THEY WANTED TO REMEMBER ME THE WAY I WAS...⟩

⟨TAKE YOUR TIME.⟩

⟨YOU DON'T HAVE TO TALK TO EACH PERSON IF YOU DON'T FEEL UP FOR IT.⟩

⇥COUGH⇤
⇥COUGH⇤

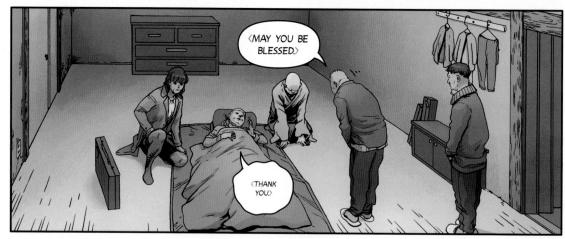
⟨MAY YOU BE BLESSED.⟩

⟨THANK YOU.⟩

⟨OH, MY GOODNESS.⟩

⟨WOW...⟩

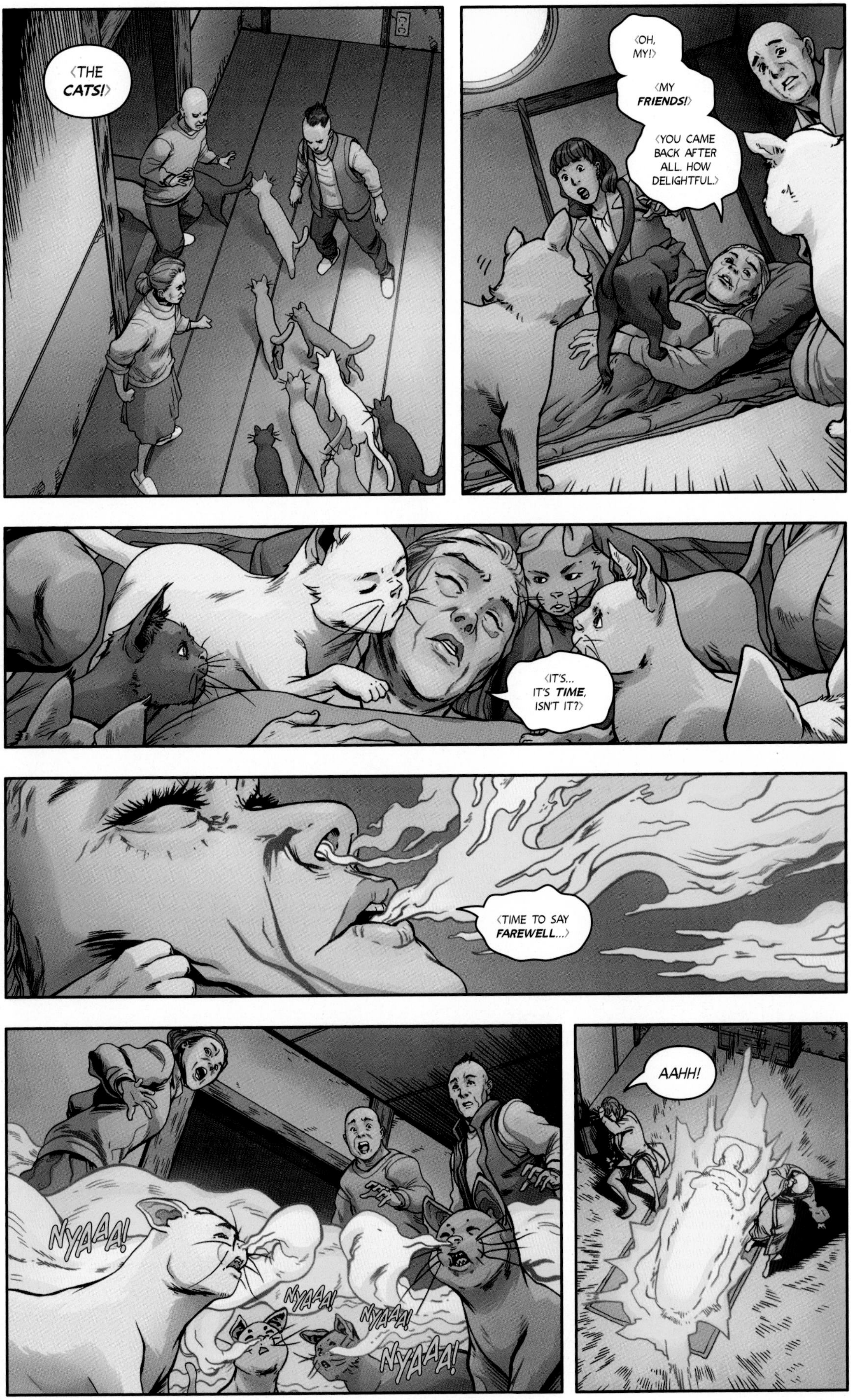

‹THE CATS!›
‹OH, MY!›
‹MY FRIENDS!›
‹YOU CAME BACK AFTER ALL. HOW DELIGHTFUL.›
‹IT'S... IT'S TIME, ISN'T IT?›
‹TIME TO SAY FAREWELL...›
NYAAA!
NYAAA!
NYAAA!
NYAAA!
AAHH!

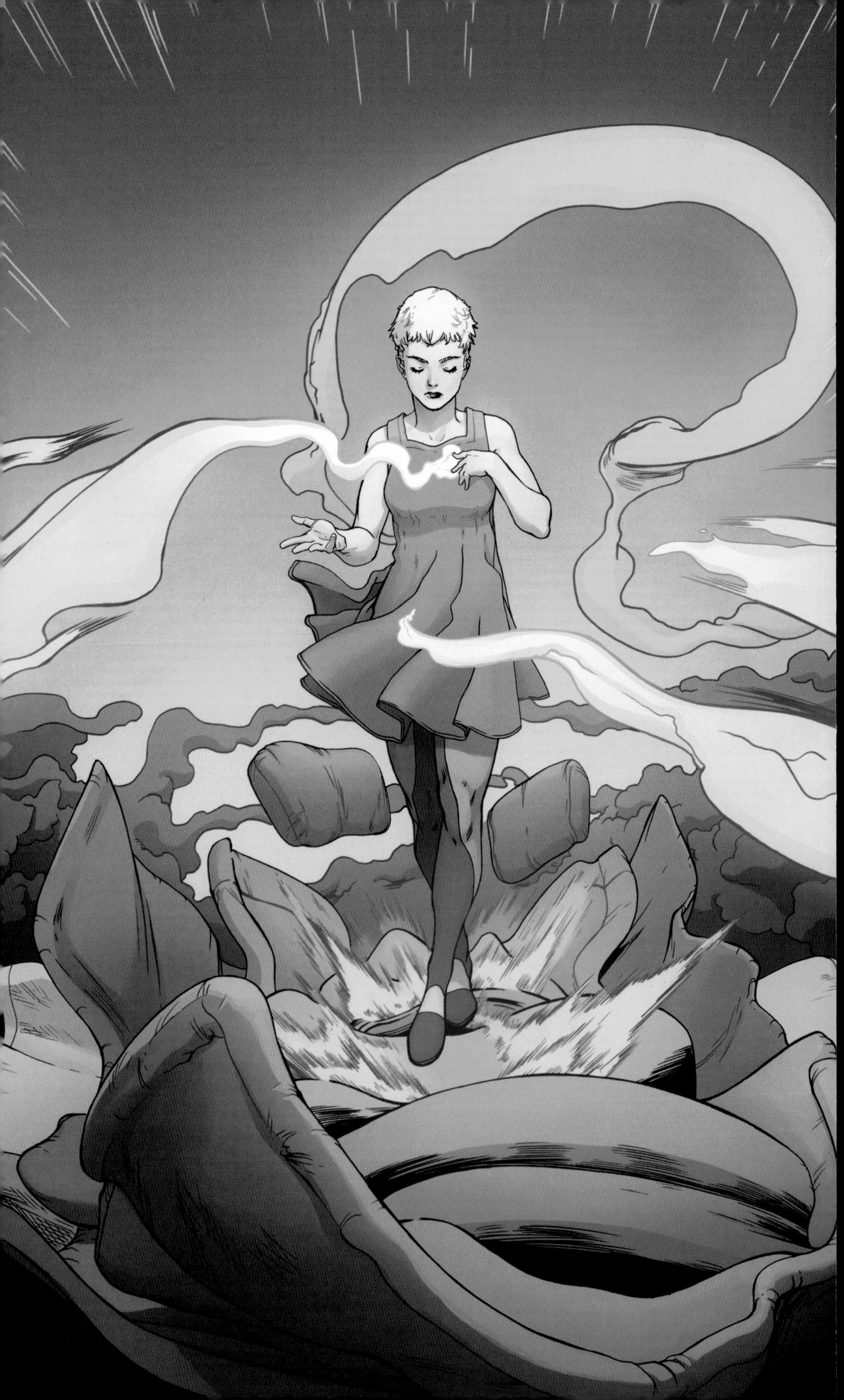

‹THANKS FOR BEING NICE TO THE **OLD LADY**.›

‹HMMM... FEELS LIKE SOMETHING'S **MISSING**...›

‹SEARCHING, SEARCHING...›

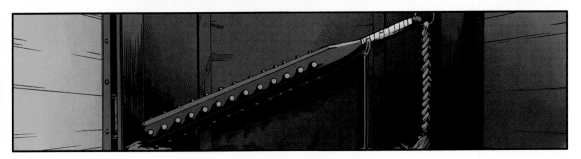

‹**THERE!** PERFECT FOR **KILLING** THOSE FUCKING **YOKAI!**›

‹I'M GONNA TAKE THIS, OKAY?›

‹I... I GUESS SO...›

‹OKAY, BYE FOR NOW!›

‹IF YOU SEE ME AGAIN I'LL PROBABLY BE COVERED IN **BLOOD!**›

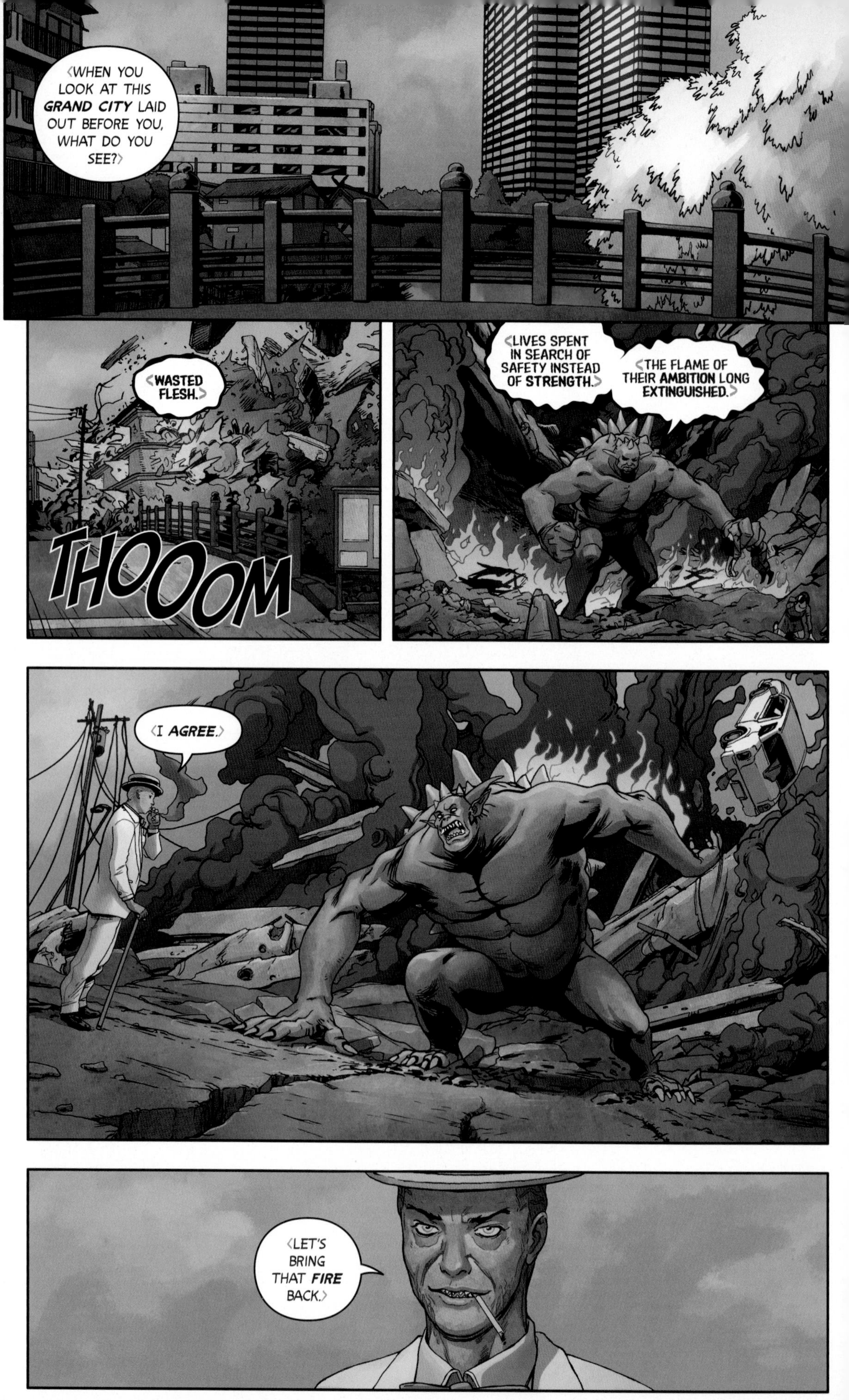

<WHEN YOU LOOK AT THIS GRAND CITY LAID OUT BEFORE YOU, WHAT DO YOU SEE?>
<WASTED FLESH.>
THOOOM
<LIVES SPENT IN SEARCH OF SAFETY INSTEAD OF STRENGTH.>
<THE FLAME OF THEIR AMBITION LONG EXTINGUISHED.>
<I AGREE.>
<LET'S BRING THAT FIRE BACK.>

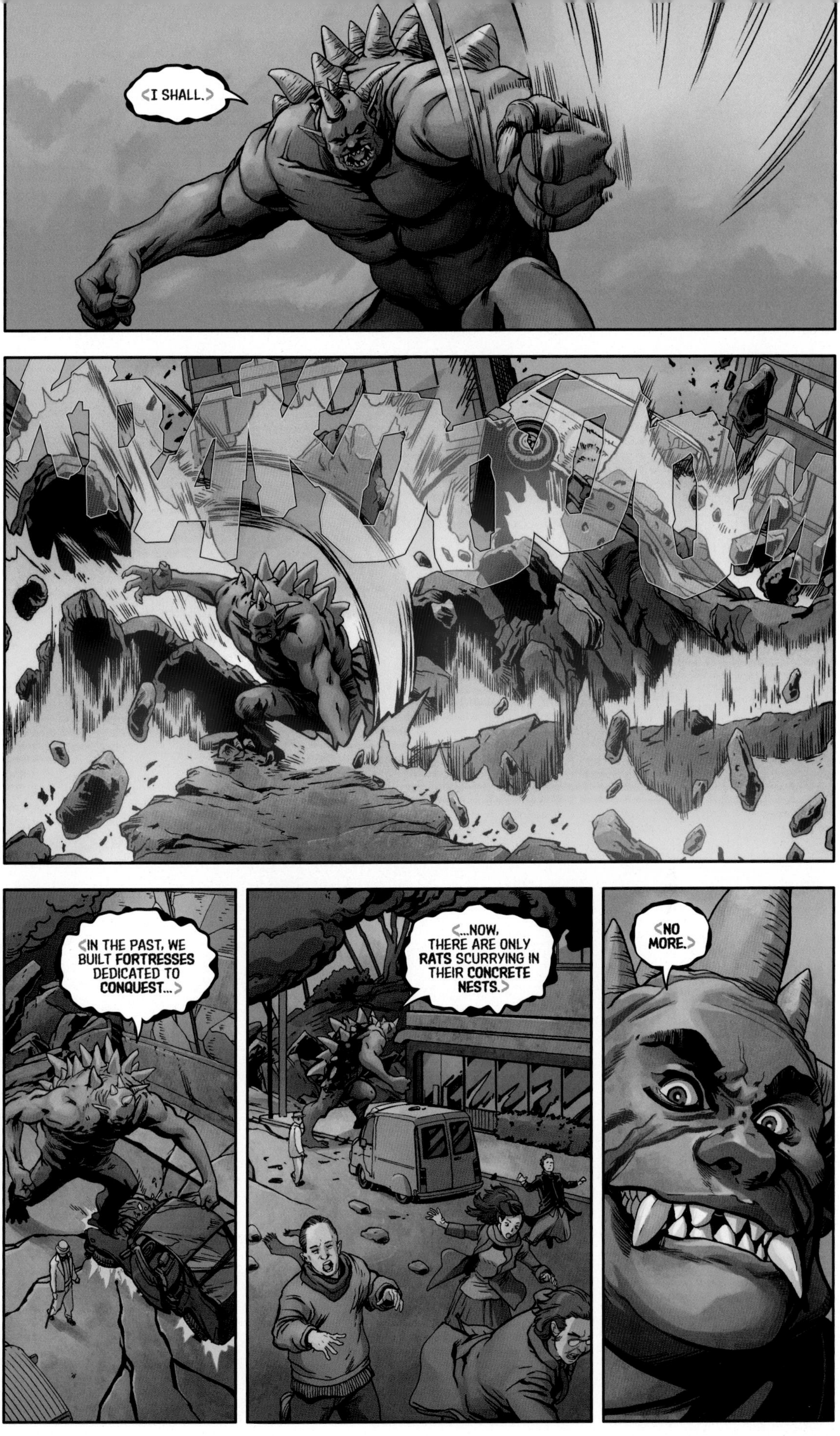
<I SHALL.>
<IN THE PAST, WE BUILT FORTRESSES DEDICATED TO CONQUEST...>
<...NOW, THERE ARE ONLY RATS SCURRYING IN THEIR CONCRETE NESTS.>
<NO MORE.>

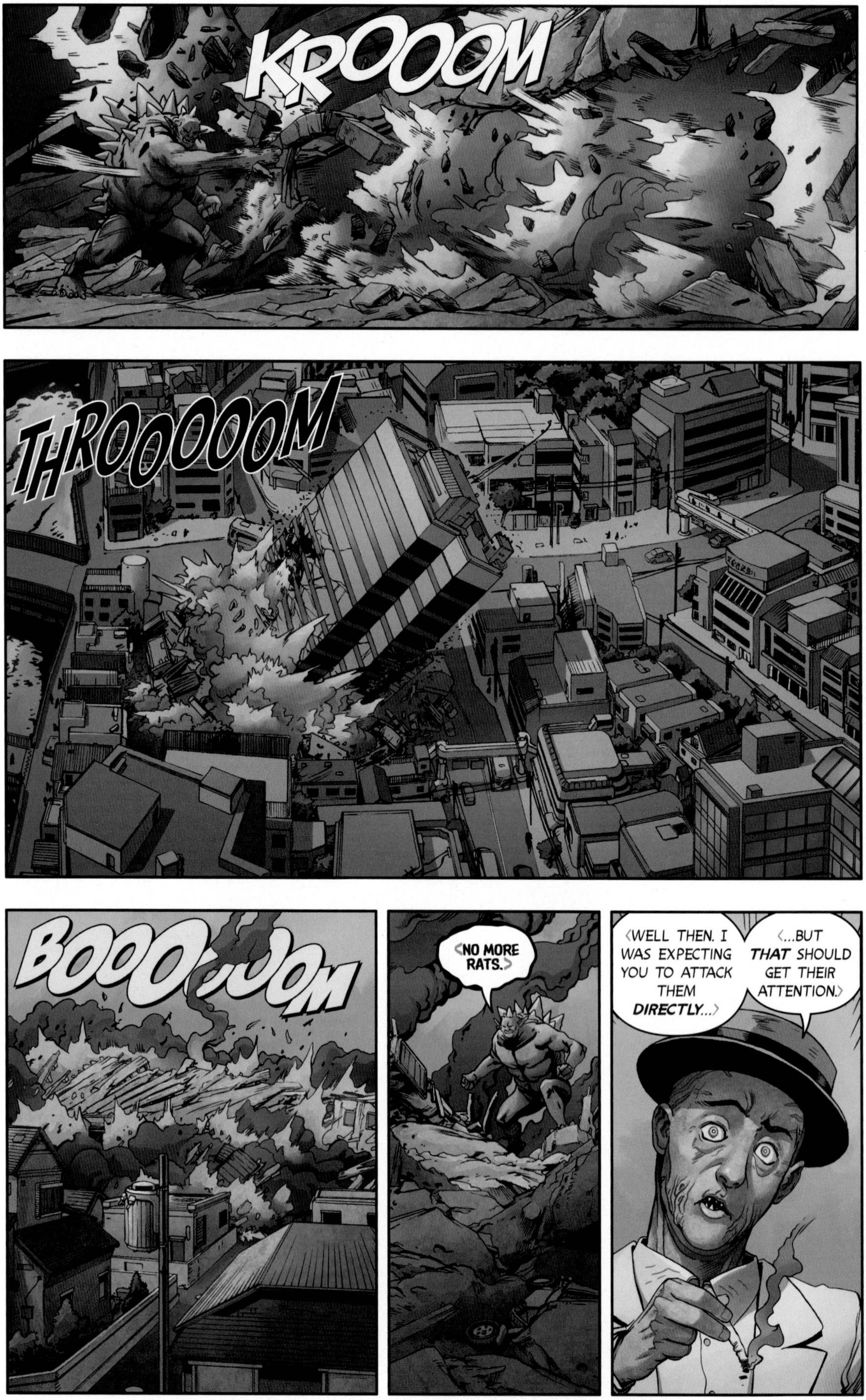
KROOOM
THROOOOOM
BOOOOOOM
‹NO MORE RATS.›
‹WELL THEN. I WAS EXPECTING YOU TO ATTACK THEM *DIRECTLY*...›
‹...BUT *THAT* SHOULD GET THEIR ATTENTION.›

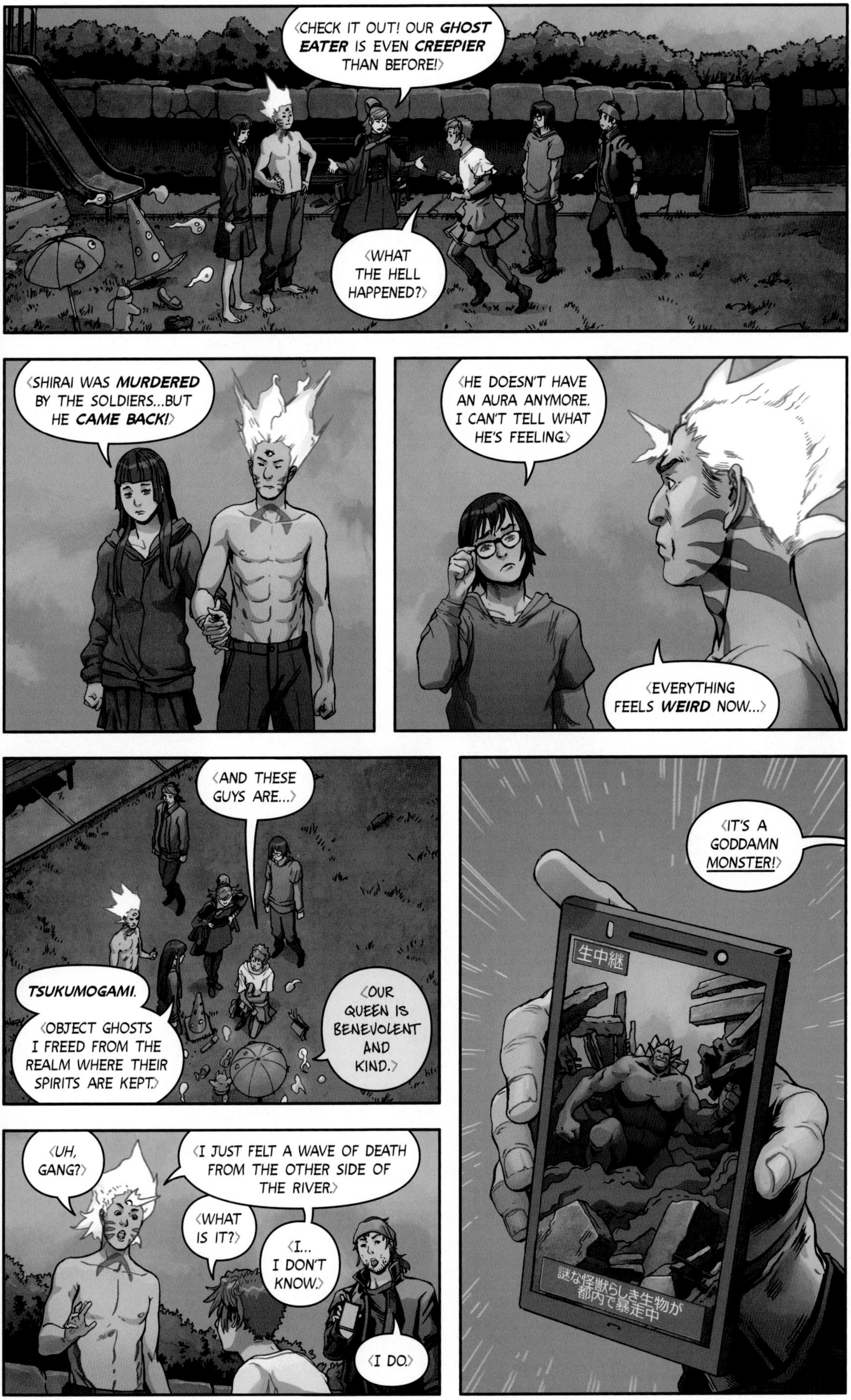
〈CHECK IT OUT! OUR **GHOST EATER** IS EVEN **CREEPIER** THAN BEFORE!〉
〈WHAT THE HELL HAPPENED?〉
〈SHIRAI WAS **MURDERED** BY THE SOLDIERS...BUT HE **CAME BACK!**〉
〈HE DOESN'T HAVE AN AURA ANYMORE. I CAN'T TELL WHAT HE'S FEELING.〉
〈EVERYTHING FEELS **WEIRD** NOW...〉
〈AND THESE GUYS ARE...〉
TSUKUMOGAMI.
〈OBJECT GHOSTS I FREED FROM THE REALM WHERE THEIR SPIRITS ARE KEPT.〉
〈OUR QUEEN IS BENEVOLENT AND KIND.〉
〈IT'S A GODDAMN MONSTER!〉
生中継
謎な怪獣らしき生物が
都内で暴走中
〈UH, GANG?〉
〈I JUST FELT A WAVE OF DEATH FROM THE OTHER SIDE OF THE RIVER.〉
〈WHAT IS IT?〉
〈I... I DON'T KNOW.〉
〈I DO.〉

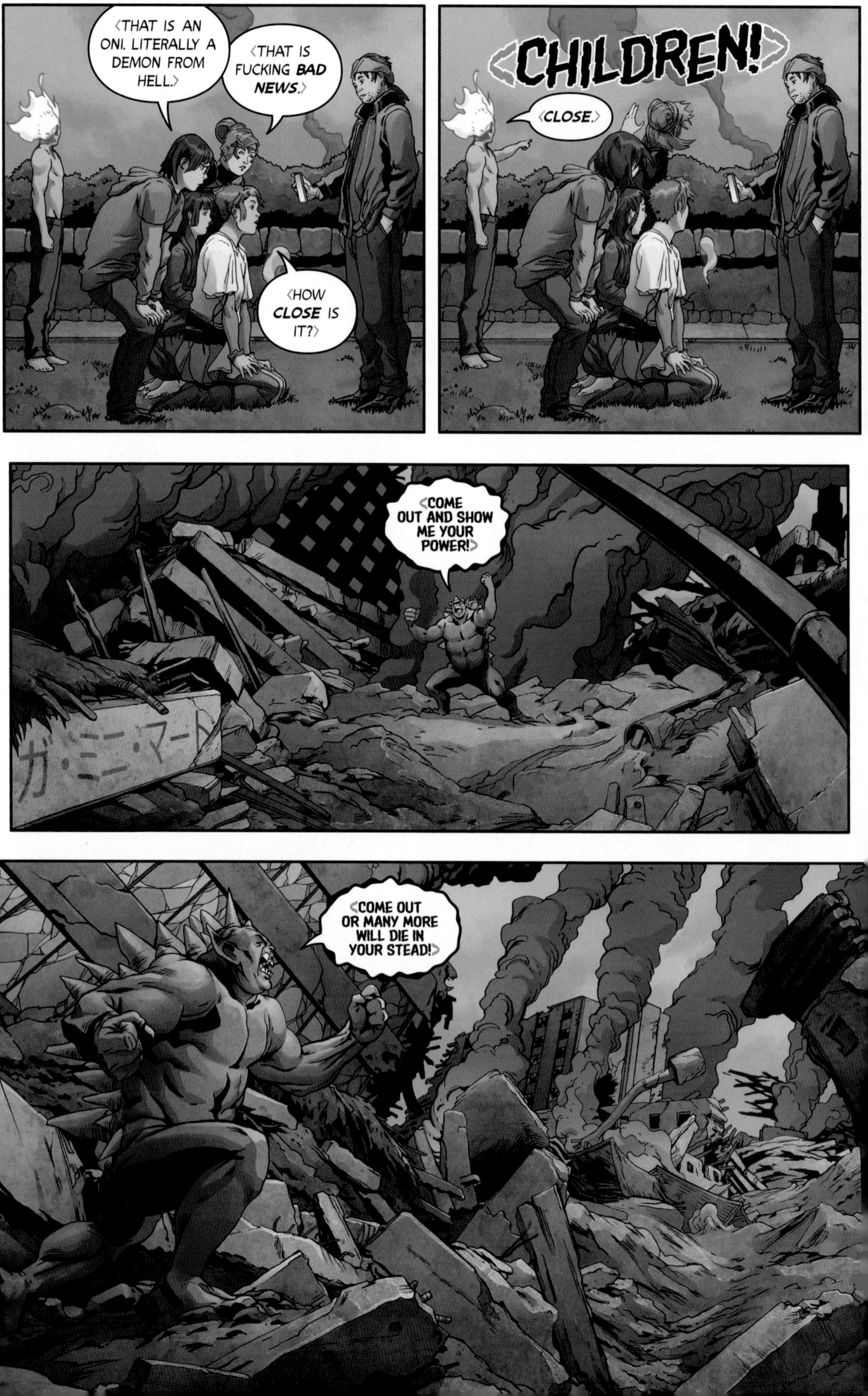
〈THAT IS AN ONI. LITERALLY A DEMON FROM HELL.〉
〈THAT IS FUCKING **BAD NEWS**.〉
〈HOW **CLOSE** IS IT?〉
〈CHILDREN!〉
〈**CLOSE**.〉
〈COME OUT AND SHOW ME YOUR POWER!〉
ガ・ミニ・マート
〈COME OUT OR MANY MORE WILL DIE IN YOUR STEAD!〉

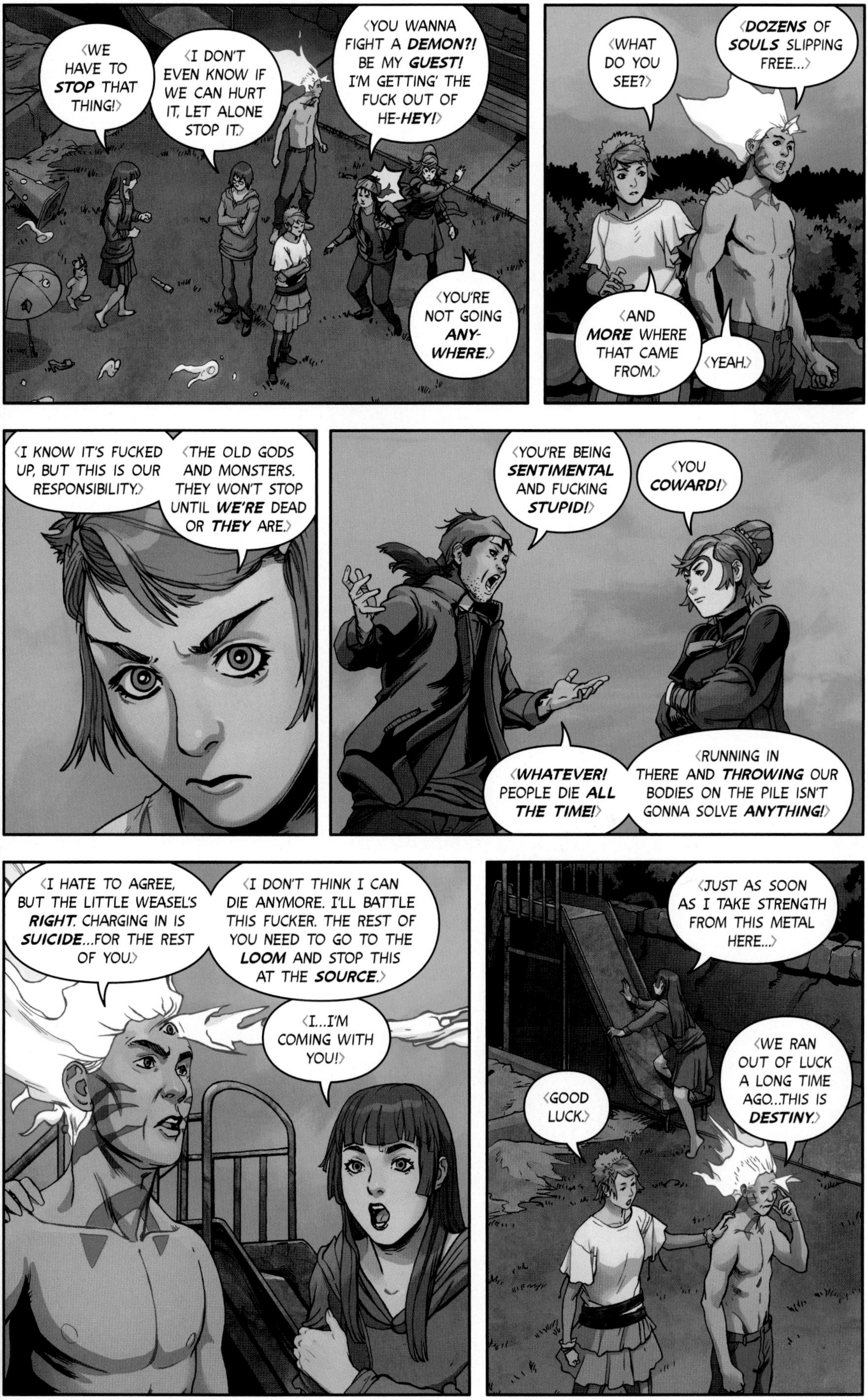
‹WE HAVE TO STOP THAT THING!›
‹I DON'T EVEN KNOW IF WE CAN HURT IT, LET ALONE STOP IT.›
‹YOU WANNA FIGHT A DEMON?! BE MY GUEST! I'M GETTING' THE FUCK OUT OF HE-HEY!›
‹YOU'RE NOT GOING ANY-WHERE.›
‹WHAT DO YOU SEE?›
‹DOZENS OF SOULS SLIPPING FREE...›
‹AND MORE WHERE THAT CAME FROM.›
‹YEAH.›
‹I KNOW IT'S FUCKED UP, BUT THIS IS OUR RESPONSIBILITY.›
‹THE OLD GODS AND MONSTERS. THEY WON'T STOP UNTIL WE'RE DEAD OR THEY ARE.›
‹YOU'RE BEING SENTIMENTAL AND FUCKING STUPID!›
‹YOU COWARD!›
‹WHATEVER! PEOPLE DIE ALL THE TIME!›
‹RUNNING IN THERE AND THROWING OUR BODIES ON THE PILE ISN'T GONNA SOLVE ANYTHING!›
‹I HATE TO AGREE, BUT THE LITTLE WEASEL'S RIGHT. CHARGING IN IS SUICIDE...FOR THE REST OF YOU.›
‹I DON'T THINK I CAN DIE ANYMORE. I'LL BATTLE THIS FUCKER. THE REST OF YOU NEED TO GO TO THE LOOM AND STOP THIS AT THE SOURCE.›
‹I...I'M COMING WITH YOU!›
‹JUST AS SOON AS I TAKE STRENGTH FROM THIS METAL HERE...›
‹GOOD LUCK.›
‹WE RAN OUT OF LUCK A LONG TIME AGO...THIS IS DESTINY.›

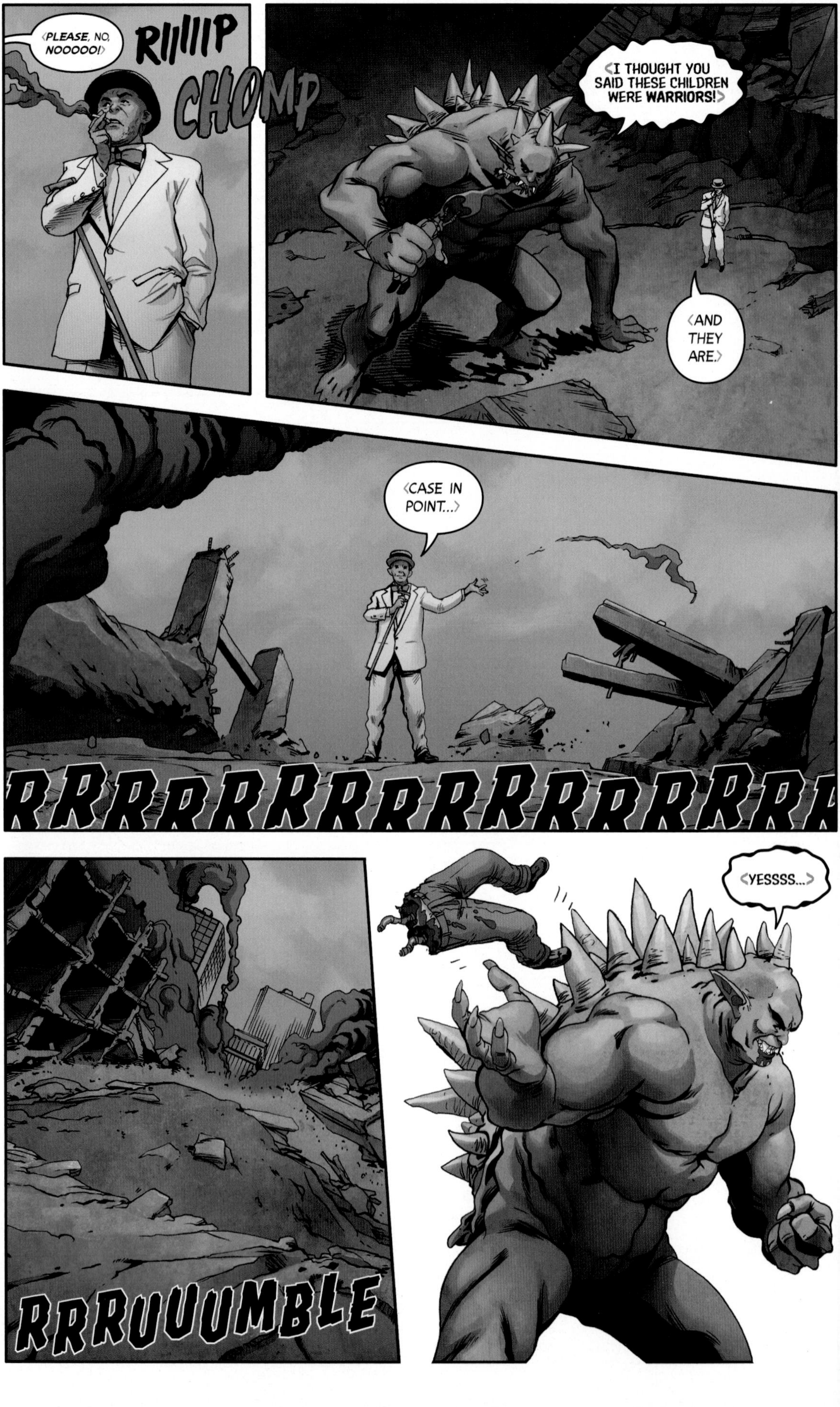

<PLEASE, NO, NOOOOO!>
RIIIIIP
CHOMP
<I THOUGHT YOU SAID THESE CHILDREN WERE WARRIORS!>
<AND THEY ARE.>
<CASE IN POINT...>
RRRRRRRRRRRRRRR
RRRUUUMBLE
<YESSSS...>

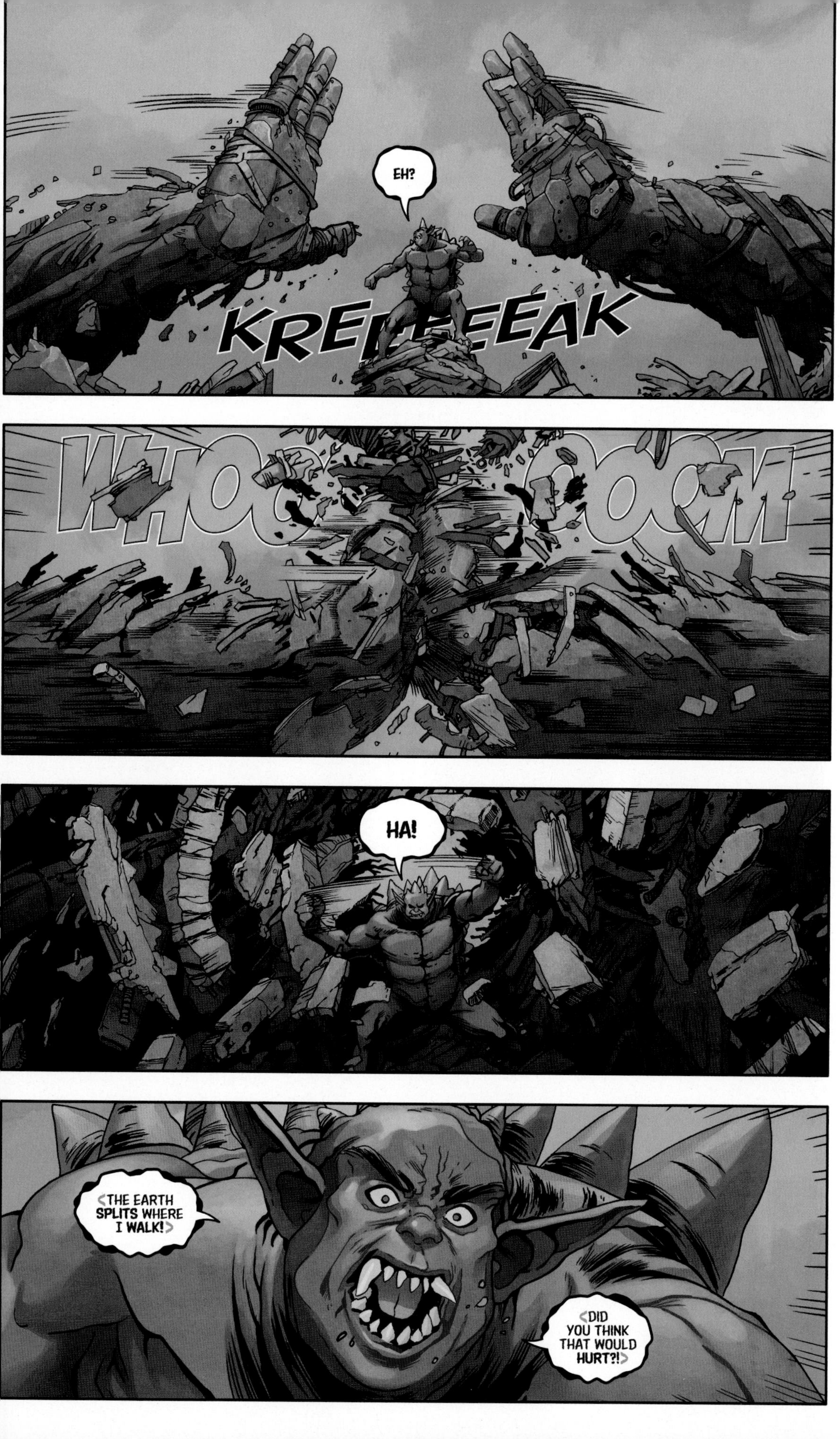
EH?
KREEEEAK
HA!
<THE EARTH SPLITS WHERE I WALK!>
<DID YOU THINK THAT WOULD HURT?!>

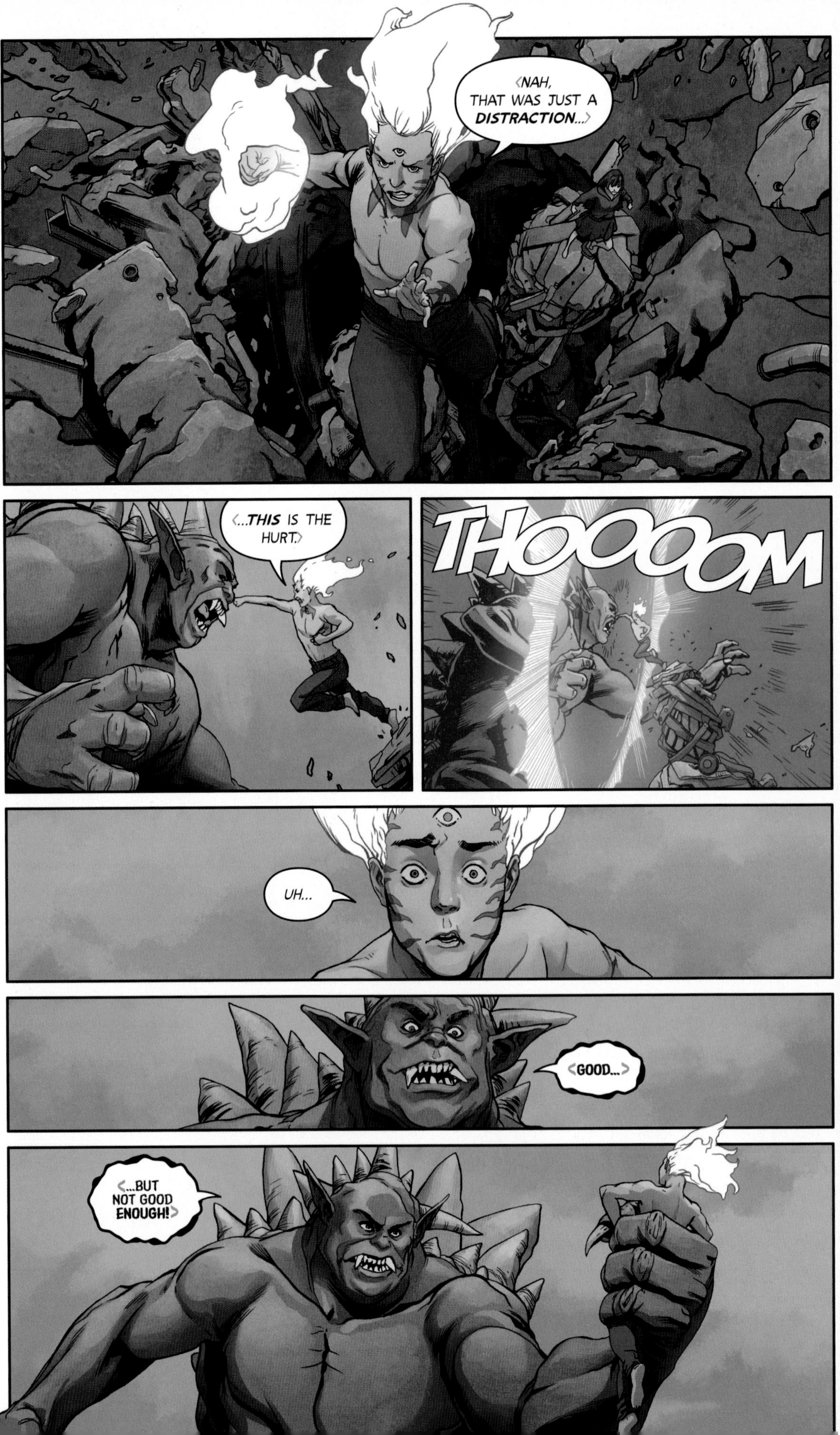
‹NAH, THAT WAS JUST A DISTRACTION...›
‹...THIS IS THE HURT.›
THOOOOM
UH...
‹GOOD...›
‹...BUT NOT GOOD ENOUGH!›

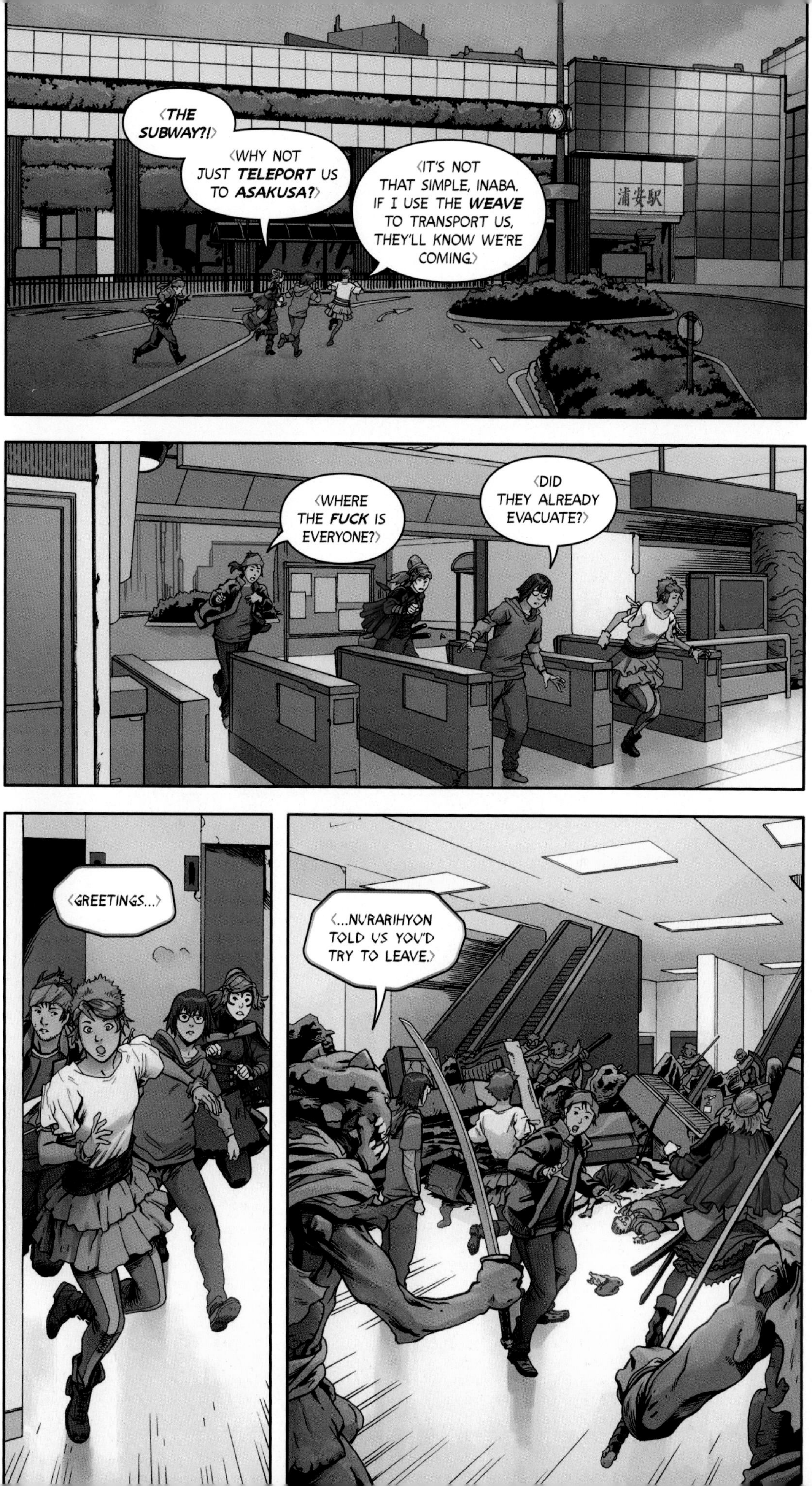
〈THE SUBWAY?!〉
〈WHY NOT JUST TELEPORT US TO ASAKUSA?〉
〈IT'S NOT THAT SIMPLE, INABA. IF I USE THE WEAVE TO TRANSPORT US, THEY'LL KNOW WE'RE COMING.〉
浦安駅
〈WHERE THE FUCK IS EVERYONE?〉
〈DID THEY ALREADY EVACUATE?〉
〈GREETINGS...〉
〈...NURARIHYON TOLD US YOU'D TRY TO LEAVE.〉

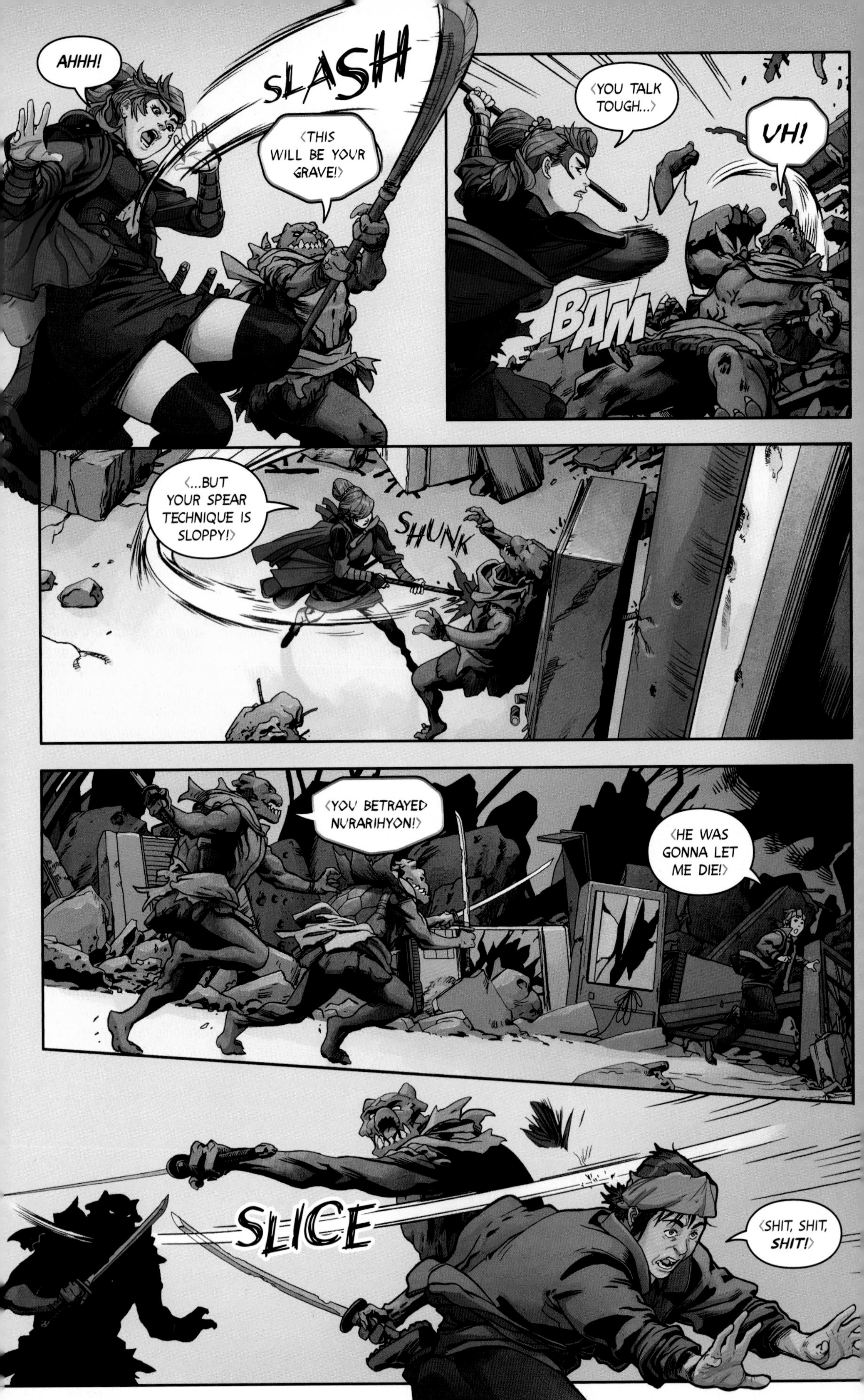
AHHH!
SLASH
‹THIS WILL BE YOUR GRAVE!›
‹YOU TALK TOUGH...›
UH!
BAM
‹...BUT YOUR SPEAR TECHNIQUE IS SLOPPY!›
SHUNK
‹YOU BETRAYED NURARIHYON!›
‹HE WAS GONNA LET ME DIE!›
SLICE
‹SHIT, SHIT, SHIT!›

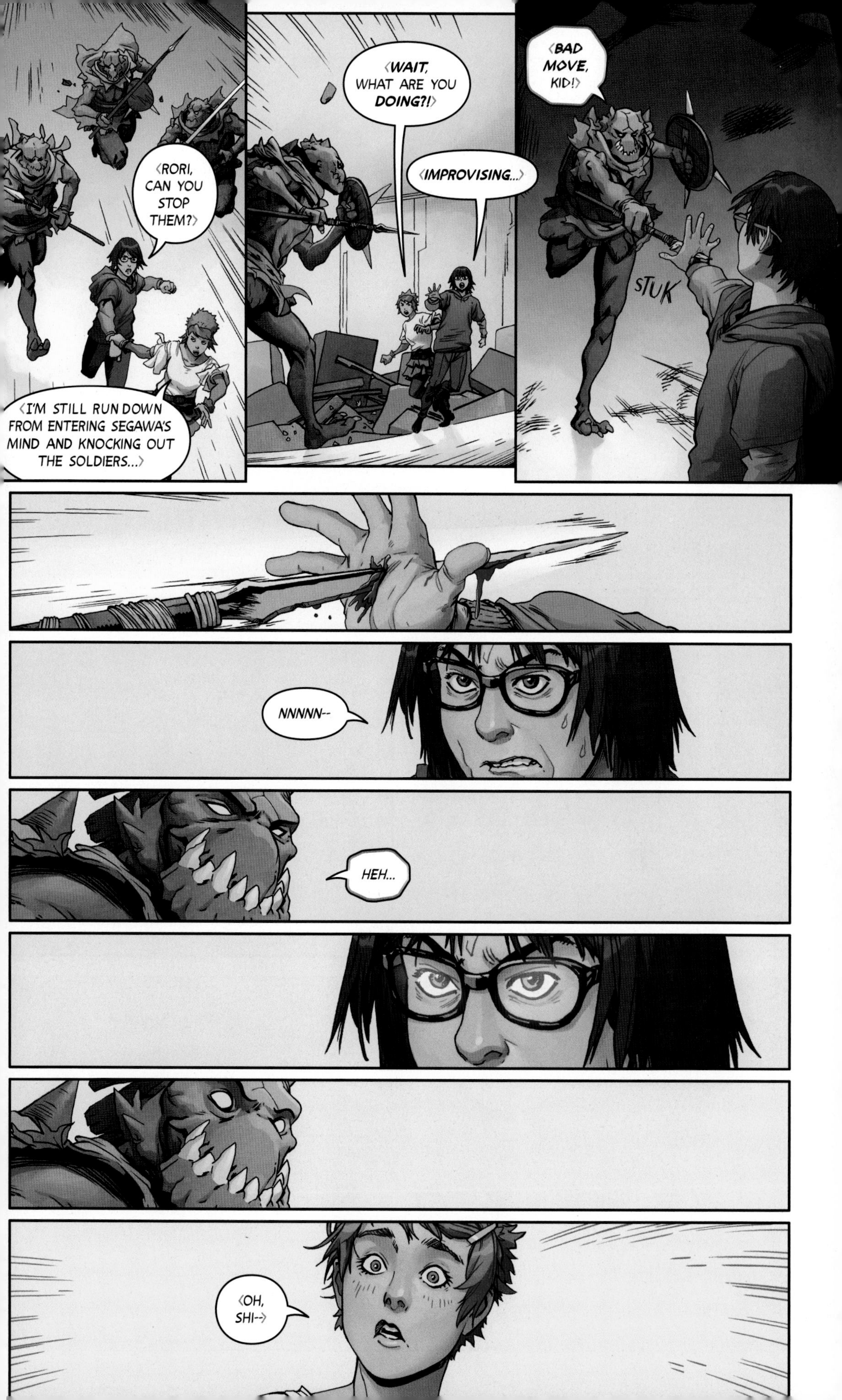

‹RORI, CAN YOU STOP THEM?›
‹I'M STILL RUN DOWN FROM ENTERING SEGAWA'S MIND AND KNOCKING OUT THE SOLDIERS...›
‹WAIT, WHAT ARE YOU DOING?!›
‹IMPROVISING...›
‹BAD MOVE, KID!›
STUK
NNNNN--
HEH...
‹OH, SHI--›

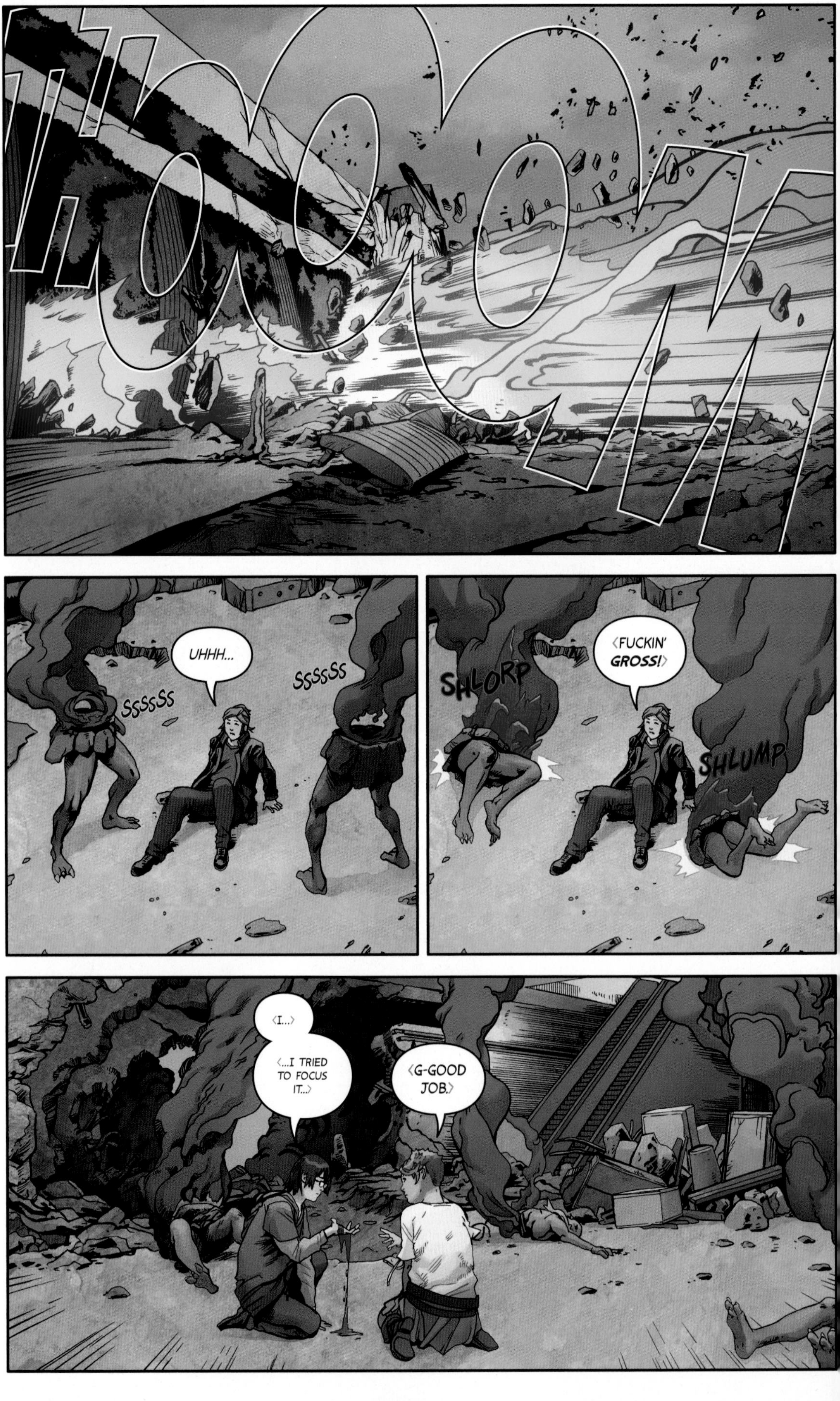
THOOOOM
UHHH...
SSSSSS
SSSSSS
SHLORP
<FUCKIN' **GROSS!**>
SHLUMP
<I...>
<...I TRIED TO FOCUS IT...>
<G-GOOD JOB.>

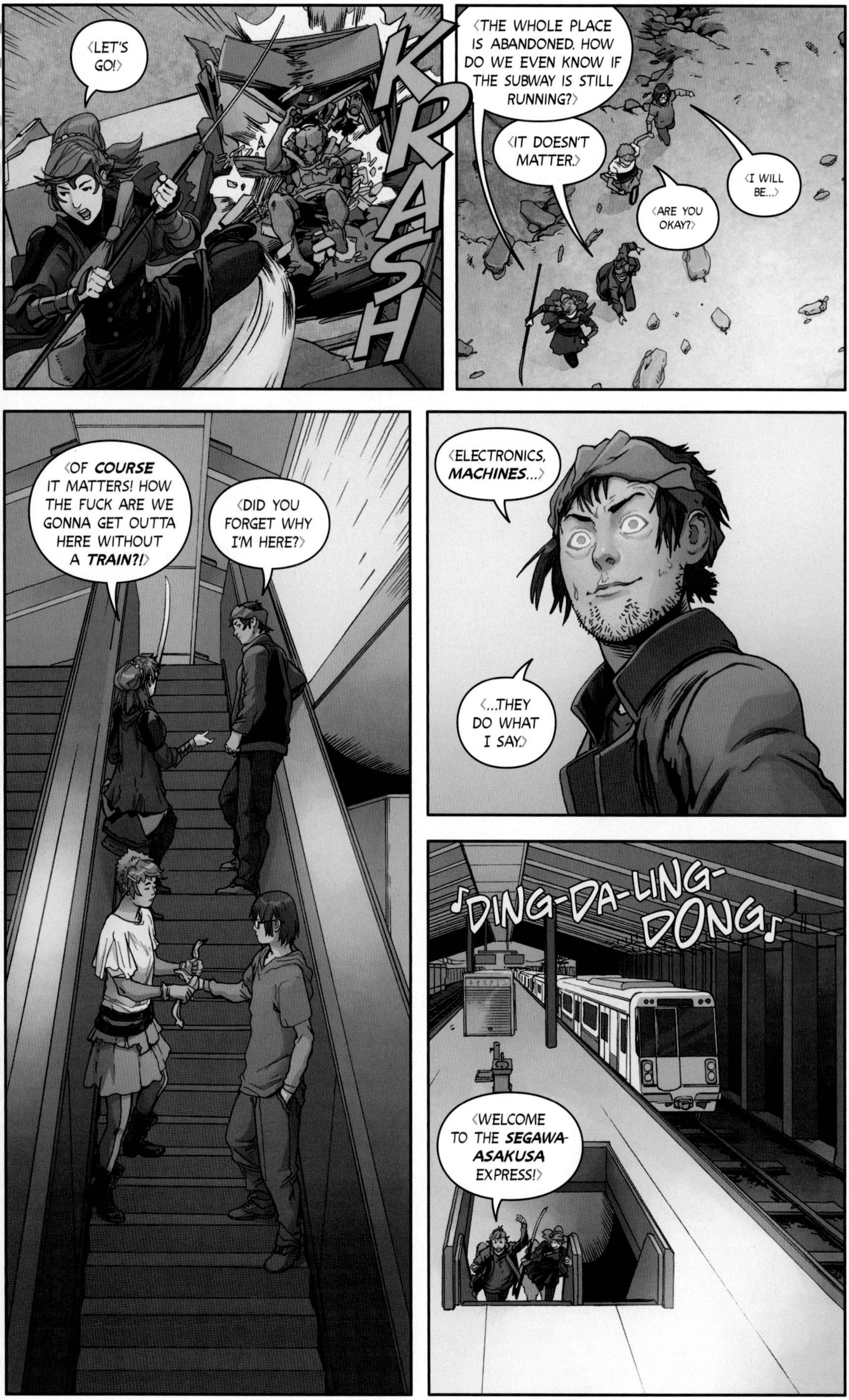
‹LET'S GO!›
KRASH
‹THE WHOLE PLACE IS ABANDONED. HOW DO WE EVEN KNOW IF THE SUBWAY IS STILL RUNNING?›
‹IT DOESN'T MATTER.›
‹ARE YOU OKAY?›
‹I WILL BE...›
‹OF COURSE IT MATTERS! HOW THE FUCK ARE WE GONNA GET OUTTA HERE WITHOUT A TRAIN?!›
‹DID YOU FORGET WHY I'M HERE?›
‹ELECTRONICS, MACHINES...›
‹...THEY DO WHAT I SAY.›
♪DING-DA-LING-DONG♪
‹WELCOME TO THE SEGAWA-ASAKUSA EXPRESS!›

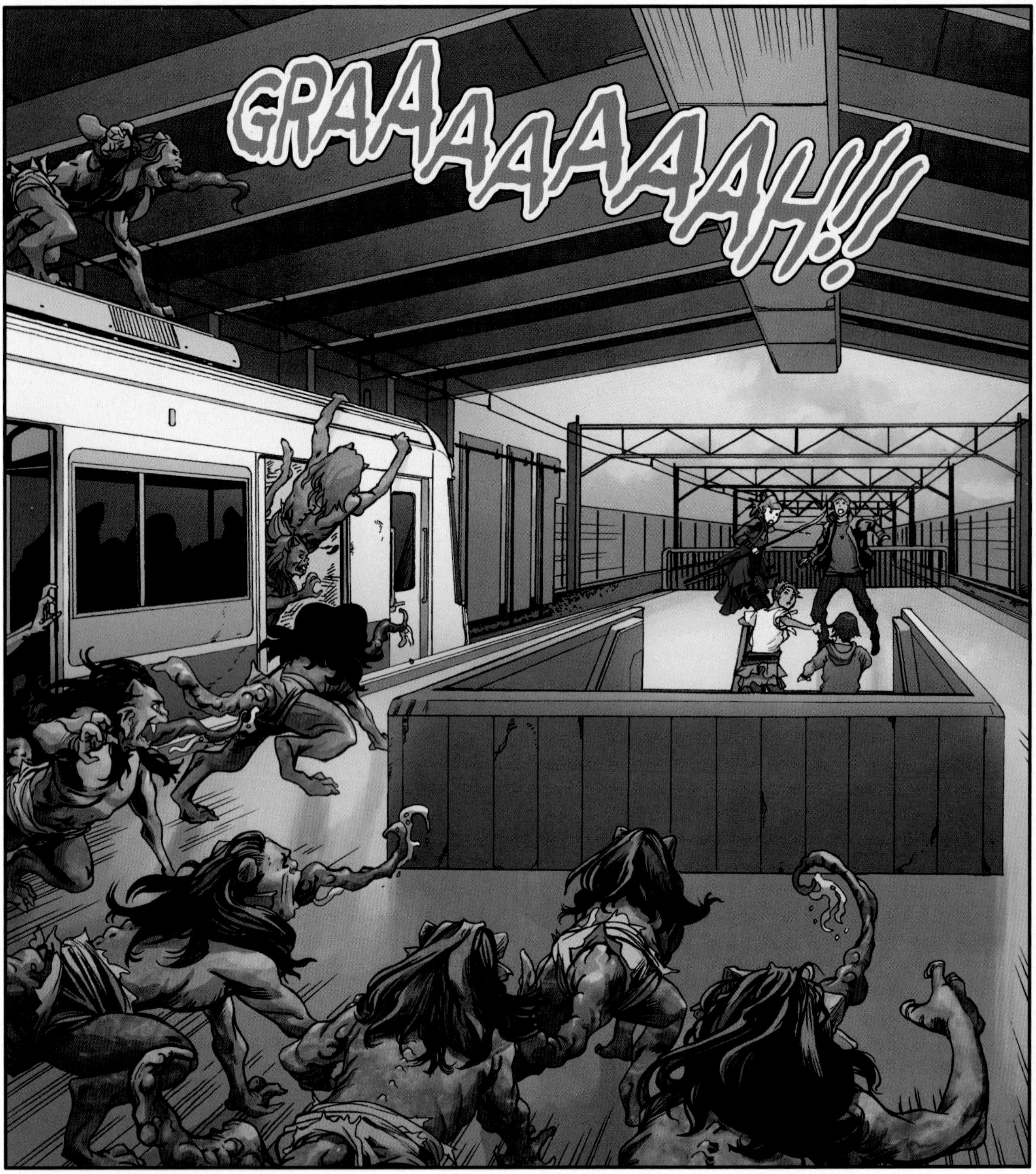
GRAAAAAAAH!!

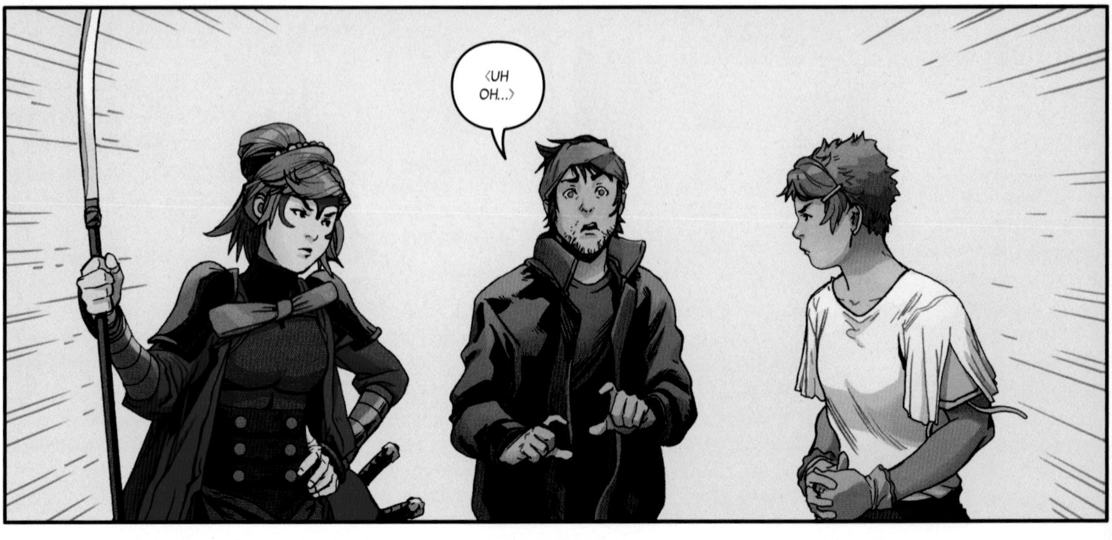
‹UH OH...›

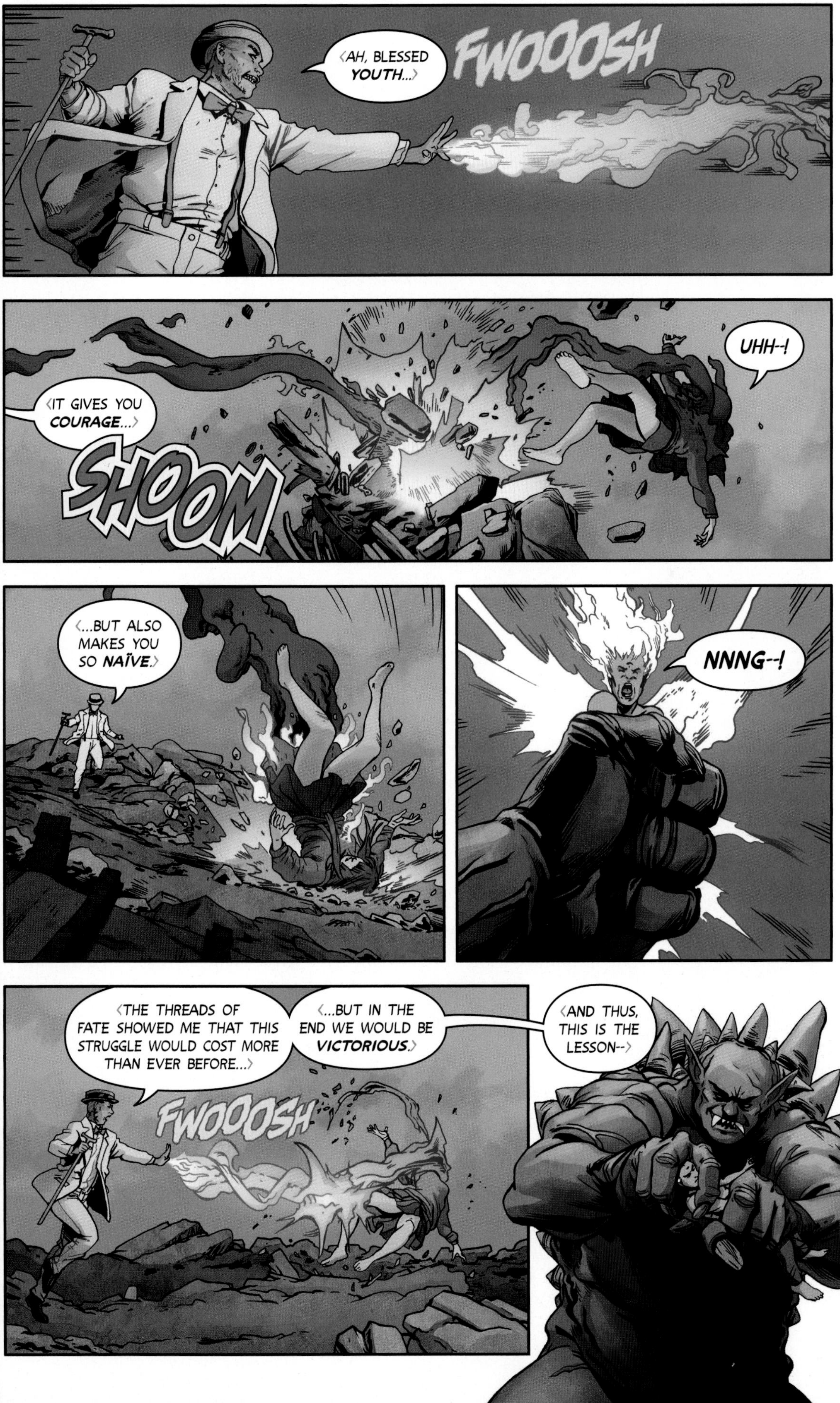

⟨AH, BLESSED **YOUTH**...⟩
FWOOOSH
⟨IT GIVES YOU **COURAGE**...⟩
UHH--!
SHOOM
⟨...BUT ALSO MAKES YOU SO **NAÏVE**.⟩
NNNG--!
⟨THE THREADS OF FATE SHOWED ME THAT THIS STRUGGLE WOULD COST MORE THAN EVER BEFORE...⟩
⟨...BUT IN THE END WE WOULD BE **VICTORIOUS**.⟩
⟨AND THUS, THIS IS THE LESSON--⟩
FWOOOSH

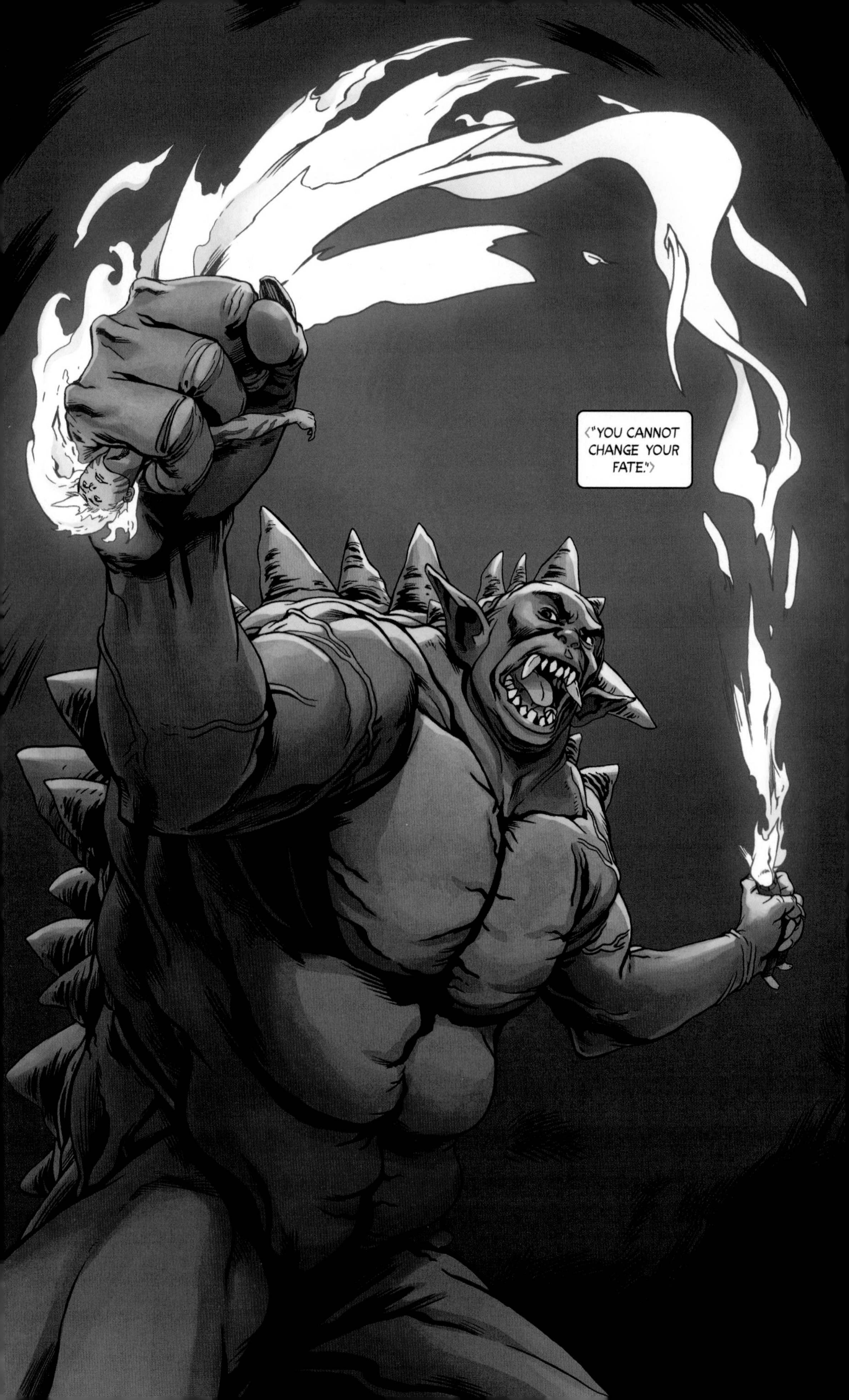
"YOU CANNOT CHANGE YOUR FATE."

Chapter Twenty-Nine

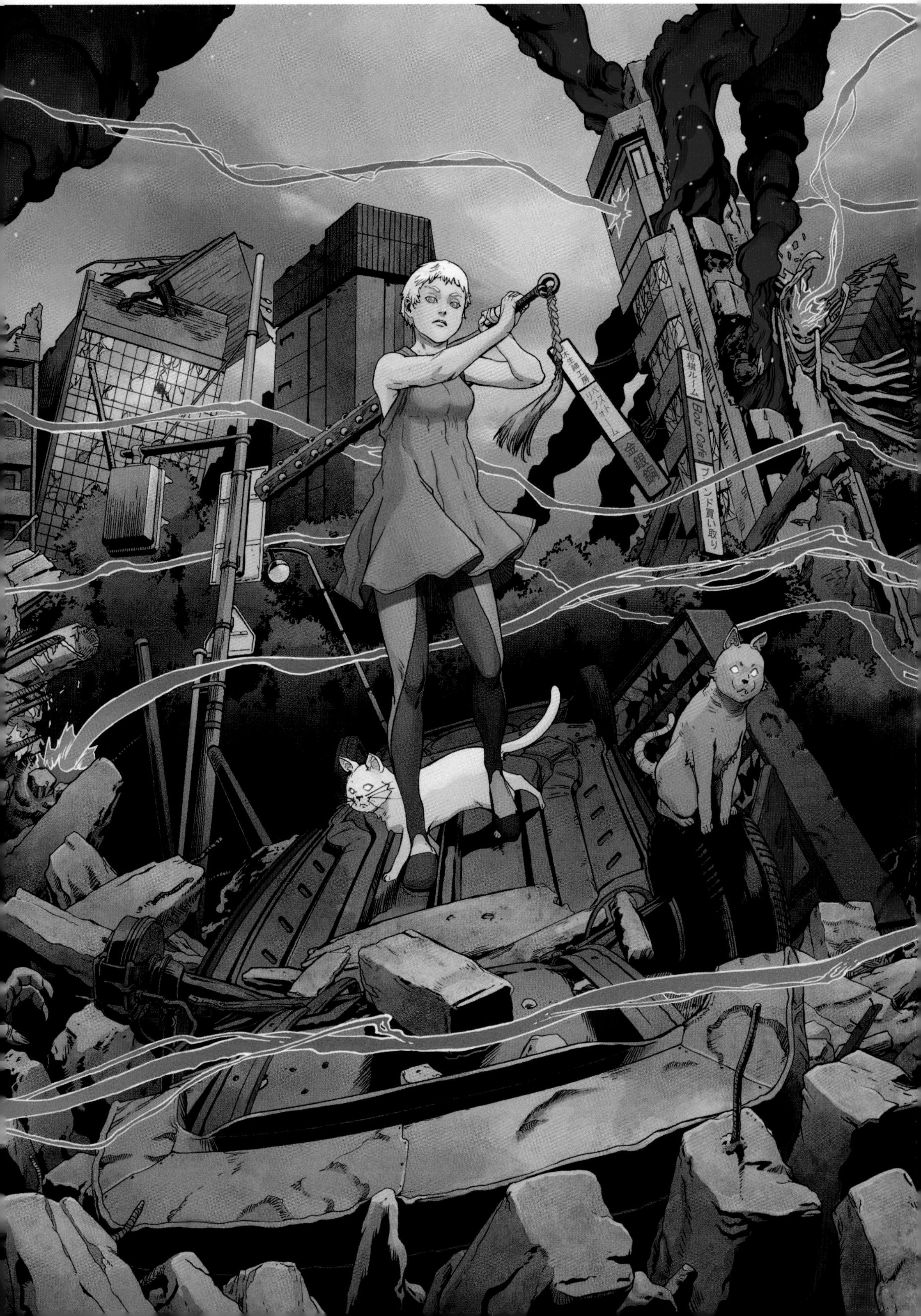
将棋ルーム
Bob・Café
金銀銅

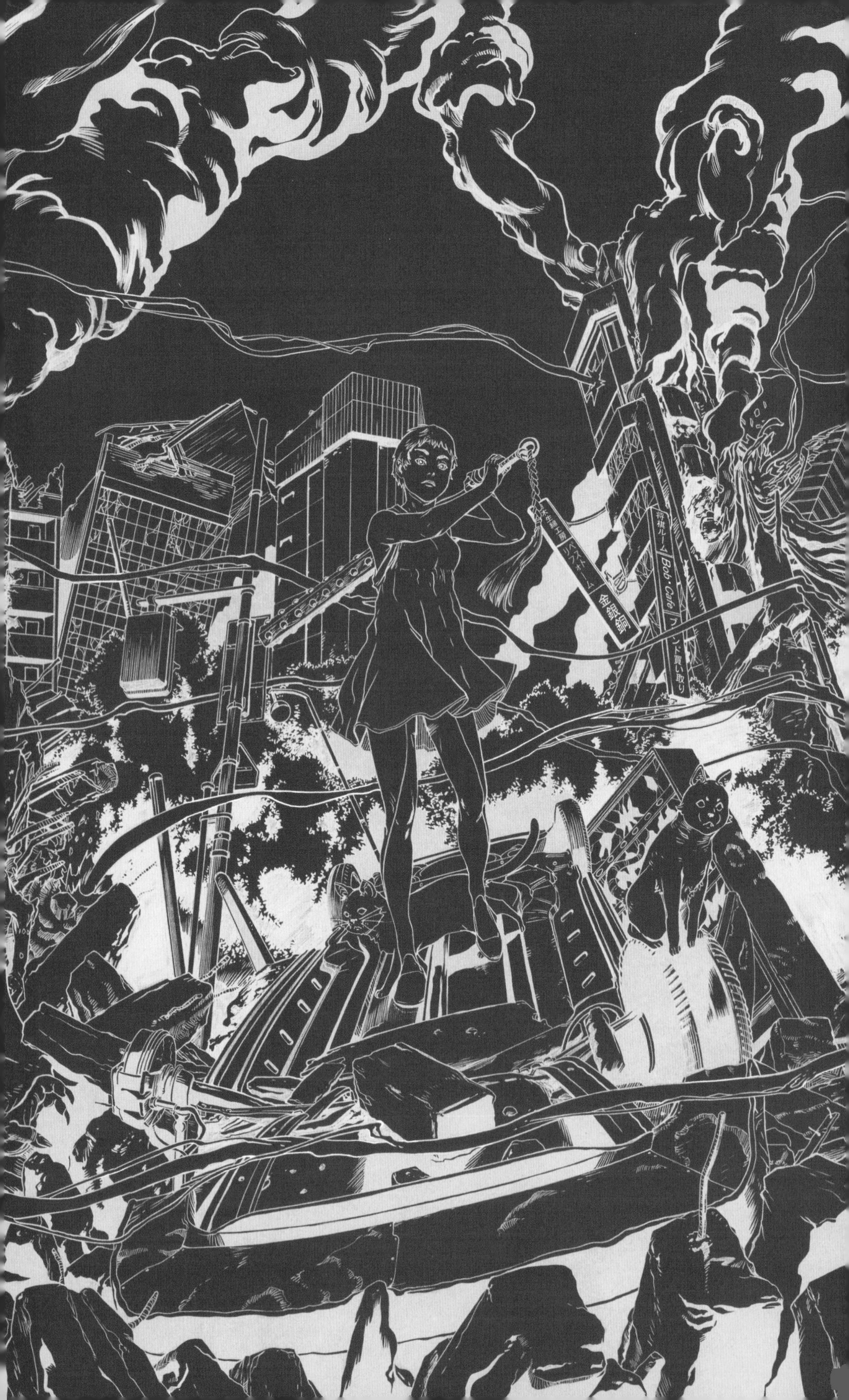
金銀銅
将棋ルーム
Bob・Cafe

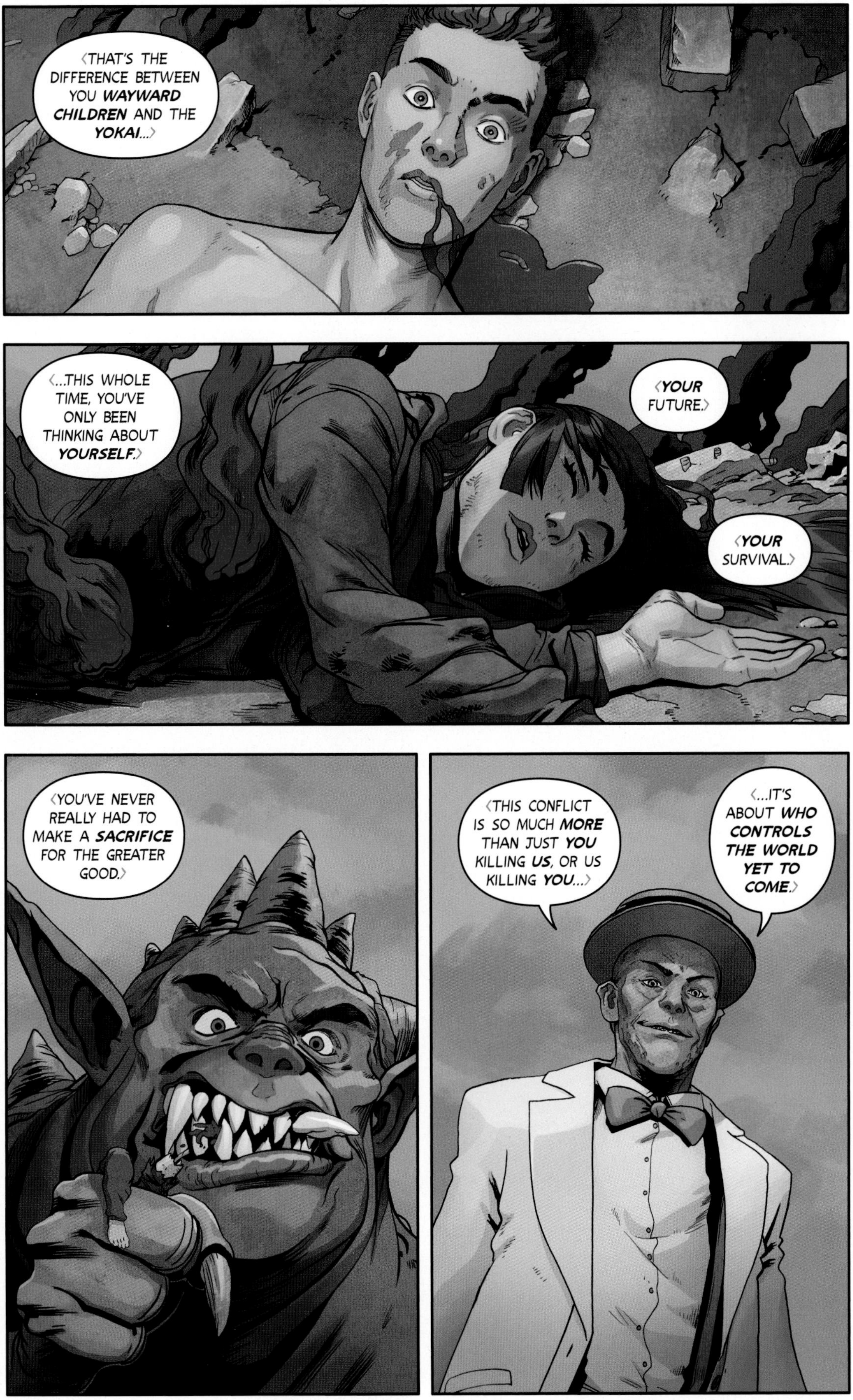

⟨THAT'S THE DIFFERENCE BETWEEN YOU **WAYWARD CHILDREN** AND THE **YOKAI**...⟩
⟨...THIS WHOLE TIME, YOU'VE ONLY BEEN THINKING ABOUT **YOURSELF.**⟩
⟨**YOUR** FUTURE.⟩
⟨**YOUR** SURVIVAL.⟩
⟨YOU'VE NEVER REALLY HAD TO MAKE A **SACRIFICE** FOR THE GREATER GOOD.⟩
⟨THIS CONFLICT IS SO MUCH **MORE** THAN JUST **YOU** KILLING **US**, OR US KILLING **YOU**...⟩
⟨...IT'S ABOUT **WHO CONTROLS THE WORLD YET TO COME.**⟩

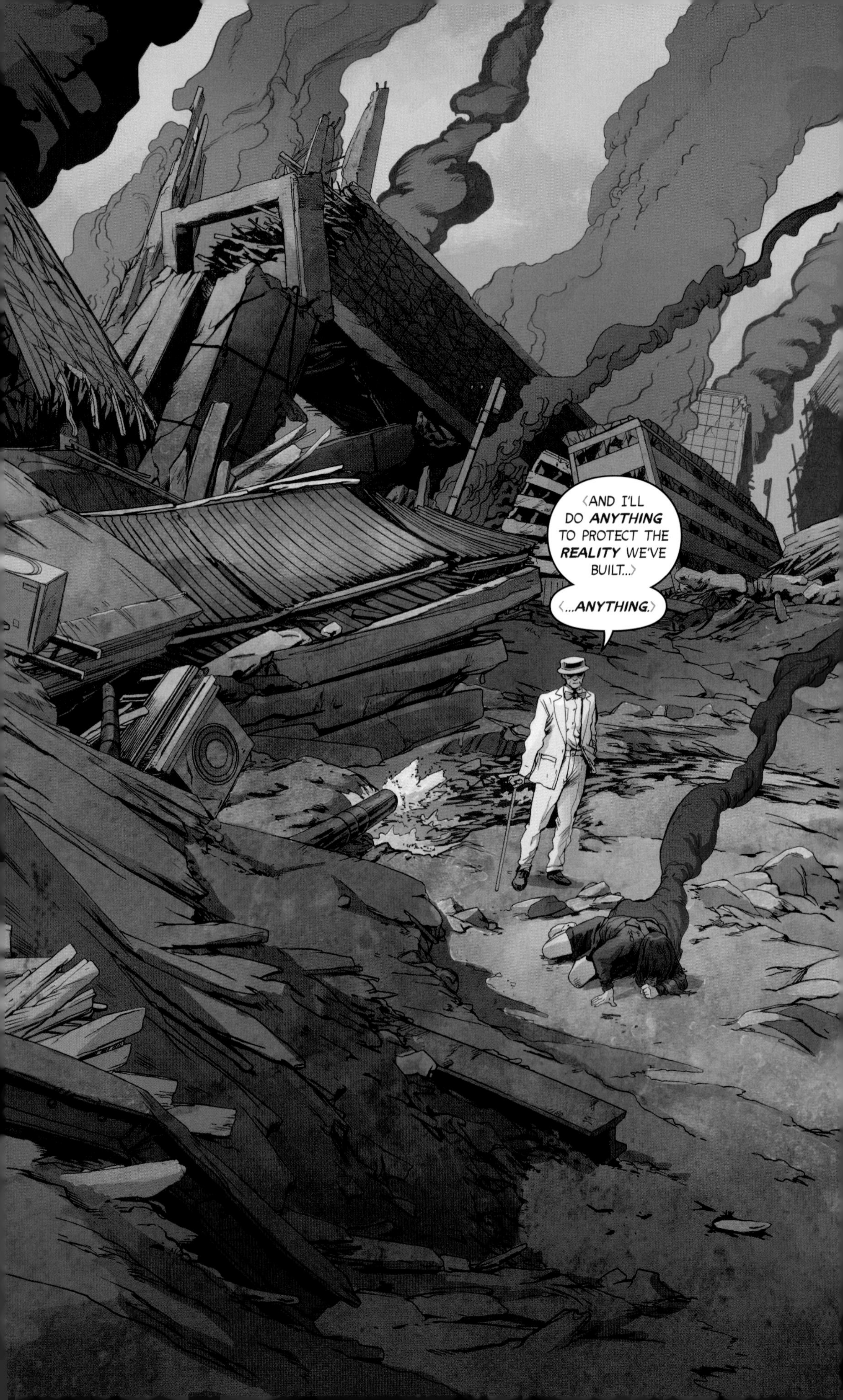
〈AND I'LL DO **ANYTHING** TO PROTECT THE **REALITY** WE'VE BUILT...〉
〈...**ANYTHING.**〉

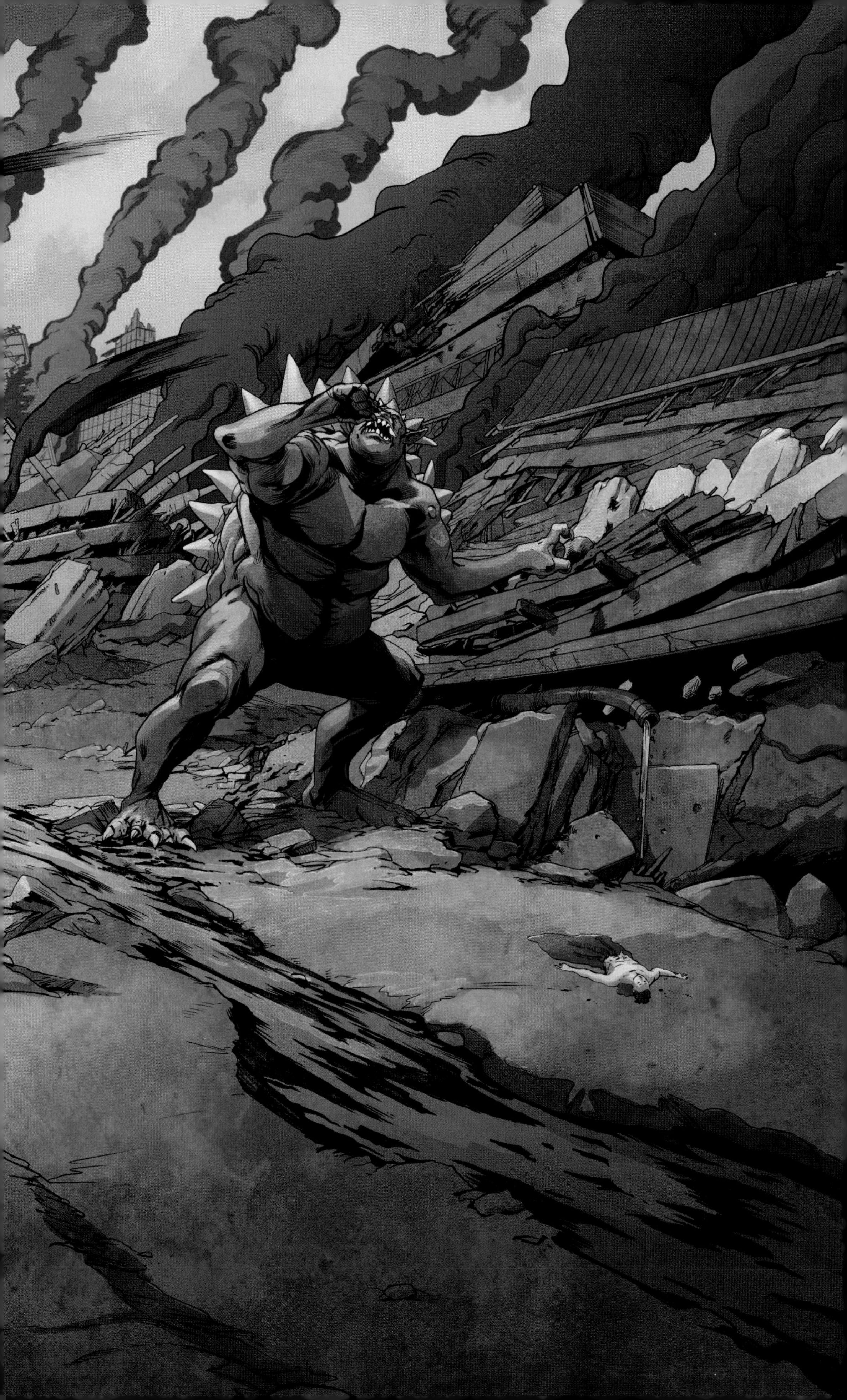

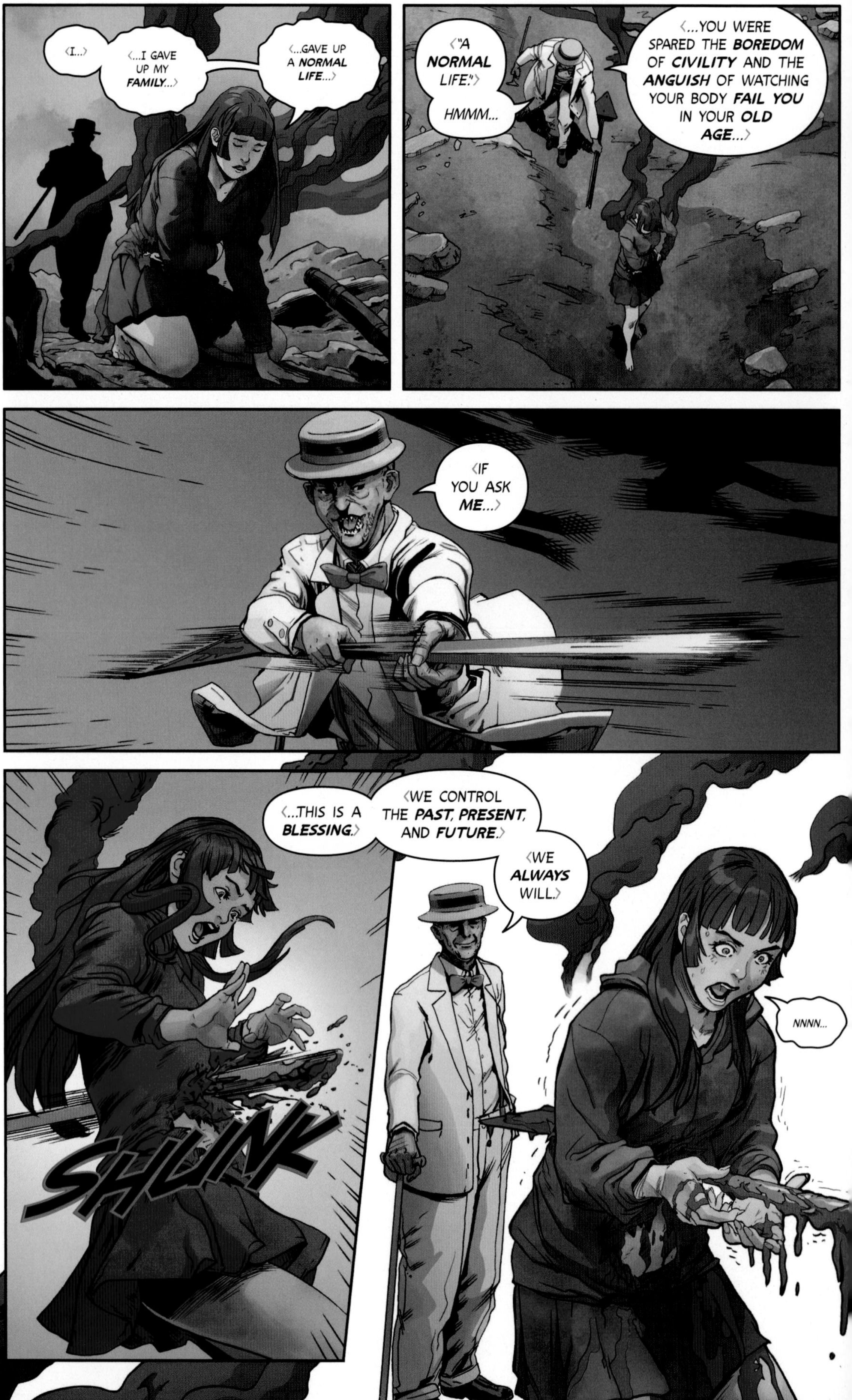
‹I...›
‹...I GAVE UP MY FAMILY...›
‹...GAVE UP A NORMAL LIFE...›
‹"A NORMAL LIFE."›
HMMM...
‹...YOU WERE SPARED THE BOREDOM OF CIVILITY AND THE ANGUISH OF WATCHING YOUR BODY FAIL YOU IN YOUR OLD AGE...›
‹IF YOU ASK ME...›
‹...THIS IS A BLESSING.›
‹WE CONTROL THE PAST, PRESENT, AND FUTURE.›
‹WE ALWAYS WILL.›
SHUNK
NNNN...

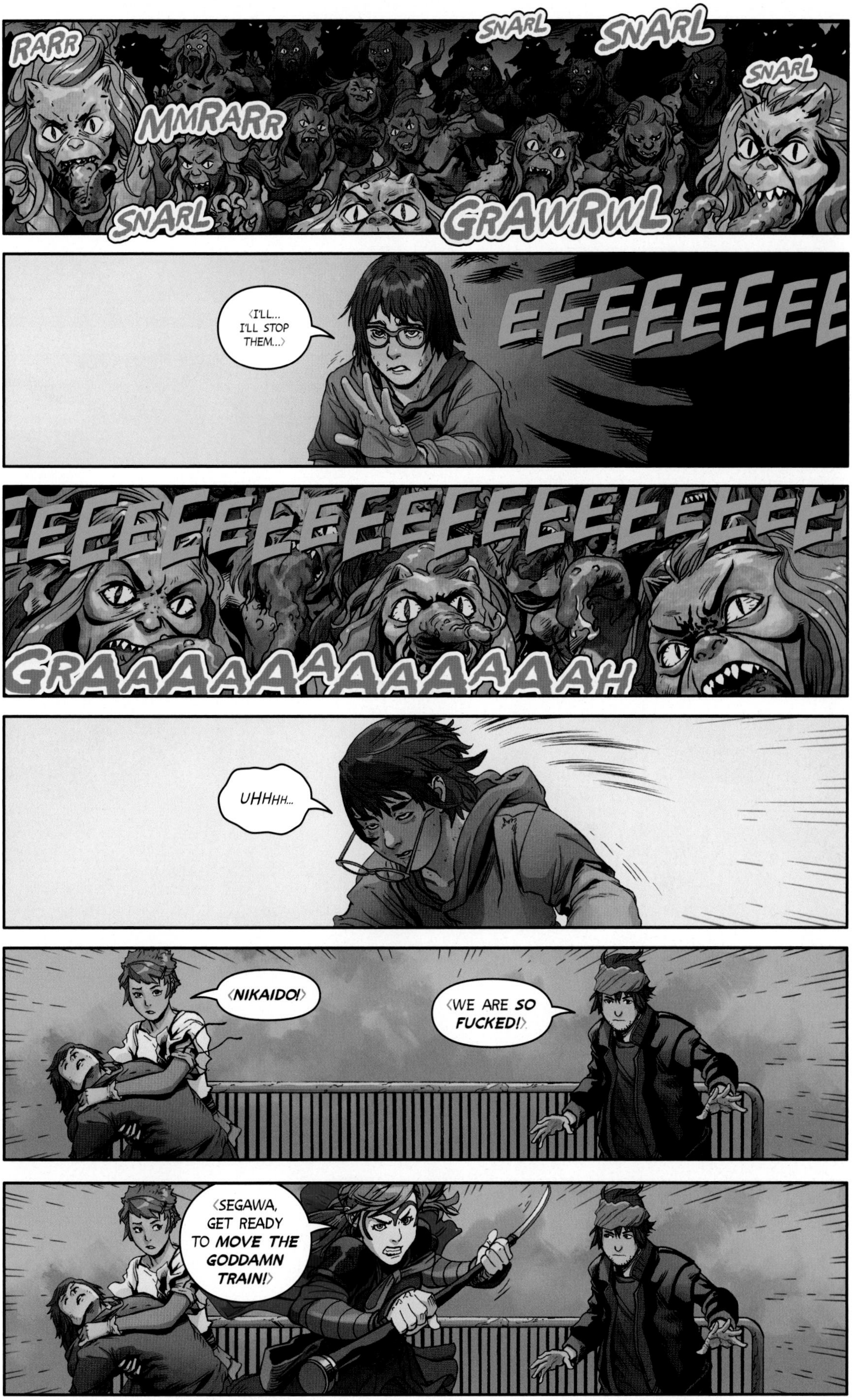
RARR
MMRARR
SNARL
SNARL
SNARL
SNARL
GRAWRWL
〈I'LL... I'LL STOP THEM...〉
EEEEEEEE
EEEEEEEEEEEEEEEEEE
GRAAAAAAAAAAAAH
UHHHH...
〈NIKAIDO!〉
〈WE ARE SO FUCKED!〉
〈SEGAWA, GET READY TO MOVE THE GODDAMN TRAIN!〉

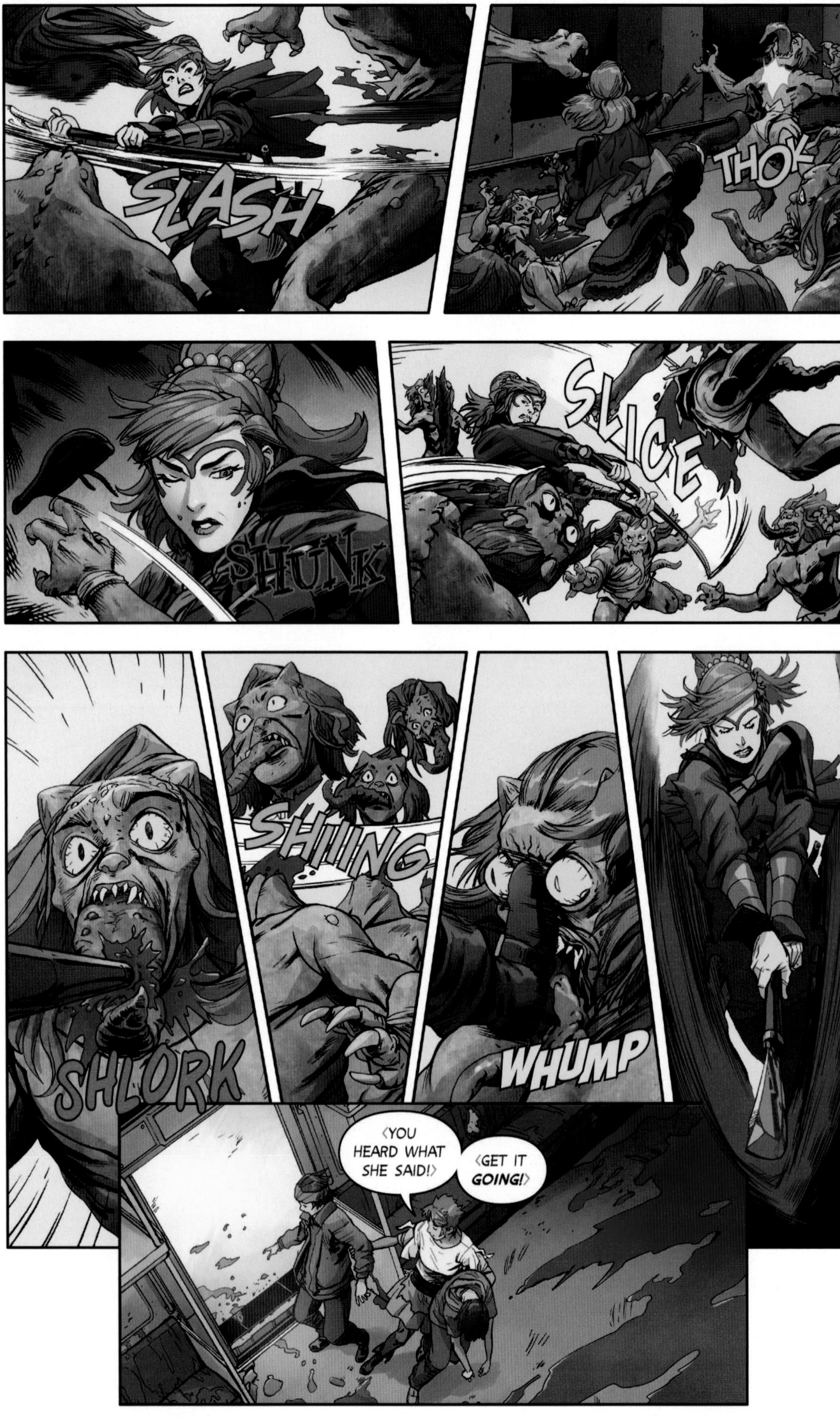
SLASH
THOK
SHUNK
SLICE
SHLORK
SHIIING
WHUMP
‹YOU HEARD WHAT SHE SAID!›
‹GET IT GOING!›

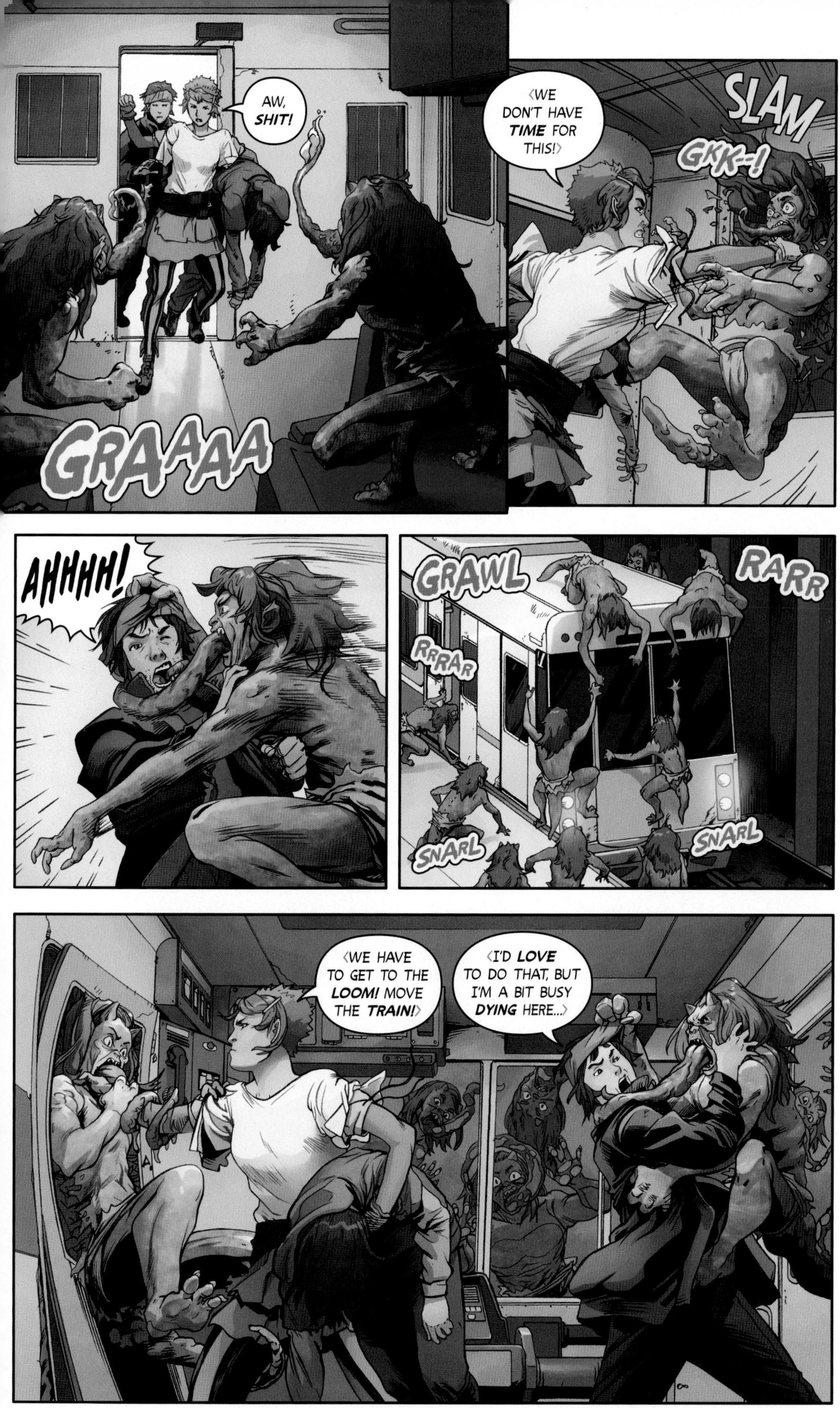

AW, SHIT!
GRAAAA
‹WE DON'T HAVE TIME FOR THIS!›
SLAM
GKK--!
AHHHH!
GRAWL
RARR
RRRAR
SNARL
SNARL
‹WE HAVE TO GET TO THE LOOM! MOVE THE TRAIN!›
‹I'D LOVE TO DO THAT, BUT I'M A BIT BUSY DYING HERE...›

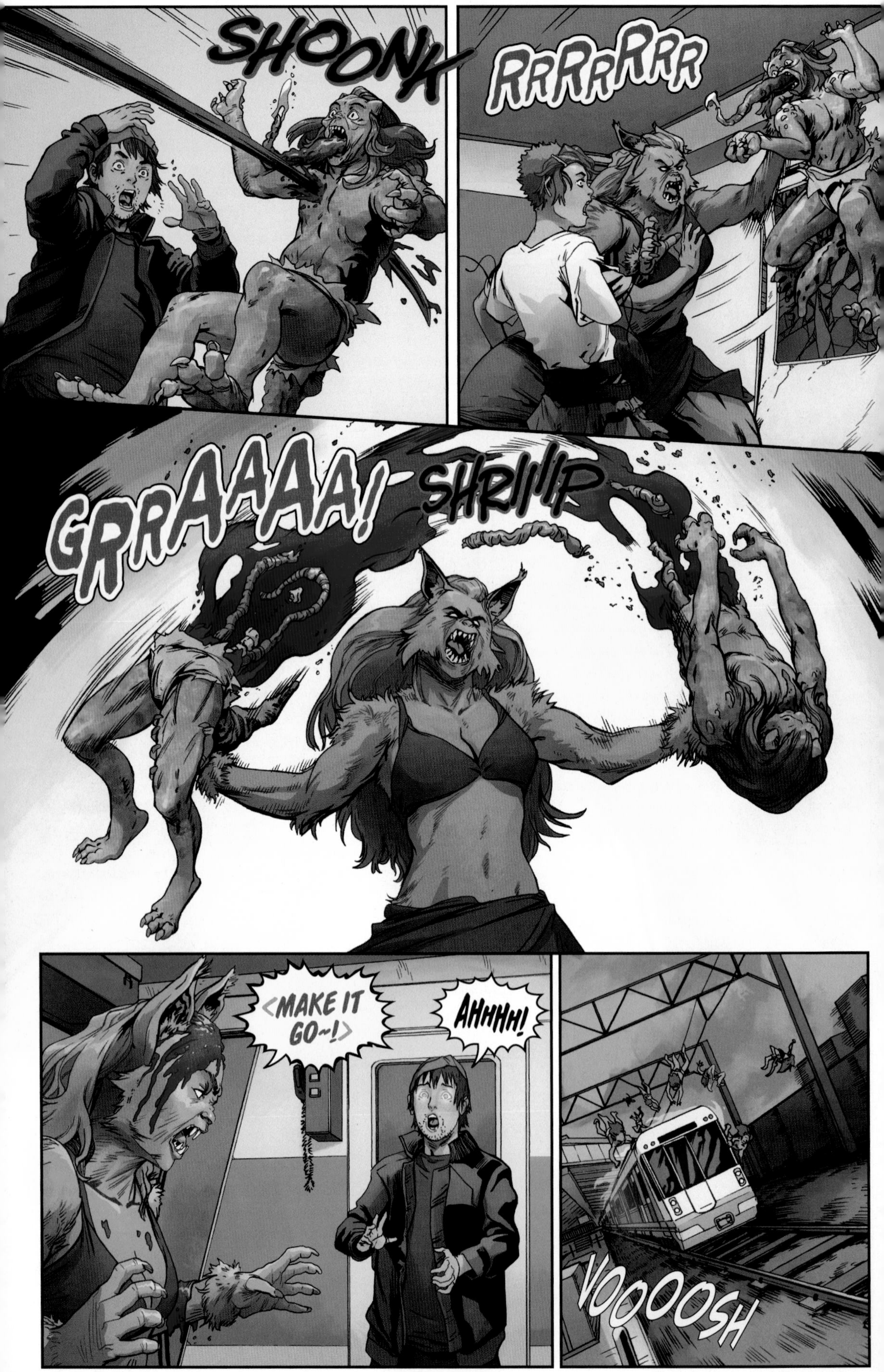
SHOONK
RRRRRRR
GRRAAAA!
SHRIIIP
<MAKE IT GO~!>
AHHHH!
VOOOOSH

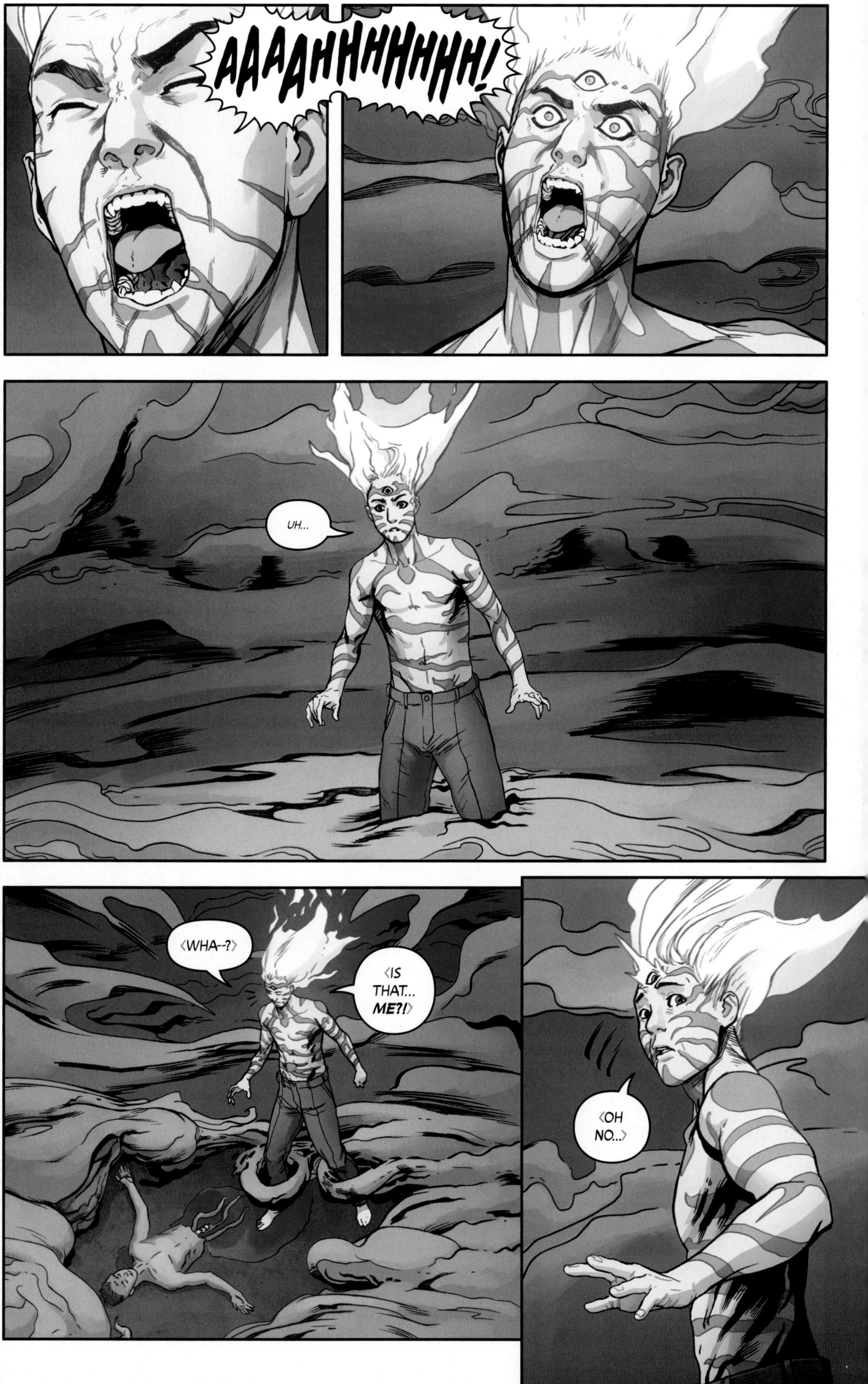
AAAAHHHHHHH!
UH...
‹WHA--?›
‹IS THAT... ME?!›
‹OH NO...›

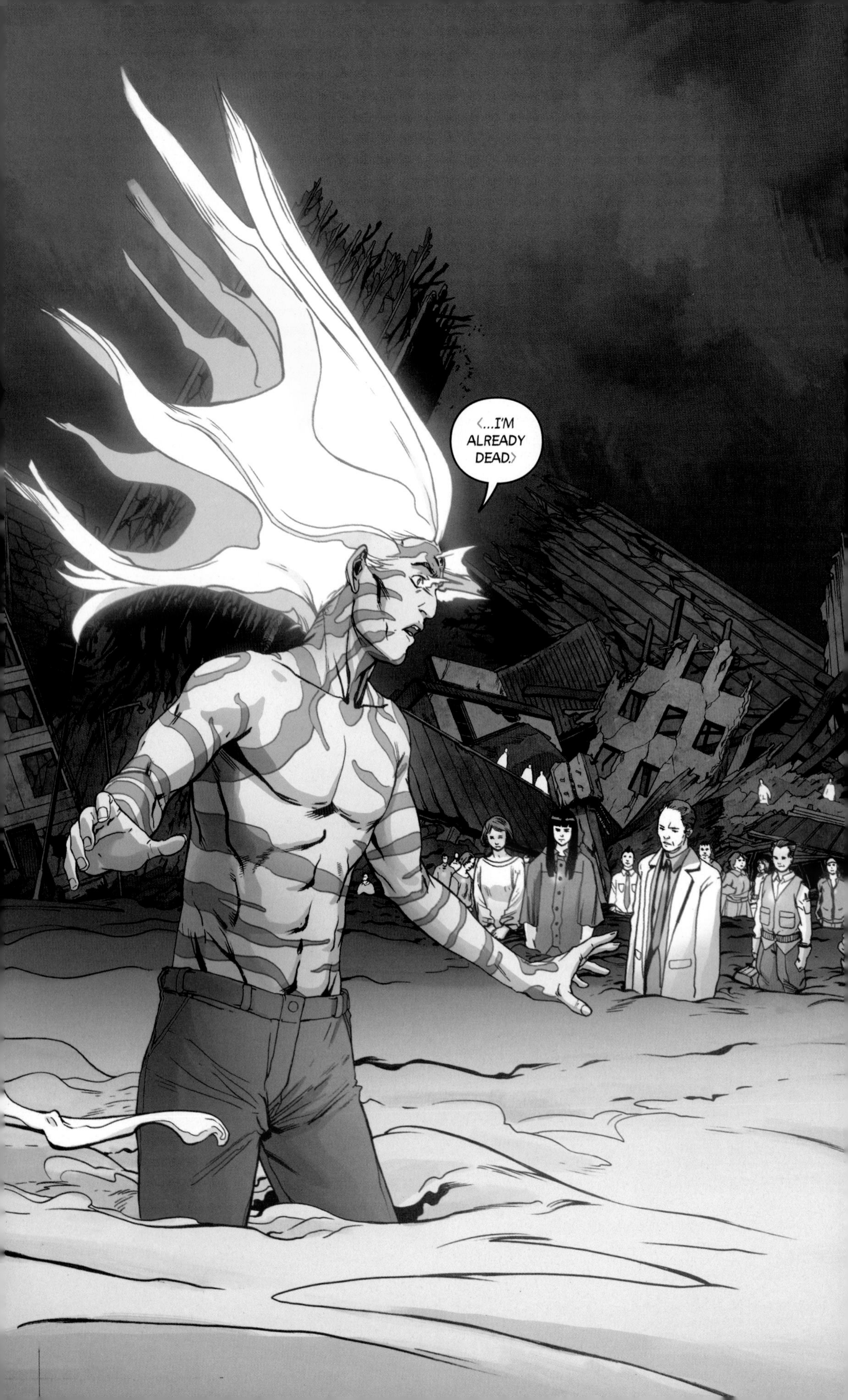
<...I'M ALREADY DEAD.>

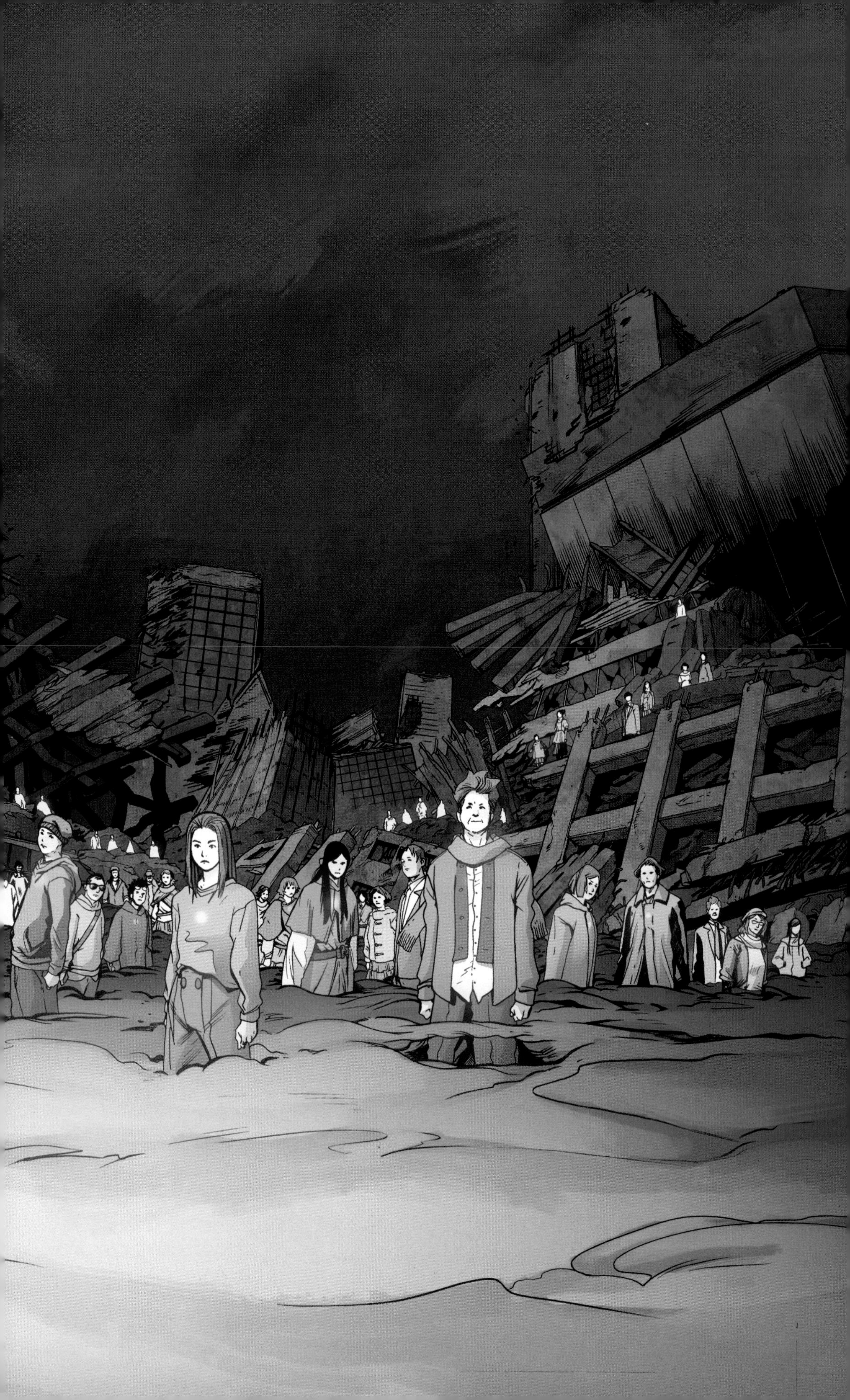

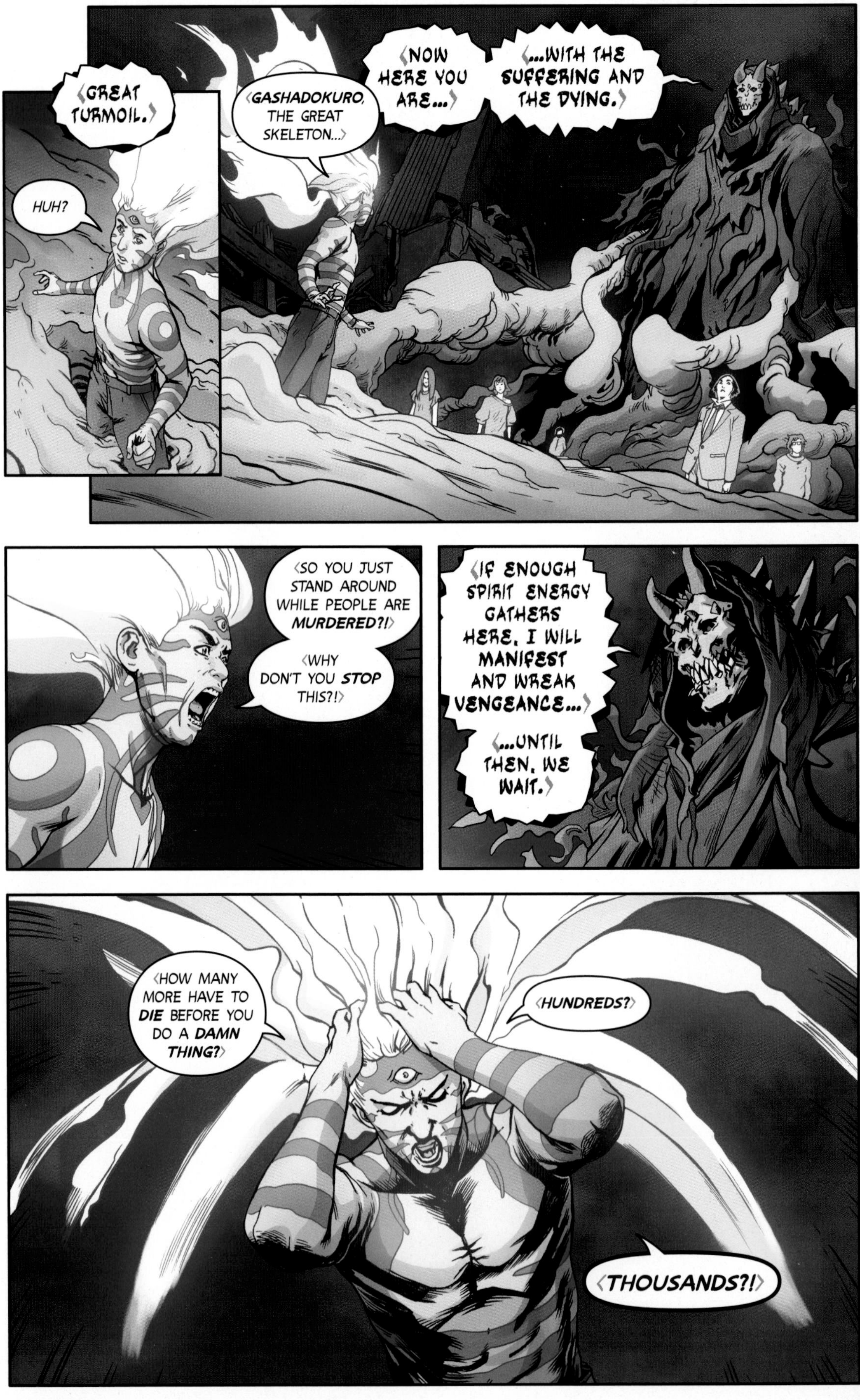

⟨GREAT TURMOIL.⟩
HUH?
⟨GASHADOKURO, THE GREAT SKELETON...⟩
⟨NOW HERE YOU ARE...⟩
⟨...WITH THE SUFFERING AND THE DYING.⟩
⟨SO YOU JUST STAND AROUND WHILE PEOPLE ARE MURDERED?!⟩
⟨WHY DON'T YOU STOP THIS?!⟩
⟨IF ENOUGH SPIRIT ENERGY GATHERS HERE, I WILL MANIFEST AND WREAK VENGEANCE...⟩
⟨...UNTIL THEN, WE WAIT.⟩
⟨HOW MANY MORE HAVE TO DIE BEFORE YOU DO A DAMN THING?⟩
⟨HUNDREDS?⟩
⟨THOUSANDS?!⟩

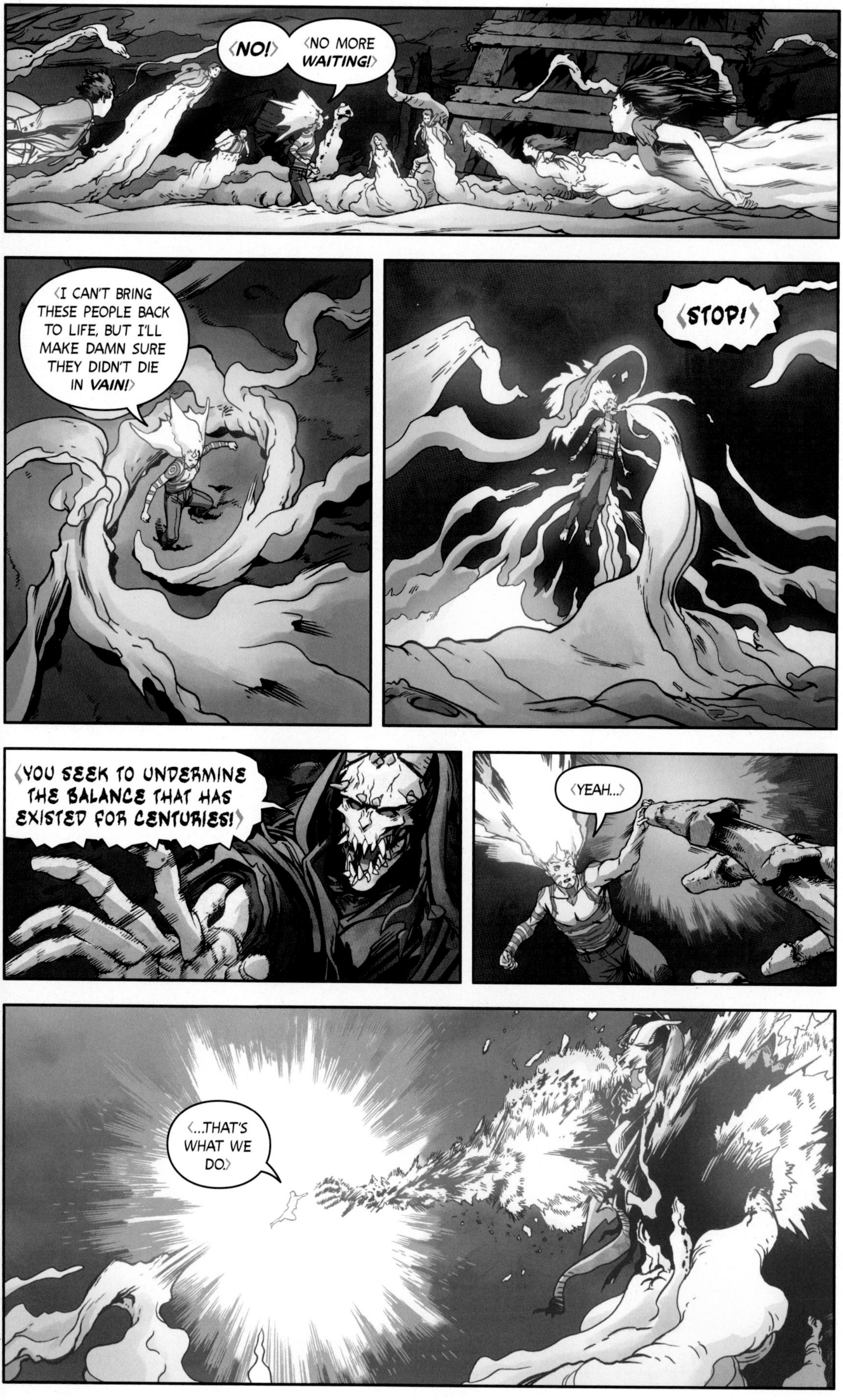
‹NO!›
‹NO MORE WAITING!›
‹I CAN'T BRING THESE PEOPLE BACK TO LIFE, BUT I'LL MAKE DAMN SURE THEY DIDN'T DIE IN VAIN!›
‹STOP!›
‹YOU SEEK TO UNDERMINE THE BALANCE THAT HAS EXISTED FOR CENTURIES!›
‹YEAH...›
‹...THAT'S WHAT WE DO.›

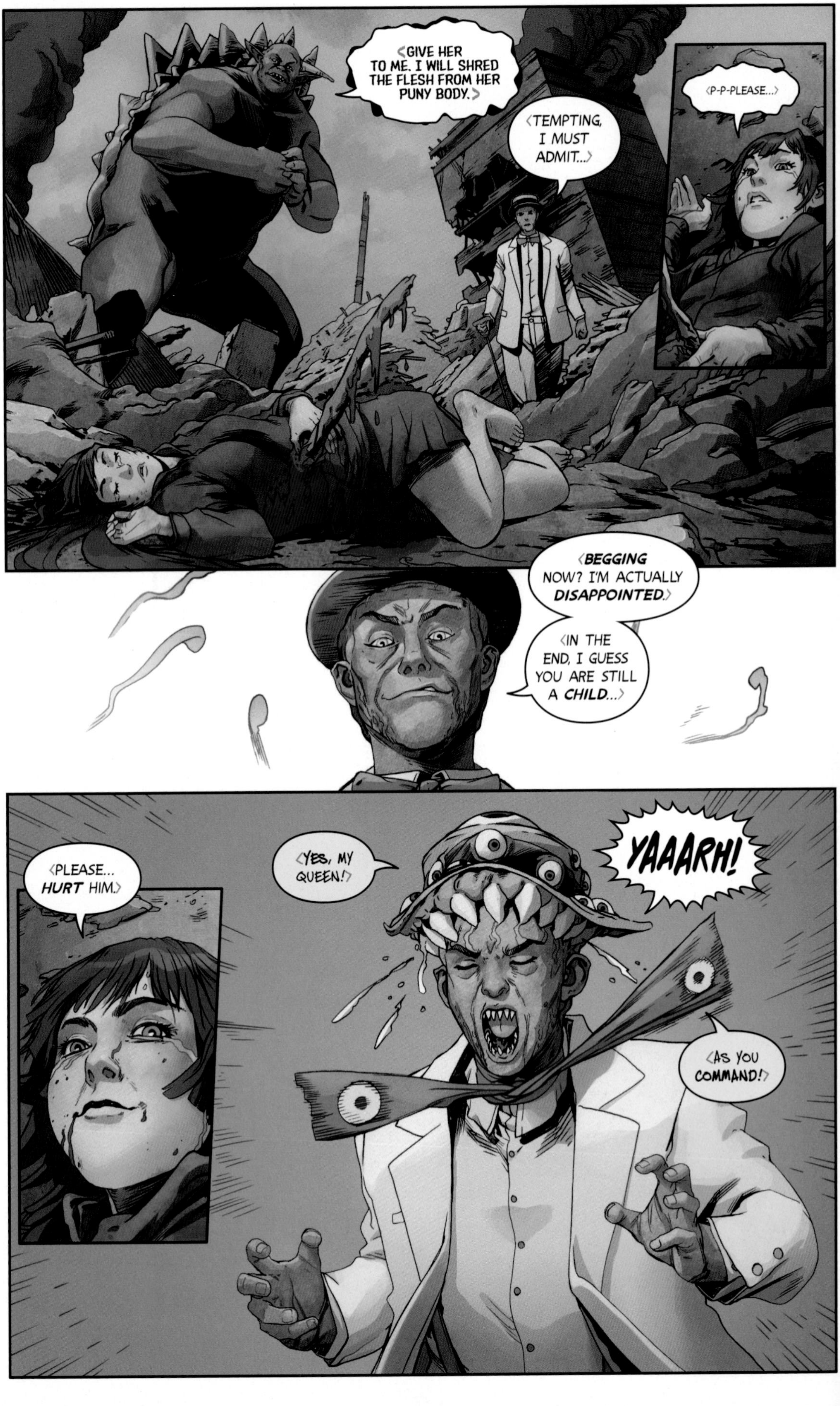
<GIVE HER TO ME. I WILL SHRED THE FLESH FROM HER PUNY BODY.>
<TEMPTING, I MUST ADMIT...>
<P-P-PLEASE...>
<BEGGING NOW? I'M ACTUALLY DISAPPOINTED.>
<IN THE END, I GUESS YOU ARE STILL A CHILD...>
<PLEASE... HURT HIM.>
<YES, MY QUEEN!>
YAAARH!
<AS YOU COMMAND!>

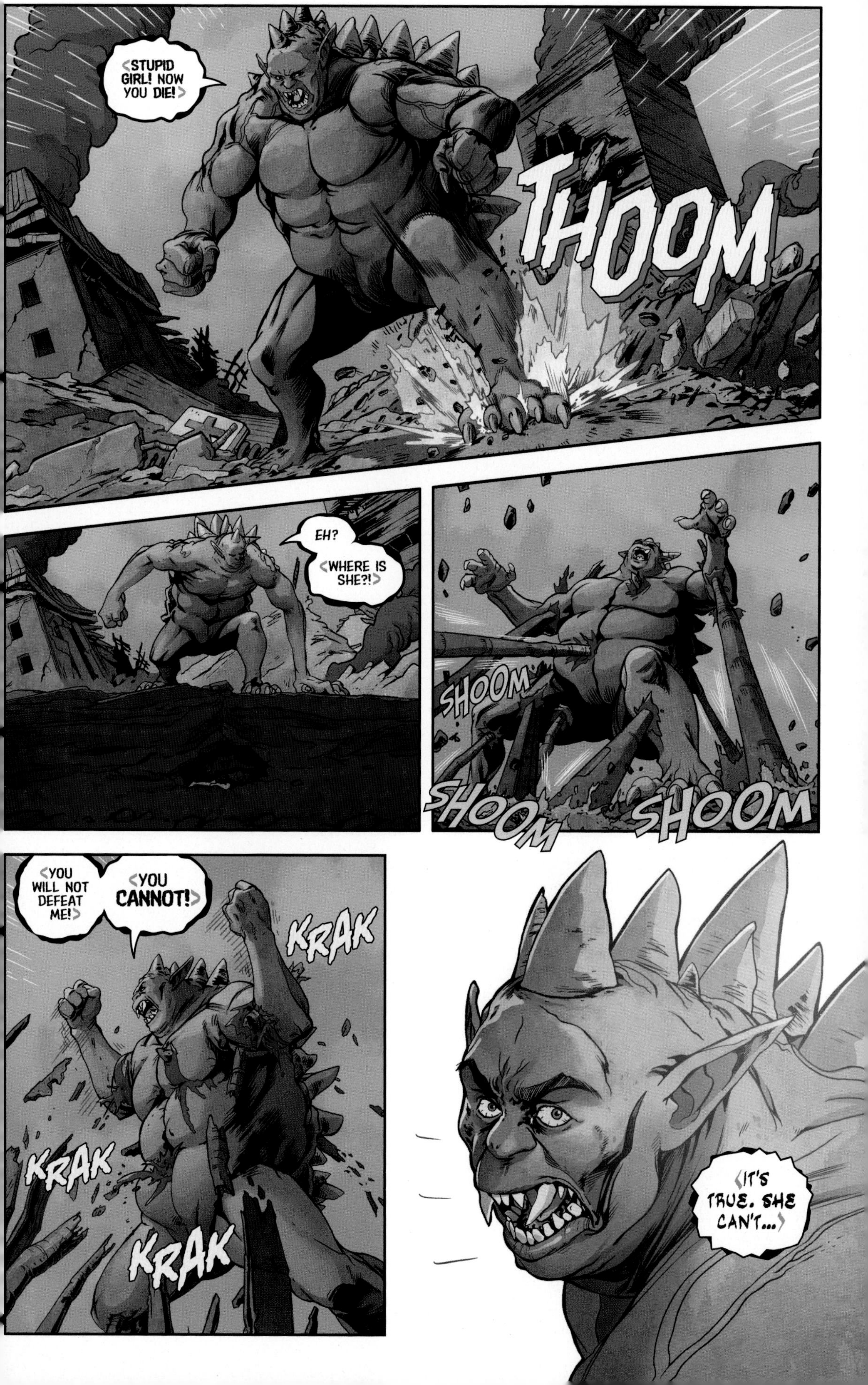
<STUPID GIRL! NOW YOU DIE!>
THOOM
EH?
<WHERE IS SHE?!>
SHOOM
SHOOM
SHOOM
<YOU WILL NOT DEFEAT ME!>
<YOU CANNOT!>
KRAK
KRAK
KRAK
<IT'S TRUE. SHE CAN'T...>

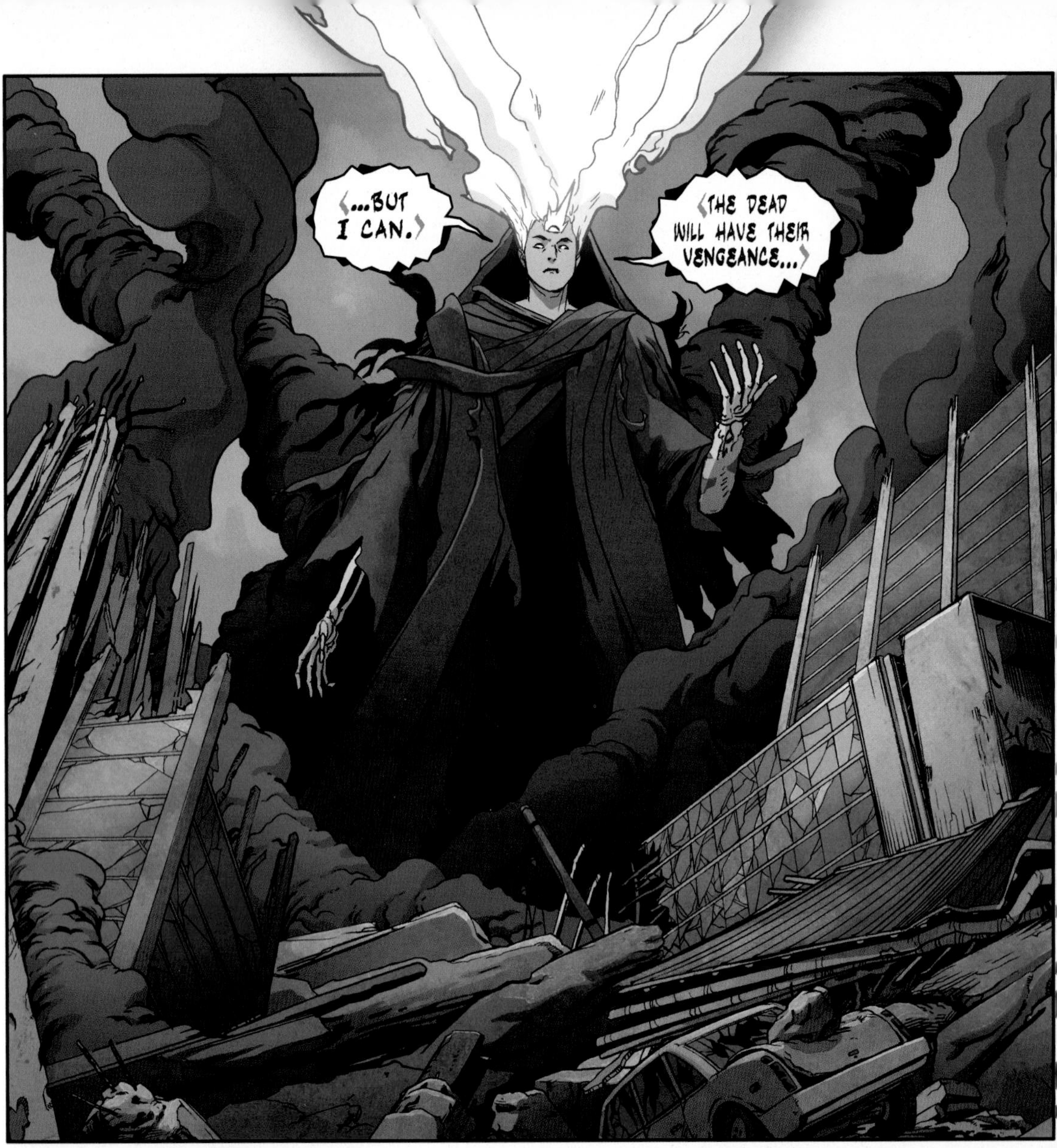
‹...BUT I CAN.›
‹THE DEAD WILL HAVE THEIR VENGEANCE...›

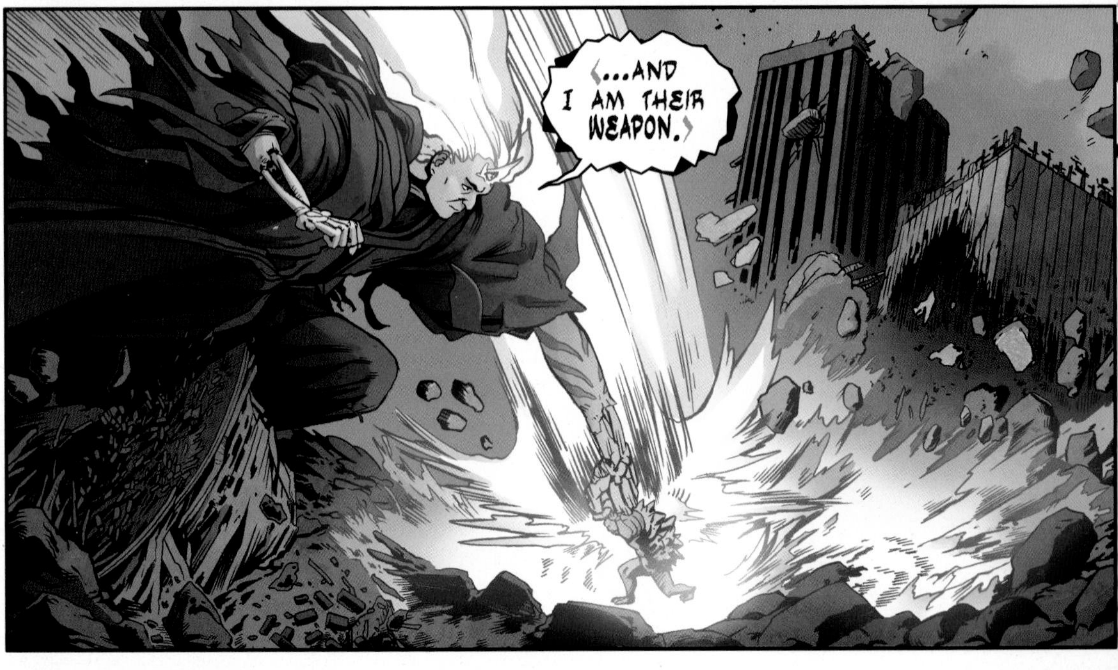
‹...AND I AM THEIR WEAPON.›

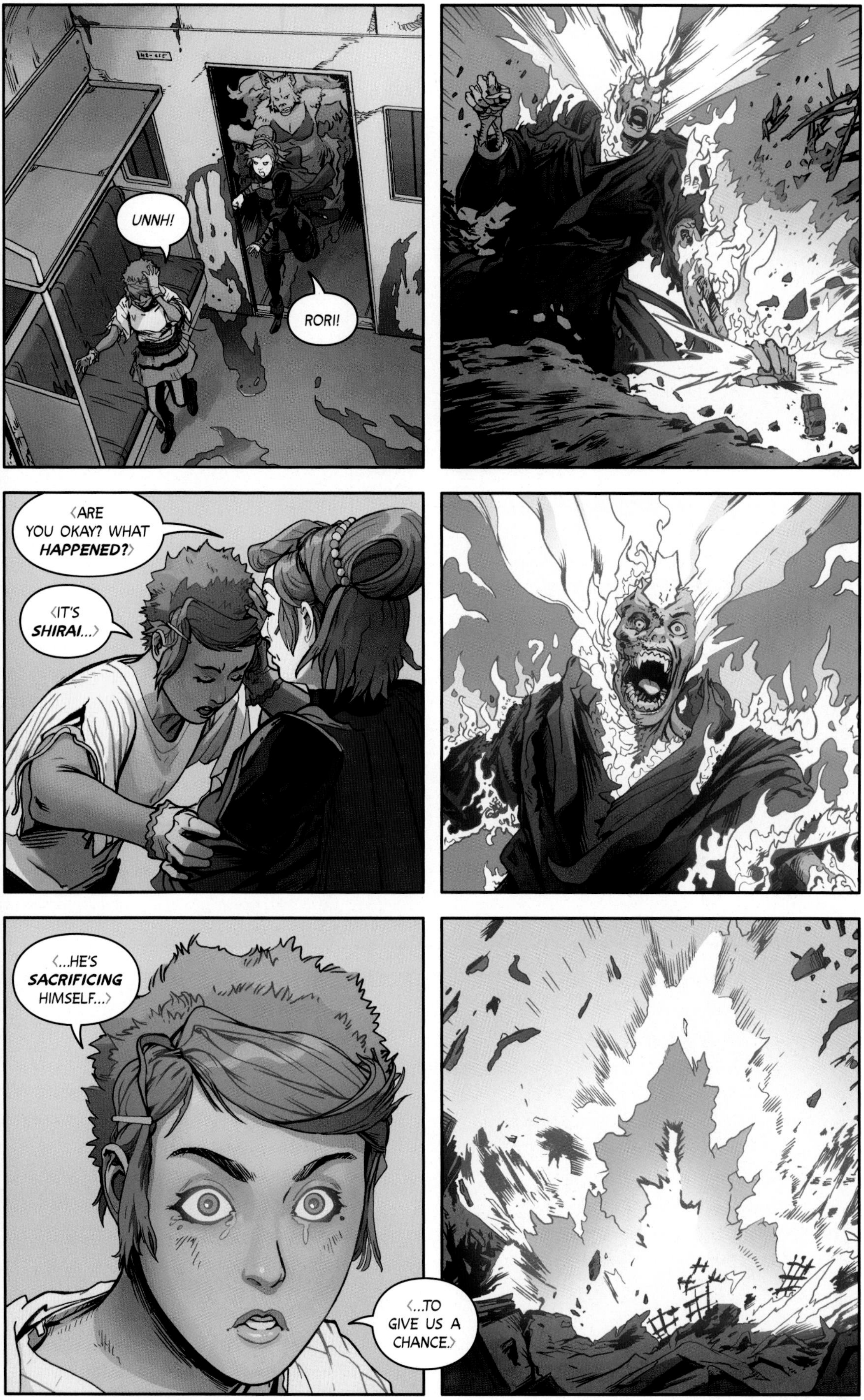
UNNH!
RORI!
‹ARE YOU OKAY? WHAT HAPPENED?›
‹IT'S SHIRAI...›
‹...HE'S SACRIFICING HIMSELF...›
‹...TO GIVE US A CHANCE.›

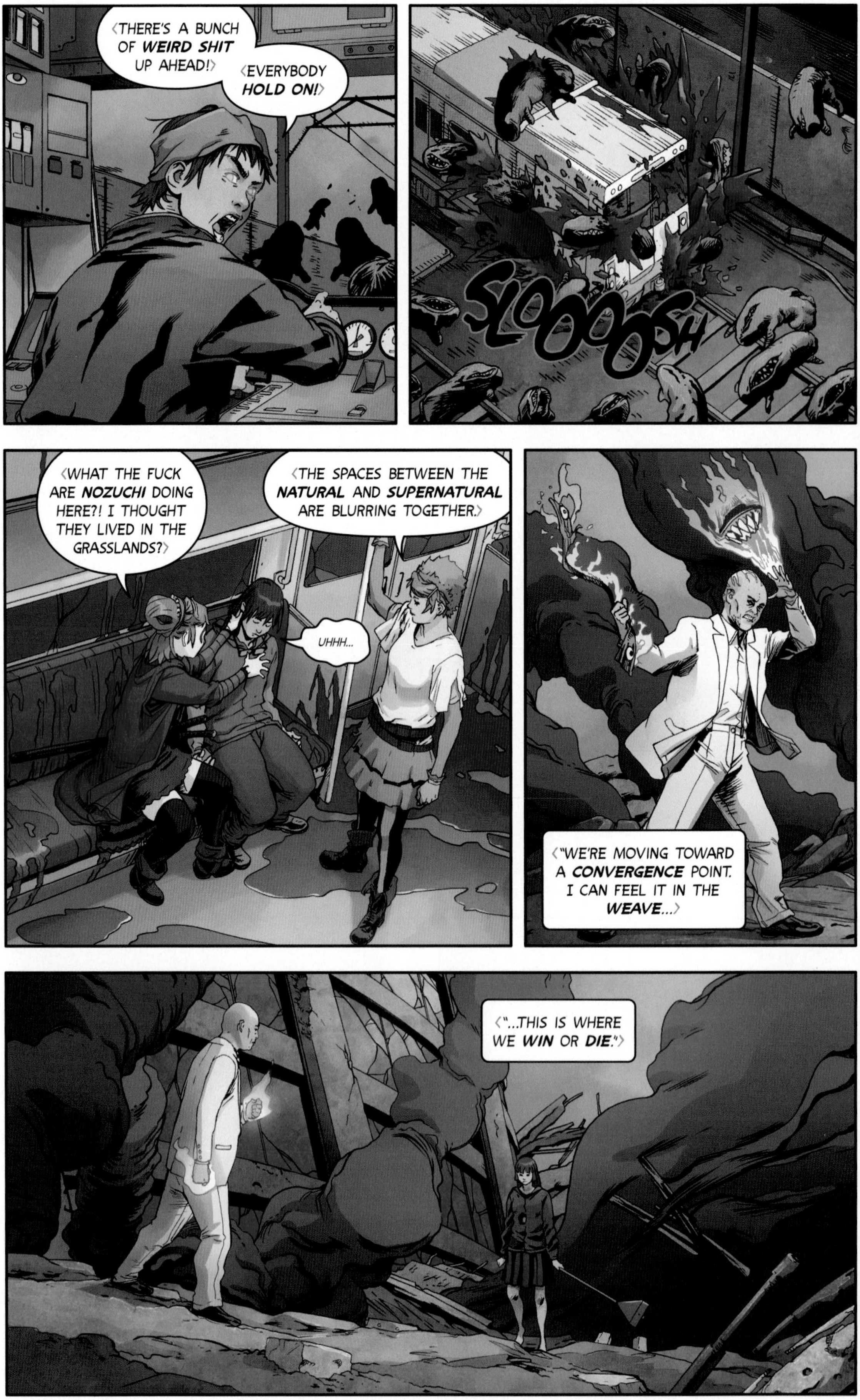

‹THERE'S A BUNCH OF WEIRD SHIT UP AHEAD!›
‹EVERYBODY HOLD ON!›
SLOOOOOSH
‹WHAT THE FUCK ARE NOZUCHI DOING HERE?! I THOUGHT THEY LIVED IN THE GRASSLANDS?›
‹THE SPACES BETWEEN THE NATURAL AND SUPERNATURAL ARE BLURRING TOGETHER.›
UHHH...
‹"WE'RE MOVING TOWARD A CONVERGENCE POINT. I CAN FEEL IT IN THE WEAVE...›
‹"...THIS IS WHERE WE WIN OR DIE."›

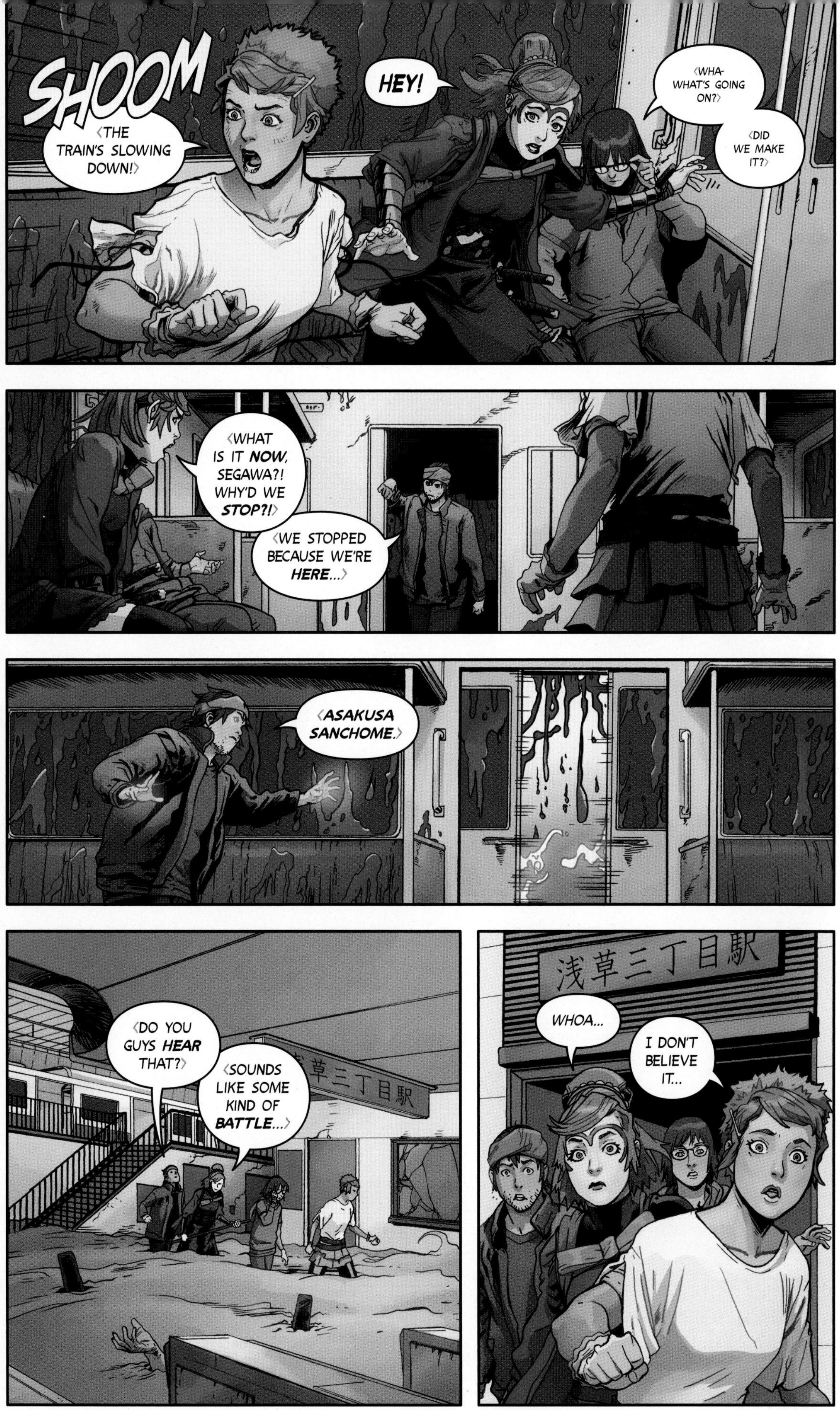
SHOOM
‹THE TRAIN'S SLOWING DOWN!›
HEY!
‹WHA- WHAT'S GOING ON?›
‹DID WE MAKE IT?›
‹WHAT IS IT NOW, SEGAWA?! WHY'D WE STOP?!›
‹WE STOPPED BECAUSE WE'RE HERE...›
‹ASAKUSA SANCHOME.›
‹DO YOU GUYS HEAR THAT?›
‹SOUNDS LIKE SOME KIND OF BATTLE...›
浅草三丁目駅
WHOA...
I DON'T BELIEVE IT...

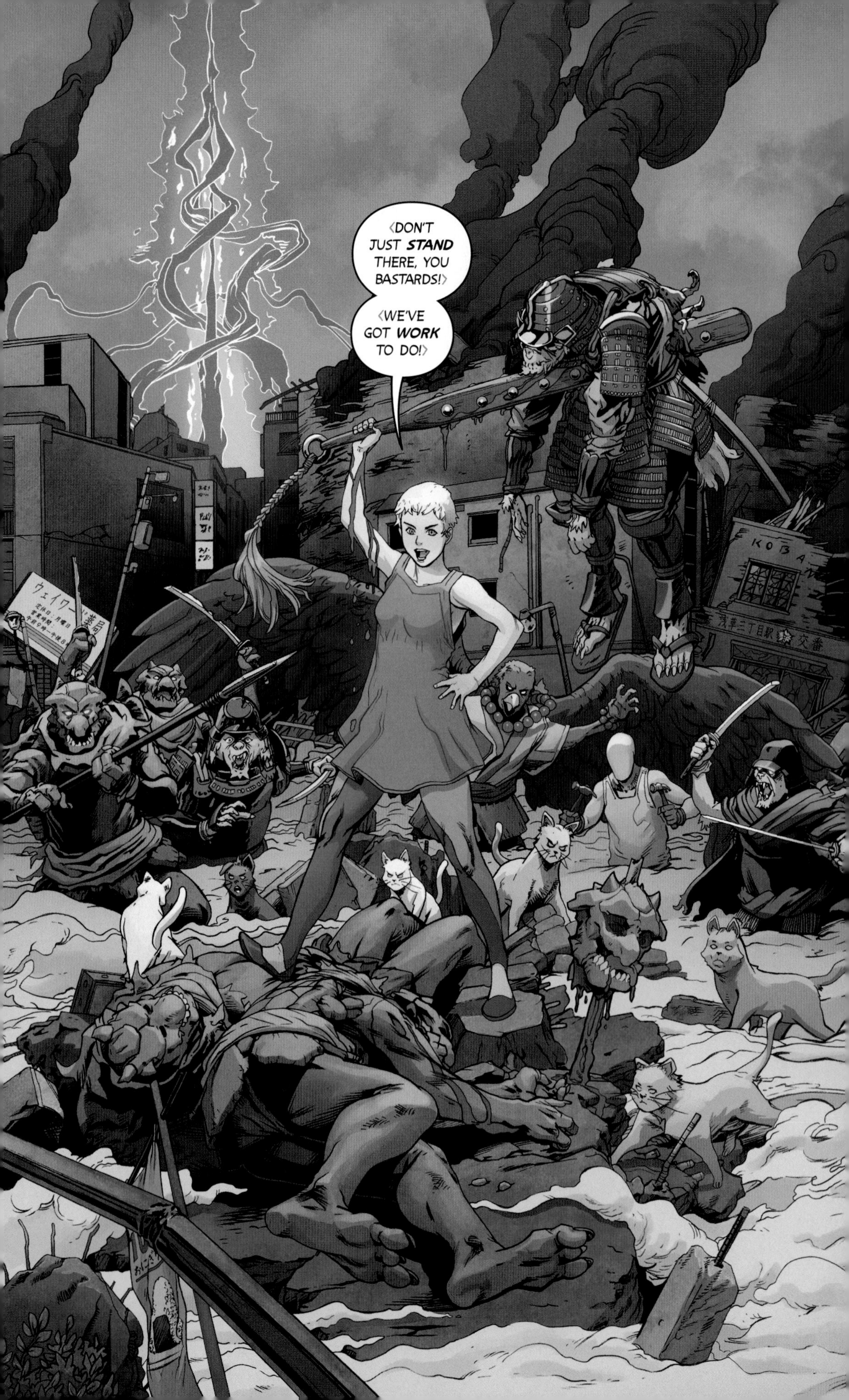
‹DON'T JUST **STAND** THERE, YOU BASTARDS!›
‹WE'VE GOT **WORK** TO DO!›
KOBA
浅草三丁目駅
交番

Chapter Thirty

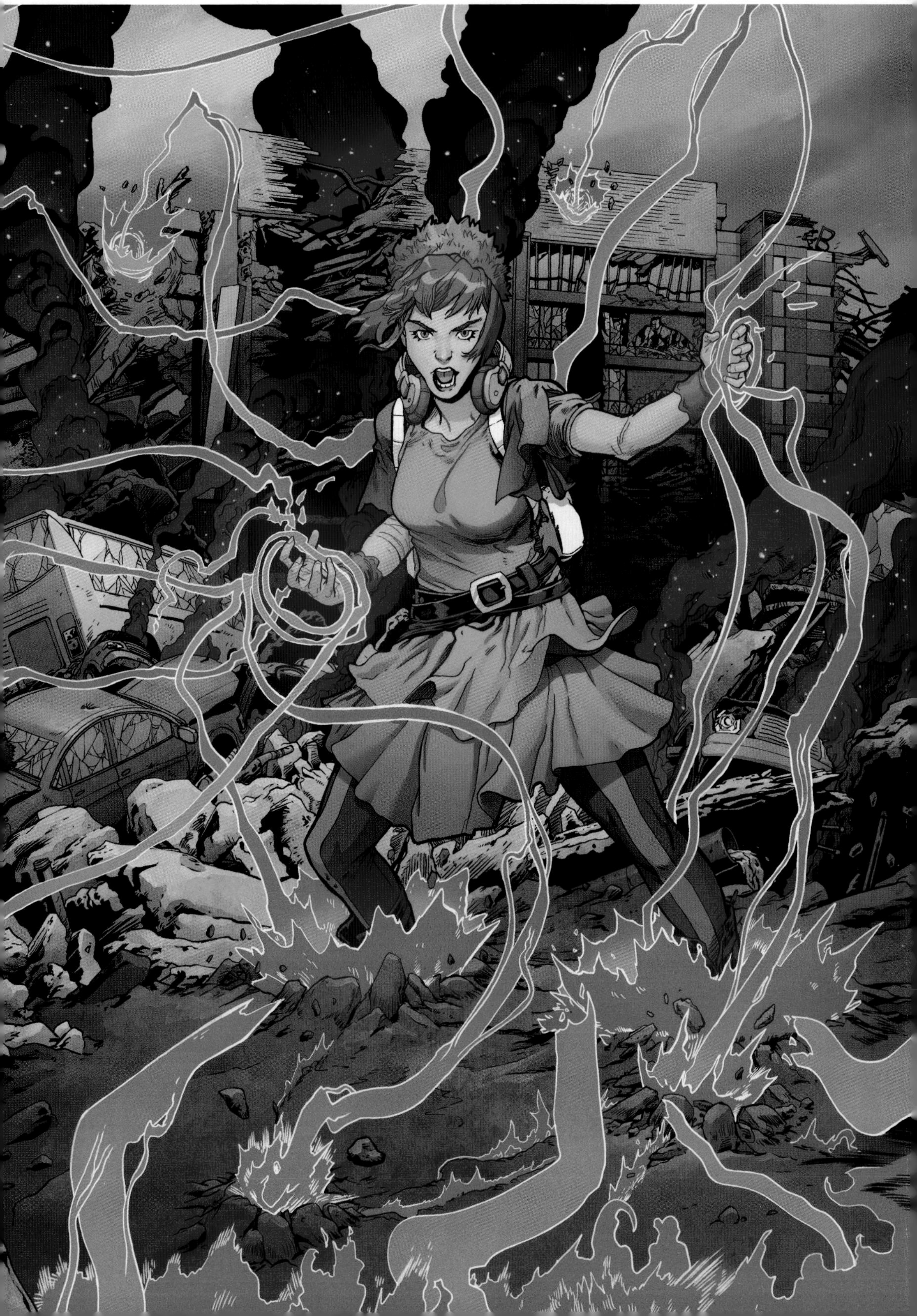

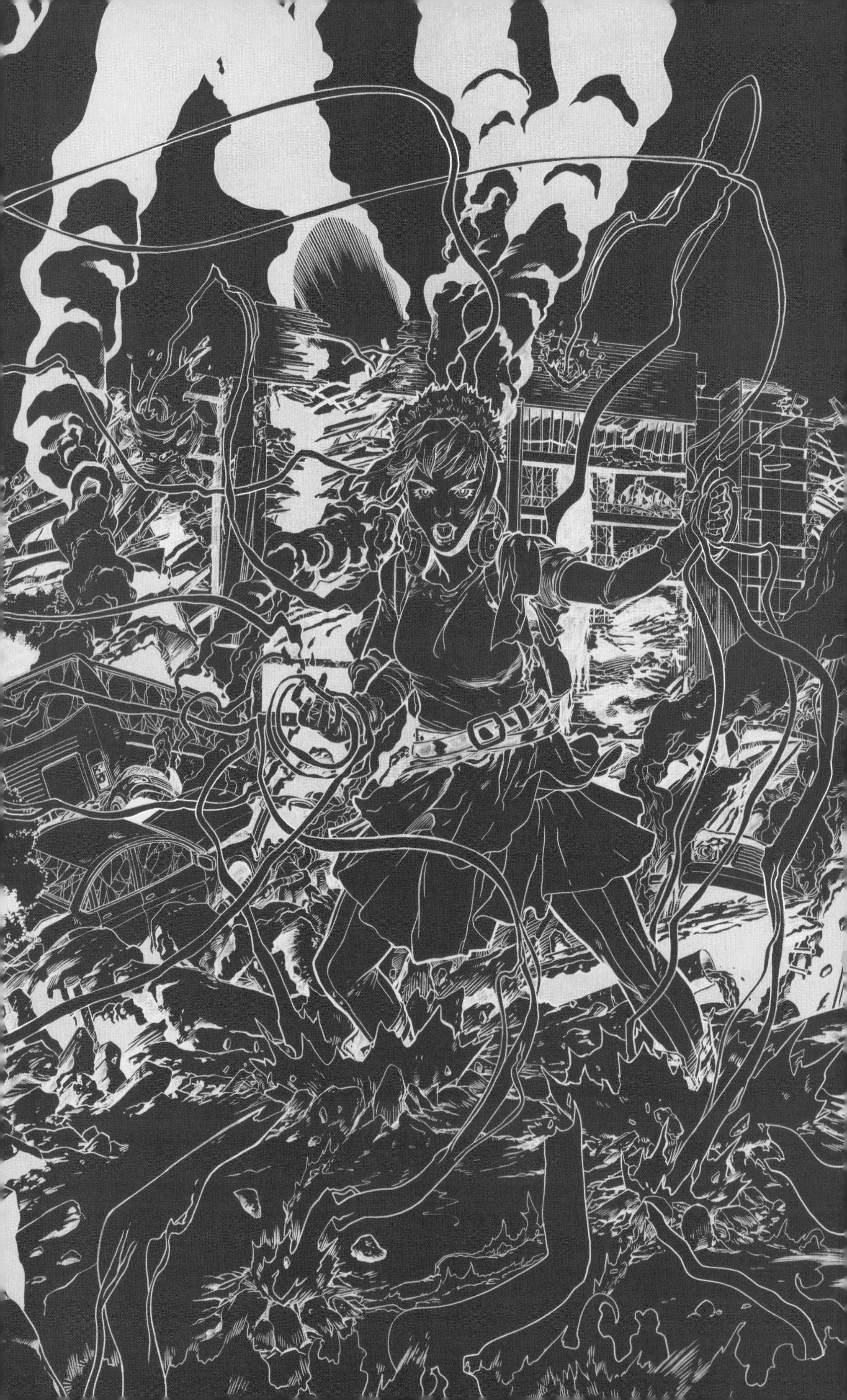

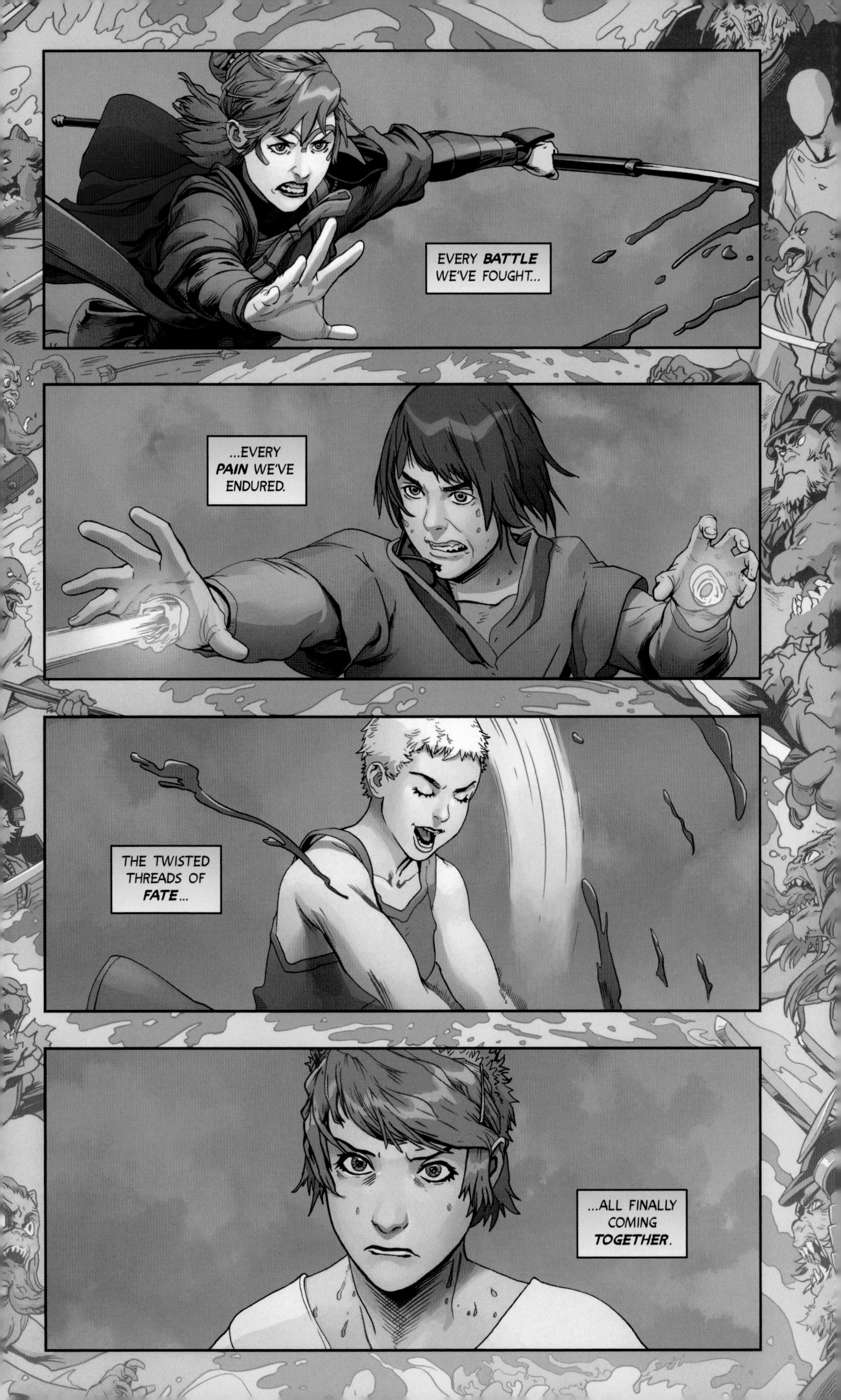
EVERY BATTLE WE'VE FOUGHT...
...EVERY PAIN WE'VE ENDURED.
THE TWISTED THREADS OF FATE...
...ALL FINALLY COMING TOGETHER.

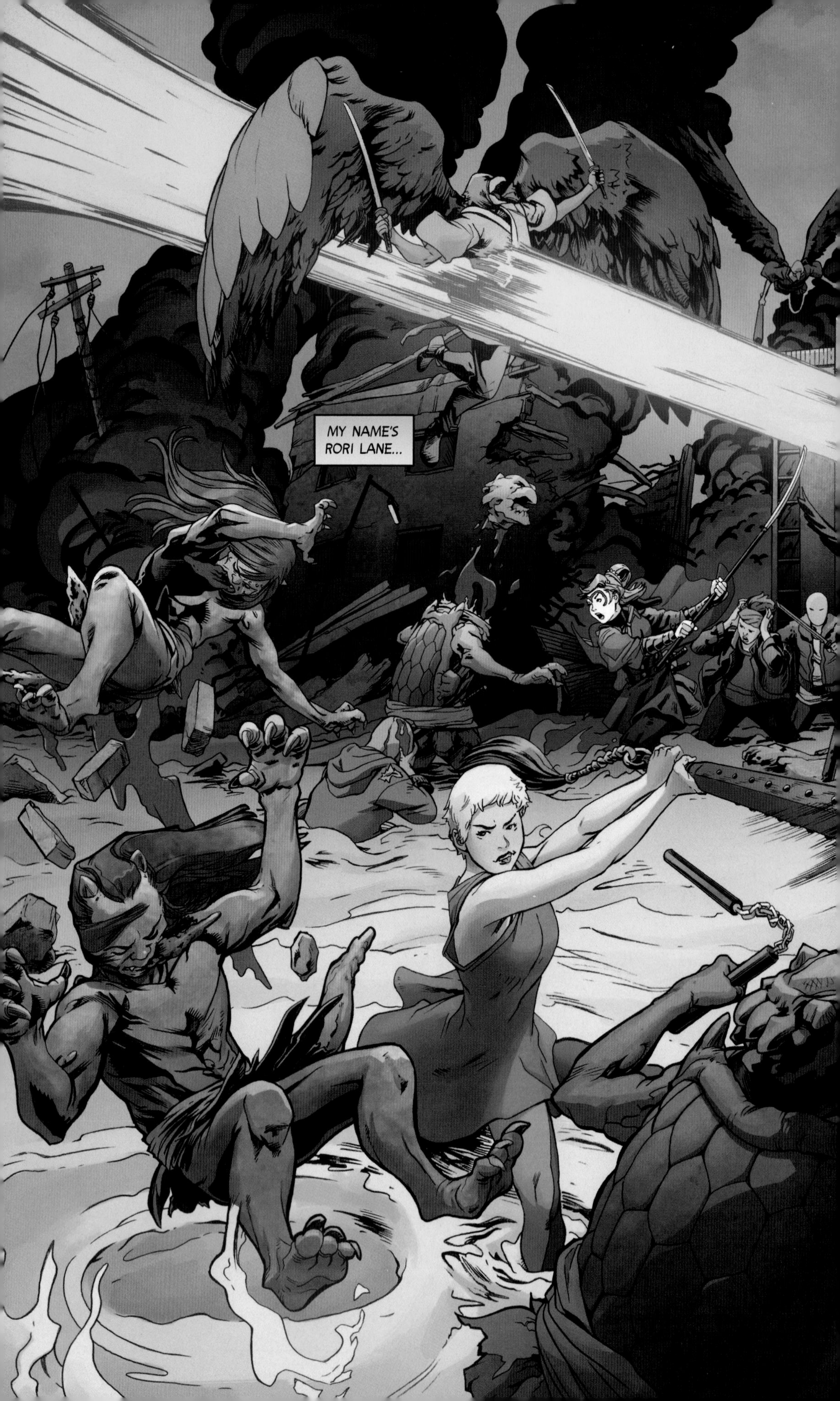
MY NAME'S
RORI LANE...

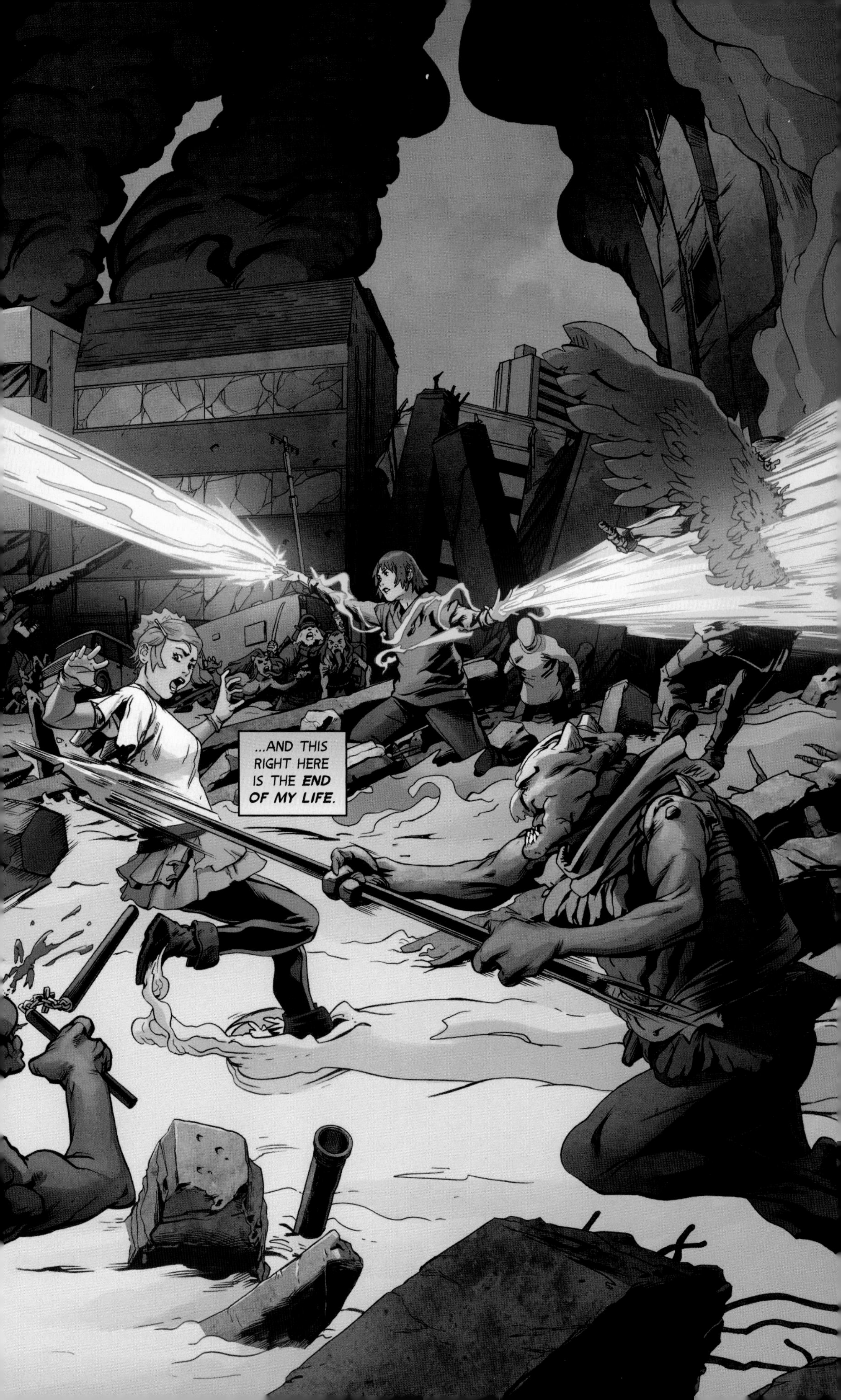
...AND THIS RIGHT HERE IS THE END OF MY LIFE.

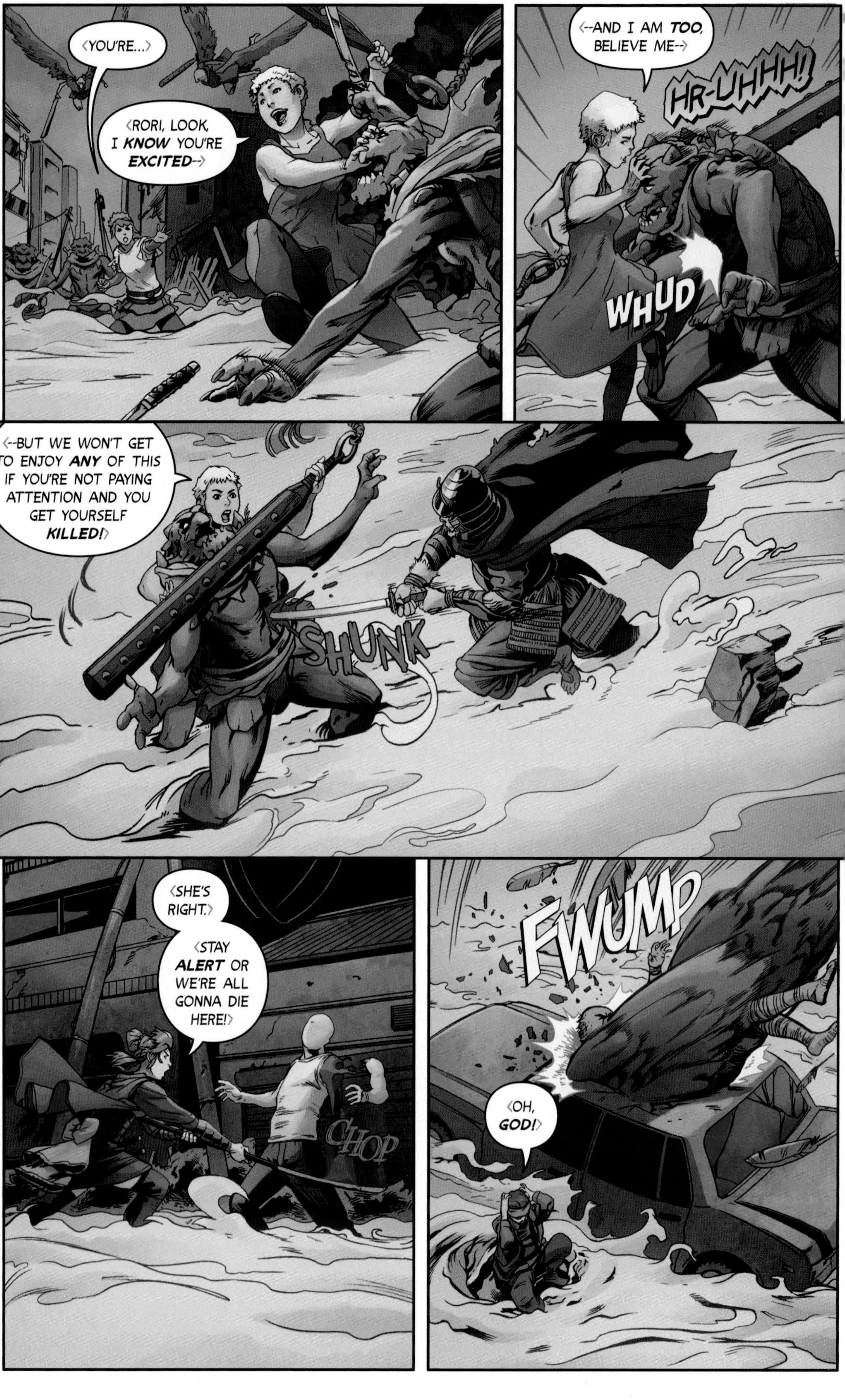

‹YOU'RE...›
‹RORI, LOOK, I KNOW YOU'RE EXCITED--›
‹--AND I AM TOO, BELIEVE ME--›
HR-UHHH!
WHUD
‹--BUT WE WON'T GET TO ENJOY ANY OF THIS IF YOU'RE NOT PAYING ATTENTION AND YOU GET YOURSELF KILLED!›
SHUNK
‹SHE'S RIGHT.›
‹STAY ALERT OR WE'RE ALL GONNA DIE HERE!›
CHOP
FWUMP
‹OH, GOD!›

SHUNK

THE LOOM.

‹WE'VE LOST ANY HOPE OF **SURPRISE**, SO NOW IT'S A FUCKING **BLOODBATH** ALL THE WAY TO THE **LOOM!**›

A NEXUS **POINT OF CONTROL** BUILT BY THE YOKAI TO MANIPULATE STRINGS OF DESTINY THAT DEFINE THE **SUPERNATURAL WORLD.**

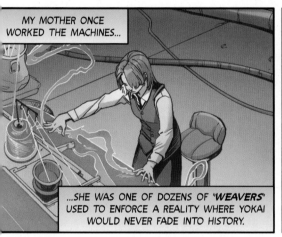

MY MOTHER ONCE WORKED THE MACHINES...

...SHE WAS ONE OF DOZENS OF "**WEAVERS**" USED TO ENFORCE A REALITY WHERE YOKAI WOULD NEVER FADE INTO HISTORY.

SEGAWA AND I HAVE TO REACH THE LOOM AND SHUT IT DOWN.

IT'S THE ONLY WAY TO BREAK THEIR HOLD ON OUR LIVES.

‹FOCUS!›

KER-CHUNK

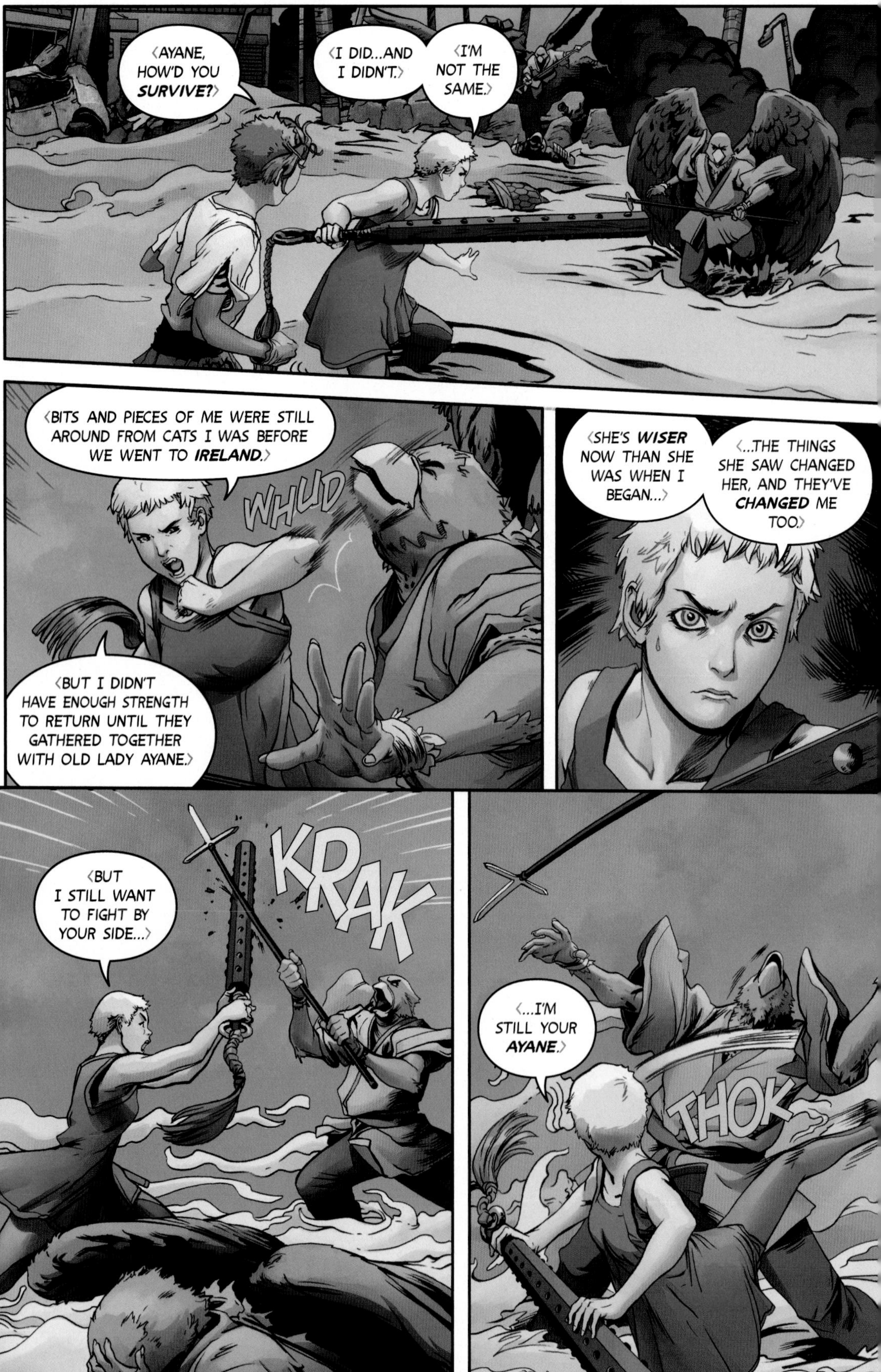
<AYANE, HOW'D YOU *SURVIVE?*>
<I DID...AND I DIDN'T.>
<I'M NOT THE SAME.>
<BITS AND PIECES OF ME WERE STILL AROUND FROM CATS I WAS BEFORE WE WENT TO *IRELAND.*>
WHUD
<BUT I DIDN'T HAVE ENOUGH STRENGTH TO RETURN UNTIL THEY GATHERED TOGETHER WITH OLD LADY AYANE.>
<SHE'S *WISER* NOW THAN SHE WAS WHEN I BEGAN...>
<...THE THINGS SHE SAW CHANGED HER, AND THEY'VE *CHANGED* ME TOO.>
<BUT I STILL WANT TO FIGHT BY YOUR SIDE...>
KRAK
<...I'M STILL YOUR *AYANE.*>
THOK

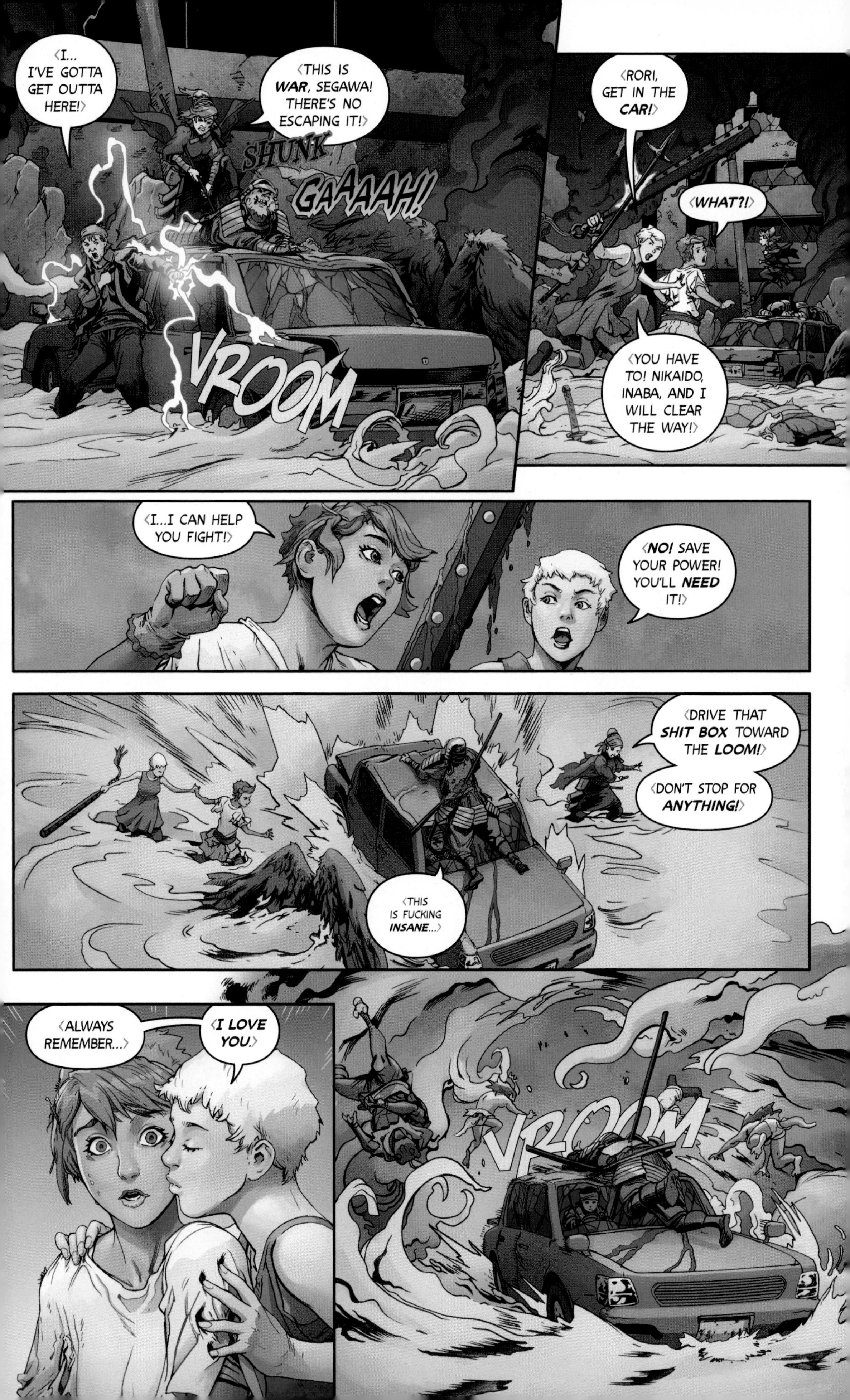

⟨I... I'VE GOTTA GET OUTTA HERE!⟩
⟨THIS IS WAR, SEGAWA! THERE'S NO ESCAPING IT!⟩
SHUNK
GAAAAH!
VROOM
⟨RORI, GET IN THE CAR!⟩
⟨WHAT?!⟩
⟨YOU HAVE TO! NIKAIDO, INABA, AND I WILL CLEAR THE WAY!⟩
⟨I...I CAN HELP YOU FIGHT!⟩
⟨NO! SAVE YOUR POWER! YOU'LL NEED IT!⟩
⟨DRIVE THAT SHIT BOX TOWARD THE LOOM!⟩
⟨DON'T STOP FOR ANYTHING!⟩
⟨THIS IS FUCKING INSANE...⟩
⟨ALWAYS REMEMBER...⟩
⟨I LOVE YOU.⟩
VROOM

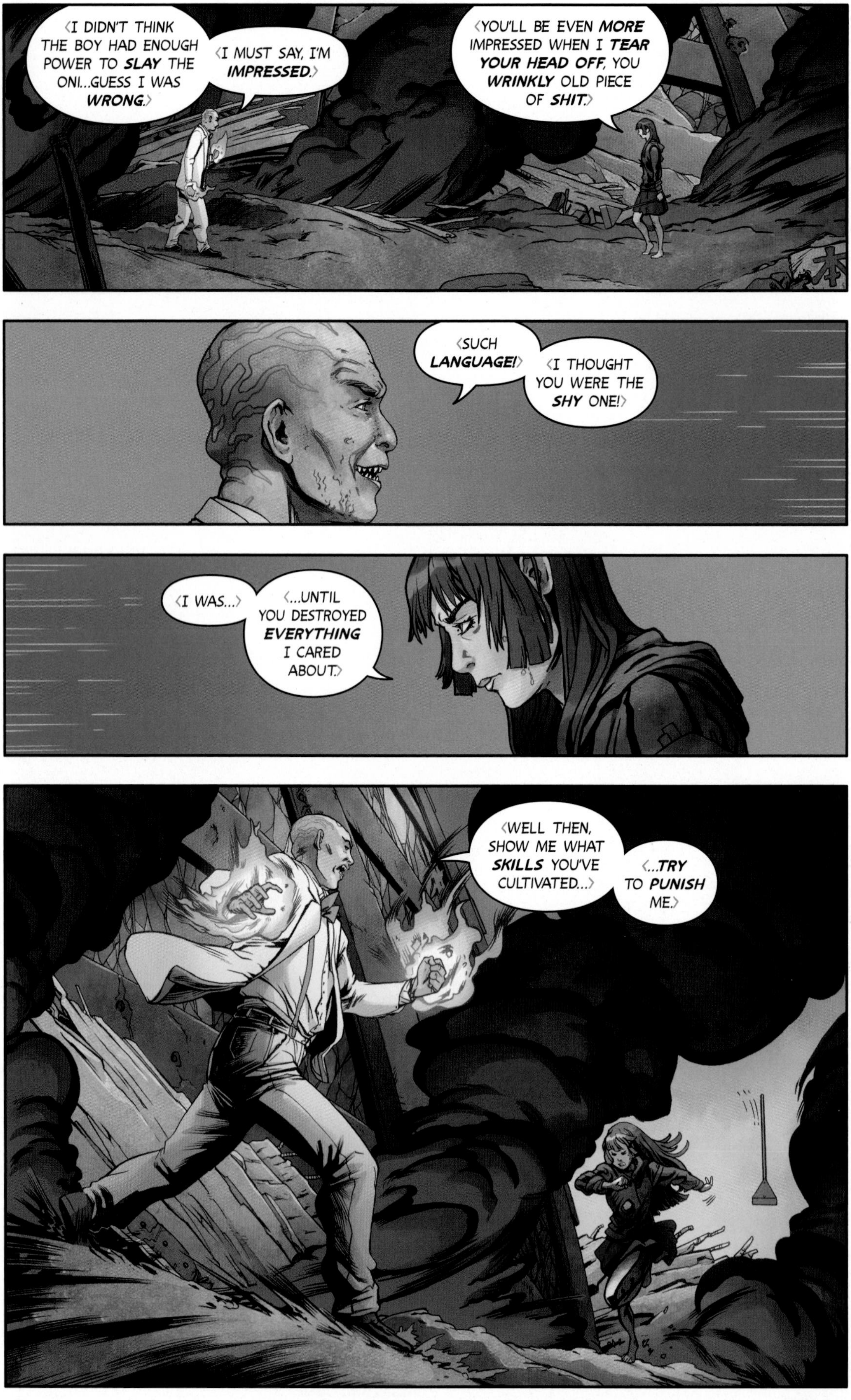

<I DIDN'T THINK THE BOY HAD ENOUGH POWER TO **SLAY** THE ONI...GUESS I WAS **WRONG**.>
<I MUST SAY, I'M **IMPRESSED**.>
<YOU'LL BE EVEN **MORE** IMPRESSED WHEN I **TEAR YOUR HEAD OFF**, YOU **WRINKLY** OLD PIECE OF **SHIT**.>
<SUCH **LANGUAGE!**>
<I THOUGHT YOU WERE THE **SHY** ONE!>
<I WAS...>
<...UNTIL YOU DESTROYED **EVERYTHING** I CARED ABOUT.>
<WELL THEN, SHOW ME WHAT **SKILLS** YOU'VE CULTIVATED...>
<...**TRY** TO **PUNISH** ME.>

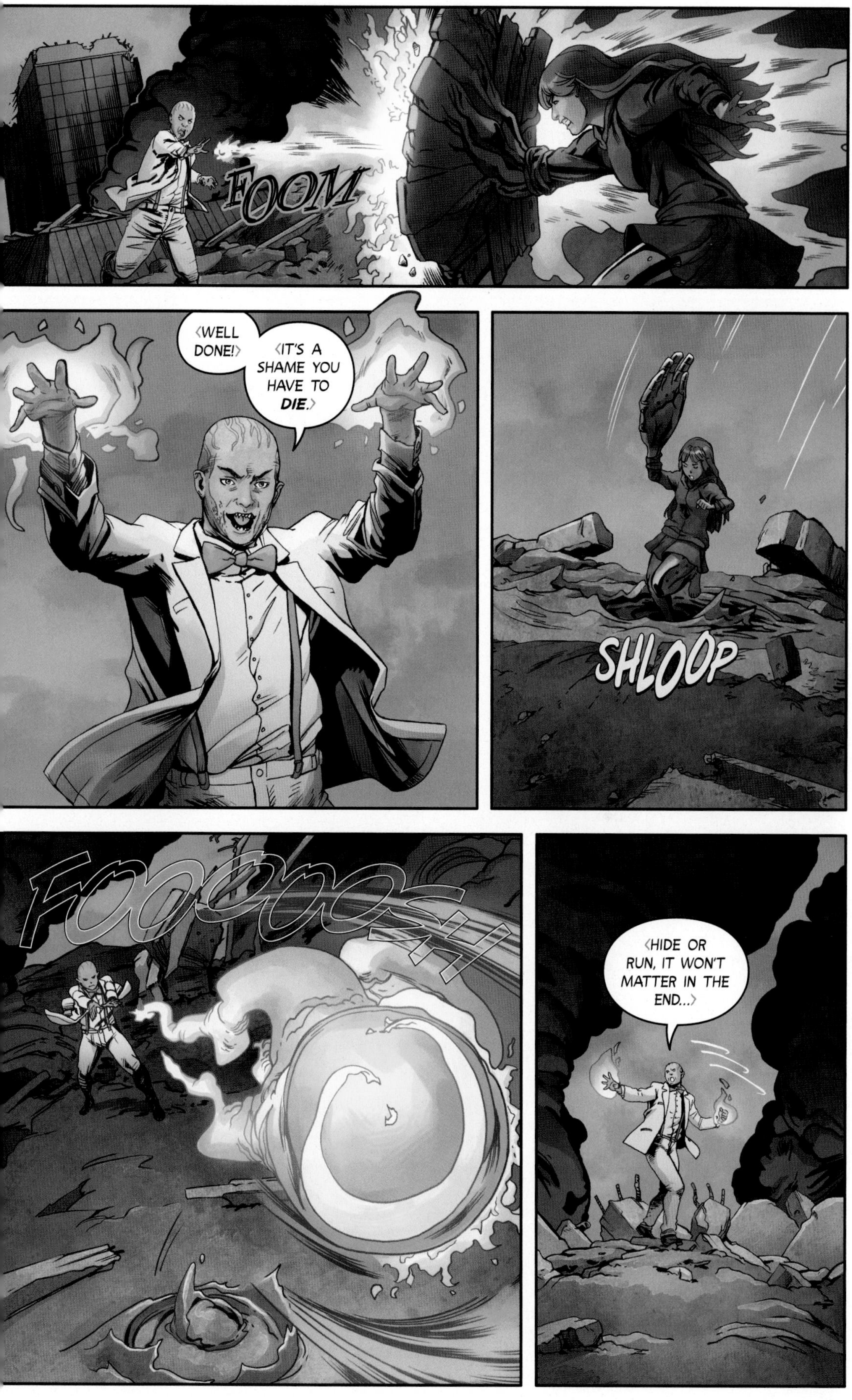
FOOM
⟨WELL DONE!⟩
⟨IT'S A SHAME YOU HAVE TO *DIE*.⟩
SHLOOP
FOOOOOSH!
⟨HIDE OR RUN, IT WON'T MATTER IN THE END...⟩

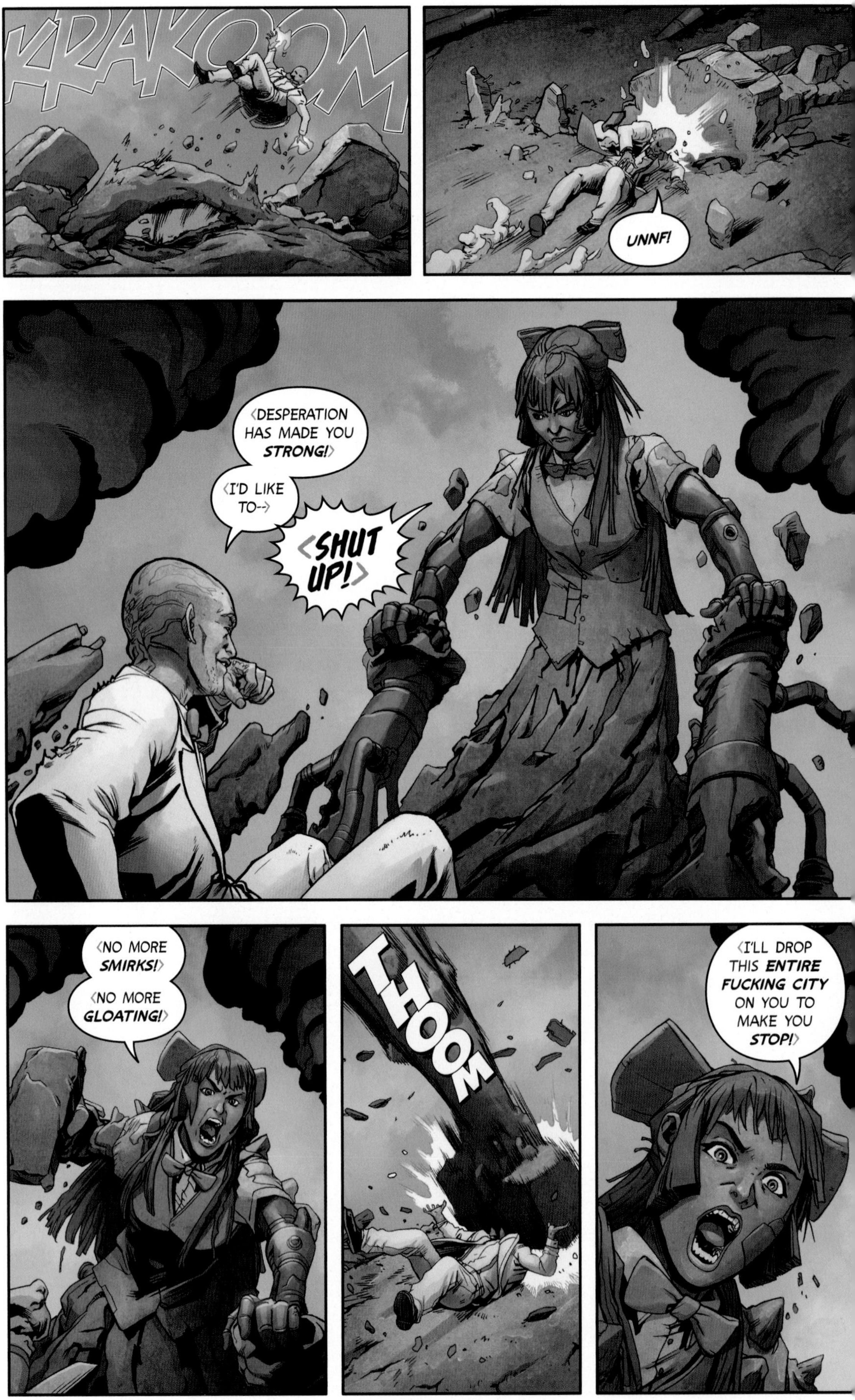
KRAKOOM
UNNF!
<DESPERATION HAS MADE YOU STRONG!>
<I'D LIKE TO-->
<SHUT UP!>
<NO MORE SMIRKS!>
<NO MORE GLOATING!>
THOOM
<I'LL DROP THIS ENTIRE FUCKING CITY ON YOU TO MAKE YOU STOP!>

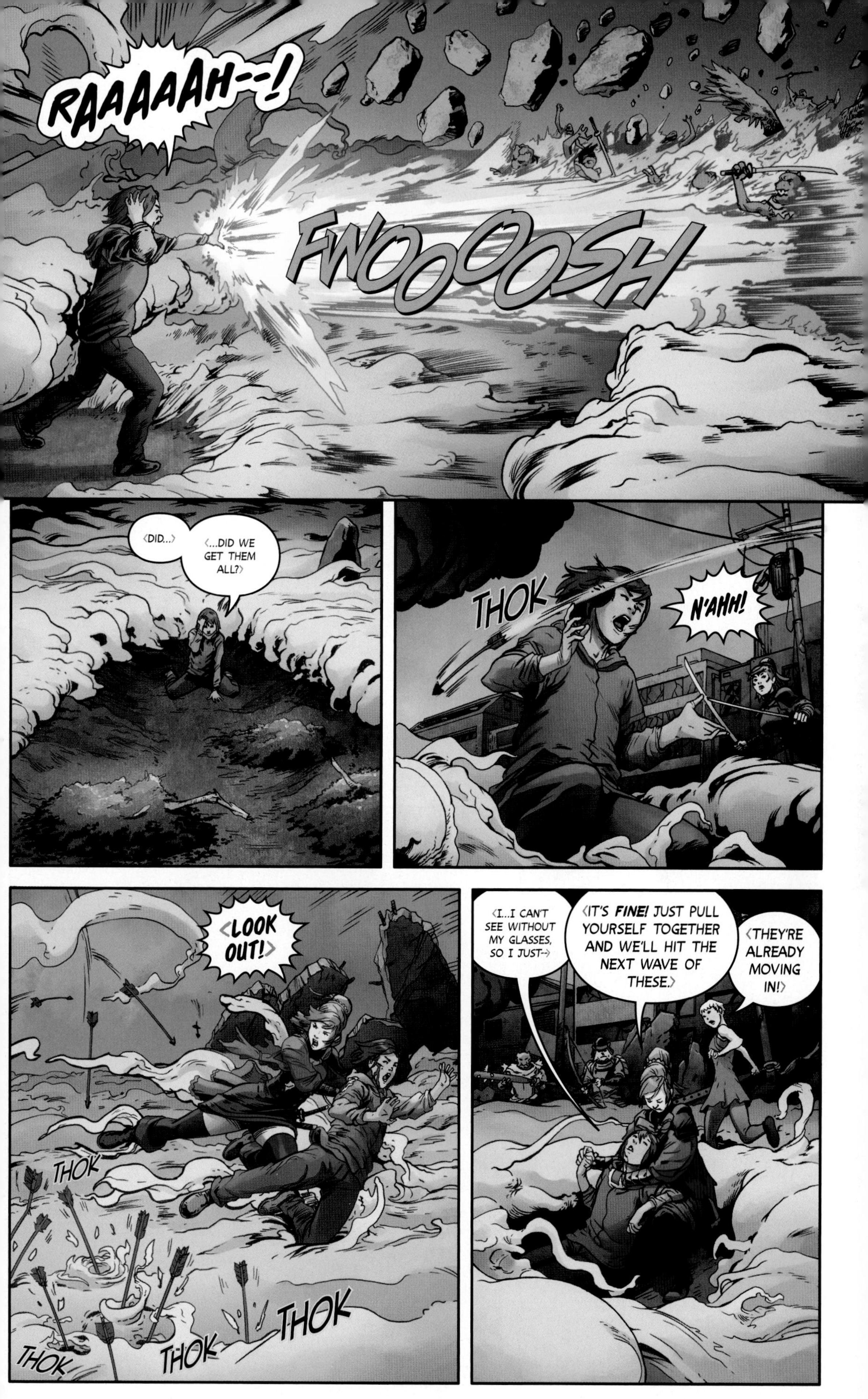
RAAAAAH--!
FWOOOOOSH
‹DID...›
‹...DID WE GET THEM ALL?›
THOK
N'AHH!
‹LOOK OUT!›
THOK
THOK
THOK
THOK
‹I...I CAN'T SEE WITHOUT MY GLASSES, SO I JUST--›
‹IT'S FINE! JUST PULL YOURSELF TOGETHER AND WE'LL HIT THE NEXT WAVE OF THESE.›
‹THEY'RE ALREADY MOVING IN!›

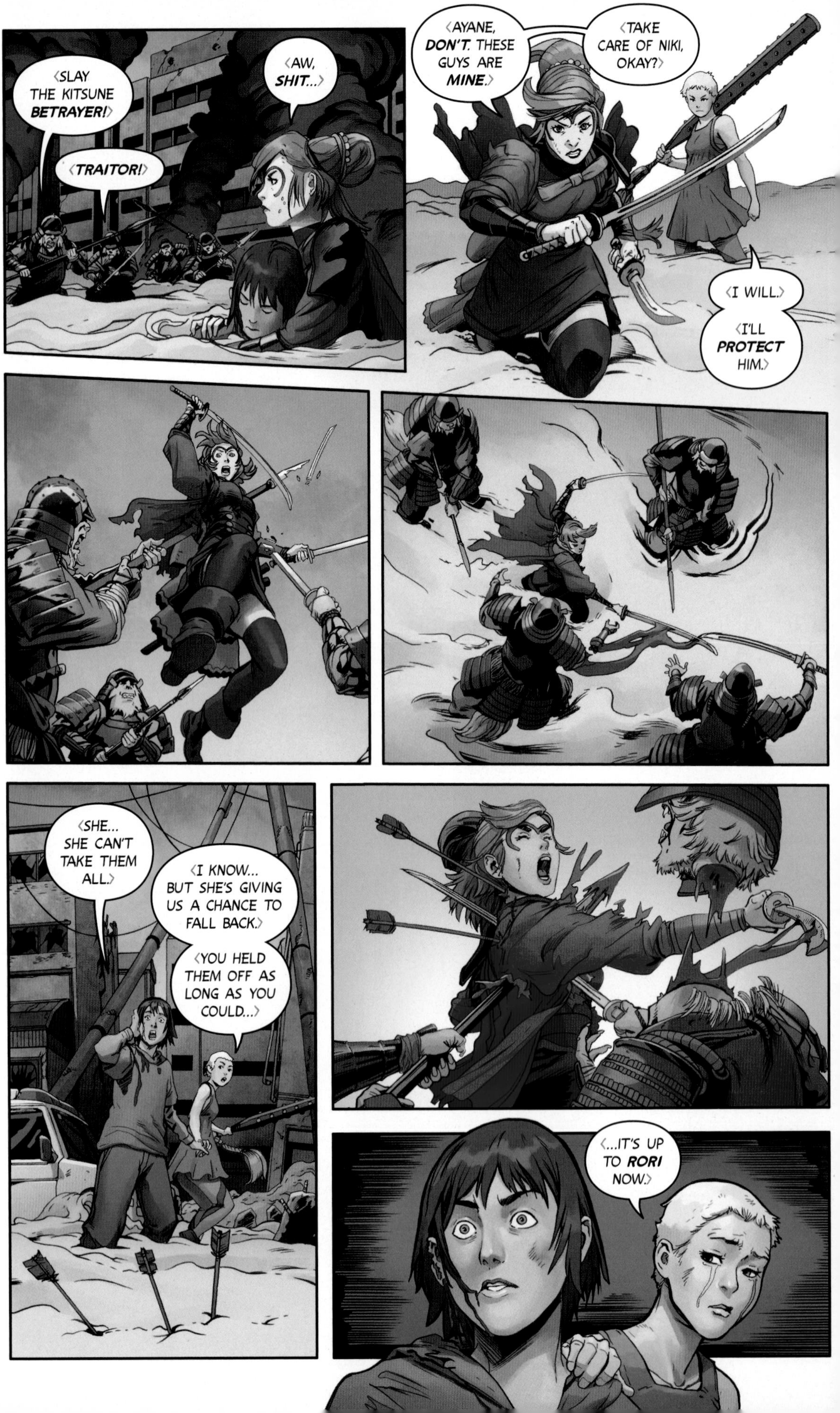

⟨SLAY THE KITSUNE BETRAYER!⟩
⟨TRAITOR!⟩
⟨AW, SHIT...⟩
⟨AYANE, DON'T. THESE GUYS ARE MINE.⟩
⟨TAKE CARE OF NIKI, OKAY?⟩
⟨I WILL.⟩
⟨I'LL PROTECT HIM.⟩
⟨SHE... SHE CAN'T TAKE THEM ALL.⟩
⟨I KNOW... BUT SHE'S GIVING US A CHANCE TO FALL BACK.⟩
⟨YOU HELD THEM OFF AS LONG AS YOU COULD...⟩
⟨...IT'S UP TO RORI NOW.⟩

NOT EXACTLY A *CLASSY* ARRIVAL, BUT IT DOES THE JOB.

CRASH

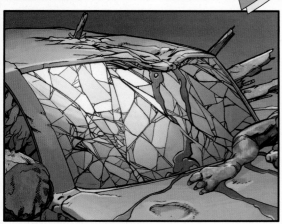

⟨YOU WANTED THE *LOOM*...⟩ ⟨...*THIS* IS THE *PLACE!*⟩

KA-CHASH

I CAN FEEL THE *WEAVE*...LOUDER AND BRIGHTER THAN I'VE EVER FELT BEFORE.

IT'S HORRIBLE, WONDERFUL, AND EVERYTHING IN BETWEEN...

⟨UH, *RORI*...YOU OKAY?⟩

⟨YOU'RE NOT GONNA *KILL* ME OR ANYTHING, ARE YOU? 'CAUSE YOU'RE EXTRA *FREAKY* RIGHT NOW AND--⟩

⟨LET'S GO.⟩

BEYOND THIS DOOR, IT ALL CHANGES...

BEYOND THIS DOOR...

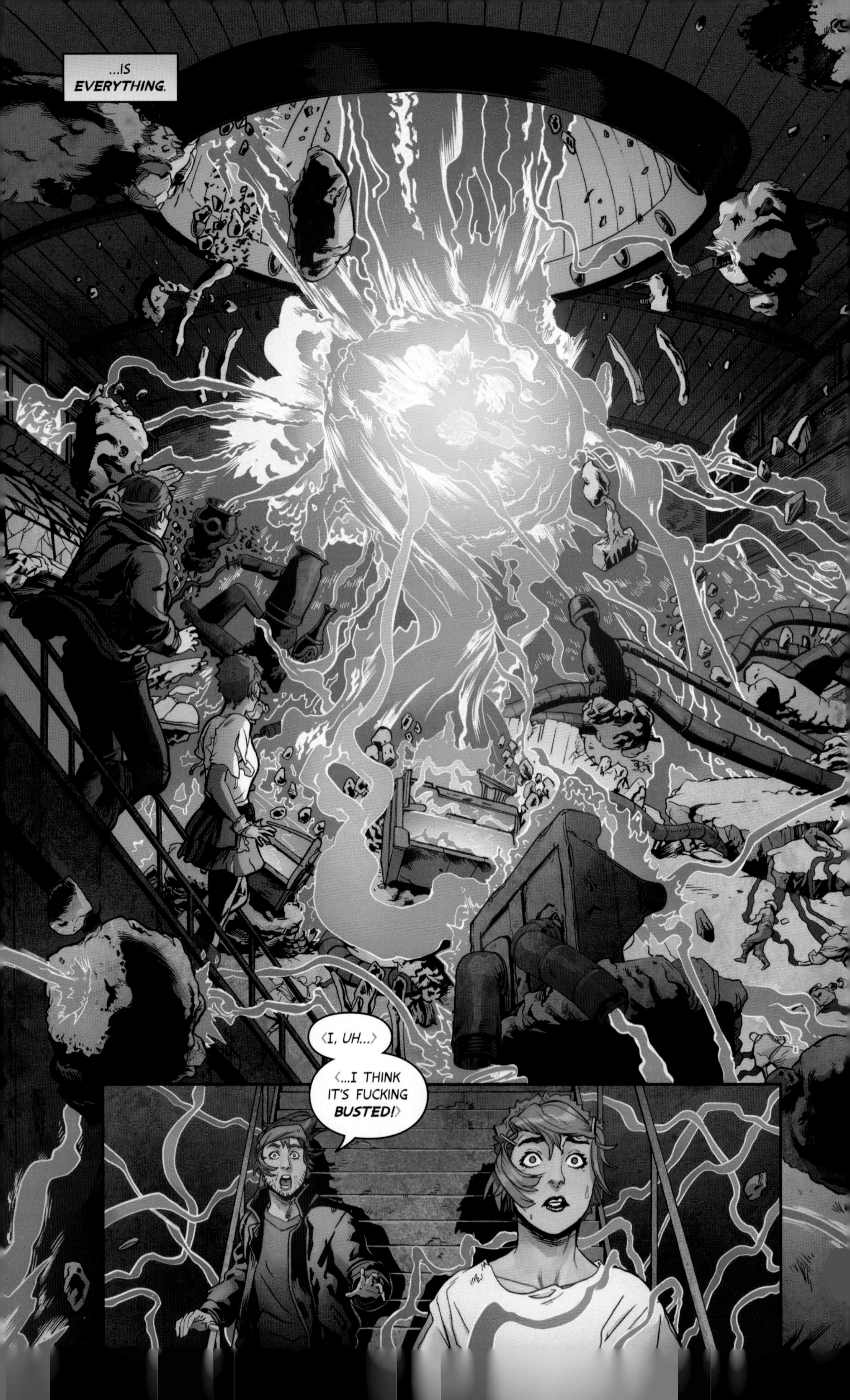
...IS
EVERYTHING.
‹I, UH...›
‹...I THINK
IT'S FUCKING
BUSTED!›

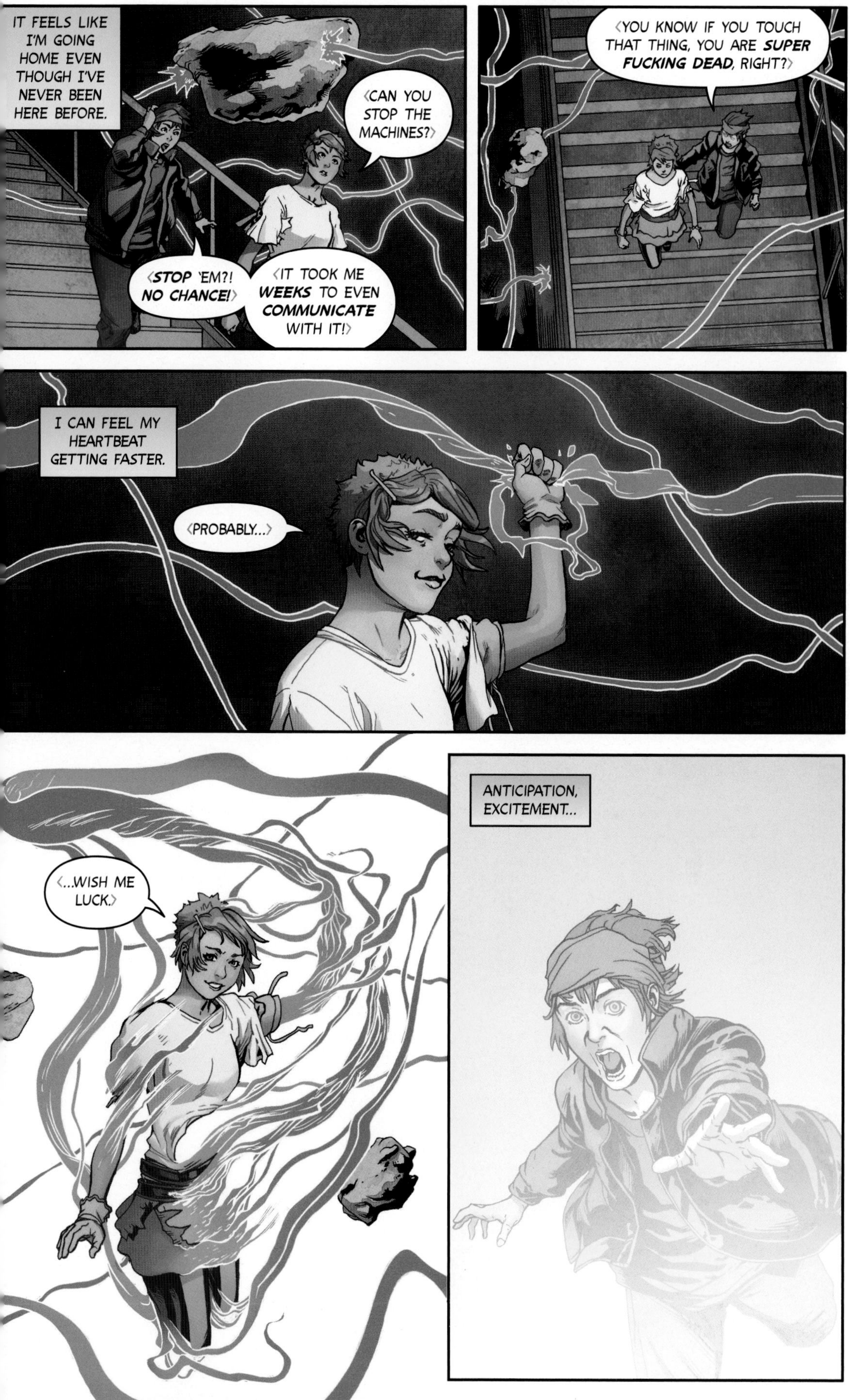
IT FEELS LIKE I'M GOING HOME EVEN THOUGH I'VE NEVER BEEN HERE BEFORE.
‹CAN YOU STOP THE MACHINES?›
‹STOP 'EM?! NO CHANCE!›
‹IT TOOK ME WEEKS TO EVEN COMMUNICATE WITH IT!›
‹YOU KNOW IF YOU TOUCH THAT THING, YOU ARE SUPER FUCKING DEAD, RIGHT?›
I CAN FEEL MY HEARTBEAT GETTING FASTER.
‹PROBABLY...›
‹...WISH ME LUCK.›
ANTICIPATION, EXCITEMENT...

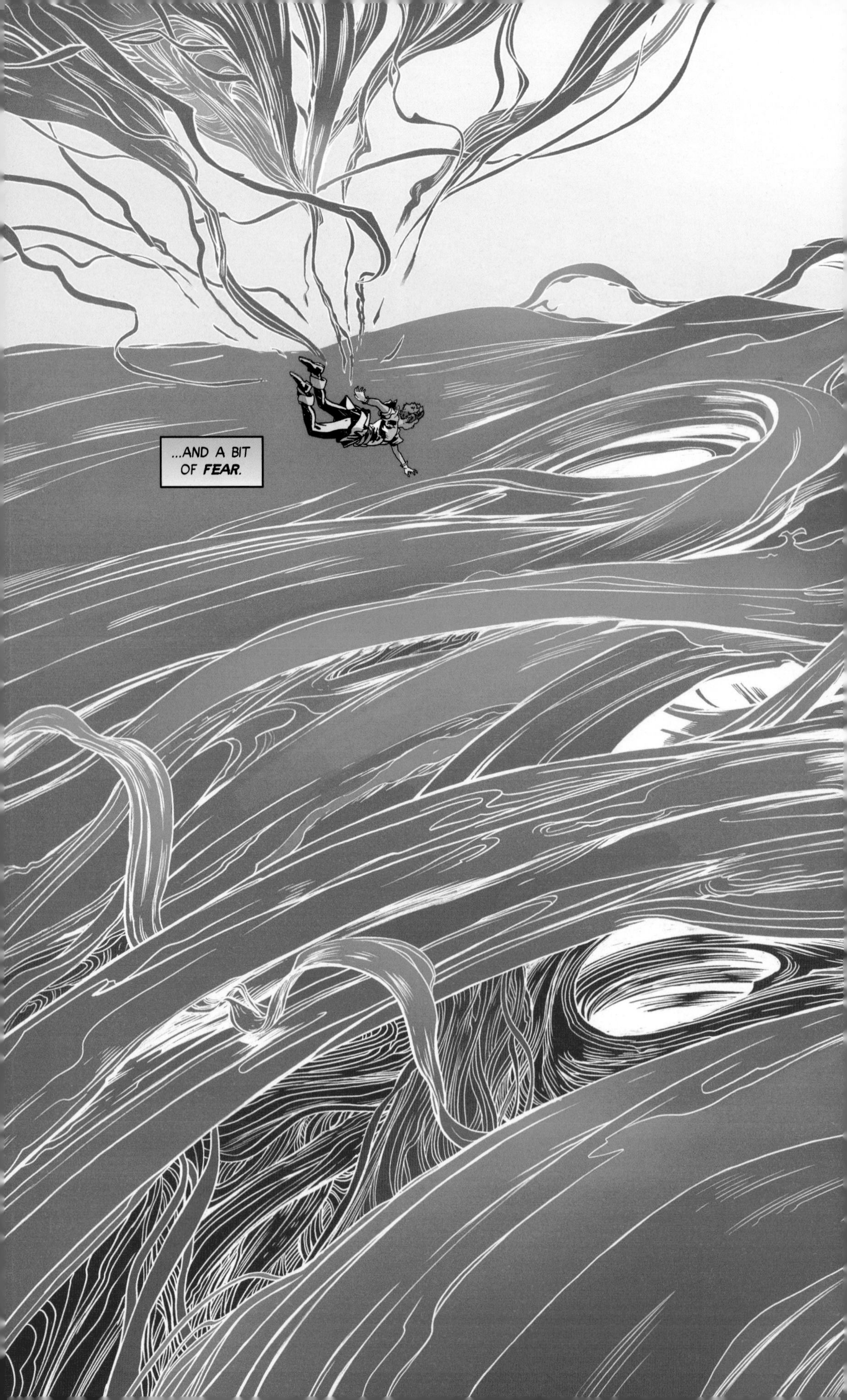
...AND A BIT OF FEAR.

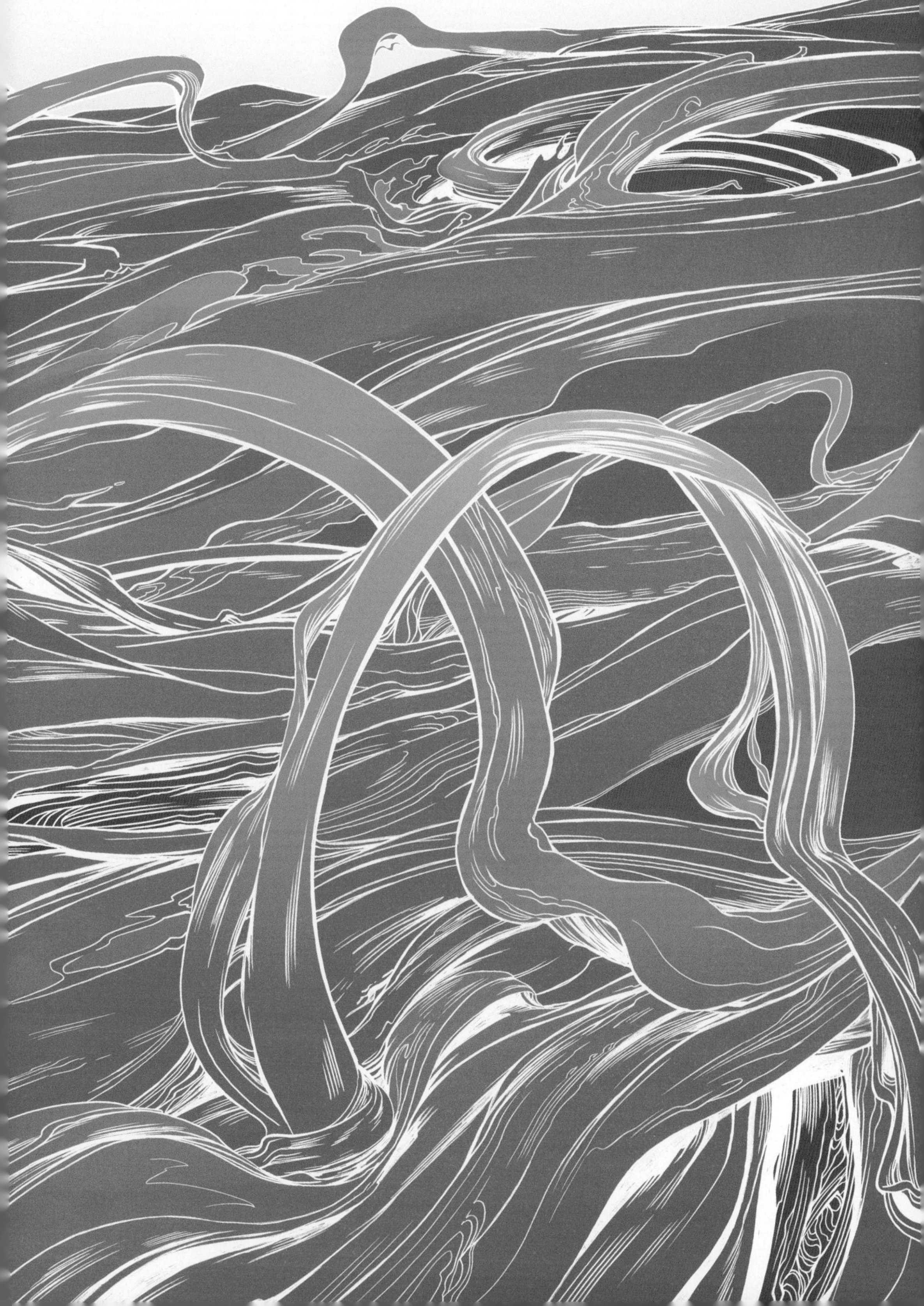

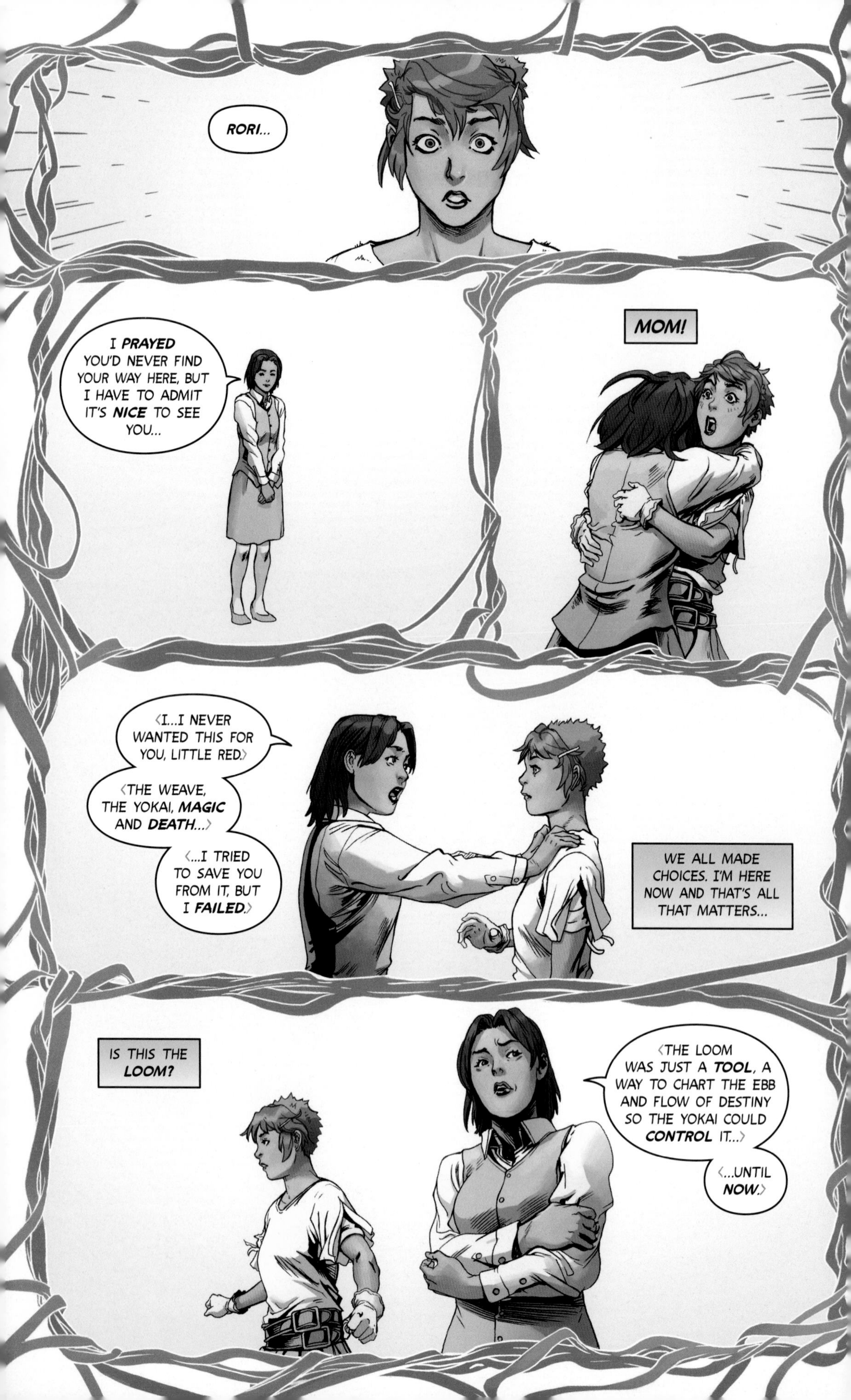
RORI...
I PRAYED YOU'D NEVER FIND YOUR WAY HERE, BUT I HAVE TO ADMIT IT'S NICE TO SEE YOU...
MOM!
<I...I NEVER WANTED THIS FOR YOU, LITTLE RED.>
<THE WEAVE, THE YOKAI, MAGIC AND DEATH...>
<...I TRIED TO SAVE YOU FROM IT, BUT I FAILED.>
WE ALL MADE CHOICES. I'M HERE NOW AND THAT'S ALL THAT MATTERS...
IS THIS THE LOOM?
<THE LOOM WAS JUST A TOOL, A WAY TO CHART THE EBB AND FLOW OF DESTINY SO THE YOKAI COULD CONTROL IT...>
<...UNTIL NOW.>

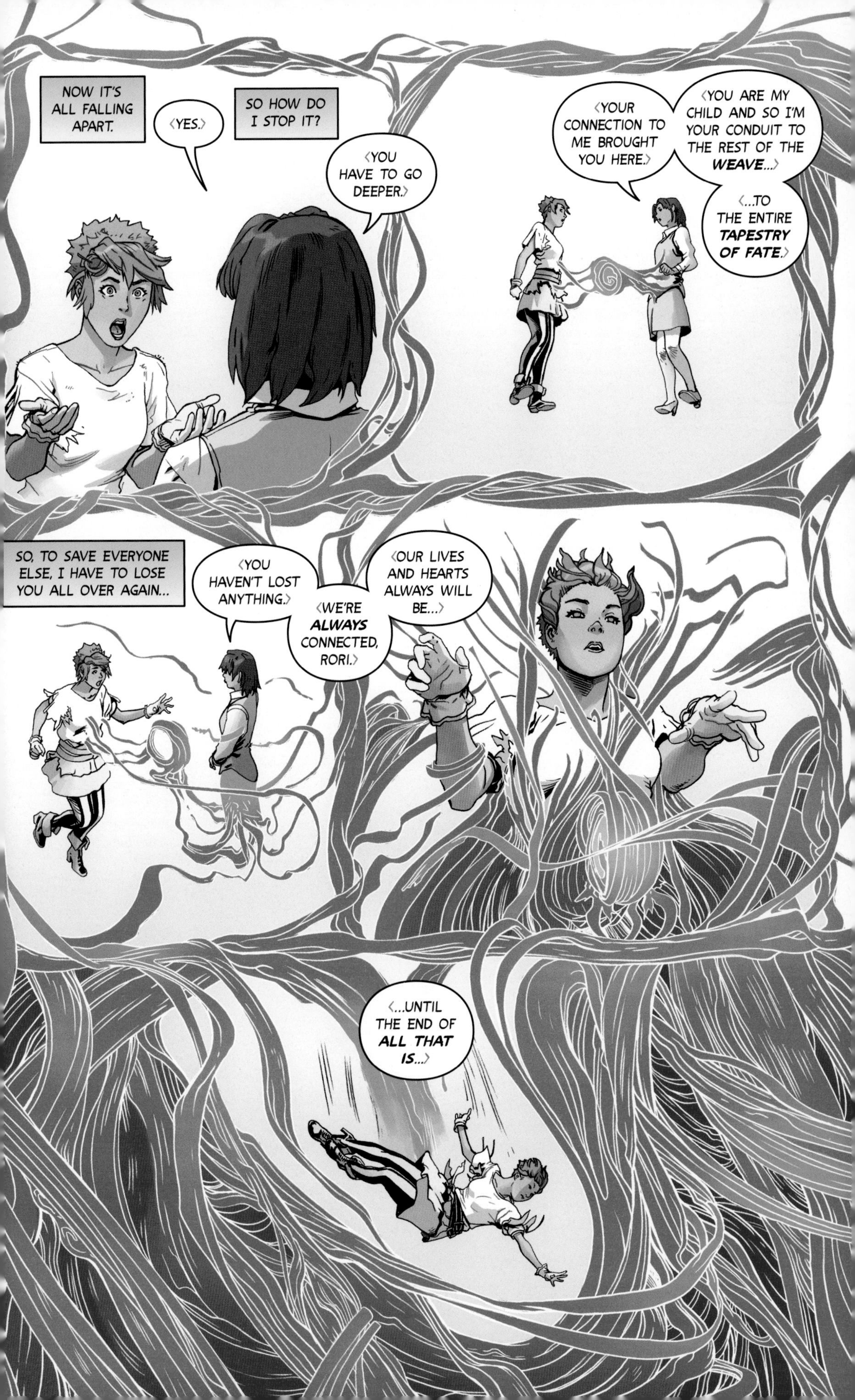
NOW IT'S ALL FALLING APART.
‹YES.›
SO HOW DO I STOP IT?
‹YOU HAVE TO GO DEEPER.›
‹YOUR CONNECTION TO ME BROUGHT YOU HERE.›
‹YOU ARE MY CHILD AND SO I'M YOUR CONDUIT TO THE REST OF THE **WEAVE**...›
‹...TO THE ENTIRE **TAPESTRY OF FATE.**›
SO, TO SAVE EVERYONE ELSE, I HAVE TO LOSE YOU ALL OVER AGAIN...
‹YOU HAVEN'T LOST ANYTHING.›
‹WE'RE **ALWAYS** CONNECTED, RORI.›
‹OUR LIVES AND HEARTS ALWAYS WILL BE...›
‹...UNTIL THE END OF **ALL THAT IS**...›

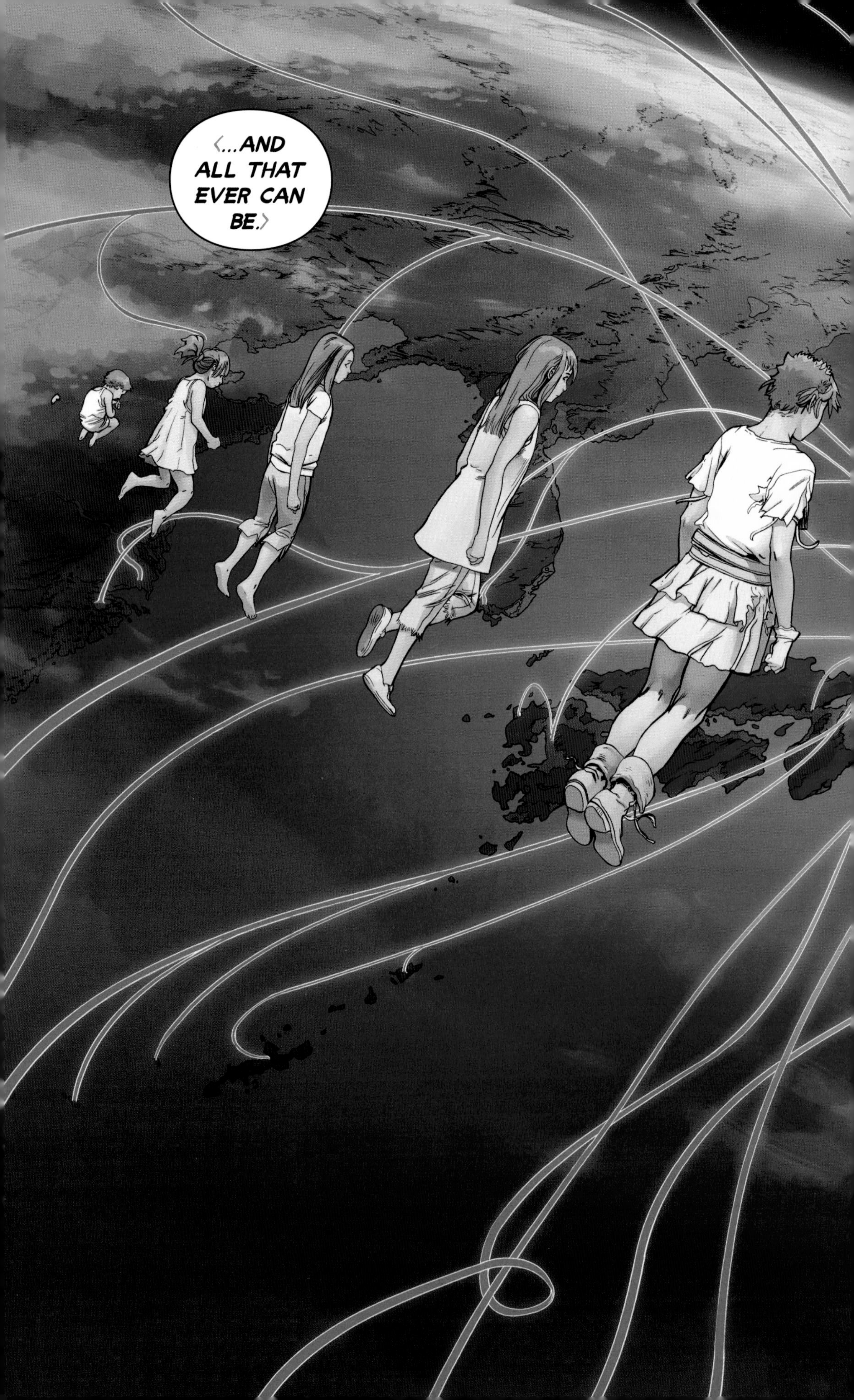
〈...AND ALL THAT EVER CAN BE.〉

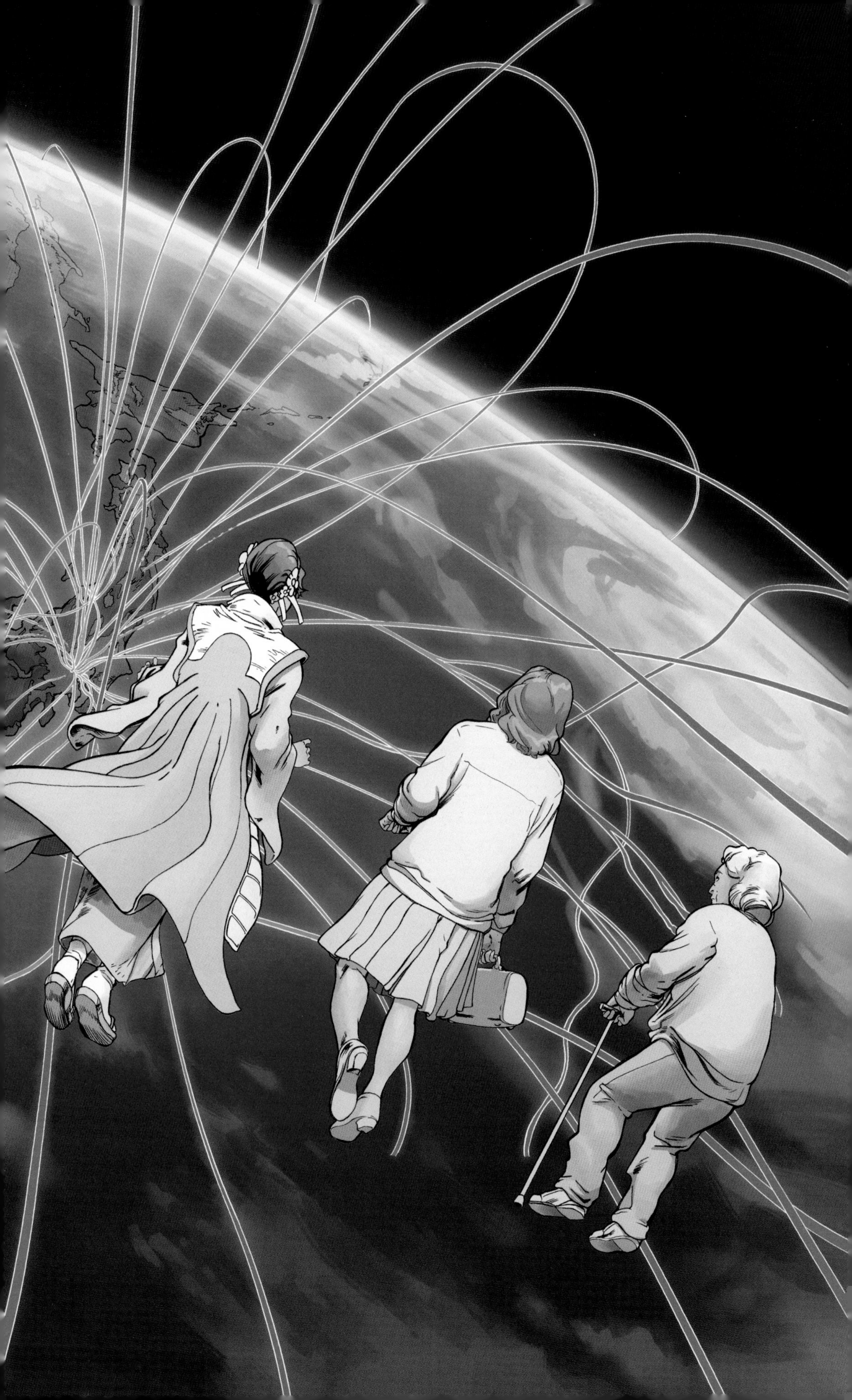

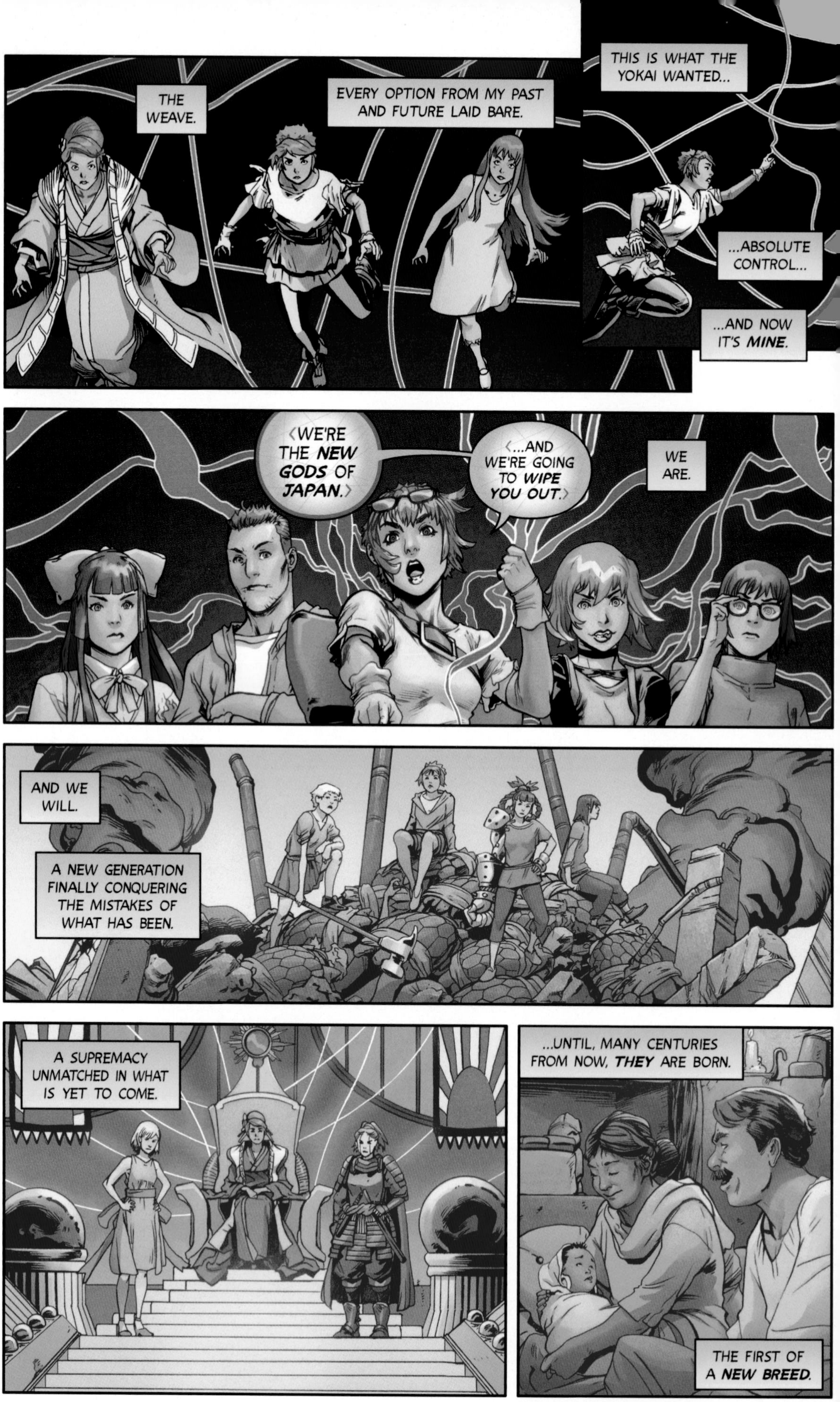
THE WEAVE.
EVERY OPTION FROM MY PAST AND FUTURE LAID BARE.
THIS IS WHAT THE YOKAI WANTED...
...ABSOLUTE CONTROL...
...AND NOW IT'S MINE.
‹WE'RE THE NEW GODS OF JAPAN.›
‹...AND WE'RE GOING TO WIPE YOU OUT.›
WE ARE.
AND WE WILL.
A NEW GENERATION FINALLY CONQUERING THE MISTAKES OF WHAT HAS BEEN.
A SUPREMACY UNMATCHED IN WHAT IS YET TO COME.
...UNTIL, MANY CENTURIES FROM NOW, THEY ARE BORN.
THE FIRST OF A NEW BREED.

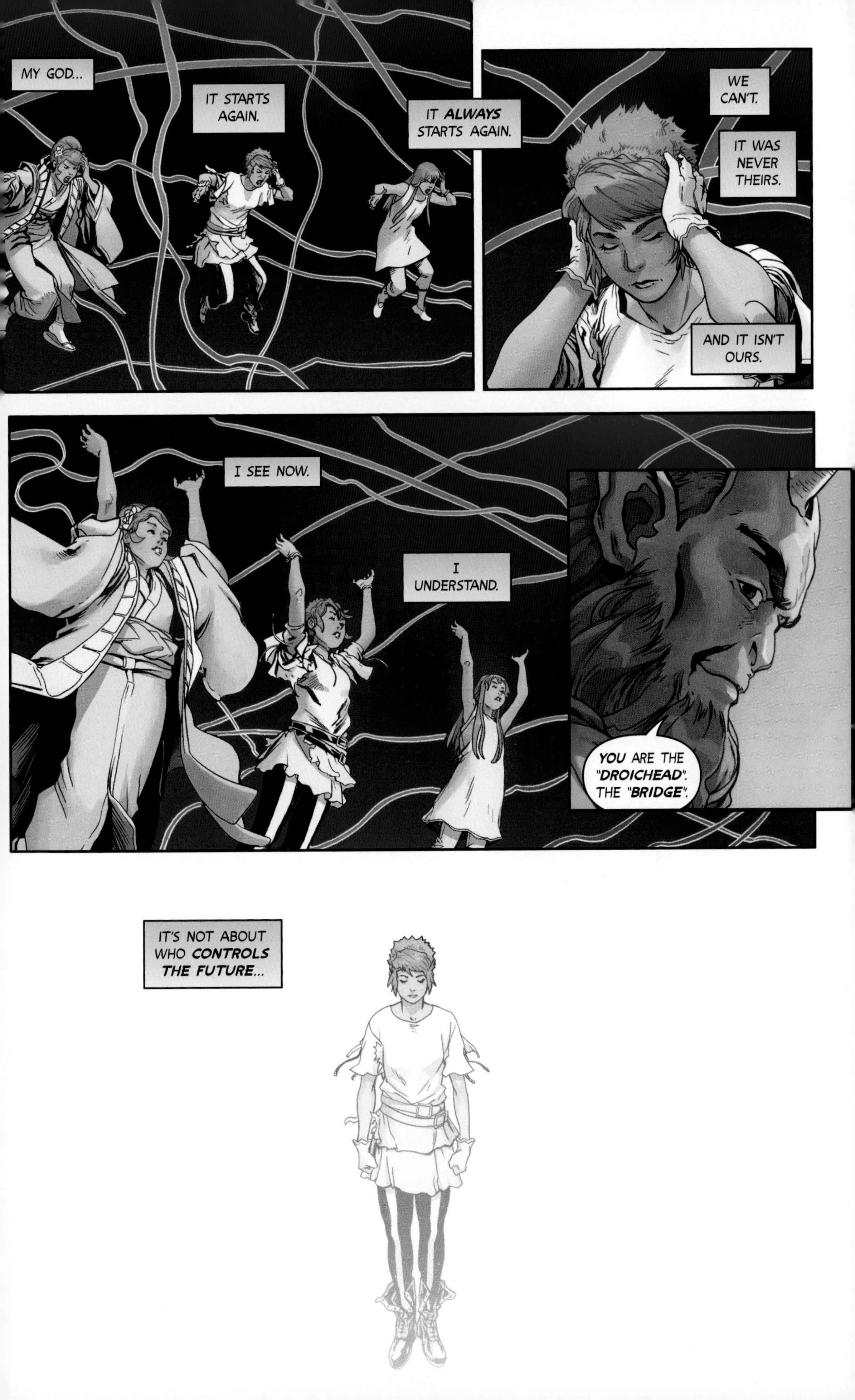
MY GOD...
IT STARTS AGAIN.
IT ALWAYS STARTS AGAIN.
WE CAN'T.
IT WAS NEVER THEIRS.
AND IT ISN'T OURS.
I SEE NOW.
I UNDERSTAND.
YOU ARE THE "DROICHEAD". THE "BRIDGE".
IT'S NOT ABOUT WHO CONTROLS THE FUTURE...

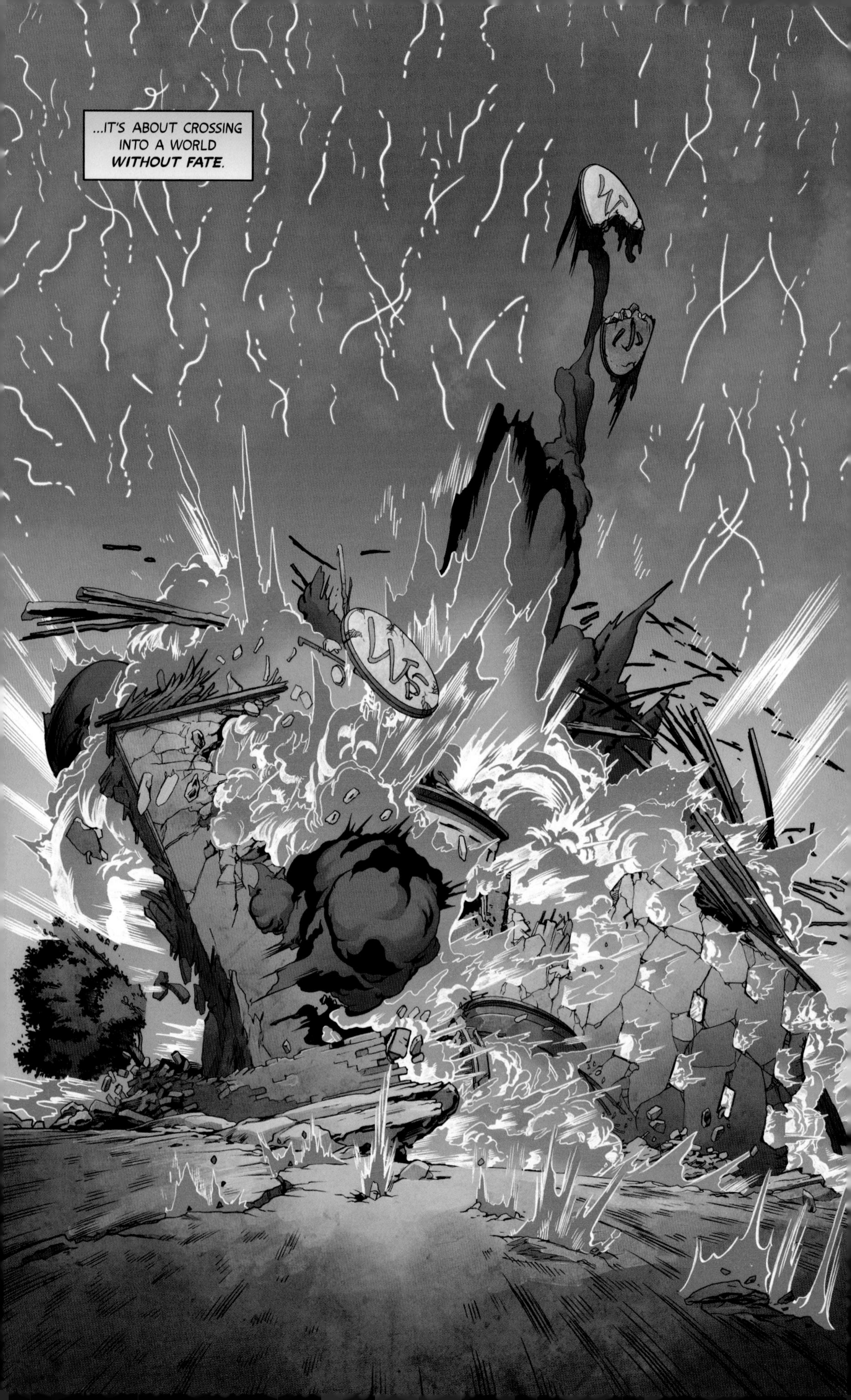
...IT'S ABOUT CROSSING INTO A WORLD ***WITHOUT FATE.***

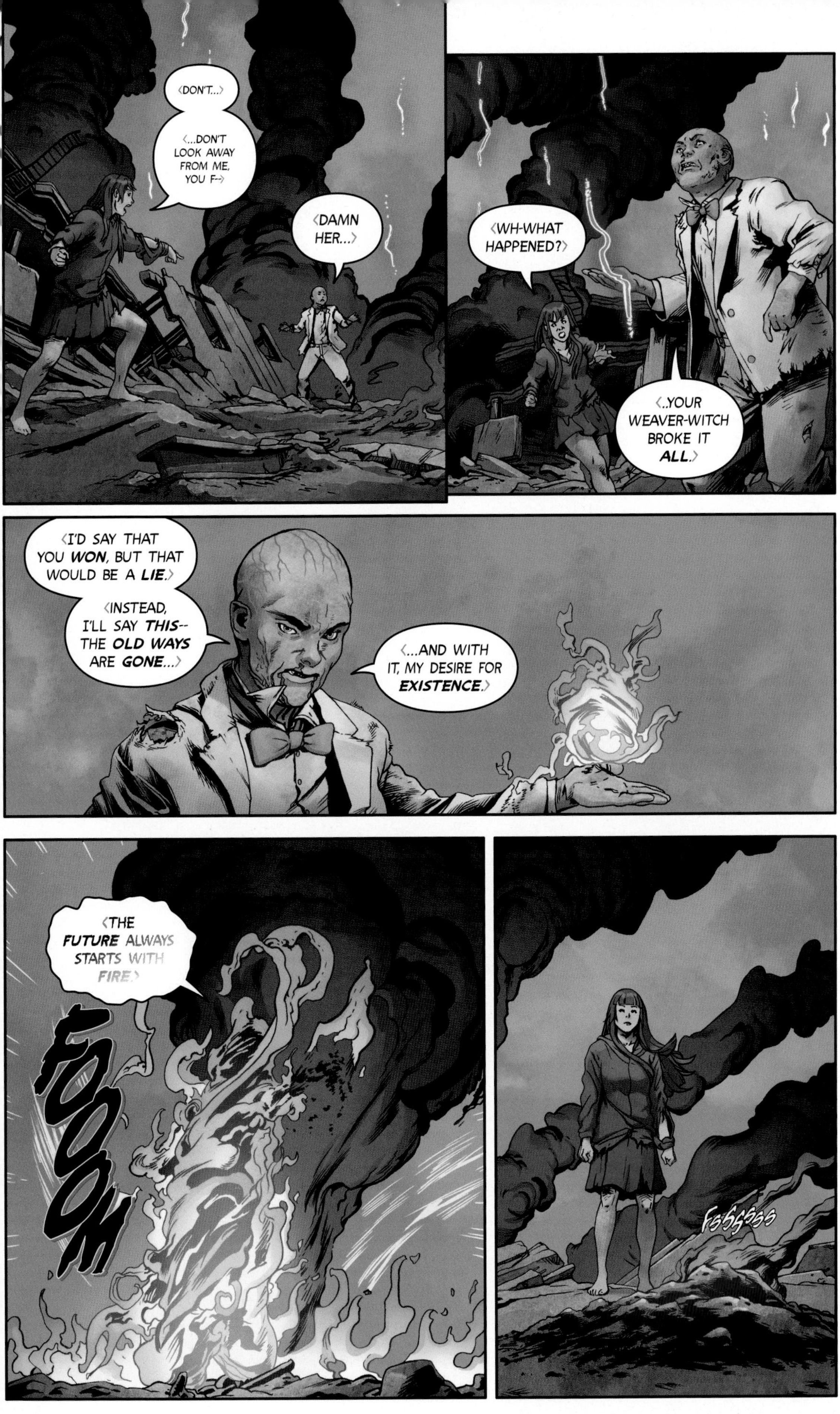

‹DON'T...›
‹...DON'T LOOK AWAY FROM ME, YOU F--›
‹DAMN HER...›
‹WH-WHAT HAPPENED?›
‹..YOUR WEAVER-WITCH BROKE IT ALL.›
‹I'D SAY THAT YOU WON, BUT THAT WOULD BE A LIE.›
‹INSTEAD, I'LL SAY THIS-- THE OLD WAYS ARE GONE...›
‹...AND WITH IT, MY DESIRE FOR EXISTENCE.›
‹THE FUTURE ALWAYS STARTS WITH FIRE.›
FOOOOM
FSSSSSS

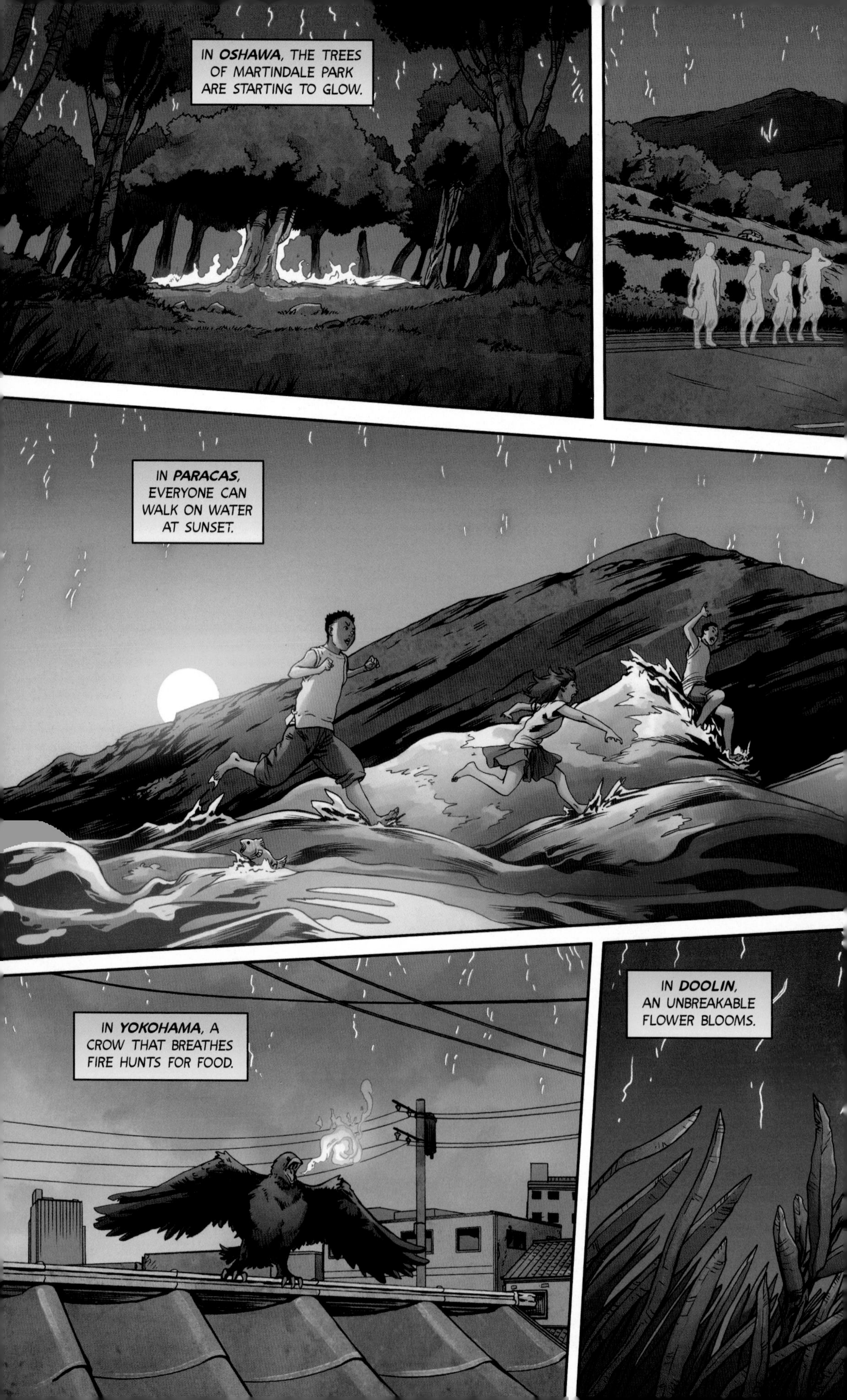
IN *OSHAWA*, THE TREES OF MARTINDALE PARK ARE STARTING TO GLOW.
IN *PARACAS*, EVERYONE CAN WALK ON WATER AT SUNSET.
IN *YOKOHAMA*, A CROW THAT BREATHES FIRE HUNTS FOR FOOD.
IN *DOOLIN*, AN UNBREAKABLE FLOWER BLOOMS.

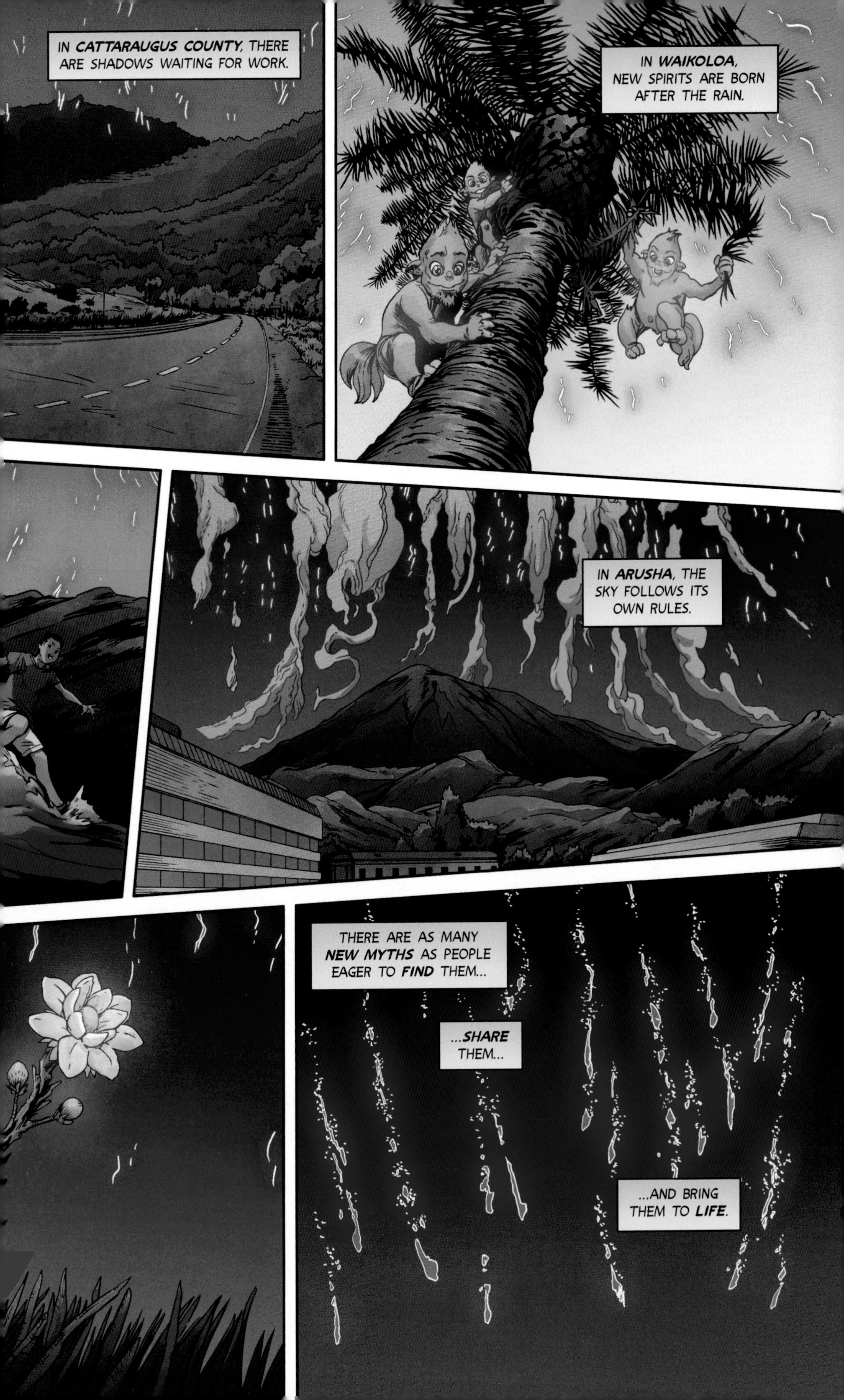
IN CATTARAUGUS COUNTY, THERE ARE SHADOWS WAITING FOR WORK.
IN WAIKOLOA, NEW SPIRITS ARE BORN AFTER THE RAIN.
IN ARUSHA, THE SKY FOLLOWS ITS OWN RULES.
THERE ARE AS MANY NEW MYTHS AS PEOPLE EAGER TO FIND THEM...
...SHARE THEM...
...AND BRING THEM TO LIFE.

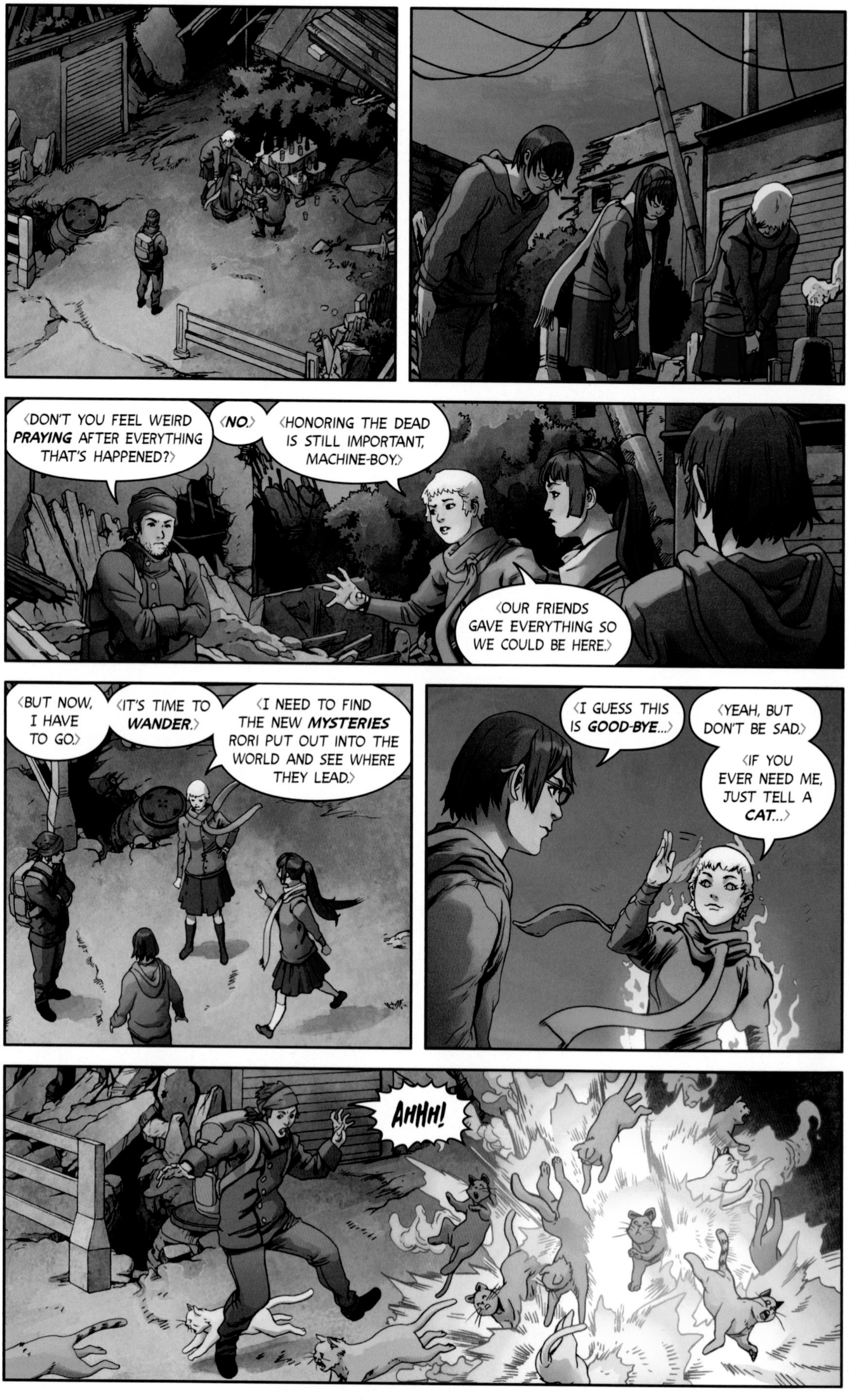
〈DON'T YOU FEEL WEIRD **PRAYING** AFTER EVERYTHING THAT'S HAPPENED?〉
〈**NO.**〉
〈HONORING THE DEAD IS STILL IMPORTANT, MACHINE-BOY.〉
〈OUR FRIENDS GAVE EVERYTHING SO WE COULD BE HERE.〉
〈BUT NOW, I HAVE TO GO.〉
〈IT'S TIME TO **WANDER**.〉
〈I NEED TO FIND THE NEW **MYSTERIES** RORI PUT OUT INTO THE WORLD AND SEE WHERE THEY LEAD.〉
〈I GUESS THIS IS **GOOD-BYE**...〉
〈YEAH, BUT DON'T BE SAD.〉
〈IF YOU EVER NEED ME, JUST TELL A **CAT**...〉
AHHH!

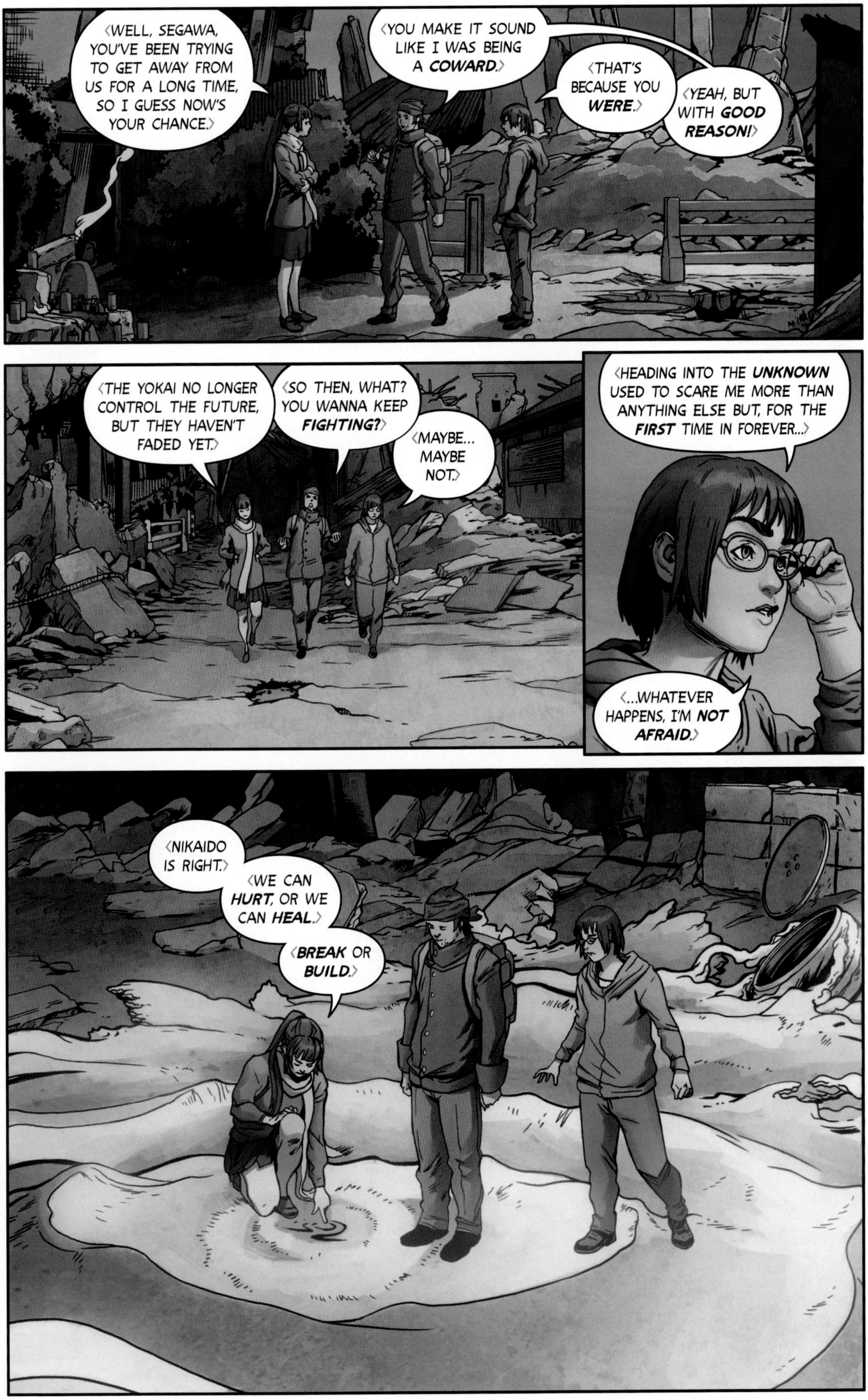
‹WELL, SEGAWA, YOU'VE BEEN TRYING TO GET AWAY FROM US FOR A LONG TIME, SO I GUESS NOW'S YOUR CHANCE.›
‹YOU MAKE IT SOUND LIKE I WAS BEING A COWARD.›
‹THAT'S BECAUSE YOU WERE.›
‹YEAH, BUT WITH GOOD REASON!›
‹THE YOKAI NO LONGER CONTROL THE FUTURE, BUT THEY HAVEN'T FADED YET.›
‹SO THEN, WHAT? YOU WANNA KEEP FIGHTING?›
‹MAYBE... MAYBE NOT.›
‹HEADING INTO THE UNKNOWN USED TO SCARE ME MORE THAN ANYTHING ELSE BUT, FOR THE FIRST TIME IN FOREVER...›
‹...WHATEVER HAPPENS, I'M NOT AFRAID.›
‹NIKAIDO IS RIGHT.›
‹WE CAN HURT, OR WE CAN HEAL.›
‹BREAK OR BUILD.›

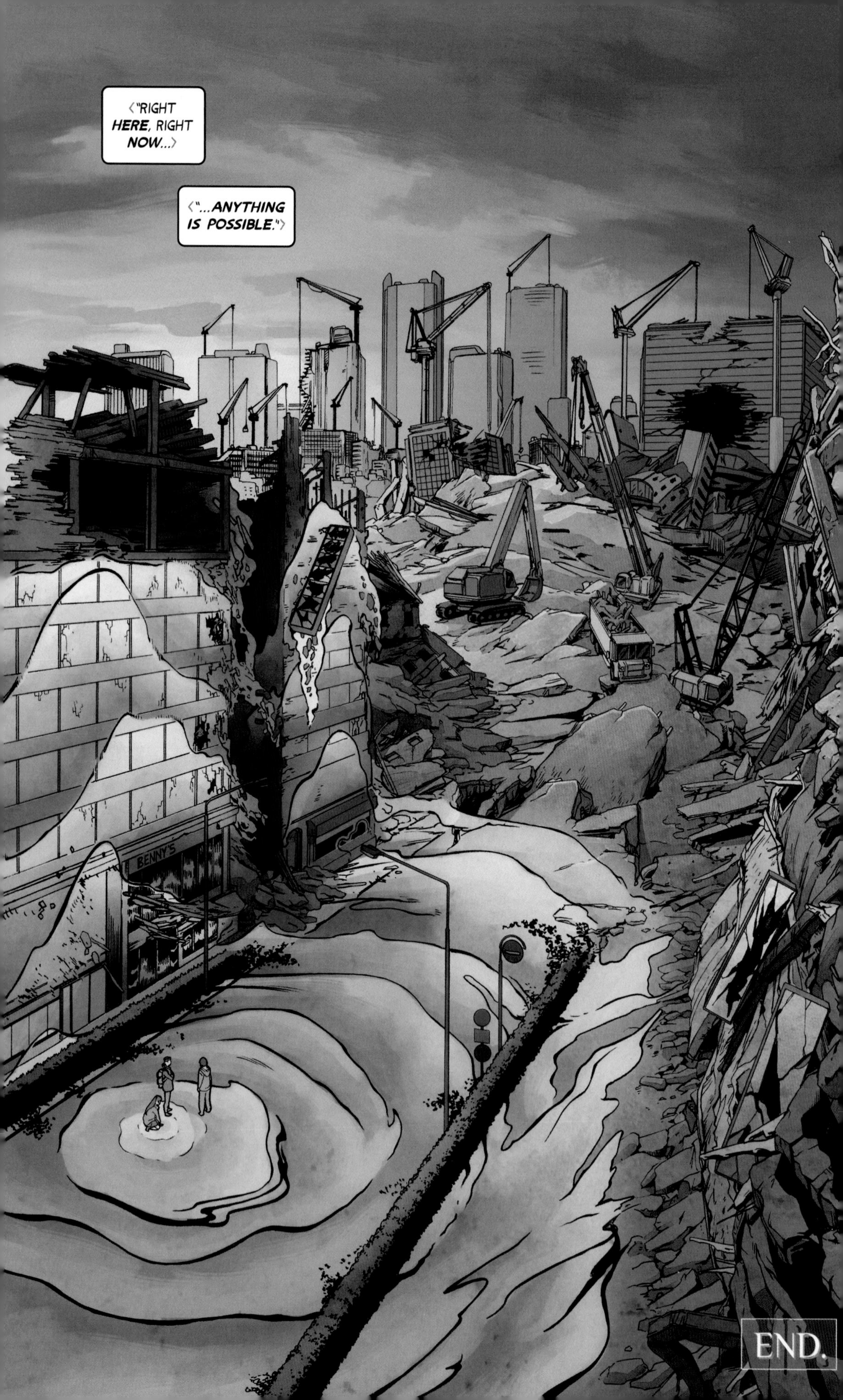

<"RIGHT HERE, RIGHT NOW...>
<"...ANYTHING IS POSSIBLE.">
BENNY'S
END.

ウェイワード

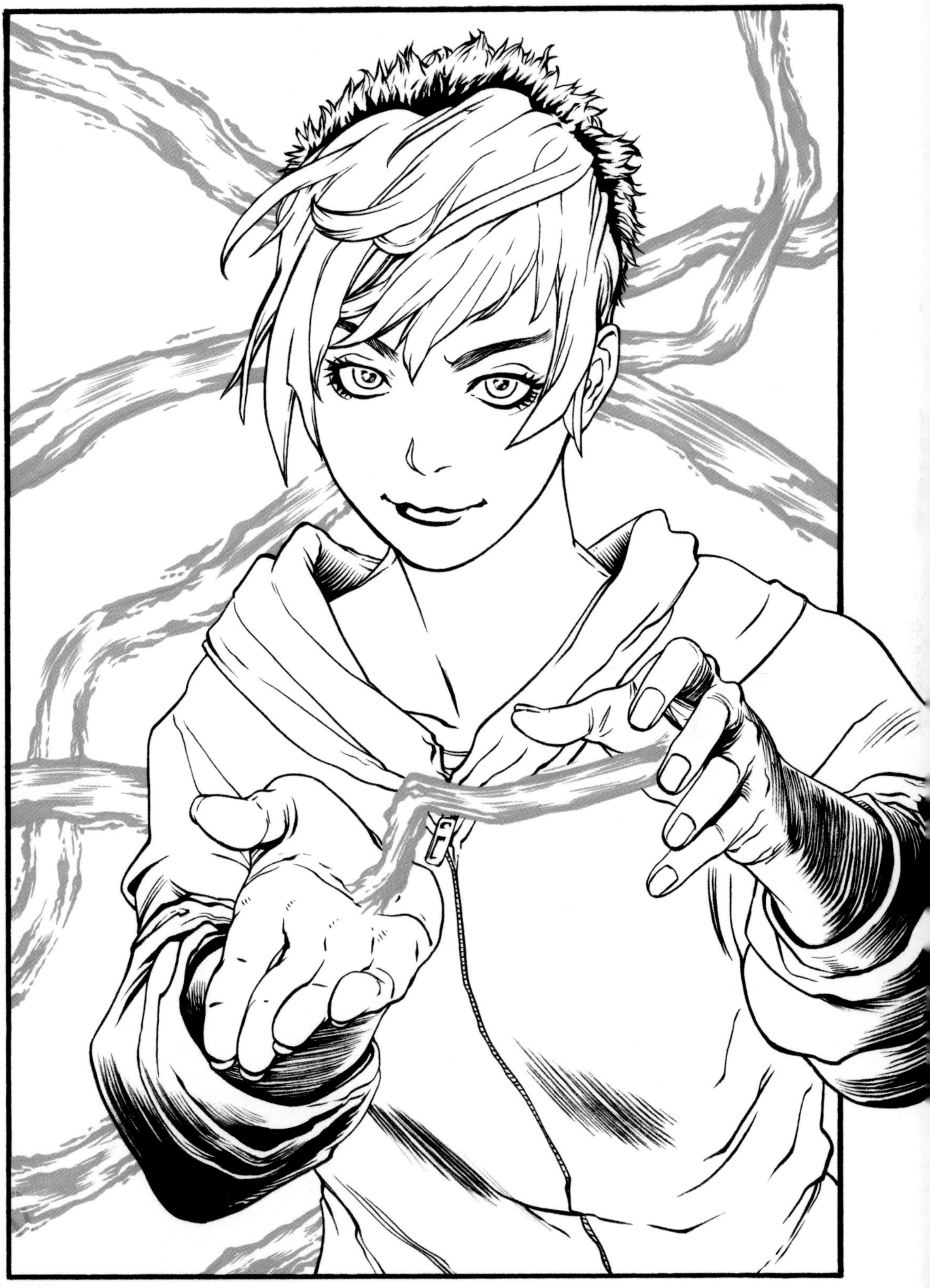

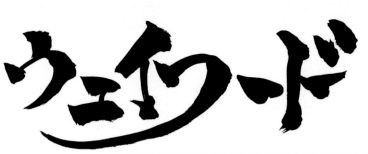

Farewell To Weird Japan

The story of Yokai never ends.

Around April 2006, rumors spread across the popular 2chan message board of a summoning ritual. The rules were complicated and shockingly specific: Take a stuffed animal or doll, something that has limbs and could walk. Using a knife, slit it open and remove the stuffing. Repack it full of uncooked rice and your own nail clippings. Once you have it full, sew the doll back up with red thread. Tie up the doll with any remaining red thread. Once this is complete, go to the bathtub and fill it with water. Choose what will be your hiding place and put a cup of salt water there along with the knife you used to cut the doll. Lastly, name your creation. The name can be any other than your own.

When the preparation is done, wait until 3am. Look the doll in the eyes and call it by name. Tell the doll "You're it." Tell it three times. Now go to the bathroom and submerge the doll in the filled tub. Turn off all the lights and return to your hiding spot. Close your eyes and count to ten. That done, grab the knife and go back to the bathroom. Take the doll out of the tub, tell it "I've found you" and stab the knife into its chest. Now tell the doll, "It's my turn to be it." Go back to your hiding place and hide.

While hiding, pour half the glass of salt water into your mouth. It is important to keep the liquid in your mouth and not swallow or spit it out. Count to ten while you hide. Now, go look for the doll. Carry the remaining glass of salt water with you. The doll will not necessarily be where you left it, so be prepared to search. The water in your mouth is essential. It will act as your protection.

When you find the doll, pour the remaining salt water over its head, then spit the water from your mouth out onto its face. Tell the doll "I win." Tell it three times. Then, the ritual is complete.

This is called *Hitori Kakurenbo* (ひとりかくれんぼ), meaning *one-person hide-and-seek*. The cursed doll created by the evocation is among the latest of new yokai to enter Japan's pantheon of monsters. The complicated summoning ritual is the direct descendant of Edo period beliefs like *Ushi no Koku Mairi* (丑の刻参り), the *Shrine Visit at the Hour of the Ox*. Like any good folklore, it takes elements of the old and combines them with the new. The time, 3am, is the "Hour of the Ox" by the old celestial clock and is considered Japan's Witching Hour. The doll is a modern update on the *waraningyo* straw effigies that feature in Heian and Edo period magic. The red thread is an element of Buddhism. The rice evokes Shinto. The toenail clippings? To be honest, those are just creepy.

The story of Yokai never ends.

There is a tendency for folklorist and researchers to revel in the past. Looking at folklore can be like an archeological dig, stripping aside layer after layer. For the next book I am writing, I went on a hunt for one of Japan's most popular folktales, *Bunbuku Chagama*. I found the oldest extant version in the footnotes of a diary kept by an Edo period

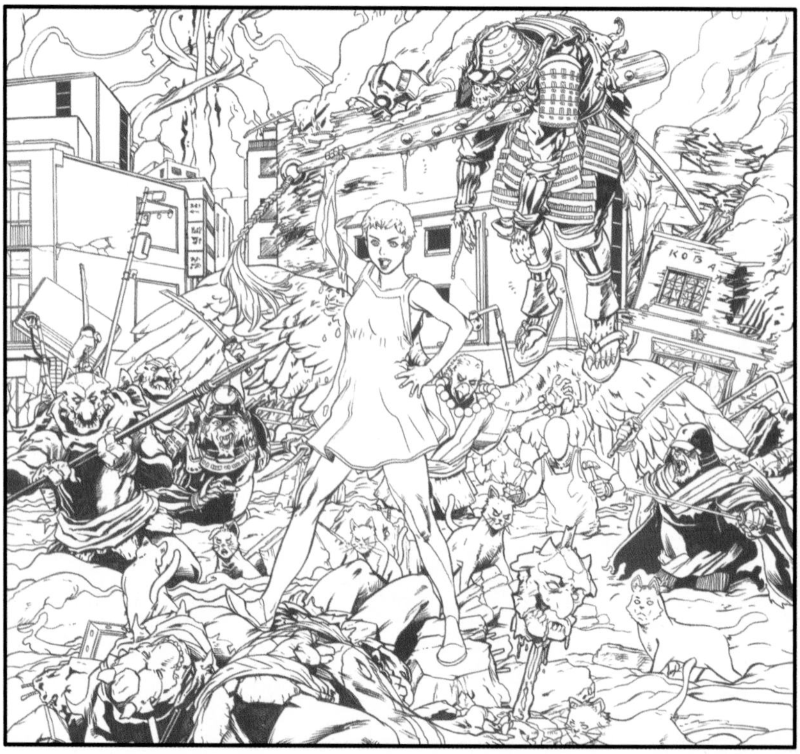
KOBA

samurai lord. It was an ecstatic find. But...it was looking backwards, not forwards. As exciting as it is to find the origins of notorious legends, digging too far into the past can blind you to the present.

Yokai live in dark corners. They exist in the liminal spaces, the in-betweens. They are the unknown. Every time science or reason shines a light on the dark corners of the world, they create new shadows—and here there be monsters. Each successive generation finds its own devils.

In the west, Dracula and Frankenstein's Monster have lost their edge. Familiarity breeds contempt. As one boggart loses its powers, new horrors arise. Slender Man slinks from the depths. Candle Cove is a haunted TV show that everyone remembers from their childhood, but no one can find evidence of. In Japan, no longer afraid of kappa or tengu, horrors like Teke Teke spring forth, a young woman sliced in half by a train. The Jinmenken—human-faced dogs—are escaped scientific experiments that hunt in Tokyo's urban sprawl.

With the pleasure districts of Edo long gone, many modern Yokai spring from the wild digital frontier, the internet. Since the early 2000s, there have been rumors of a secret website called the Red Room. If you find your way there, it means your death. The next day your body will be found in a room painted without your own blood. Another whispered tale tells of Gozu, meaning The Cow's Head. This story, supposedly authored by science fiction writer Sakyo Komatsu, is so terrifying that anyone who reads it falls into a catatonic fit and dies.

The story of Yokai never ends.

Much has changed since Wayward began. *Yo-Kai Watch* debuted in English, meaning we no longer need to explain what the word "Yokai" means.

Japan's great folklorist and arbiter of Yokai, Shigeru Mizuki, died at 93 years old. For the first time ever, Mizuki's creation *Kitaro* is available in both comic book form and an animated series in English at the same time. On the television show *Constantine*, the main character battled a kuchi-sake onna. On *Teen Wolf*, kitsune fought against western werewolves. Yokai seem to be popping up everywhere.

I like to think we played some small part in that, as have you readers who journeyed with us through Weird Japan. It is a unique place with unique monsters and there are a million more to explore. (I never did convince Jim and Steve to include *Shirime* in the series. Oh well, there's always hope for a sequel.) After all, although Wayward may be saying farewell to Weird Japan...

The story of Yokai never ends.

皆様、読んでくれて誠に有難うございます。これからも妖怪の世界が待っています

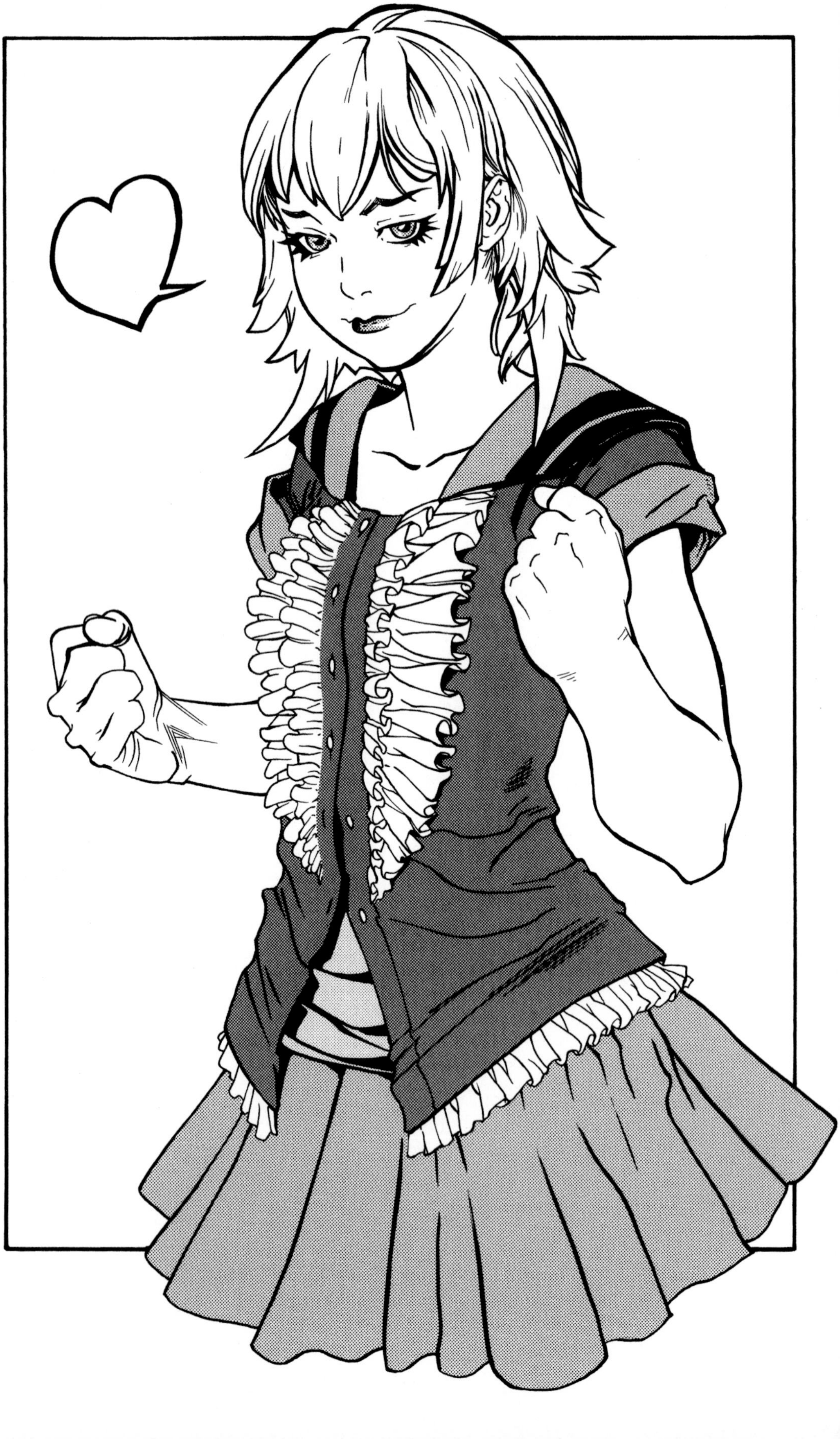

Farewell To Wayward

I sent Steven an email back in July 2013 proposing a story about supernatural stuff happening in Tokyo. The idea for it came from story bits I had been brainstorming about mythology in the modern world mixed with a cool illustration Steven had done years earlier in an art book called *Vent*.

Over five years later, here we are with thirty issues under our belt and a big crazy story about myth, destiny, and finding your way in a changing world.

I knew how the broad elements would come together for the finale and that we'd break the chains of fate, but I wasn't sure if the ending would end up being optimistic or something grim. Thankfully, a hopeful tone won out in the end and, rereading it now, it feels right.

The unknown is scary, but it also carries great potential. Our past informs who we are, but it's not the sum total of who we will be in the future.

Going on this journey with our creative team has been an incredible honor. Steven Cummings and I worked together on opposite sides of the world, keeping production going around the clock. I'd pop onto Google Hangouts late in the evening as he woke up to start another day of art production. We'd check in and encourage each other as we plugged away on each issue, each arc, year after year. Like any creative endeavor, it was stressful at times, but also a constant source of joy.

Tamra Bonvillain came on board to color *Wayward* at the end of our first arc and stuck with us until the end. Her ability to bring out the best in Steven's line work and take it to a higher level with mood and atmosphere still makes me smile. She brought a distinct look to the series that kept us competitive with any other title on the stands.

Marshall Dillon has been with me on every creator-owned series I've done and with good reason. His work effortlessly enhances each page, keeping readers focused and moving through the story in a way that's easy to take for granted. That's what great lettering does.

Zack Davisson and Ann O'Regan brought their knowledge and research skills to the mix in a way that helped us stand out in a crowded field. Our back matter essays were educational without being preachy, fascinating and always relevant. The reference material they provided helped ground our supernatural story in the real world and brought added value to our single issues and collections.

Wayward gave me the opportunity to dig into my love of Japan in a way I hadn't ever thought possible. It has forged lifelong friendships, enabled trips around the globe and enriched my life, time and time again.

Thank you to my wife Stacy for her endless editorial support and love, to the crew at Image Comics for helping us every step of the way, and to the many retailers and reviewers who enthusiastically told people about what we were doing as we built our readership.

Thank you for supporting us. Every day I'm thankful I get to make comics and none of it would be possible without great people like you.

Right here, right now...Anything is possible.

-Jim Zub

My journey with *Wayward* started years ago when Jim and I had a talk about what we could do with a creator-owned story. The black and white illustration I drew for the Udon Entertainment artbook *Vent* of a girl with cats got brought into the conversation and, after ideas began to be thrown around, *Wayward* was born. In that entire process I never expected what it became...a tale stretching out over six story arcs and thirty issues, different countries, endless property damage, crazy monsters, not to mention the cats. Lots and lots of cats. So many cats.

Did I mention I am incredibly allergic to cats?

Wayward was a fun ride that kept up the excitement right to the very end and I couldn't have done it without the help of my partner Jim Zub and the rest of our comic crew; Marshall Dillon, Tamra Bonvillain, and Zack Davisson. Their hard work helped bring this project to life on the page and in the hearts of our readers and I am grateful for their cooperation. Guys, I just want to say thank you!! As I look back on what we did together I am incredibly proud of what we accomplished and I will fondly remember all the work that went into the book.

Except drawing all those cats.

I also want to thank each and every person who tried out our monthly issues and helped spread the word about *Wayward* by telling their friends. Readers like you are what makes a comic book a success. We most definitely could not have done this without all of you.

-Steven Cummings
(still in Wayward land)

Steven has drawn the last page, Tamra is putting the finishing touches on the colors. Zack has likely been done with his part for a while now. Jim has given me the final lettering notes. Stacy is waiting to give it all one final read. And then we'll be done. *Wayward* will pass on into the library of history. The thread will be severed.

I am grateful to have been part of this project and I'm excited to see where our threads lead. I hope they weave back together in interesting ways as we write and rewrite the histories and the futures of our own lives.

Thank you to the readers, thank you to Steven, Tamra, Zack, Ann, and Stacy, and thank you to Jim for including me in another of his wonderful creative webs. We've done an incredible amount of work together over the years and I'm proud of every single balloon.

Love to you all,
Marshall Dillon

Wayward has been one of the most challenging and rewarding projects I've worked on in comics, and I've been so wrapped up in the grind, it's kind of surreal that it's ending!

I appreciate Jim and Steven bringing me on board. I always tell people *Wayward* is the hardest book I work on, but I feel like it's pushed me to get better and faster and has opened up many other opportunities for me as well. After four years, it's going to be weird letting go of *Wayward*, but I'm very proud of all the work I've done with Jim, Steven, Marshall, Zack, Ann, Brittany, and Ludwig!

Tamra Bonvillain

It's a cliché, I know. But that doesn't make it any less true. The best thing about *Wayward* was the people I met along the way.

When that first email came in from Jim Zub he was a stranger. I'd never worked on a Western comic before and was unfamiliar with everyone on the team. Now I have spent countless hours next to Jim and Tamra at conventions, had late night chats with Steven, and met hundreds of wonderful fans who have enjoyed and been touched by *Wayward*. Strangers became friends. A fan (me) became a legitimate "comics pro." It has been an incredible journey and one I will always be thankful for being a part of. What an amazing team. And what amazing readers.

Thank you all so much for coming along into the wide, weird world of yokai. I hope to see you again.

Zack Davisson

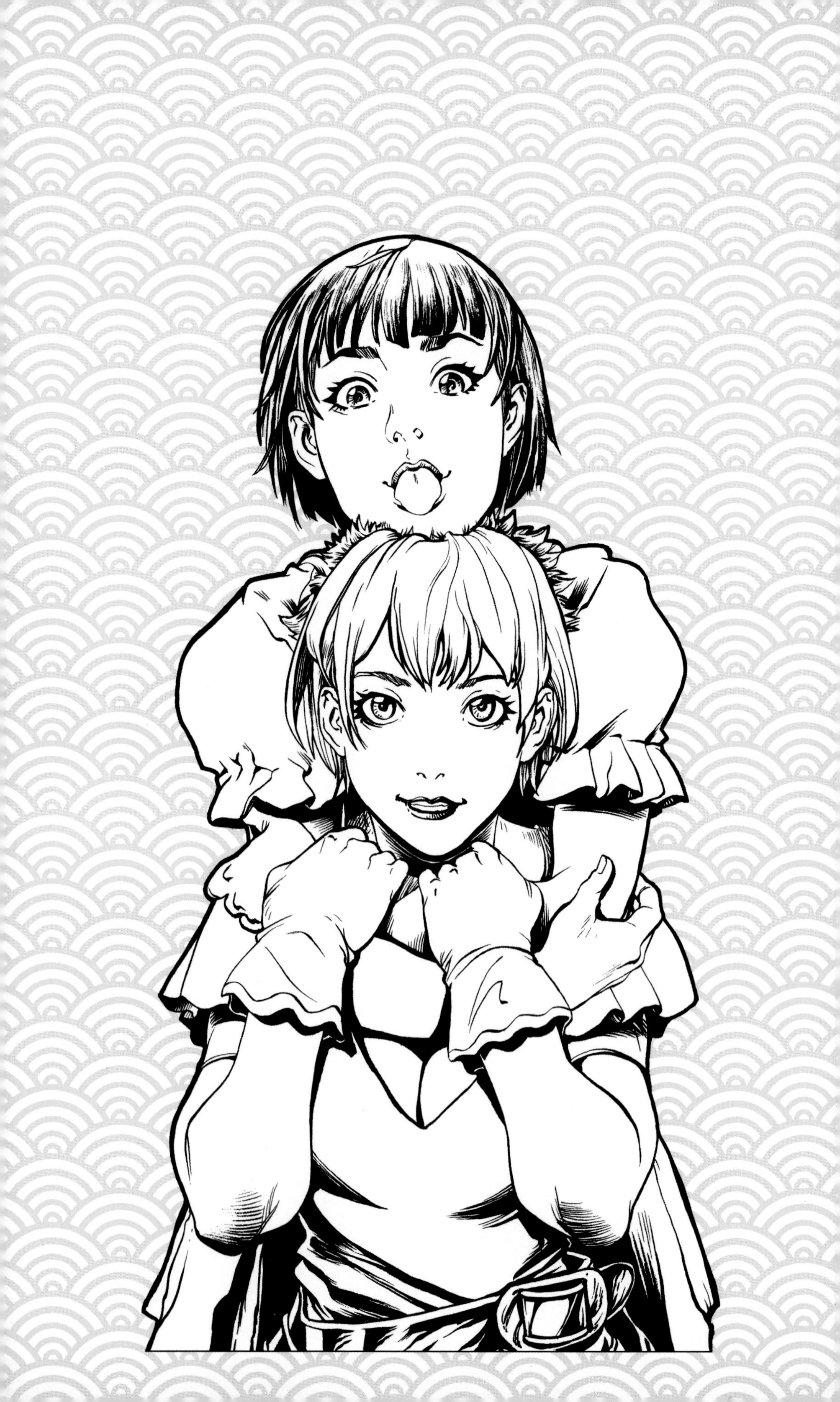